Means

MAUREEN CHILD
KRISTI GOLD
YVONNE LINDSAY

MILLS
BOON

First Published in Great Britain 2016
By Mills & Boon, an imprint of HarperCollins*Publishers*
1 London Bridge Street, London, SE1 9GF

HIS BY ANY MEANS © 2016 Harlequin Books S. A.

The Black Sheep's Inheritance, From Single Mum to Secret Heiress
and *Expecting the CEO's Child* were first published in Great Britain by
Harlequin (UK) Limited.

The Black Sheep's Inheritance, © 2014 Harlequin Books S. A.
From Single Mum to Secret Heiress © 2014 Harlequin Books S. A.
Expecting the CEO's Child © 2014 Harlequin Books S. A.

Special thanks and acknowledgement are given to Maureen Child,
Kristi Gold and Yvonne Lindsay for their contributions to the
His By Any Means series

ISBN: 978-0-263-92091-8

05-1216

Our policy is to use papers that are natural, renewable and recyclable products and made from wood grown in sustainable forests. The logging and manufacturing processes conform to the legal environmental regulations of the country of origin.

Printed and bound in Spain
by CPI, Barcelona

THE BLACK SHEEP'S INHERITANCE

BY
MAUREEN CHILD

Maureen Child writes for the Mills & Boon Desire line and can't imagine a better job. Being able to indulge your love for romance, as well as being able to spin stories just the way you want them told is, in a word, perfect.

A seven-time finalist for the prestigious Romance Writers of America RITA® Award, Maureen is the author of more than one hundred romance novels. Her books regularly appear on the bestseller lists and have won several awards, including a prism, a national readers' Choice Award, a Colorado romance Writers Award of excellence and a Golden Quill.

One of her books, *The Soul Collector*, was made into a CBS TV movie starring Melissa Gilbert, Bruce Greenwood and Ossie Davis. If you look closely, in the last five minutes of the movie you'll spot Maureen, who was an extra in the last scene.

Maureen believes that laughter goes hand in hand with love, so her stories are always filled with humor. The many letters she receives assures her that her readers love to laugh as much as she does.

Maureen Child is a native Californian, but has recently moved to the mountains of Utah. She loves a new adventure, though the thought of having to deal with snow for the first time is a little intimidating.

To Stacy Boyd and Charles Griemsman,
two editors who make writing Desires
such a terrific experience

his arm thrown protectively around her shoulders. He wore a leather jacket tossed on over a long-sleeved white shirt. Dark blue jeans and boots completed the outfit, and the gray Stetson he was never without was balanced on one knee. He was a cowboy down to his bones and the manager of J.D.'s thirty-thousand-acre ranch, Big Blue.

"You have any idea what the bequests are?" Dylan asked. "Couldn't get a thing out of Walter."

"Not surprising," Sage remarked with a sardonic twist of his lips. Walter Drake was not only J.D.'s lawyer, but practically his clone. Two more stubborn, secretive men he'd never met. Walter had made calls to all of them, simply telling them when and where to show up and not once hinting at what was in J.D.'s will. Logan Whittaker, another partner in the firm, was also working on J.D.'s will but he hadn't been any more forthcoming than Walter.

Sage wasn't expecting a damn thing for himself. And it wasn't as if he needed money. He'd built his own fortune, starting off in college by investing in one of his friends' brilliant ideas. When that paid off, he invested in other dreamers, and along the way he'd amassed millions. More than enough to make him completely independent of the Lassiter legacy. In fact, he was surprised he had been asked to be here at all. Long ago, he'd distanced himself from the Lassiters to make his own way, and he and J.D. hadn't exactly been close.

"Have you talked to Angelica since this all happened?" Dylan frowned and glanced to where their sister sat beside her fiancé, Evan McCain, her head on his shoulder.

"Not for long." Sage frowned, too, and thought about the sister he and Dylan loved so much. Her much-anticipated wedding had been postponed because of their father's death and who knew when it would happen now. Angelica's big brown eyes were red rimmed from crying and there were lavender shadows beneath those eyes that told Sage she wasn't sleeping much. "I went to see her a couple of days ago, hoping I could talk to her, but all she did was bawl." His scowl deepened. "Hate seeing her like that, but I don't know what the hell we can do for her."

"Not much really," Dylan agreed. "I saw her yesterday, but she didn't want to talk about what happened. Evan told me she's not sleeping, hardly eating. She's taking this really hard, Sage."

Nodding, he told his brother, "She and the old man were so close, of course she's taking it hard. Not to mention, J.D. collapsing at her rehearsal dinner adds a whole new level of misery. We've just got to make sure she gets past this. We'll tag team her. One of us going to see her at least every other day…"

"Oh," Dylan said, chuckling, "Evan will love having us around all the time."

"He's the one so hell-bent on marrying into the Lassiter family," Sage pointed out wryly. "If he takes one of us, he gets all of us. Best he figures that out now anyway."

"True." Dylan nodded then sat back in his chair. "Okay, then. We'll keep an eye on Angelica."

Dylan kept talking, now about his plans for the restaurant he was opening, but Sage had stopped listening. Instead, he watched Colleen Falkner, J.D.'s private nurse, slip quietly into the room, then make her way to the front, where she took a seat beside Marlene. The older woman gave her a watery smile of welcome and took her hand in a firm grip.

Sage narrowed his gaze on Colleen and felt a hard jolt of awareness leap to life inside him—just as it had the night of the rehearsal dinner. The same night J.D. died.

That night, he'd really *noticed* her for the first time. They'd met in passing of course, but on that particular night, there had been something different about her. Something that tugged at him. Maybe it had been seeing her long, amazing hair loose, cascading down her back in beautiful shimmering waves. Maybe it had been the short red dress and the black heels and the way they'd made her legs look a mile long. All he knew for sure was when he'd caught her eye from across the room, he'd felt a connection snap into place between them. He had started toward her, determined to talk to her—then J.D.'s heart attack had changed everything.

She wasn't wearing party clothes today, though. Instead, she wore baggy slacks, a sapphire-blue pullover sweater and her long, dark blond hair was pulled back into a braid that hung down between her shoulder blades. She had wide blue eyes that were bright with unshed tears and a full, rich mouth that tempted a man to taste it.

If he hadn't seen her in a figure-skimming red dress at the party—a dress that remained etched into his memory—Sage never would have guessed at the curves she kept so well hidden beneath her armor of wool and cotton.

He hadn't had much interaction with Colleen, since he and J.D. hadn't exactly been on the best of terms, so Sage didn't spend much time on Big Blue. But that night at the party, she'd intrigued him. Not only was she beautiful, but when J.D. collapsed, she had sprung into action, shouting orders like a general and taking charge until the paramedics showed up.

She had been devoted to J.D., had earned the family's affections—as evidenced by the way Marlene reached out to take the woman's hand—yet through it all had remained a bit of a mystery. Where was she from? Why had she taken a job working for a grumpy old man on a remote, if luxurious, ranch? And why the hell did he care?

"Colleen do something to you?"

He glanced at Dylan. "What?"

"Well, you're staring at her hard enough to set her hair on fire. What's up?"

Irritated to have been caught out, Sage muttered, "Shut up."

"Ah. Good answer." Dylan just smiled, shook his head and leaned forward to ask Chance something.

Sage let his gaze slide carefully back to Colleen. She bent her head to whisper something to Marlene, and he watched that long, silky braid slide across her shoulder, baring the nape of her neck. Soft blond curls brushed against her skin and he suddenly had the urge to touch her. To stroke that skin, to slide his fingers through her hair, to— He cut that thought off as fast as he could and scowled to himself.

The only possible reason she had for being here was if she was mentioned in J.D.'s will. Sure, J.D. had needed a nurse over his last few months, with his health failing, but such a beautiful one? Was that why she'd taken the job of caring for the old man? Had she been hoping for a nice payoff someday? Maybe he should spend a little time looking into Colleen Falkner, he thought. Do some checking. Make sure—

"You're looking at her again," Dylan pointed out.

Glaring at his brother and ignoring the smile on the man's face, Sage grumbled, "Don't you have something else to do?"

"Not at the moment."

"Lucky me."

"I just think it's interesting how fascinated you seem to be by Colleen."

"I'm not fascinated." *Much.* He shifted uncomfortably in his chair and told himself to stop thinking about her. How could the woman have gotten to him so easily? Hell, he hadn't even really *talked* to her.

"Not what it looks like from where I'm sitting."

"Then maybe you should sit somewhere else." He wasn't fascinated. He was…interested. Attracted. There was a difference.

Dylan laughed shortly. True to form, Sage's younger brother was almost impossible to insult. He was easygoing, charming and sometimes Sage thought his younger brother had gotten all the patience in the family. But he was also stubborn and once he got his teeth into something, he rarely let it go.

Like now, for example.

"She's single," Dylan said.

"Great."

"I'm just sayin'," his brother continued, "maybe you could leave your ranch once in a while. Have an actual date. Maybe with Colleen."

Sage drew his head back and stared at his brother. "Are you running a dating service I don't know about?"

"Fine," Dylan muttered, sitting back in his chair. "Have it your way. Be a hermit. End up becoming the weird old guy who lives alone on an isolated ranch."

"I'm not a hermit."

"Yeah? When's the last time you had a woman?"

Frowning, Sage said, "Not that it's any of your business, but I get plenty of women."

"One-night stands? Nice."

Sage preferred one-night stands. He didn't do commitment, and spending time with women who felt the same way avoided a lot of unnecessary hassle. If his brother wanted to look for more in his life, he was welcome to. As for Sage, he liked his life just the way it was. He came and went as he pleased. When he wanted a woman, he went and found one. When he wanted to be left the hell alone, he had that, too.

"Now that you mention it," he said quietly, "I haven't noticed you busy developing any serious relationships, either."

Dylan shrugged, folded his arms across his chest and said, "We're not talking about *me*."

"Yeah, well, we're done talking about *me,* too."

Then the office door opened, and lawyer Walter Drake stepped inside and announced, "All here?" He swept the room with a sharp-eyed gaze and nodded to himself. "Good. Then we can get started."

"I don't know if I'm ready for this," Dylan grumbled.

Sage was more than ready. He wanted this day done and finished so he could get back to his ranch.

After settling himself behind a wide oak desk, Walter, an older man who looked like the stereotypical image of an "old family retainer"—handsome, gray haired and impeccably dressed—picked up a stack of papers and straightened them unnecessarily. That shuffle of paper and the rattle of the window panes as a cold wind gusted against it were the only sounds in the room. It was as if everyone had taken a breath and held it.

Walter was clearly enjoying his moment in the spotlight. Every eye in the room was on him. Once again, his gaze moved over the people gathered there and when he finally came to Angelica, he gave her a sad, sympathetic smile before speaking to the room. "I know how hard this is on all of you, so I'll be as brief as possible."

Sage would be grateful.

"As you all know, J.D. and I knew each other for more than thirty years." Walter paused, smiled to himself and added, "He was a stubborn man, but a proud one, and I want you all to know that he took great care with his will. He remade it just a few months ago because he wanted to be sure to do the right thing by all of you."

Scraping one hand across his face, Sage shifted in the uncomfortable chair. He flicked a quick glance out the window and saw dark clouds rushing across the sky. *April in Wyoming,* he mused. It could be sunny in the morning and snowing by afternoon. And right now, it looked as though a storm was headed their way. Which only fed the urge to get back to his ranch before the bad weather hit.

"There are a lot of smaller provisions made to people J.D. thought well of over the years," Walter was saying. "I won't be reading them aloud today. Nor will I make mention of other estate business that will be handled separately."

Sage frowned thoughtfully and shifted his gaze to Walter. Handled separately? Why? What was the lawyer trying to hide? For that matter, what had *J.D.* been trying to hide? He braced his elbows on his thighs and leaned forward, keeping his gaze fixed on Walter as if the man was about to saw a woman in half. Or pull a dove from a magic hat.

"That part of the will is, at this time, not to be shared with the family."

"Why not?" Sage's question shattered the stillness left in the wake of Walter's startling statement.

The older man met Sage's gaze squarely. "Those were J.D.'s wishes."

"How do we know that?" An insulting question and he knew it, but Sage didn't stop himself. He didn't like secrets.

Dylan jammed his elbow into Sage's side, but he didn't so much as flinch. Just kept staring at the lawyer waiting for an answer.

"Because I tell you so," Walter said, stiffening in insult.

"C'mon, Sage," Dylan muttered. "Let it go for now."

He didn't want to, but he would. Only because Marlene had turned in her seat to give him a worried frown. Damned if he'd do anything to upset her any further than she already was. Nodding to the woman he thought of as a mother, he promised himself that he'd keep his silence for now, but that didn't mean this was the end of it.

"Now," Walter said firmly, "if that's settled, I'd like to continue. After all, the heart and soul of the will is what we're here to discuss today." He paused only long enough to smooth one hand across his neatly trimmed silver beard. "I appreciate you all coming in on such short notice, and I promise to get through this as quickly as possible."

Sage didn't know if the man was deliberately trying to pump up the suspense in the room or if he was just a naturally dramatic lawyer. But either way, it was working. Everyone there shifted uncomfortably in their seats as Walter read aloud the strange, coma-inducing legal phrases leading up to the actual bequests. One or two of those phrases resonated with Sage.

Sound in mind and body. Well, in mind, anyway, Sage told himself. J.D. had been sick for a while, but the old man's brain was as sharp the day he died as it was when he was nothing but a kid starting out. Which meant J.D. had had a reason for keeping these so-called secrets from the family even after his death. A flicker of anger bristled inside him, and Sage admitted silently that it sucked to be angry at a dead man, because you had no way of confronting him. J.D. was probably loving this, he thought. Even after he was gone, he was still running the show.

But as soon as he had the chance, Sage promised himself a long talk with J.D.'s lawyer.

"To my dear sister-in-law, Marlene..." Walter paused to smile at the woman in question. "I leave a ten-percent share in the Big Blue ranch along with ownership of the main ranch house for as long as she lives. I also leave her enough cash to maintain her lifestyle—" Walter broke off and added, "J.D. got tired of all the 'legal speak,' as he called it, and had me write the rest down just as he spoke it." He took a breath and continued, "Marlene, I want you to have some fun. Get on out there and enjoy your life. You're a good-looking woman and too damn young to fold up and die alone."

Marlene sniffed, then laughed shortly and mopped at her tears. The rest of the room chuckled with her, and even Sage had to smile. He could hear the old man's gruff voice as if he were there with them. J.D. and Marlene had been an unofficial couple for years. More than that though, Marlene had been a rock to three motherless young kids and to a man who had lost the love of his life.

"To Chance Lassiter, my nephew, I leave a sixty-percent share in Big Blue and enough cash to take some time and enjoy yourself a little." Walter paused and added, "The cash amounts mentioned in the will are specific and will be discussed privately with each of you at a later date."

Chance looked stunned and Sage was glad for him. The man loved that ranch and cared for it every bit as meticulously as J.D. had himself.

"You take care of Blue, Chance," Walter kept reading, "and she'll do the same for you."

"To Colleen Falkner," he went on and Sage shifted his gaze to the blonde. "I leave the sum of three million dollars."

Colleen gasped and rocked back in her chair. Blue eyes wide, mouth open, she stared at Walter as if he had two heads. If she was acting then send her an Oscar fast, Sage thought dryly. She looked as genuinely surprised as he was. J.D. had left three million dollars to his *nurse?*

Walter kept reading. "Colleen, you're a good girl and with this money, I want you to go on and chase your dream down. Don't wait until it's too late."

"Oh, my—" She shook her head in disbelief, but Walter was moving on already and Sage braced himself for whatever came next.

"To my son Dylan Lassiter, I leave controlling interest in Lassiter Grill Group, and enough cash to tide you over while you take it to the top. Oh, and I'm giving you ten-percent share of the Big Blue, too. It's your home, never forget that."

Beside Sage, Dylan looked shell-shocked and he

couldn't blame him. Hell, the man was now the owner of one of the fastest-growing restaurant groups in the country. If that didn't stop your heart a little, you weren't human.

"My son Sage Lassiter—"

Sage tensed for whatever was coming. He wouldn't have put it past J.D. to take one last swipe at him from the grave. To remind him publicly of the distance that had grown between them over the years. Like oil and water, Sage thought, he and J.D. had just never managed to mix well together.

"Sage," Walter read with a shake of his head, "you're my son and I love you. We butted heads too many times to count, but make no mistake, you're a Lassiter through and through. I'm leaving you twenty-five-percent interest in Lassiter Media, a ten-percent share in Big Blue—to remind you that's always your home—and lastly some cash that you won't want and don't need."

Surprised and touched, Sage snorted.

Walter continued word for word, "You're building your ranch your own damn way, just like I did. I admire that. So take this cash and buy something for that ranch. Something that will always remind you that your father loved you. Whether we could get along together or not."

Damn. The old man had surprised him one last time, was all Sage could think. His throat felt like a fist was squeezing, closing off his air. If he didn't get out of here soon, he was going to make a damn fool of himself. How the hell did J.D. know how to touch him, even from beyond the grave? How had he scripted words in a will months ago that could reach out long after he was gone to do what he hadn't been able to do in life?

"And lastly," Walter was saying, "I come to my beloved daughter, Angelica Lassiter. You are my heart and soul and the light of my life."

Sage glanced at his sister and saw her beautiful face crumple into tears again.

"And so," Walter read, "I leave you, Angelica, a ten-percent share of Big Blue, just like your brothers, the Lassiter estate in Beverly Hills, California, enough cash for you to spoil yourself some and finally, a ten-percent share in Lassiter Media."

"What?" Sage jumped to his feet, outraged, and Dylan was just a breath behind him. All of the warm feelings for his adoptive father vanished in a blink. How could he do that to Angelica? He'd groomed his daughter for years to take over the day-to-day operations of Lassiter Media, a conglomerate of radio, TV, newspapers and internet news outlets. Hell, she'd practically been running the damn thing on her own since J.D. got sick. And now he cut her out of the thing she loved?

"You can't be serious," Sage argued hotly, with a quick look at his sister's shocked, ashen features. "She's been running Lassiter Media for J.D. He left *me* more interest than Angie? That's insane!"

"We'll challenge the damn will," Dylan was saying, moving toward his sister to lay one hand on her shoulder in a show of solidarity.

"Damn straight," Sage agreed, glaring at the lawyer as if it were all his fault.

"There's more," Walter said, clearing his throat uncomfortably. "And I warn you, try to challenge this will and you might all be sorry—but more about that later. For now, voting control with forty-one-percent share of Lassiter Media, chairmanship and title of CEO, I leave to Evan McCain."

"Evan?" Angelica pulled away from her fiancé even as he was rising to his feet, stunned speechless.

"What the hell is going on here, Walter?" Sage demanded, coming around the corner of the man's desk to snatch up the will and read the terms himself.

"J.D. knew what he wanted to do and he did it," the lawyer argued.

"Well, it won't stand," Marlene said.

"Damn right it won't," Dylan piped up, charging the desk and snatching the will from his brother's grasp.

"It's not right." Chance came to his feet slowly, his calm, quiet voice nearly lost in the confusion.

"I can't believe it," Angelica murmured, looking at her fiancé as if she'd never seen him before.

"I swear I don't know anything about this," Evan said, taking a step toward her only to stop when she backed away from him.

"Well, somebody does, and I'm going to find out what's going on," Sage promised, then snapped his gaze to the door. Colleen Falkner was slipping out of the office like a damn ghost.

She'd gotten what she wanted, he told himself. He only wondered what she'd had to do for three million dollars. And he also had to ask himself if she'd known about J.D.'s plans. Had she been involved in his decision to rob Angelica of the very thing she cared most about?

Damned if he wouldn't find out.

Colleen leaned back against the door briefly, closing her eyes and forcing herself to drag a deep breath into her lungs. Her heart was pounding so hard and so fast she felt dizzy.

She hadn't expected anything like this.

Three million dollars?

Tears burned her eyes, but she frantically blinked them back. Now wasn't the time to indulge in tears for the loss of her friend—or for thinking about the future he had just made possible.

Behind her, she heard muffled shouts through the closed door. Sage Lassiter's voice was the most unmistakable. Though he didn't have to shout to be heard. The cold steel in his deep voice was enough to get the attention of anyone in the room.

God knew, he'd had *her* attention.

She'd felt him watching her earlier. Had sneaked a peek or two over her shoulder at him in return. He made her nervous. Always had. Which was why any time he'd come to the Big Blue ranch to visit his father—which wasn't often—Colleen had made herself scarce.

He was so…*male.*

Sage Lassiter was a force of nature. The kind of man women drooled over. And she was the kind of woman men like him never noticed. Well, not usually. He'd certainly noticed her today, though. And he hadn't looked very happy about it.

Tossing a quick look at the closed door behind her, Colleen hurried down the long beige hallway toward the elevators. She wanted to be long gone before Sage left that room.

Two

She made it as far as the parking lot.

"Colleen!"

Standing beside her car, Colleen took a breath and braced herself. That deep voice was unmistakable.

Goose bumps broke out on her arms and it wasn't because of the icy wind buffeting her. Blast Wyoming weather anyway. One day it was spring and the next, it was winter again. But the cold was the least of her worries.

It was him. Colleen had only been close to Sage Lassiter one time before today. The night of Angelica's rehearsal dinner. From across that crowded restaurant, she'd felt him watching her. The heat of his gaze had swamped her, sending ribbons of expectation unfurling throughout her body. He smiled and her stomach churned with swarms of butterflies. He headed toward her, and she told herself to be calm. Cool. But it hadn't worked. Nerves fired, knees weakened.

And just as he was close enough to her that she could see the gleam in his eyes, J.D. had his heart attack and everything had changed forever.

Looking back on that night, she told herself she was being silly even thinking that Sage might have been interested in her. He'd probably only wanted to ask her questions about his father's care. Or where the restrooms were.

In her own mind, she'd built up the memory of that night into something magical. But it was time to remember that she simply wasn't the kind of woman a man like him would ever notice. Sadly, that didn't stop *her* from noticing *him* and she hadn't been able to stop thinking about him since that night.

Now he was here, and she had to battle down a flurry of nerves. She turned and brushed a few stray, wind-blown hairs out of her face as she watched him approach.

Her heartbeat sped up at the picture he made. Sage Lassiter *stalked* across the parking lot toward her. It was the only word that could describe that long, determined stride. He was like a man on a mission. He wore dark jeans, boots and an expensively cut black sports jacket over a long-sleeved white shirt. His brown hair flew across his forehead and his blue eyes were narrowed against the wind. His long legs closed the distance between them in a few short seconds and then he was there. Right in front of her.

She had to tip her head back to meet his gaze and when she did, nerves skated down along her spine. For three months, she'd listened to J.D. Lassiter as he talked about his family. Thanks to those chats, she knew that

Sage was ruthless in business, quiet, hardheaded and determined to make his own way rather than capitalize on the Lassiter name. And though that last part had irritated J.D., she knew that he'd also admired Sage for it. How could he not? The older man had done the same thing when he was starting out.

Still, being face-to-face with the man who had filled her mind for weeks was a little unnerving. Maybe if she hadn't spent so much time daydreaming about him, she wouldn't feel so awkward right now. Colleen took another deep breath and held it for a moment, hoping to calm herself. But there was a flash of something she couldn't quite read in his eyes and the nerves won.

Wind slid down off the mountain, wrapped itself around them briefly then rushed on, delivering chills to the rest of Cheyenne. Ridiculously, Colleen was grateful for the cold wind. It was like a slap of common sense and though it wasn't enough to completely dampen her hormones, her next thought absolutely was.

The only reason she and Sage were here, about to talk, was because they had both attended the reading of his father's will. Remembering that helped her keep her voice steady as she gave him a smile and blurted, "I'm so sorry about your father."

A slight frown crossed his face briefly. "Thanks. Look, I wanted to talk to you—"

"You did?" There went her silly heart again, jumping into a gallop. He really was impossibly handsome, she thought absently—tall, dark and glower-y. There was an aura of undeniable strength that emanated from him. He was the kind of man other men envied and women wanted. Herself included. A brand-new flock of butterflies took off and flew in formation in the pit of her stomach. "You want to talk to me?"

"Yes," he said, his voice a deep rumble that seemed to roll across every one of her nerve endings. "I've got a couple questions…"

Fascination dissolved into truth. Instantly, Colleen gave herself a mental kick. Here she was, daydreaming about a gorgeous man suddenly paying attention to her when the reality was, he'd just lost his father. She knew all too well that the families left behind after a loss often had questions. Wanted to know how their loved one had been feeling. What they'd been thinking. And as J.D.'s private nurse, she had been with him the most during those final days.

And now that reality had jumped up to slap her, she was forced to acknowledge that Sage Lassiter had probably planned to talk to her the night of the party for the same reason. What had she been thinking? She'd half convinced herself that the rich, gorgeous Sage Lassiter was interested in *her*. God, what an idiot. Embarrassment tangled with a wash of disappointment before she fought past both sensations, allowing her natural empathy to come rushing to the surface.

"Of course you do." Instinctively, she reached out, laid her hand on his and felt a swift jolt of electricity jump from his body to hers. Totally unexpected, she felt the heat from that brief contact sizzle inside her. It was so strong, so real, she wouldn't have been surprised to actually *see* the arc of light shimmering between them. Quickly, she drew her hand back, then curled her fingers into her palm, determined to ignore the startling sensation.

His eyes narrowed further and she knew he'd felt it,

too. Frowning a little, he pushed one hand through his hair, fixed his gaze on hers and let her know immediately that whatever he might have felt, he was as determined as she to ignore it.

Shaking his head, he said, "No. I don't have any questions about J.D. Actually, *you're* the mystery here."

"Me?" Surprised, Colleen stared up at him, practically mesmerized by those cool blue eyes of his. "You think I'm a mystery? I'm really not."

"Oh, I don't know," he mused. "You went from nurse to millionaire in a few short months."

"What?" Confused now, she shook her head as if that might help clear things up a little. It didn't.

His lips curved but the smile didn't reach his eyes. "Sure, it's a big step, isn't it? I just wanted to say congratulations."

"Con—what? Oh. What?" Colleen's mind was slowly working its way past the hormonal surge she'd first felt when Sage had walked up to her. And now that she was able to think almost clearly again, it finally dawned on her what he was talking about. The bequest. The money J.D. had left her. He was making it sound…ugly.

Stung, she said quietly, "I don't know if *congratulations* is the right word."

"Why not?" He set one hand on the roof of her old, but completely reliable, Jeep and leaned in closer. "From private nurse to millionaire in one easy step. Not many people could have pulled that off."

Cold slithered through her and it was an icier feeling than anything the weather could provide. She glanced around the nearly empty parking lot. Only a half dozen or so cars were sprinkled around the area. The law office adjoining the lot seemed to loom over her, so for a second or two, she let her gaze drift past the city to the mountains in the distance. Sunlight glanced off the snow still covering the peaks. Gray clouds scudded across the deep blue sky and the ever-present wind tugged at her hair.

Just like always, the view of the mountains soothed her. She and her mother had moved to Cheyenne several years ago, and from the moment they arrived, Colleen had felt at home. She hadn't missed California and the beaches. It was the mountains that called to her. The wide-open spaces, the trees, the bite of cold in the air. In a moment, she was ready to face the man glaring at her. "I don't know what you mean."

But she did. She really did. His eyes were icy, detached and a muscle in his jaw ticked as if he were biting back all kinds of words he really wanted to say. J.D. had told her so much about Sage, and for the first time, she was seeing the less than pleasant aspects. *Ruthless. Hard.*

He was more different now from the man who had flirted with her from across a crowded room not two weeks ago than she would have thought possible. Did he really believe she had somehow engineered this bequest? That she'd tricked J.D. into leaving her money?

"I think you know exactly what I mean." His head tilted to one side as he studied her. "I just find it interesting that J.D. would bequeath three million dollars to a woman he didn't even know three months ago."

While she stood there, pinned in place by the sheer power of his gaze, Colleen felt like a bug on a glass slide under a microscope. The cold inside her began to melt beneath the steam of insult. She was still feeling a little shaky over J.D.'s death and the fact that he'd remembered her in his will. Now, staring up into Sage's eyes, seeing the flash of accusation gleaming there, she had to wonder if others would be thinking the same thing. What about the rest of the Lassiter family? Did they feel the same way? Would they also be looking at her with suspicion? Suddenly, she had a vision of not just the Lassiters but the whole town of Cheyenne whispering about her, gossiping.

That thought was chilling. She'd made Cheyenne her home and she didn't want her life destroyed by loose tongues spreading lies. Anger jumped to life inside her. She'd done nothing wrong. She'd helped an old man through his last days and she'd enjoyed his company, too. Since when was that a crime?

Gorgeous or not, Sage Lassiter had no right to imply that she'd somehow tricked J.D. into leaving her money in his will. Lifting her chin, she glared at him. "I didn't know he was going to do that."

"And you would have stopped him if you *had* known?"

The sarcasm in his tone only made the sense of insult deeper. She met his gaze squarely. On this, she could be completely honest. And she would keep being honest until people believed her. "I would have tried."

"Is that right?"

"Yes, it is," she snapped, and had the satisfaction of seeing surprise flicker in his eyes. "Whatever you might think of me, I'm very good at my job. And I don't ordinarily receive gifts from my patients."

"Really?" He snorted. "You consider three million dollars a *gift?*"

"What it represents was the gift," she countered, then

stopped herself. She didn't owe him an explanation and if she tried, he probably wouldn't accept it.

His features looked as if they'd been carved from marble. There was no emotion there, nothing to soften the harsh gaze that seemed to bore right through her as if he were trying to read everything she was.

Colleen fought past the temper still bubbling into a froth in the pit of her stomach and tried to remember that people grieved in different ways. He'd lost a father he'd been estranged from. There had to be conflicting emotions roiling inside him and maybe it was easier for Sage to lash out at a stranger than to deal with what he must be feeling at the moment. Though she knew from her many long talks with J.D. that he and his oldest son weren't close, Sage was clearly still dealing with a loss he hadn't been prepared for. That was bound to hit him hard and it was scarcely surprising that he wasn't acting rationally at the moment.

With that thought in mind, the tension inside her drained away. "You don't know me, so I can understand how you might feel that way. But what J.D. did was as big a shock to me as it was to you."

A long second or two ticked past as he watched her through those deep blue eyes of his. She couldn't help wondering what he was thinking, but his features gave her no clue at all. Seconds ticked past as the wind blew, the sky grew darker and the silence between them stretched taut. Finally, he straightened up and away from the car, shoved both hands into his pockets and allowed, "Maybe I was a little harsh."

She gave him a tentative smile that wasn't returned. Despite his words, he wasn't really bending. Sighing, she said, "A little. But it's understandable, considering what you're going through. I mean…I understand."

"Do you?" Still watching her, though the ice in his eyes had melted a bit.

"When my father died," she said, sliding back into her own memories, "it was horrible, despite the fact that we knew for months that it was coming. Even when death is expected, it's somehow a surprise when it actually happens. It's as if the universe has played a dirty trick on you. I was so angry, so sorry to lose him—I needed someone to blame." She paused and met his gaze. "We all do."

He snorted. "A nurse *and* a psychologist?"

She flushed. "No, I just meant…"

"I know what you meant," he said shortly, effectively shutting her down before she could offer more sympathy he clearly didn't want.

And just like that, the ice was back in his eyes. Then he glanced over his shoulder, noted that his family was walking out of the office building behind them and turned back to her. "I have to go."

She looked to where Marlene and Angelica were holding onto each other while Chance, Dylan and Evan squared off, obviously arguing. "Of course."

"But I'd like to talk to you again," he said, catching her by surprise.

"Sure, I—"

"About J.D.," he added.

A tiny flicker of something lovely disappeared in a wash of sympathy. Of course he wanted to talk to her about his father. He wanted to hear from the woman who had spent the most time with him in his last several months. Ridiculous to have ever thought that he

might be interested in *her*. Sage Lassiter dated women
who were socialites or celebrities. Why on earth would
he ever be attracted to a private nurse who didn't even
own a bottle of nail polish?

"Sure," she said, giving him another smile that went
unreturned. "Anytime."

He nodded, then turned and strode across the parking lot toward his family.

Alone in the quickening wind, Colleen threw one
look up at the sky and realized that a storm was coming.

"What was he *thinking?*" Dylan took a sip of his beer
and set the bottle back onto the table. "Cutting Angie
out like that? Dad had been grooming her for years to
take over Lassiter Media."

They were at a small bar on the edge of the city. Marlene had taken Angelica off for a spa day, hoping to relax
her. Evan had gone back to the office and Chance was
at the ranch. Left to their own devices, Sage and Dylan
had opted for drinks, and the chance to talk things over,
just the two of them.

The customers here were locals, mostly cowboys,
ranch hands and a few cops and firemen. It was a comfortable place that didn't bother trying to be trendy.
The owner didn't care about attracting tourists. He just
wanted to keep his regulars happy.

So the music was loud and country, blasting from a
jukebox that was older than Sage. The floorboards were
scarred from wooden chairs scraping across them for
the past fifty years. The bar top gleamed and the rows
of bottles behind the bar were reflected in a mirror that
also displayed the image of the TV playing on the opposite wall. People came here to have a quiet drink. They

weren't looking to pose for pictures or listen to tourists talking excitedly about "the Old West." This was modern-day Cheyenne, yet Sage had the feeling quite a few people rode into town half expecting stagecoaches and more than just the staged gunfights in the streets.

"I don't know," Sage muttered, unnecessarily answering his brother's rhetorical question.

Dylan kept talking, but Sage wasn't really listening. Instead he was remembering the look in Colleen's eyes when he'd confronted her in the parking lot. He'd wanted to talk to her. To see what she knew. To find out if she'd had any idea what J.D. had been up to.

Instead, he'd put her on the defensive right from the jump. He hadn't meant to just launch into an attack. But with the memory of his sister's tears still fresh in his mind, he'd snapped at Colleen.

Scrubbing one hand across his face, he realized that he was going to have to use a completely different tactic the next time he talked to her. And there *would* be a next time. Not only did she intrigue him on a personal level but there were too many questions left unanswered. Had she swayed J.D. into leaving her the money? Did she know why Angelica had lost everything? Did she maybe know something that might help him invalidate the will? His brain was racing.

"Angie was looking at Evan like he was the enemy instead of the man she loves."

"Hard not to," Sage said, mentally dragging himself back to the conversation at hand. "In one swipe, Evan took everything Angie thought was hers."

"Well, it's not like he stole it or anything," Dylan told him. "J.D. *left* it to him."

"Yeah," he grumbled. "J.D. was just full of surprises,

wasn't he? Still, doesn't matter how it happened. Bottom line's the same. Angie's out and Evan's in. Not surprising that she's angry at him."

"True." Dylan picked up his beer for another sip, then held the bottle, rubbing his thumb over the label.

"It was always tricky, the two of them engaged and working for the same company. But now that Angie's not even the boss anymore?" Sage shook his head grimly. "I just hope this will doesn't cause a breakup."

"Worst part is, I don't know what we can do about it. From the little Walter said, I don't think we'll be able to contest the will without everyone losing."

"That's Walter's opinion. We need to check into that with an impartial lawyer."

"If there is such a beast," Dylan muttered.

"I know." Sage lifted his glass and took a slow sip of very old scotch. The heat swarmed through his system, yet did nothing to ease the tight knot in the pit of his stomach.

His sister had been crushed by their father's will. His aunt Marlene was happy with her bequest but naturally worried for Angie. Chance was good, of course. Big Blue ranch was his heart and soul. Evan had looked as though he'd been hit in the head with a two-by-four, but once the shock eased, Sage couldn't imagine the man complaining about the inheritance. Except for how it was affecting Angie.

There was going to be tension between Evan and her. But Sage hoped to hell they could work it out and find their way past all of this. But for now, their wedding was still postponed and after the will reading, Sage had no idea how long that postponement was going to last.

As for himself, Sage was still staggered by his bequest from J.D. Hell, he'd gotten a bigger share of Lassiter Media than Angie had—and that just wasn't right. Every time he thought about this, he came back to one question: What the hell had J.D. been thinking? And the only way he had even the slightest chance of figuring that out was by getting close to Colleen.

She was the one who had spent the most time with J.D. in the past few months. Sage had heard enough about the young, upbeat, efficient nurse from Marlene and Angie to know that she had become J.D.'s sounding board. He'd talked to her more than he had to anyone else in the last months of his life. And maybe that was because it was easier to talk about your problems to a stranger than it was to family.

But then, J.D. had always been so damned self-sufficient, he'd never seemed to need anyone around him. Until he got sick. That was the one thing he and Sage had always shared in common—the need to go it alone. Maybe that was why they'd never really gotten close. Both of them were too closed off. Too wrapped up in their own worlds to bother checking in with others.

He scowled at the thought. Funny, he'd never before considered just how much he and his adoptive father were alike. Went against the grain admitting it now, because Sage had spent so much of his life rebelling against J.D.

Yes, he knew that Colleen was the one person who might help him make sense of all this. But he hadn't been prepared for that spark of something hot and undeniable that had leaped up between them when she touched him. Sure, he had been interested in her the night of the rehearsal dinner—a beautiful woman, alone, looking uncomfortable in the crowd. But he hadn't had a chance to talk to her, let alone touch her, before everything had changed in an instant. Now he thought again of that flash of heat, the surprise in her eyes, during their confrontation a little while ago, and had to force himself to shove the memory aside. It was clear just by looking at her that she wasn't a one-night-stand kind of woman—but that could change, he assured himself. He couldn't get the image of her out of his mind. Her wide blue eyes. The sweep of dark blond hair. A soft smile curving a full mouth that tempted a man. His body tightened in response to his thoughts. The attraction between them was hot and strong enough that he couldn't simply ignore it.

"So what were you talking to Colleen about?"

"What?" He snapped his gaze up to meet Dylan's, shoving unsettling thoughts aside. "I…uh…" Uncomfortable with the memory of his botched attempt at getting close to the woman, Sage scrubbed one hand across the back of his neck.

"I know that look," his brother said. "What did you do?"

"Might have gotten off on the wrong foot," he admitted, remembering the look of shock on Colleen's face when he'd practically accused her of stealing from J.D. Was she innocent? Or a good actress?

"Why'd you hunt her down in the first place?"

"Damn it, Dylan," he said, leaning across the table and lowering his voice just to be sure no one could overhear them. "She's got to know something. She spent the most time with J.D. Hell, he left her three million dollars."

"And?"

"And," he admitted, "I want to know what she knows. Maybe there's something there. Maybe J.D. bounced ideas off of her and she knew about the changes to the will."

"And maybe it'll snow in this bar." Dylan shook his head. "You know as well as I do that J.D. was never influenced by anyone in his life. Hell," he added with a short laugh, "you're so much like him in that it's ridiculous. J.D. made up his own mind, right or wrong. No way did his *nurse* have any information that we don't."

He had to admit, at least to himself, that Dylan had a point. But that wasn't taking into consideration that the old man had known he was getting up there in years and he hadn't been feeling well. Maybe he started thinking about the pearly gates and what he should do before he went. That had to change things. If it did, who better to share things with than your nurse?

No, Sage told himself, he couldn't risk thinking Dylan was right. He had to know for sure if Colleen Falkner knew more than she was saying. "I'm not letting this go, Dylan. But it's going to be harder to talk to her now, though, since I probably offended the hell out of her when I suggested that maybe she'd tricked J.D. into leaving her that much money."

"You *what?*" Dylan just stared at him, then shook his head. "Have you ever known our father to be tricked into *anything?*"

"No."

Still shaking his head, Dylan demanded, "Does Colleen seem like the deadly femme fatale type to you?"

"No," he admitted grudgingly. At least she hadn't today, bundled up in baggy slacks and a pullover sweater. But he remembered what she'd looked like the night of the party. When her amazing curves had been on display in a red dress that practically screamed *look at me!*

"You've been out on your ranch too long," Dylan was saying. "That's the only explanation."

"What's that got to do with anything?"

"You used to know how to charm people. Especially *women*. Hell, you were the king of schmooze back in the day."

"I think you're thinking of yourself. Not me," Sage said with a half smile. "I don't like people, remember?"

"You used to," Dylan pointed out. "Before you bought that ranch and turned yourself into a yeti."

"Now I'm Sasquatch?" Sage laughed shortly and sipped at his scotch.

"Exactly right," Dylan told him. "You're practically a legend to your own family. You're never around. You spend more time with your horses than you do people. You're a damn hermit, Sage. You never come off the mountain if you don't have to, and the only people you talk to are the ones who work for you."

"I'm here now."

"Yeah, and it took Dad's *death* to get you here."

He didn't like admitting, even to himself, that his brother was right. But being in the city wasn't something he enjoyed. Oh, he'd come in occasionally to meet a woman, take her to dinner, then finish the evening at her place. But the ranch was where he lived. Where he most wanted to be.

He shifted in his chair, glanced uneasily around the room, then slid his gaze back to his brother's. "I'm not a hermit. I just like being on the ranch. I never was much for the city life that you love so much."

"Well, maybe if you spent more time with people instead of those horses you're so nuts about, you'd have done a better job of talking to Colleen."

"Yeah, all right. You have a point." Shaking his head, he idly spun the tumbler of scotch on the tabletop. He studied the flash of the overhead lights in the amber liquid as if he could find the answers he needed. Finally, he lifted his gaze to his brother's and said, "Swear to God, don't know why I started in on her like that."

Dylan snorted, picked up his beer and took a drink. "Let's hear it."

So he told his brother everything he'd said and how Colleen had reacted. Reliving it didn't make him feel any better.

When he was finished, a couple of seconds ticked past before Dylan whistled and took another sip of his beer. "Man, anybody else probably would have punched you for all of that. I know I would have. Lucky for you Colleen's so damn nice."

"Is she?"

"Marlene loves her," Dylan pointed out. "Angie thinks she's great. Heck, even Chance has had nothing but good things to say about her, and you know he doesn't hand out compliments easy."

"All true," Sage agreed.

And yet…Sage's instincts told him she was exactly what she appeared to be. A private nurse with a tantalizing smile and blue eyes the color of a lake in summer. But he couldn't overlook what had happened. What J.D. had done in his will. And the only person around who might have influenced the old man was the one woman who had spent the most time with him. He had to know. Had to find out what, if anything, she knew about the changes to J.D.'s will.

And if she had had something to do with any of this, he would find a way to make her pay.

Three

The Big Blue ranch seemed empty without the larger-than-life presence of J.D. Lassiter. Colleen glanced out the window of the bedroom that had been hers for the past several weeks and smiled sadly. She was going to miss this place almost as much as she would miss J.D. himself.

But it was always like this for her, she thought sadly. As a private nurse, she slipped into the fabric of families—sometimes at their darkest hours. And when her job was done, she left, moving on to the next client. The next family.

She tugged on the zipper of her suitcase, flipped the lid open and then sighed. Colleen hated this part of her assignments. The packing up of all her things, the saying goodbye to another chapter in her life. Positioning these memories onto a high shelf at the back of her mind, where they could be looked at later but would be out of the way, making room for the next patient.

Only this time…maybe there wouldn't be another family.

She shook her head and realized that the silence of the big house was pressing down on her. The only other people at Big Blue right now were the housekeeper and the cook, and it was as if the big house was…lonely. It wouldn't be for long, though. Soon, Marlene, Angelica and Chance would be returning, and she wanted to be gone before they got home. They didn't need her here anymore. By rights, she should have left two weeks ago after J.D.'s death, but she'd stayed on at Marlene's request, to help them all through this hard time.

Colleen walked to the closet and gathered an armful of clothes, carrying them back to the bed. On autopilot, she folded and then stacked her clothing neatly in the suitcase and then went back for more. It wouldn't take long to empty the closet and the dresser she had been using. She'd only brought a few things with her when she moved into the guest room.

Normally, she didn't live in when she took a private client. But J.D. had wanted her close by and had been willing to pay for the extra care, to spare his family having to meet all of his needs. In the past couple of months, Colleen had grown to love this place. The ranch house was big, elegant and yet still so cozy that it wasn't hard to remember that it was, at its heart, a family home.

At that thought, Sage crept back into her mind. He, his brother and sister had all grown up here on this ranch, and if she listened hard enough, she was willing to bet she would be able to hear the long-silent echoes of children playing.

And strange, wasn't it, how her mind continually drifted back to thoughts of Sage? To be honest, he had been on her mind since the rehearsal dinner. He starred nightly in her dreams and even his coldly furious outburst that morning hadn't changed anything. In fact, it had only made her like him more. That outburst had shown her just how much he had cared for his father, despite their estrangement. And the sympathy she felt for the loss he'd suffered was enough to color his accusations in a softer light.

Her brief conversation with Sage Lassiter had left Colleen more shaken than the news that she was now a millionaire. Maybe because the thought of so much money was so foreign to her that her brain simply couldn't process it. But having the man of her dreams actually speak to her was so startling, she couldn't seem to think of anything but him. Even though he'd insulted her.

"Not his fault," she assured herself again as she folded her clothes and stuffed them into the suitcase. "Of course he'd be suspicious. He doesn't know me. He just lost his father. Why should he trust me?"

All very logical.

And yet the sting of his words still resonated with her. Because she couldn't get past the thought that everyone else would believe what he'd blurted out. That somehow she had tricked a sick old man into leaving her money. Maybe she *should* turn it down. Go back to the lawyer, tell him to donate the money to charity or something.

Releasing a breath, she stopped packing and lifted her gaze to the window of the room that had been home for the past three months. The view outside was mesmerizing, as always.

There were no curtains on the windows at Big Blue.

In the many talks Colleen and J.D. had had, she'd learned that was a decree from J.D.'s late wife, Ellie. She'd wanted nothing to stand between her and the amazing sweep of sky. There were trees, too—all kinds of trees. Pines, oaks, maples, aspen. There was a silence in the forest that was almost breathtaking. She loved being here in the mountains and wasn't looking forward to going back to her small condo in a suburb of Cheyenne.

But, a tantalizing voice in her mind whispered, *with your inheritance, you could buy a small place somewhere out here. Away from crowds. Where you could have a garden and trees of your own and even a dog.* A dog. She'd wanted one for years. But she hadn't gotten one because first, her father had been sick, and then when she and her mother moved to Cheyenne, they'd lived in apartments or condos. It hadn't seemed fair to her to leave an animal cooped up all day while she and her mom were at work.

Now, though…her mind tempted her with the possibilities that had opened up to her because of J.D. She could quit her job, focus on getting her nurse practitioner's license and start living the dream that had been fueling her for years. More than that, she could help her mom, make her life easier for a change. That thought simmered in her mind, conjuring up images that made her smile in spite of everything.

The winters in Cheyenne were beginning to get to Colleen's mother. Laura Falkner was always talking about moving to Florida to live with her widowed sister and maybe the two of them taking cruises together. Seeing the world before she was too old to enjoy it all.

With this inheritance, Colleen could make not only her own dreams come true, but her mother's, as well.

Her hands fisted on the blue cotton T-shirt she held. Should she take the money as the gift it had been meant to be? Or should she reject it because she was afraid what small-minded people might say?

"Wouldn't that be like a slap in the face to J.D.?" she asked aloud, not really expecting an answer.

"Lots of people wanted to slap J.D. over the years."

She whirled around to face Sage, who stood in the open doorway, one shoulder braced against the doorjamb. He leaned there casually, looking taller and stronger and somehow more intimidating than he had in the parking lot. And that was saying something. His cool blue gaze was locked on hers and Colleen felt the slam of that stare from all the way across the room.

Her heartbeat jumped into a gallop, her mind went blessedly blank for a second or two and her mouth dried up completely. There was a buzzing sensation going on inside her, too, and it was tingling long-comatose parts of her body back into life. What was it about this man that could turn her into such a hormonal wreck just by showing up?

"What? I mean," she muttered, irritated that once again she felt tongue-tied around him. She'd always thought of herself as a simple, forthright kind of woman. Before now, she had never had trouble talking to anyone. But all Sage had to do was show up and her mouth was so busy thinking of doing other more interesting things that it couldn't seem to talk. "I didn't know you were there."

"Yeah," he said, pushing away from the wall and strolling confidently into the room. "You seemed a little...distracted." He glanced around the sumptuous room, taking in the pale blue quilt, the dozen or more pillows stacked against a gleaming brass headboard and the brightly colored throw rugs covering the polished wood floor. "This place has changed some."

"It's a lovely room," she said, again feeling a pang about leaving.

He glanced at her and shrugged. "When I was a kid, this was my room."

His room. Oh, my. A rush of heat swept through her system so completely, she felt as if she'd gotten a sudden fever. She'd been living in Sage's room for the past few months. If she'd known that before, she might not have been able to sleep at all.

She smiled hesitantly. "I'm guessing it looks a lot different to you, then."

"It does." He walked to the window, looked out, and then turned back to her with a quick grin. "The trellis is still there, though. You ever climb down it in the middle of the night?"

"No, but you did?"

"As often as possible," he admitted. "Especially when I was a teenager. J.D. and I…" His voice trailed off. Then he cleared his throat and said, "Sometimes I just needed to get out of the house for a while."

Colleen tried to imagine Sage as an unhappy boy, escaping out a window to claim some independence. But with the image of the strong, dynamic man he was now, standing right in front of her, it wasn't easy.

"So," he said abruptly, "what do you want to slap J.D. for?"

The sudden shift in conversation threw her for a second until she remembered that he'd been listening when she was talking to herself.

"I don't. I mean…" She blew out a breath and said, "It's nothing."

"Didn't sound like nothing to me," he mused, turning his back on the window and the view beyond to look at her again.

Backlit against the window, he looked more broad shouldered, more powerful…just, *more*. The bedroom suddenly seemed way smaller than it had just a few minutes ago, too. Sage Lassiter was the kind of man who overtook a room once he was in it, making everyone and everything somehow diminished just with his presence. A little intimidating. And if she was going to be honest with herself, a *lot* exciting.

Which wasn't helping her breathing any. "I was thinking out loud, that's all."

"About?"

She met his gaze. "If you must know, about whether or not I should accept the money J.D. left me."

Surprise shone briefly in his eyes. "And the decision is?"

"I haven't made one yet," she admitted, dropping the T-shirt onto her half-packed suitcase. "To be honest, I don't know what I should do."

"Most people would just take the three million and run."

Colleen shrugged helplessly. "I'm not most people."

"I'm beginning to get that," he said, stuffing both hands into his jeans pockets as he walked toward her. "Look, I came on a little strong earlier—"

"Really?" She smiled and shook her head. She remembered everything he'd said that morning. Every word. Every tone. Every glittering accusation he'd shot at her from his eyes. She also remembered that electrical jolt she'd gotten when she touched him.

He nodded. "You're right. And I was wrong. J.D. wanted you to have the money. You should take it."

"Just like that?" She studied him, hoping to see some tangible sign of why he'd changed his mind, but she couldn't read a darn thing on his face. The man was inscrutable. As a businessman, the ability to blank out all expression had probably helped him amass his fortune. But in a one-on-one situation, it was extremely annoying.

"Why not?" He moved even closer and Colleen could have sworn she felt actual *heat* radiating from his body to enclose her in a cocoon of warmth. Warmth that spread to every corner of her body. She swallowed hard, lifted her chin and met his eyes when he continued. "Colleen, if you're thinking about turning down your inheritance because of what I said, then don't."

A cold breeze slipped beneath the partially open window and dissipated the warmth stealing through her. That was probably a good thing. "I admit, what you said has a lot to do with my decision. But mostly, I'm worried that other people might think the same thing."

He pulled one hand from his pocket and slapped it down on the brass foot rail. "And that would bother you?"

Stunned, she said, "Of course it would bother me. It's not *true*."

"Then what do you care what anyone else thinks?"

Did he really not see what it would be like? Were the rich really so different from everyone else? "You probably don't understand because you're used to people talking about you. I mean, the Lassiters are always in the papers for something or other."

"True," he acknowledged.

"And as for you, the press loves following you around. They're always printing stories about the black sheep billionaire." She stopped abruptly when she caught his sudden frown. "I'm sorry, it's just—"

"You seem to keep up with reports about me," he said softly.

"It's hard not to," she lied, not wanting him to know that she really did look for stories about him in the paper and magazines—not to mention online. God, she was practically a stalker! "The Lassiter family is big news in Cheyenne." She covered for herself nicely. "The local papers are always reporting about you and your family."

He snorted. "Yeah, and I'm guessing the will is going to be front-page news as soon as someone leaks the details."

Surprised, she asked, "Who would do that?"

"Any number of clerks in the law offices, I should think," he said. "The right amount of money and people will do or say anything."

"Wow...that's cynical."

"Just a dose of reality," he said, his hand tightening around the brass rail until his knuckles whitened. "I used to think most people were loyal, with a sense of integrity. Then I found out differently."

"What happened?" she asked, caught up in the glimmer of old pain and distant memories glittering in his eyes. The house was quiet, sunlight drifting in through the bedroom window, and it felt as though they were the only two people on the planet. Maybe that's why she overstepped. Maybe that's why she allowed herself to wonder about him aloud rather than just in her mind.

He almost looked as though he would tell her, then in an instant, the moment was gone. His features were once again schooled in pokerlike stillness and his eyes were shuttered. "Doesn't matter. The point is, you shouldn't let gossips rule your decisions."

Colleen was sorry their all-too-brief closeness was gone, but it was just as well. "It sounds so simple when you say it like that, but I don't like being gossiped about."

"Neither do I," he said, glancing down at her suitcase, then lifting his gaze to hers again. "Doesn't mean I can stop it."

He was right and she knew it. Still, he was a Lassiter and rumors and prying questions came with the territory. She was a nobody and she preferred it that way. "Maybe if I don't accept the inheritance, they won't bother because there would be nothing to talk about."

He smiled, but it wasn't a comforting expression. "Colleen, people are going to gossip. Whether you take the money or not, people will talk. Besides, trust me, a beautiful woman like you taking care of J.D. all these months…there's gossip already."

Beautiful? He thought she was *beautiful?* Then what he said struck home. A flush of embarrassment washed over her as she realized he was probably right. There was no doubt talk already, and with her living here at the ranch, she had fed the flames of the gossip.

"That's just awful. I was his *nurse.*"

"A young, pretty nurse with a sick old man. Doesn't take much more than that to get tongues wagging."

She argued that because she had to. For her own peace of mind. Colleen hated to think that people were making ugly accusations about a sweet old man. And oh, God, had her *mother* heard the talk? No. If she had, she would have said something, wouldn't she?

Shaking her head, Colleen said, "But J.D. wasn't my first patient. This has never happened to me before."

He shrugged the argument aside. "You'd never worked for a Lassiter before, either. I'm only surprised you haven't already heard the speculation."

She plopped down onto the edge of her mattress, her mind racing as images from the past few months flashed across her brain. She hadn't really paid attention before, but now that she was looking at things in a new light, she realized he was right. The gossip had already started. She remembered knowing winks, slow smiles and whispered conversations cut short when she entered any of the local shops.

"Oh, my God. They really think that I—that J.D.— oh, this is humiliating."

"Only if you let them win," he said quietly and she looked up at him, waiting for him to continue. "Small minds are always looking for something to occupy them. If you live your life worried about what they're saying, you won't do anything. Then they win."

"I really hate this," she murmured. He did have a point, but this was the first time in her life that she was the subject of gossip. She'd led a fairly quiet existence until she'd taken the job with J.D.

Sage was looking at this from an entirely different angle. The truth was, as a Lassiter, he was insulated from the nastiest rumors and innuendos. He didn't have to worry about what people were saying about him, because his career was already made, and he had a powerful family name behind him. Besides, how bad was it to have people discussing how incredibly gorgeous you were?

No, this was different. If people were talking about her, it could affect her work. Her life. If the nursing agency she worked for got wind of any of this, they might be reluctant to send her out on other assignments—and that made her cringe. On the other hand, if she simply accepted J.D.'s generosity, she could make her own way. Though she would still, as a nurse practitioner, have to work through local doctors and hospitals.

"My head hurts," she muttered.

He laughed and it was such a rich, surprising sound, it startled her. Looking up at him, she saw that his eyes were shining and the wide smile on his face displayed a dimple she was fairly certain didn't show up very often.

"You're thinking about this too much."

"It's very hard not to," she told him, shaking her head. "I've never been in this position before and I'm not really sure what to do about it."

"Do what you want to do," he advised.

Want was a big word. She *wanted* a lot of things. World peace. Calorie-free chocolate. Smaller feet. Her gaze drifted to Sage's mouth and locked there. And she *really* wanted to kiss him.

As that thought settled into the forefront of her mind, Colleen cleared her throat and tried for heaven's sake to get a grip. Honestly, she'd been alone so long, was it really so surprising that a man like Sage Lassiter would tangle her up into knots without even trying?

"Everything okay?" He was frowning now.

"Fine. Fine." She breathed deeply and repeated, "What I want. Do what I want."

"Not so hard, is it?"

"You wouldn't think so…" But she'd been raised to consider more than her wants. There was doing the right thing, and in this case, she just didn't know what that was.

"You know," he murmured, "once you show people you don't care what they think, they usually stop talking about you."

Wryly, she asked, "And if you *do* care what they're saying?"

His lips quirked into a quick half smile that tugged at something inside her. "Well, that's a different story, isn't it? But why would you care?"

"Because I have to work here. Live here. If people think—" She swallowed hard. Everything she'd worked toward, everything she'd built in the past five years. Her reputation…her hopes and dreams. It could all disappear.

Suddenly, the windfall from J.D. looked like more of a curse than a blessing.

"You're giving other people all the power here," Sage said, drawing her attention away from her thoughts.

"I don't want to, but…" Shaking her head, she folded her hands together on her lap. "Ever since this morning, my mind's been filled with questions. And now I don't know what to do about this."

"Not much you can do about it." Sage walked around her, pushed the open suitcase out of his way and took a seat beside her on the bed. "The will's a done deal."

"But I could donate the money."

He shrugged. "People would still talk. The only difference would be you wouldn't have the money."

She sighed heavily and turned to look at him. He was so close to her, his muscular thigh was just a bare inch from brushing against hers. Heat rushed through her and

Colleen forced a deep breath as she met his gaze. His eyes weren't as frosty as they had been earlier, yet they were still unreadable. As if he'd drawn shutters down, to keep others from sensing his emotions. He was so closed off—much like J.D. had been when she'd first come to take care of him. But, she reminded herself, it hadn't taken her long to bypass the older man's defenses and get him to really talk to her.

The difference was, Sage wasn't her patient. He was a strong, completely masculine male who made her feel things she hadn't felt in far too long. Which was, of course, not only ridiculous, but inappropriate. He was the son of her patient. A family member who'd just gone through a devastating loss. He wasn't interested in her and she would only do herself a favor if she found a way to tamp down the rush of attraction she felt every time he came close. Of course, *way* easier said than done.

"Look," he said, his voice quiet, "why don't we have dinner tonight? Give us a chance to talk some more."

She blinked at him, so stunned she could hardly manage to croak, "You're asking me out?"

One corner of his mouth lifted. "I'm asking you to have dinner with me."

Not a date. Of course it wasn't a date. Idiot.

"Why?" *And why are you questioning it,* her mind demanded.

"Well, I still want to talk to you about J.D.," he said. "And it's been a long day. For both of us."

Of course. That explained it, Colleen told herself firmly. He wanted to talk about his father and all she'd managed to do was talk his ear off about *her* problems.

"Okay," she said after a long moment. "That would be nice."

"Great." He stood up and looked down at her. "I'll pick you up at seven."

"I'll give you my address."

"I know where you live," he told her. "I'll see you tonight."

He knew where she lived. What was she supposed to make of that?

"Can I carry your suitcase down to the car?"

"What? Oh. No, thank you." She glanced around the room. "I've still got a few things to pack up."

"All right then, I'll leave you to it," he said, heading for the doorway. When he got there, he paused, turned around and speared her with an unfathomable look. "See you tonight."

When he left, Colleen stared after him for a long minute. Her heartbeat was racing and her knees felt a little wobbly. Her reaction to Sage was so staggering, she wasn't really sure how to deal with it. However, as the sound of his footsteps faded away, Colleen told herself that she couldn't really be blamed for her response to his presence. He was like a force of nature. Sage Lassiter was a gorgeous steamroller, flattening everything in his path.

And Colleen realized that now, for whatever reason, *she* was in his path.

Four

"So how's the rest of dealing with the will going, Walter?" Sage drove straight from Big Blue to the lawyer's office. He wanted a chance to talk to J.D.'s lawyer without the explosive release of emotion that had happened when the family was gathered together. Not that he'd been able to dismiss the anger churning inside him. The plan had been to arrive, calm and cool, and outstare the older man. That didn't happen though, because he was far from feeling cool and detached.

Tension played in every one of his muscles and tugged at the last threads of his patience. Being with Colleen had ramped his body up to the point where he'd practically had to limp his way out of the ranch house. Just sitting beside her on the bed in her room had tested his self-control, because what he'd really wanted to do was lay her back on the mattress and explore those amazing curves she kept so carefully hidden.

Instead, he'd talked to her. And talking to Colleen hadn't solved a damn thing—it had only muddied waters that were already so damn thick it might as well have been concrete. He couldn't make her out. Was she the innocent she seemed to be? Or was she working him as she had worked J.D.? He had to find out…but that was for later. Right now, he had a couple of questions for his late father's lawyer.

"It's coming along but I'm not discussing it with you, Sage, and you damn well know it." Walter Drake steepled his fingers, leaned back in his leather chair and looked at Sage with the barely hidden impatience he would have shown a five-year-old. "J.D.'s will is a private matter. I've already read publicly the parts that affect the family. As for the rest…"

Sage jumped out of his chair and stalked to the far window. Yeah, he was too on edge to be facing down a lawyer. He should have known better than to come here today, but damn it, there were just too many questions about the will.

Looking down on the street below, he focused for a second on the traffic, the pedestrians wandering along the sidewalks and even the mountains jutting into the sky in the distance. He looked anywhere but into the smug features of J.D.'s lawyer.

Going in, Sage had guessed that Walter wouldn't talk. Hell, he wouldn't have even if he *could*. The man liked holding all the power here. Liked having information that no one else did. And getting anything out of him would probably require dynamite—or someone with far more patience than Sage possessed. Fine, then. He'd back off the topic of the rest of the will for the moment and try a different tack. Half turning, he faced the man watching him through hooded eyes.

"All right," Sage said, "never mind."

Walter nodded magnanimously.

"But there's still the matter of J.D. leaving control of Lassiter Media to Evan instead of Angelica."

Walter frowned at him, sat up and braced both elbows on his desktop. "J.D. had reasons for everything he ever did, Sage. You know that."

J.D. had sure thought so. But Sage had given up trying to figure out the old man years ago. The whole time he was growing up, the two of them hadn't even been able to be in the same room together without snarling and growling like a couple of alpha dogs fighting for territory.

But Angelica was different. Right from the start, she had been J.D.'s shining star. So how he could have cut her out of her rightful inheritance was beyond Sage. "Yeah, but what reason could he have for cheating his daughter out of what should have been hers?"

"I can't tell you that."

"Can't?" Sage demanded, walking back to stand opposite the man's desk. "Or won't?"

"Won't." Walter stood up, since staying in his chair required him to look up at Sage, and he clearly didn't enjoy that. "J.D.'s my client, Sage, dead or alive. Not you. Not the Lassiter family."

"And you'll protect him from his damn *family* even after his death?"

"If I have to," Walter said softly.

Frustration clawed at him. "None of this makes sense. You know as well as I do that J.D. had been grooming Angie for years, getting her ready to run Lassiter Media."

"True…"

"So does it seem rational to you that he would leave the company to Angie's fiancé?" There went his grasp on the last slippery thread of temper.

The lawyer only stared at him for a long minute or two. "If you're trying to insinuate that J.D. wasn't competent to make this will, you're wrong. And that allegation would never stand in a court."

"I'm not talking about court." *Yet.* "I'm talking about your knowledge of J.D."

"As I've already said, J.D. had reasons for everything he did, and this is no different."

Sage had no idea why J.D. would have done this. It made no sense at all.

The lawyer's deliberate refusal to give anything away just increased the sense of outrage snarling inside him.

"This isn't getting either of us anywhere, Sage. So if you'll excuse me, I've got business to take care of and—"

"I'm not done with this, Walter," Sage promised. "We all want answers."

For the first time, a flicker of something that might have been sympathy shone in the other man's eyes. "And I wish I could give them to you," he said. "But it's out of my hands."

Frustrated, Sage conceded defeat. At least for now. "Fine. I'll go. But once the family gets over the shock of all of this, I won't be the only one showing up here demanding answers. I hope you're ready for that."

At any other time, Sage might have laughed at the beleaguered expression on the man's face. But right now he just wasn't in the mood to be amused.

Once out in the parking lot, Sage hunched deeper into his black coat as a cold mountain wind pushed at him. Even nature was giving him a hard time today. He crossed to his black Porsche and climbed in. During the winter, this car spent most of its time locked away in a temperature-controlled garage on his ranch. Right now, he was glad he had the sports car. He had a driving need to push the car to its limits, wanting the speed, needing the rush of the moment.

He peeled out of the lot, drove through Cheyenne, and once he was free of the city, cut the powerful engine loose. He backtracked, headed to the Big Blue ranch. By now, Colleen would be gone, but Marlene and Angie would be there. And he had to see his sister. Find out for himself if she was okay. But how could she be? She'd been betrayed by someone she trusted. And Sage knew just how that felt.

The growl of the engine seemed to underscore the rage pumping just below the surface of his mind. Speeding along the road to the ranch forced him to focus, to concentrate on his driving, which gave him a respite from everything else tearing through his brain. He steered the car through the wide ranch gates, kicked up gravel along the winding drive and then parked outside the front doors.

From the stable area came the shouts of men hard at work. He caught a glimpse of a horse in a paddock, running through the dirt, and realized that J.D. being gone hadn't stopped *life* from going on. This ranch would go on, too. The old man had seen to that. But what the hell had he been thinking about the rest of it?

Sage climbed out of the car and paused long enough to take a quick look around the familiar landscape. Much like Sage's own ranch, there were plenty of outbuildings, barns, cabins for the wranglers who lived and worked on the ranch, guest cabins, and even a saltwater pool surrounded by grass, not cement, so that it looked like a natural pond. His gaze fixed on the ancient oak that shaded the pond and a reluctant smile curved his mouth. He, Dylan and Angelica had spent hours out here when they were kids, swinging from a rope attached to one of the oaks' heavy limbs to drop into the cold, clear water.

So much of his life had been spent here on this ranch, and in spite of his estrangement from J.D., there were a lot of *good* memories here, too. He shifted his gaze to the house. Built from hand-cut logs, iron and glass, it was two stories high and boasted wraparound porches with hand-hewn wood railings on both levels. Those porches provided Adirondack chairs with colorful cushions and views of the mountains from almost everywhere.

Sage took a breath. He'd left here only a couple hours ago, but it felt like longer. After mentally dueling with a crafty lawyer, he wanted nothing more than a drink and some quiet. The minute he entered the ranch house, though, he knew the quiet was something that would elude him.

"Why would he do this to me?" Angelica demanded, her voice carrying through the cavernous house.

Three or four people answered her at once and Sage followed the voices to the great room. The heart of the house, the main room was enormous, with honey-toned wood floors, log walls and what seemed like acres of glass windows affording views of the ranch and the wide blue sky that had given the ranch its name above. He'd heard the story often enough to know it by heart.

J.D. and his wife, Ellie, had bought this ranch, then

only two hundred acres, and Ellie had so loved the expanse of deep blue sky that J.D. had decreed the ranch would be named Big Blue, after the sky overhead. Here they'd begun the Lassiter dynasty. Over the years J.D. had added to the property, expanding the ranch into the state's largest cattle herd and building the land holdings up to more than thirty thousand acres. They'd put their stamp on Wyoming and in Cheyenne, the Lassiter name was damn near legend.

Maybe that was part of what Sage had rebelled against all these years. The Lassiter name and what it had meant to J.D. What it had been like to not be born a Lassiter, but *made* into one. With that thought simmering in his brain, he took another step into the chaos.

"Thank heaven," Marlene muttered. "Sage, help me convince your sister that her father wasn't angry at her about anything."

He glanced quickly around the familiar room. The massive stone fireplace, the wide French doors that led to a flagstone patio, the oversize leather couches and chairs dotting the shining wood floor. And the family members scattered across the room, all looking at him.

"What other reason could there be?" Angie asked, throwing both hands high only to let them fall to her sides again. Flipping her dark hair back out of her face, she looked at her oldest brother and said, "I thought he was proud of me. I thought he *believed* in me."

"He did, Angie," Chance put in and she turned on her cousin.

"This is an odd way to show it, don't you think?"

Chance sighed and scrubbed one hand over his face impatiently. Sage could sympathize. The poor guy had probably been trying to cheer Angie up for hours with no success.

"Angie." Evan McCain spoke up then and all eyes turned to him. "You're overreacting."

"Am I?" Shaking her head, Angie looked at the man she had been poised to marry only two weeks ago and it was as if she'd never seen him before. The wedding had been postponed after J.D.'s death, but the two of them had remained close. Until today. Until Evan had been given the company Angie loved. "He gave the company—*my* company—to you, Evan." She slapped one hand to her heart. "I was his daughter and he left it to *you*."

Evan shoved one hand through his hair and looked to Sage for help. But hell, Sage didn't know what he could do. He didn't believe that Evan had tried to undermine Angie. But who the hell knew anymore? Mysterious benefactors. Nurses who inherited three million dollars. A daughter who got cheated out of what should have been hers. None of this made a damn bit of sense.

Still, if they went to war with each other over it, that wouldn't solve a thing either—it would just splinter them when they needed each other most.

"Angie, taking it out on Evan isn't going to help," Sage finally said and he caught a brief look of relief on Evan's face. "We just have to try to figure out what was in J.D.'s mind and then do what we can to change things."

"Can we change anything?" Marlene looked worried, her gaze darting from Angelica to Evan and back again. "The will is done. And even though J.D. was sick, he was mentally competent right up until his last day."

"I know." Sage walked to the woman who had been a mother in all but name to him since he was a kid and wrapped one arm around her shoulders. The scent of her perfume drifted up to him and colored his mind with memories. Marlene had been the one stabilizing influence in his life. Through all of his rebellion with J.D., his aunt was there, talking him down, trying to build a bridge between Sage and his adoptive father. That bridge had never really materialized, but it hadn't been for lack of trying on her part.

Sage dropped a kiss on the top of her head, then looked across the room to Dylan, sprawled in one of the oversize leather chairs.

"You don't have anything to say?"

"I've said plenty," his brother countered, then shifted a glare to their sister. "I was shouted down."

"I didn't shout," Angie argued.

"Like a fishwife," Dylan told her, then glanced at Evan. "If you still want to marry her, you're either brave or brain-dead."

"You're not helping," Sage said.

"Yeah, I heard that from our darling sister an hour ago," Dylan told him tiredly.

"You don't understand how this feels, Dylan," Angelica said, giving him a look that should have set fire to his hair. "Dad didn't take away the business you love, did he?"

"No, he didn't," he admitted.

"Angie," Evan said, stepping toward his fiancée and laying both hands on her shoulders. "I love you. We're getting *married*. Nothing's changed."

She slipped out from under his grip and shook her head. "Everything's changed, Evan. Don't you see that?"

"I don't want to run your company, Angie. You'll

still be doing the day-to-day," he argued. "You're still in charge."

"I don't have the title. I don't have the power. The only reason I would still be in charge is because you *allow* it." She shook her head and bit down hard on her bottom lip before saying, "It's not the same, Evan."

"We'll figure this out," he countered, but Angelica didn't look convinced.

Sage wondered suddenly if maybe J.D. hadn't done all this just so he could hang around as a damn ghost and watch his family jump through the hoops he'd left behind.

"I think we've all had enough for one day," Marlene announced, interrupting what looked as though it could turn into a battle. She walked over to give Angelica a hug, then smoothed a stray lock of her dark brown hair back with gentle fingers. Giving the younger woman a smile, she spoke to the room at large.

"Why don't we all go into the kitchen? We'll have some coffee. Something to eat. It's been a hard day but I think we all have to remember—" she paused, letting her gaze slide around the room "—that we're *family*. We're the *Lassiters*. And we will come through this. Together."

"There's no reason to be so nervous." Jenna Cooper took a sip of her white wine and smiled as Colleen changed clothes for the third time in a half hour.

"I'm not nervous," she replied, "I'm just hyperalert."

Jenna chuckled and curled up into a corner of her chair. Colleen met her friend's amused gaze in the mirror and released a sigh. "Fine. Maybe I'm a little nervous, but there's no reason to be. This is not a date. It's just dinner with a family member of a patient I've lost."

"Uh-huh."

"You might sound a little more convincing when you're placating me."

"I'll work on it," her friend said, still laughing.

Jenna Cooper lived next door, with her husband and adorable three-year-old twin boys, Carter and Cade. At five foot two, Jenna looked like a pixie with very short black hair that curled around her elfin features. Her green eyes were always shining and she and Colleen had been good friends since the second week Colleen had lived in the condo complex two years before.

Knowing Colleen was a nurse, Jenna had come to her door in a panic late one night because one of the boys had had a fever seizure. Colleen had recognized it for what it was immediately and helped them lower Carter's temperature, then she had stayed at the house with a sleeping Cade while Jenna and her husband took Carter to the E.R. to be checked out, just to be on the safe side.

Jenna took a sip of her wine and murmured, "I still can't get over Mr. Lassiter leaving you so much money."

Colleen's stomach churned uneasily and she slapped one hand to her abdomen in a futile attempt to stop it. "Neither can I."

She'd had several hours to think about it, yet it still didn't seem real. Though everything Sage had said to her earlier kept replaying in her mind. The thought of gossip gave her cold chills, but...

"So, have you told your mother yet?"

"About the money?" She shook her head and then frowned at her reflection. Tugging at the scooped bodice, she tried to pull it a little higher, but no matter what she did, you could see cleavage. A *lot* of cleavage. "I never really noticed just how big my boobs are."

"That's because you've usually got them covered up under a layer of cotton and wool." Jenna stood up, smacked Colleen's hand away from the fabric and smiled. "You look gorgeous. Stop fussing. God, that's an amazing dress."

"It is." And ordinarily, she never would have bought anything like it. But Angelica had insisted on taking Colleen shopping for the perfect dress to wear to the rehearsal dinner. Sage's sister had picked this dress out for Colleen and she'd worn it the night Sage had first noticed her. The night…her eyes widened suddenly. "Oh, God. I can't wear this dress tonight. I was wearing it the night Sage's father collapsed and *died.* What was I thinking?"

She turned to head for her bedroom and the pitiful offerings she might find in her closet, but Jenna stopped her with one hand on her arm. "You can't retire the dress, Colleen. For one thing, it didn't kill Mr. Lassiter, and it's just too amazing to be tossed into the dark abyss that is your closet."

"Thank you."

"And for another thing, trust me when I say that when Sage gets a look at you in this dress—" Jenna took a step back, swept her gaze up and down Colleen and whistled "—it won't be funerals that'll spring to mind."

A tiny thrill dazzled Colleen before she remembered that Jenna was her *friend.* Of course she was going to compliment her. *But,* she told herself firmly, *let's be realistic.* Sage Lassiter was *not* interested in her. Going to dinner with him meant absolutely nothing.

"This is crazy," she said aloud. "I'm acting like this is a date and it's not." Colleen wrung her hands together until she realized what she was doing, then she stopped that pitiful action. "Honestly. Slacks and a sweater. That's what I should wear."

"If you change one more time, I'm going to tie you to a chair," Jenna warned. "You look great, you've got a date—"

"Not a date—"

"—you're going to dinner with the most gorgeous man in Wyoming, possibly the United States—"

"I wonder what Tom would say if he heard that."

Jenna grinned. "He's not worried. My Tom's not gorgeous, but he has other…compensations."

"You're impossible." Colleen could admit silently that she felt more than a little envy of her friend's relationship with her very cute husband.

"Tom thinks so…" She grinned again and wiggled her eyebrows for emphasis.

If Colleen had half the confidence that Jenna had, she wouldn't be the slightest bit nervous about her nondate. As it was though…the bats in her stomach—too big for butterflies—were flying in tighter and tighter circles. It was as if they were winding an invisible spring inside her and Colleen was terrified that it was going to snap at just the wrong moment.

Maybe the red dress would help. It was beautiful and wearing it, she couldn't help but feel more confident. Besides, she told herself, Sage might not even remember that she was wearing this dress at the rehearsal dinner.

"Have some wine." Jenna offered her own glass and Colleen snatched at it, taking a big gulp, hoping to drown the bats. Apparently though, they knew how to swim.

"This is a mistake," she muttered and handed the glass back to her friend.

"No, it's not. You're a terrific person, Colleen. It's about time you let some man figure that out for himself."

"It's not a—"

"Yes, yes." Jenna walked back to the love seat, dropped onto the slipcovered cushions and stared up at her. "Now, tell me how my best friend becomes a millionaire and gets a date with *the* Sage Lassiter."

"Weren't you listening? It's *not* a date."

"Whatever." She patted the cushion beside her. "So how're you doing, really, with this crazy, world-shifting, life-altering day?"

Good question. "Actually, I think I'm feeling better about the money."

"Yay!"

Smiling, Colleen thought about sitting down, but she didn't want to wrinkle her dress. How did the beautiful people do this all the time? "Really, I've had all day to think about it, and you know, Sage was right. Even if I give up the money to charity, people will still talk. I'll just be poor while they're talking about me."

"He's obviously brilliant as well as gorgeous. I like him already."

Colleen did, too. Which was worrying on a whole different level. Still, first things first. Now that she'd decided to accept J.D.'s amazing gift, her life was going to change. Big-time. Laughing to herself, she said, "You know this means I can quit my job."

Jenna lifted her glass. "Excellent. Soon-to-be nurse practitioner Colleen Falkner."

Colleen put one hand to her abdomen to ease those bats that were still flying in formation in the pit of her stomach. But it was a futile gesture. Her body had been through so many ups and downs today, there was no calming it. Oddly enough, it wasn't even the money or the knowledge that she could make her dreams come true that was really affecting her. Nope, that was all Sage Lassiter. His eyes. His mouth. The deep rumble of his voice, the impossibly broad shoulders.

Oh, God.

She shouldn't be going to dinner with him. Colleen turned and glanced into the mirror again and what she saw didn't make her feel any better. Her eyes were too wide, her boobs were too big, her hair was a mass of waves on her shoulders because no matter what she'd tried, she hadn't been able to clip it up and keep it from looking like a rat's nest.

Why was she putting herself through this? What if she couldn't talk? What if staring at him across a table turned her into a mute? Or worse, her mind taunted, what if she babbled incoherently?

"Stop."

"What?" Colleen came up out of her nerve-racking thoughts like a drowning woman breaching the surface of a lake. She was practically gasping for air.

Shaking her head, Jenna said, "You're making yourself nuts. It's just dinner, Colleen. You eat dinner every day. You can do this."

Could she? She didn't think so. Heck, her last date had been…oh, God, she couldn't even *remember* when she'd dated last. All she could recall was that the guy in question had bored her to tears and then tried to grope her on her front porch. Good times. "I'm being crazy, aren't I?"

"Just a little."

"Right." Sage certainly wouldn't be boring, she told herself. And if he tried to grope her, she might just let him. Oh, boy. *Get a grip,* she told herself silently. She was making too much of this. Sage wanted to talk about his late father. All she had to do was keep remembering that and she'd be fine. By talking to him, spending time with him, she could help him get the closure he no doubt needed.

This wasn't about *her* and her fantasies. This was about a man, who in spite of his wealth and remarkable good looks, had lost a link to his past. With that thought firmly in mind, she let her sympathy for his loss rise up to drown her silly hormonal meltdown.

"You're right," she said, and reached out to take another sip of Jenna's wine. Colleen hadn't poured herself any because she hadn't wanted to risk alcohol on a nearly empty stomach. But the crisp, sharp taste of the Sauvignon Blanc felt like bliss sliding down her too-tight throat. Then the cold, wheat-colored liquid hit her stomach and immediately soothed those pesky bats.

She took a breath, handed the glass back and checked her reflection one last time. "It's just a meal with a grieving man."

"Yep. Just dinner with the gorgeous, incredibly sexy, unattainable black sheep billionaire," Jenna said with a grin. "No pressure."

Oh, God.

Five

The condo was small, even for a condo.

Sage gave it a quick once-over as he approached the front door. It was tidy, with its cream-colored paint and postage stamp–sized front garden, where spring bulbs were pushing up through the earth. There was a wreath of silk flowers hanging on her front door and when he pushed the doorbell, he wasn't even surprised to hear a series of melodic chimes sounding out from somewhere inside.

What *did* surprise him was Colleen.

She opened the door and every scrap of air escaped from his lungs. She was wearing that red dress again. The one she'd worn the night of the rehearsal dinner. The night he'd really *seen* her for the first time. That damn dress was designed to bring a man to his knees. It molded her figure, defined her luscious breasts and skimmed across rounded hips that made a man think of long, dark nights and hot, steamy sex. Her dark blond hair tumbled over her shoulders and looked like raw honey. He caught the wink of gold earrings when she tossed her hair back and then his gaze dropped lower—to the expanse of smooth, pale flesh that ended in a spectacular display of the tops of her breasts. It was all he could do to lift his gaze to meet her eyes.

"You look beautiful," he said before he could think better of it. Hell, he was always in control of any given situation, and at the moment, he felt like a teenager on his first date. Hard body and vacant mind.

She beamed at him as if he'd handed her flowers, and immediately he told himself he should have done just that. If he was trying to sway her into spilling her secrets, then he should use all the weapons he could bring to bear.

"Thank you," she said, her voice just a little breathless. "Let me get my coat."

She reached into a hall closet, pulled out a heavy black coat and slipped into it, covering herself up so thoroughly, Sage's brain was able to kick back into gear.

She stepped onto the porch, locked her front door, then joined him with another smile. "Shall we go?"

And he knew at that moment, when her blue eyes were staring into his, that this night was not going to go according to plan.

At the restaurant, Sage was grateful for the clink of fine crystal and the murmured conversations that reminded him they were in a public place. Otherwise he might have been in trouble. She was damned distracting, sitting across from him.

"This is lovely," she said, turning her head to look

around the interior of Moscone's Italian restaurant. It was filled with small round tables, covered in white linen and each boasting a single candle in the center. A sleek black-and-chrome bar stood along one wall and Italian arias played softly over the loudspeaker. The floors were tile, the waiters were all in white aprons and the scents filling the air were amazing. "I've never been here before."

"Food's good," Sage mused. "But they're going to have some serious competition when the Lassiter Grill opens up." Damn. He could hardly get words past the knot of need in his throat. Sage took a sip of the wine the waiter had poured just moments before.

"It was really nice of you to bring me here," she said, "but it wasn't necessary. We could have talked at my house."

But then she wouldn't have worn *the dress*. Sage shifted uncomfortably on the black leather bench seat. He hadn't expected to spend the night in agony, but apparently he was going to. And just by looking at her, he knew she had absolutely no idea what she was doing to him. He had to take back control of this situation or he was going to achieve nothing.

"What can you tell me?" he asked, blurting the question out to divert himself from the thoughts plaguing him.

"Anything you want to know."

Like if you talked an old man into leaving you money? Did you steer him away from giving Angelica the company she loves? Did you wear that damn dress on purpose, knowing what it would do to me?

Couldn't start with those questions, though…could

he? His brain scrambled, coming up with a different way to begin.

"First tell me about you. How long have you been a nurse?" Good. Get her talking. Then later, once she'd relaxed her guard, he'd be able to slide the more important questions in.

She took a sip of wine and he watched, hypnotized by the movement in her throat as she swallowed. Not good.

"Eleven years," she said, setting the goblet back onto the table and sliding her fingertips up and down the long, elegant stem.

Sage's gaze fixed on to that motion, and his brain fogged over even as his body went rock hard. He had to force himself to pay attention when she continued to speak quietly.

"When my father got sick, it was such a blessing to be able to help my mom take care of him." Old pain etched itself into her eyes briefly. "After he died, I realized that I was more interested in taking care of people one-on-one than in a hospital setting. I decided to become a private nurse. So I could make a real difference in the lives of families who were going through what we went through."

Was she really as selfless and kind as she appeared? He wanted to spot deception, gamesmanship in her eyes, but those soft blue depths remained as clear and guileless as ever. Was she really that good an actress, he wondered. Or was she really an innocent?

No, he mentally assured himself. There were no innocents anymore. And a woman this staggeringly beautiful had no doubt learned before she was five just how to work a man.

Pleased that he'd managed to wrest control of his

own urges, he asked, "How long ago did you lose your father?"

"Six years," she said softly and her features once again twisted with sorrow.

"Then," she added, "Mom and I both decided we needed a change, a chance to get away from the memories, so we left California and came here."

"Why Cheyenne?"

She laughed a little and her blue eyes sparkled with it. Instantly, his control drowned in a sea of pulsing desire that grabbed hold of him and wouldn't let go.

"You won't believe it."

"Try me."

"Okay." She leaned in a little closer, as if telling a funny story. Unfortunately, this increased his view of the delectable cleavage that dress displayed.

"We laid a map of the U.S. out on the dining room table and Mom closed her eyes and poked her finger down. She hit Cheyenne and here we are."

Surprise and a bit of admiration rose up inside him, however reluctantly. "Just like that. You packed up and moved to somewhere you'd never been before."

"It was an adventure," she told him with a smile. "And we both needed one. Watching someone you love die by inches is horrible. At least you were spared that. I know it's not much comfort though."

He didn't speak because, frankly, what the hell could he say? She'd obviously had a much better relationship with her father than he'd had with his.

"Although," she added, "the snow was hard to get used to. We're California girls through and through, so we needed a whole new wardrobe when we got here."

"I can imagine." His mind brought up the image of

her seeing her first snowfall, and he almost wished he'd been there to witness it.

"When your winter coat is a sweatshirt and you can wear flip-flops year-round…" Another bright smile. "Let's just say it was even more of an adventure than we'd thought it would be."

"But you enjoy it?"

"I love it," she said simply. "I'd never had a change of season before. I love the fall. And the snow is so beautiful. Then the spring when everything comes alive again. Mostly though, I love the mountains."

"Me, too." Funny, he hadn't thought they'd find common ground, but here it was. Unless, his mind chided, she was saying what she thought he wanted to hear. After all, if J.D. had talked about him as she said, then she knew Sage owned a ranch in the high country, and why else would he do that if he didn't love the mountains?

"I know… J.D. told me about your ranch."

Ha! Proof then. But he played along. "If I can help it, I rarely come down off the mountain into the city."

"I know that, too," she said, her hand stilling on the wineglass. "J.D. talked about you a lot. How you preferred your ranch to anywhere else in the world. He missed seeing you, but said that you almost never left the ranch."

A flare of something hot slashed through him. Guilt? He didn't *do* guilt. "J.D. didn't have much room to talk. You could hardly blast him off the Big Blue with a stick of dynamite."

"True," she said, agreeing with him. "He told me. Truth is, he used to worry that you were too much like him. Too ready to cut yourself off from everything."

"I'm not cut off." Hadn't Dylan said the same thing

to him just hours ago? Why did everyone assume that because a man was happy where he was that he was missing out on other things?

"Aren't you?" It was softly asked, but no less invasive.

He stiffened and the desire pumping through him edged back just a little. Sage hadn't brought her there to talk about *him*.

"No," he assured her, and even he heard the coolness in his tone. "Just because I didn't visit J.D. doesn't mean I'm a damn hermit."

Hermits had a hell of a lot more peace and quiet than he ever got. It wasn't that Sage didn't love his family, he did. He only preferred the solitude of his ranch because nothing good ever came of mixing with people—

He cut that thought off and buried it amid the rubble of his memories.

"He missed you."

Three words that hurt more than he would have thought possible. Sage and J.D. had been at odds for so many years, it was hard to remember a time when things were different. He didn't want to feel another sting of guilt, but how the hell could he avoid it? J.D. had been old and sick and still Sage hadn't been able to get past their differences. Would that haunt him for the rest of his life? Would he have yet another regret to add to the multitude he already carried?

Shaking his head, he told her, "Our arguments were legendary. J.D. and I mixed about as well as oil and water. There's just no way he missed me, so you don't have to worry about telling pretty lies and trying to make me feel better. I know the truth."

About that, anyway.

"It's not a lie," she said, pausing for another sip of her wine.

What was it about the woman's throat and the slim elegance of it that fascinated him?

"He did miss you." She smiled at him again and the warmth in her eyes washed over him. "He told me about your arguments. And really, I think he missed them. He had no one to butt heads with, and that must have been frustrating for a man as strong and powerful as he once was."

Frowning now, Sage saw that she might just have a point. Even though his relationship with J.D. had never been a close one, he knew that his adoptive father had gone through life like a charging bull. Putting his head down and rushing at problems, determined to knock them out of his way through sheer force of will.

J.D. Lassiter had been the kind of man who let nothing stand between him and his goals. He'd bent the world to his whim and pushed those around him into line—or in Sage's case, had *tried* to. For him to be reduced to a sick bed because his heart had turned on him must have been wildly frustrating. Surprisingly, Sage felt a twinge of sympathy for the old man rattle around inside him before he could stop it.

"He told me that he and his wife adopted you and Dylan when you were boys."

Seemed J.D. had talked her damn ears off. Which gave him hope that somewhere in there, he might have confessed the reasons behind his will.

"They did," he said and reluctantly was tossed into the past.

He had been six and Dylan four when they went to live on Big Blue. Their parents had just been killed in a traffic accident and they'd clung to each other in an unfamiliar world. Then J.D. and Ellie had swooped in and suddenly, everything was different. Their lives. Their home. Their parents. All new. All so damned hard to accept. At least for Sage. Dylan, maybe because he was younger, had accepted the change in their lives with much more ease.

Sage had refused to let go of his memories...of the life he'd been forced to surrender. He'd bucked against the rules, had fought with his new parents and in general been a pain in the ass, now that he thought about it. He'd grumbled about everything, comparing their new life to the old and the new always came up short.

Ellie had tried relentlessly, through patience and love, to get through to Sage and eventually she'd succeeded. But J.D. hadn't had the patience to carefully win Sage over. Instead, he'd simply demanded respect and affection and Sage had refused to give either.

The two of them had fought over everything, he remembered now. From doing chores as a kid to driving as a teenager. Sage had instinctively gone in the opposite direction of anything J.D. recommended. There'd been plenty of battles between them, with Ellie stepping in as peacemaker—until she died after giving birth to Angelica.

And the love they shared for Sage's sister was the one thing he and J.D. had ever agreed on. She had been the glue in their shattered family. Without Ellie there, they would have all floundered, but caring for Angelica kept them all afloat. Then Marlene had moved in and because she hadn't expected their love, she'd won their hearts.

Shaking his head now, Sage reached for his wine and gulped it down as if it were water. The waiter appeared, delivering their meals, and for a moment or two, there was silence. Then they were alone again and Colleen finally spoke.

"I'm sorry. I didn't mean to bring back unpleasant memories."

"You didn't," he lied, smoothing his voice out as easily as he mentally paved over memory lane.

"Okay." She took a small bite of her ravioli, then chewed and swallowed. "Well, I've been talking forever. Why don't you tell me about your ranch?"

Sage stared at her for a long minute as he tried to figure out what she was up to. But damned if he could see signs of manipulation on her features.

So he started talking, grateful to be in comfortable territory. He watched her face as she listened to him, and enjoyed the shift and play of emotions she made no attempt to hide. But as he told her about his place, Sage realized something. He wasn't going to be getting the information he needed tonight. She was either really skillful at turning the conversation away from her—or she was as sweet and innocent as she appeared to be. But either way, it was going to take longer than he'd thought to find out exactly what she knew.

Oddly enough, that thought didn't bother him at all.

"You can't be serious." Laura Falkner dropped into her favorite chair and stared up at her daughter as if she'd just sprouted another head. "Three million dollars?"

Colleen drew a deep breath and realized that over the past few days, she had actually gotten *used* to the idea of having three million dollars. Okay, it was still a little weird to know that she wasn't going to have to worry about paying her cable bill—or anything else. But she'd finally come to grips with the idea that J.D. had meant for her to have this. That he'd wanted to help her reach her dreams, and she only wished that she could look him in the eye and say *thank you*.

Now, seeing her mother's reaction to her news made Colleen excited all over again. She was so glad she'd waited a few days to tell her mom. Colleen had wanted to get everything in order, have her plan set in stone so her mom couldn't argue with her over any of it. It hadn't been easy to wait. The past three days had been a whirl-wind of activity. She'd hardly had a chance to really sit down and appreciate just how much her life had changed.

And thanks to J.D.'s generosity, her mother's life was about to change, too.

Looking around the apartment she and her mom had shared when they first moved to Cheyenne, Colleen smiled. There were good memories here, but soon her mother would be making new memories. Enjoying the dreams she'd always tucked aside. And that pleased her, even though she knew she would miss her mom being so close by.

"I'm completely serious," Colleen replied, sitting in the chair opposite her mother. She reached out and took her mom's hands in hers. "It's all true. I'm going to get my nurse practitioner's license and buy myself a cabin in the mountains as soon as possible."

"Honey, that's wonderful." Laura pulled her hands free of her daughter's grasp, then cupped Colleen's face between her palms. "It's been your dream for so long, having a rural practice." Leaning back in her chair, she smiled even more broadly. "I'm delighted for you. Of course I was so sad to hear that Mr. Lassiter had died, but it was so good of him to remember you."

"It really was." She could see that now and accept J.D.'s bequest for the gift it was. She didn't care anymore if people talked. As Sage had pointed out, either way, she couldn't stop them, so why shouldn't she be grateful to J.D. and enjoy what he'd tried to give her?

Sage.

Just the thought of his name sent ripples of anticipation racing through her. It had been three days since their dinner together, and the one-time-only night to talk about J.D. had turned into something more. Sage had taken her to a movie two nights ago, and last night to a country-western club for dancing. She still didn't understand why he wanted to spend so much time with her, but she was enjoying herself more than she would have thought possible.

Dragging herself away from thoughts of Sage, Colleen focused on what she'd come to tell her mother. "There's more, Mom."

"More?" Laura just blinked at her. "You have financial security. You're about to make your dream job a reality. What's left?"

"Your dreams."

"What?" Her mother had the wary look in her eyes that she used to get when Colleen was a child and up to something.

"You know how you're always talking about moving to Florida to live with Aunt Donna?"

The two sisters were both widows now, and they'd discussed for years how much fun it would be if they could live together. But neither of them had been able to afford the move, so it just hadn't been possible. Until now.

"Yessss…"

"Well, you're going to."

"I'm—" Her mother's mouth snapped shut. "Don't be silly."

"It's not silly." Colleen had it all worked out in her mind. In fact, since the reading of the will three days before, she'd spent a lot of time on the phone, talking to lawyers, bankers, real estate agents and travel agencies. She had wanted every detail clear in her mind before broaching the subject to her mother. It had all been worth it, too, because as she started laying out her plans, Laura was dumbstruck.

"I've found a perfect house for you and Aunt Donna. It's gorgeous and it's in this lovely retirement community outside Orlando."

"You can't do that, you don't have the money yet and—"

Colleen cut her off quickly. "It's amazing how willing banks are to give you a line of credit based on a lawyer's sworn affidavit that a will's bequest is coming."

"You didn't."

"Oh, yes, I did." Walter Drake wasn't the easiest lawyer to talk to, but he had assured Colleen that she would be able to draw on her bequest almost immediately. And he'd gone out of his way to set up the line of credit with a local bank.

Laura pushed out of the chair and walked the few steps to the narrow, galley-style kitchen. Busily, she filled a teakettle with water and set it on the stove, all the while shaking her head and muttering.

"Mom—"

"You shouldn't have done that, Colleen," her mother said, not even looking at her. She turned the fire on under the kettle, then grabbed two mugs from a cupboard and dropped a tea bag into each of them. "I don't want you spending money on me. I want you to have that money to keep you safe."

Colleen's heart turned over. Her mom was the most unselfish person she'd ever known in her life. She always gave and never once had she done anything purely for herself. Well, that was about to change, whether she liked it or not.

Joining her mother in the kitchen, Colleen gave her a hard hug, then said, "I couldn't spend all of that money if I tried and you know it."

"Just the same—"

"Mom." Colleen tried another tack. "Getting a house for you and Donna, so you can live without the snow making your arthritis worse, that makes me feel *great*. And, I only put a down payment on it. I would never buy you a house you haven't even seen."

"I don't like this…"

"You will," Colleen said, hugging her again. "And anyway, if you don't like the house, we'll find something else. I just thought it would be a good idea because this community has people to take care of your yard and watch over your house while you're traveling—"

"Traveling?"

This was so much fun, it was like Christmas morning. Colleen grinned. "Yes. You're going to travel. Just like you always wanted to."

"Honey, enough. You know I can't let you do this. Any of it." Laura finally found her voice and naturally she was using it to try to turn down her daughter's generosity.

"Too late, it's already done." Colleen hurried back into the living room, grabbed her purse and carried it back to the kitchen. She set it onto the small round table, slid one hand inside and came back up with a batch of cruise brochures. Handing them over to her mother, she tapped her index finger on the top one.

"A world cruise?" Laura dropped into one of the kitchen chairs as if she'd suddenly gone boneless.

"Yes." Colleen really did feel like Santa. A tall, busty Santa with big feet. "It doesn't leave for another three months, though, so you and Aunt Donna have plenty of time to get your passports and shopping done, and I thought we could talk about your moving to Florida as soon as you get back. Of course, if you'd rather move right away, I understand, but I don't know that I'm ready to have you leave just yet and…"

She stopped talking when she saw the tears spill from her mother's eyes and run down her cheeks. "Don't cry. You're supposed to be happy! Did I mention that you and Aunt Donna are going to be sharing the presidential suite on your cruise? There are pictures in the brochure. You have a full balcony. And butler service and twenty-four-hour room service and—"

Laura choked out a laugh, then lifted one hand to her mouth, shaking her head in disbelief.

"Mom, are you okay?"

"I don't think so," she murmured, staring down at the brightly colored brochures displaying pictures of England, Scotland, Switzerland and more. "I can't let you do this, honey…"

"Mom." Colleen hugged her mother tightly, then leaned back and looked into watery blue eyes much like her own. "You've given me everything for so long. I want to do this. I *can* do this now and if you fight me on it—"

Laura laughed a little again. "You'll what?"

"I'll hold my breath." She smiled, hoping to coax an answering smile from her mother. Holding her breath had been her threat of choice when she was a little girl and using it now was a deliberate choice.

"You never could stop talking long enough to hold your breath for long," her mother finally said, and Colleen knew she'd won.

"Well, I had very important things to say. Just like now." She plucked one of the brochures from her mother's hands and spread it open, showing the sumptuous cabin her mother and aunt would be sharing on their twelve-week cruise. "Just look at this, Mom. Can you imagine?"

"No," she said, sliding one hand across the high-gloss paper, "I really can't."

"I'm going to want lots of pictures cluttering up my in-box."

"I'll email every day." She frowned. "They do have computers on board, right?"

"Absolutely. Complete with Skype. We can talk face-to-face whenever you have time." As she thought about it, she said, "Maybe we'll get you a computer tablet, too, so you can video chat with me from Stonehenge!"

"Donna's not going to believe this," her mother whispered, unable to tear her gaze away from the pictures of a dream of a lifetime coming true.

Six

A few hours later, Colleen sat across from Sage in a local coffee shop. "You should have seen my mother's face," she said, grinning at the memory.

"She must have been shocked." He could imagine. Hearing her talk about what she'd done for her mother had stunned Sage into silence himself.

Far from the grasping, manipulative woman he'd assumed her to be, she'd arranged for her mother and aunt to have the trip they'd always dreamed instead of spending her money on herself. Admiration flowed through him, along with the desire that had become as familiar to him as breathing over the past few days.

Since that first dinner hadn't brought him any information, Sage had made it his business to spend as much time with Colleen as possible. Though they hadn't been able to speak at the movies, watching her reaction to the drama playing out on the screen had fascinated him. Tears, laughter, a jolt of surprise at the happy ending—she was so easy to read and at the same time, so damn complicated he didn't know what to make of her.

Long ago, he had decided that women weren't to be trusted. That they turned their emotions on and off at whim, the better to acquire whatever they happened to be after at the time. Tears were a woman's best weapon, as he'd discovered early on. But on the surface, at least, Colleen seemed…different.

And that both intrigued and worried him.

"Oh, she really was." Shaking her head, she picked up her burger and took a bite, still smiling. "Mom and Aunt Donna have been planning fantasy trips for years. They go back and forth, deciding what hotels they'll stay in, what countries they'll see. They go online and look up cruise packages, just to torture themselves." She took a breath and sighed happily. "Knowing that they're going to actually get to go and *experience* everything they've always talked about is just…amazing."

"*You're* amazing," he murmured, thinking his voice was so soft it would be lost in the clatter and noise from the rest of the patrons surrounding them.

He should have known she'd hear him.

"Why?"

Sage shrugged, sat back in the booth and draped one arm along the back. "Most people, receiving a windfall like you did? They'd go out and buy themselves fast cars, a house that's too big and too expensive, all kinds of things. But you didn't. You bought your mother's dreams."

She smiled. "What a nice way to put it."

Her eyes were shining and that smile lit her face up

like a damn beacon. Something inside him turned over and he was pretty sure it was his heart. That was unsettling. Sage had spent most of his life carefully building a wall around his heart, keeping out anything that might touch him too deeply. His family was one thing. His brother and sister were a part of him, and he accepted the risk of loving them because there was no way he could live without them.

But to love a woman? To trust love? No. He'd nearly made that mistake years ago, and he'd steered clear of it ever since. He'd had a narrow escape and hadn't come away unscathed even at that. So the women he allowed into his life now were nothing like Colleen. They were temporary distractions…just blips on a radar that was finely tuned for self-protection. Colleen was something different. If she was who he now believed her to be, then he had no business being around her. But for the life of him, he couldn't stay away.

Frowning now, he said, "What about your plans? Your dreams?"

She picked up her iced tea and took a long drink. "Well, I already told you my main goal. I'm going to get my nurse practitioner's license."

"Because?"

"Because what I'd really like to do is have a rural practice," she said, leaning toward him over the table.

He caught himself wishing she was wearing that red dress again so he could get another peek at her luscious breasts. Instead though, she wore an emerald-green sweater over a white T-shirt with a slightly V-shaped neckline. Her jeans were soft and faded and hugged her curves like a lover's hands. And even the casual clothing couldn't dispel the desire that pumped through him just sitting across from her.

For a man who prided himself on his rational thinking and ability to concentrate on the task at hand, it grated that while she talked, all he could think about was laying her down atop the table and burying himself deep inside her.

"There are a lot of people in the high country who live so remotely it's hard to get into town to see a doctor," she was saying and he could read the excitement on her face with every word she spoke. "Or if they can, they can't afford it."

She kept surprising him.

Wanting to devote herself to a rural practice would be a hard, even dangerous way to build a career. Why wasn't she like other women? Why wasn't she making plans for spa trips and exclusive shopping excursions? Hell, she'd bought her mother and aunt an around-the-world cruise. But for herself, she wanted to live and work in the wilderness areas?

That thought settled in his mind and his brain drew up a series of uncomfortable images. Colleen trying to dig her way out of a blizzard. Colleen's little Jeep careening off a mountain road and sailing down into a rock-strewn canyon. Colleen freezing to death in her car because she'd gotten lost.

His stomach twisted into knots and he told himself that it was none of his business if she wanted to risk her life by working somewhere she had no knowledge of. He was only with her to find out what she knew. There was no real relationship between them. She wasn't his to protect.

But damn it, *someone* had to set her straight.

"Driving up into the mountains from Cheyenne is going to make for a hell of a commute. Especially in winter," he pointed out, with a warning note in his tone that he hoped would get past the spirit of adventure he saw so clearly in her eyes.

Colleen flashed him a smile that shone from those cornflower-blue eyes and hit him like a sledgehammer.

"That's part two of my plan," she said, clearly pleased with herself. "I'm not going to be commuting every day. That would be silly and time-consuming. Instead, I'm selling my condo and I'm going to buy a cabin or a small house higher up in the mountains."

Those mental images rose up again, only this time, he saw Colleen in a remote cabin, no help for miles around. An icicle dropped down his spine.

"And live there by yourself?" He didn't like the sound of that. Not that there were a million crazies running around the mountains or anything, but hell, you didn't need a human enemy to worry about. Nature could kill you just for the hell of it. And nature in the wilderness had attitude.

"I'm a big girl," she countered, airily brushing aside his concerns. "I can take care of myself."

"No doubt," he said, though he doubted it very much. "In the city. Where there are police to call if you need help. Neighbors right next door. Grocery stores. Not to mention that you grew up in California. What do you know about digging yourself out of ten-foot snowdrifts or how to stockpile firewood for winter? What do you know about driving on roads that haven't been cleared by the county after a storm?"

She frowned a little, then took a breath and admitted,

"Okay, there's a learning curve. But I can adapt. I'll figure it out as I go. It'll be another adventure."

"Learning as you go can turn it into a *final* adventure."

Sighing, Colleen pushed her lunch plate to one side, apparently losing her appetite as they talked. She took another sip of her iced tea, then set the glass down. "Why are you raining on my parade, Sage? You live up on the mountain and you love it."

"This isn't about shooting down your dreams, Colleen," he said tightly. "This is about being realistic. Thinking things through."

"I have thought it through. I've *been* thinking about this for years." She leaned even closer and Sage was caught in her eyes. "I could make a real difference in people's lives."

"Or end your own," he told her, hating that the shine in her eyes dimmed a little at his words. But better she be disappointed than in danger. "I was raised up there, Colleen. I know how to survive bad weather. More than that, I know not to turn my back on the mountain. I don't take anything for granted."

"You weren't born knowing all of that, though," she said, determination clear in her voice. "You learned. So can I."

Sage tore his gaze from hers and glanced around the coffee shop. He needed a minute to get ahold of himself. To keep from *ordering* her to stay off the damn mountain. Conversations rose and fell from the dozens of customers gathered in the sunlit restaurant. An occasional burst of laughter rang out, and the scent of coffee and hamburgers hung in the air. Coming here to the coffee shop had seemed like a good idea at the time. With the amount of tension he'd been living with the past few days, he'd figured that taking Colleen to a crowded place in the middle of the day was one way to help him keep a tight grip on his control. Naturally, that wasn't working out as he'd planned. Pretty much nothing had since he'd first met Colleen.

Shaking his head grimly, Sage noticed the number of strange faces among the crowd. Tourists were streaming into Cheyenne already, clogging up the streets and making the restaurants even more crowded than usual. Soon, the summer crowds would be arriving. By the end of July, thousands would be here for Cheyenne Frontier Days, reliving the Old West and enjoying the world's largest outdoor rodeo. There would be ten days of parades, carnivals and food fairs. For a second, he thought about the rodeo itself and remembered what it had been like to ride in front of thousands of cheering people.

Of course, it wasn't just the rodeo that drew people to Cheyenne. Summer was filled with tourist attractions from the eight-foot-tall painted fiberglass cowboy boots situated all over the city to the carefully staged, G-rated "gunfights" acted out daily by the Cheyenne Gunslingers. There were tours, art festivals and so many other activities, people came to Cheyenne and poured hundreds of thousands of dollars into the local economy.

As for Sage, he tried to stay on the mountain to avoid all of those people. He spent summers working with the horses and trying to forget that there was a world outside his ranch. Right now, though, summer was still months away and Sage's mind was preoccupied by the thought of Colleen, midwinter, all alone on the mountain. Cold dropped into the pit of his stomach and stayed there.

He shifted his gaze back to hers and barked, "You can't do it."

"Excuse me?" Her face went blank for an instant, and then her cheeks flushed with color and her eyes started firing sparks at him.

"Maybe I put that the wrong way," he allowed, since he hadn't been thinking at all when the words shot from his throat.

"You think?"

Colleen felt a quick spurt of irritation, then squashed it again quickly. Yes, Sage was being a little authoritarian, but he had backed off quickly, too, hadn't he? It was in his nature to take command. She could tell that by the way he stood, so tall and alert, his gaze constantly darting around his surroundings, as if checking for any problem that might arise. He was the kind of man who would always do what he could to keep people safe— whether they appreciated it or not.

And now, he was trying to protect *her*. Which made her feel good enough that she was willing to overlook the fact that he was also trying to keep her from doing what she'd always dreamed of doing. Actually, she could hardly believe she was out with him. Again. And the past few times she'd been with him had absolutely been dates.

Even Jenna agreed that this had moved way beyond him wanting closure after his father's death. There was something else going on here. They rarely talked about J.D. anymore, instead sharing stories about their lives and talking about everyday things. So if it wasn't about his dad, what else could it be? She wasn't sure, but she had decided to simply enjoy this time with Sage for as long as it lasted. Because she knew, at the heart of it, she just wasn't the kind of woman to capture and hold the interest of a man like him.

"I didn't mean that you *can't*," he was saying and Colleen came up out of her thoughts to focus her attention on him. "What I meant was that you can't just decide to live in what could be dangerous terrain while knowing nothing about survival." Colleen couldn't help it—she laughed. He looked so serious. So…growly. A small, tiny part of her thrilled to hear him trying protect her. But the reality was, she took care of herself very well.

"You make it sound as though I'm talking about moving to the middle of nowhere. This isn't the frontier, Sage. I'll be perfectly safe."

"Probably," he agreed, "but the country—especially the *high* country—can be dangerous."

She shook her head, then pushed her hair back from her face and gave him a patient smile. "How dangerous can it be, really?"

"Bears?" he fired back.

Before she could react to that disturbing thought, he continued.

"Mountain lions? Snakes? Blizzards?" He picked up his coffee and took a drink. "You're not in any way prepared for that kind of life, Colleen. You're asking for trouble if you do this."

He was right. She hadn't really considered any of that, and she could admit, at least to herself, that the thought of facing any *one* of those dangers on her own was… intimidating. All right, terrifying. But there had to be a way to make this work. "Fine, I admit you have a point."

He nodded.

"*But* if I knew how to handle myself in those situations, I'd be okay, right?"

"Sure," he said, one corner of his mouth curving up. "*If.* And that's a big *if.*"

"You could teach me."

"What?" He paused, coffee cup halfway to his mouth.

The idea had just leaped into her mind, but now that it was there, she ran with it. J.D. had told her so much about Sage—there was no one she would trust more to show her what she needed to know. "I promise, I'm a quick study. And you said yourself that you grew up in the mountains. No one knows them better than you do, right?"

"I suppose…" He set his still-steaming mug of coffee down onto the table and stared at her. And that penetrating stare was so…disconcerting, it was hard to draw an easy breath. His eyes were just hypnotic. At least to Colleen. Honestly, she was proud of herself just for being able to speak coherently while looking into those deep blue eyes of his. His jaw was tight, his dark brown brows drawn into a scowl, and still she thought he was the most gorgeous man she'd ever seen.

Every time he looked at her, she felt that swirl of batwings in the pit of her stomach—not to mention heat that burned just a bit lower. She'd never been so aware of herself as a woman as she was when she was with Sage Lassiter. He made her feel things she'd never experienced before and *want* things she knew she shouldn't.

Being with him was a kind of pleasurable torture, which had to be an oxymoron or something, but she really couldn't think of another way to put it. She enjoyed his company, but her body was constantly buzzing out of control around him, too. Which left her breathless, on edge and in a constant state of excitement. It was the most alive she'd felt in years.

"What do you think, Sage?" She kept her gaze fixed on his. "Will you show me what I need to know?"

His features froze and she watched a muscle in his jaw twitch spasmodically. His fingers drummed against the tabletop and he shifted in his seat. He was thinking about it, and Colleen anxiously waited to see what he would say.

Finally, her patience was rewarded.

"You want to learn to survive on the mountain."

"Yes." She bit her bottom lip.

"Fine," he said. "I'll teach you."

A wash of relief and something that felt like eager anticipation swept through her. "That's *great,* thank you."

He laughed shortly. "Save your thanks. By the time we're finished, you'll probably be cursing me."

"No, I won't." She shook her head and reached across the table to cover one of his hands with hers. "J.D. always told me how kind you were and I've really seen that for myself in the past few days."

He just stared at her through eyes that had been carefully shuttered. "J.D. was wrong. I'm not kind, Colleen."

His features were hard, his body language cold. He was pulling back from her even while he was within reach. She didn't know why. "If it's not kindness," she asked quietly, "what is it?"

He just looked at her for a long moment and she had the feeling he was trying to decide whether to answer her or not. Then she got her answer.

"You said you don't have a job to go to anymore, right?"

"No, I don't. I turned in my resignation at the agency." And hadn't that felt incredible? She had liked her job well enough, but now that her dream was within her reach, she didn't mind at all saying goodbye to the private agency. "Until I get my practitioner's license, I'm officially unemployed."

"All right then," he said, coming to some internal decision. "We'll start day after tomorrow. You come up to my ranch and stay for a few days. We'll go up the mountain from there."

"Stay? At your ranch?" Heat sizzled through her veins, and even while a delicious tingle settled deep inside her, Colleen felt a tiny niggle of worry.

He was going to teach her to survive in the mountains. But who could teach her how to survive a broken heart when this time with him was over?

Logan Whittaker was handsome, friendly and professional. Late thirties, he was tall, with nearly black hair, warm brown eyes and when he smiled, a disarming pair of dimples appeared in his cheeks. He wore a sports coat over a pair of black jeans and a long-sleeved white shirt, black cowboy boots betraying his Texas heritage.

As a partner at Drake, Alcott and Whittaker, he was able to meet with Colleen the next morning, when Walter Drake was busy elsewhere.

She walked into his office and took a quick, admiring look around. The room was huge, befitting a partner. Neutral colors, with navy blue accents, including a navy blue sofa and matching visitor chairs situated on one side of his massive desk. There was a blue-and-white-tiled fireplace on one wall with an empty mantel over it. No family pictures to clutter up his office.

The windows along the hallway boasted electric shades that were in a halfway-down position. It was all very businesslike but hospitable, much like Logan himself seemed to be.

"I really appreciate you seeing me on such short notice."

"Not a problem," Logan said, stepping forward to take her hand in a firm shake before steering her toward one of the visitor's chairs. "Walter and I are sort of working a tag team on the Lassiter will. We're each dealing with different angles, and sometimes the lines cross."

She had to smile. The slight hint of a Texas accent flavored his speech, but couldn't hide the fact that he seemed agitated and a little harried. "Having some trouble with J.D.'s will?"

He blew out a breath, took a seat in his chair behind the wide desk and then shot her a heart-stopping grin. "Is it that obvious?" A short laugh rumbled from his throat as he shook his head. "Let's just say there are some issues with the estate that I'm not at liberty to discuss and leave it at that."

"Well, that sounds frustrating."

"Oh, it is." He pushed one hand through his hair and said, "But I'll get it done."

The look in his eyes was sheer determination, and Colleen didn't doubt for a minute that he would succeed.

"Now, how can I help you, Ms. Falkner?"

"Colleen, please." She scooted forward to the edge of the leather chair and leaned her forearm on his desk. "Walter helped me set up a line of credit at a local bank, but—"

"What is it?" He gave her his full attention, and Colleen thought at any other time, she might have been mesmerized by his eyes. The man was exceptionally good-looking and when he looked at a woman with his complete concentration, she could only assume that most women melted into a puddle at his feet. As it stood now, though, Logan Whittaker, as handsome and compelling as he was, couldn't hold a candle to Sage Lassiter.

Letting go of that train of thought, she brought herself back to the business at hand. The reason she'd come here.

"I really just wanted to make sure everything is going through without any trouble." Shrugging, she added, "I'm about to sell my condo so I can buy something closer to where I will be working, and—"

He gave her a knowing smile. "And you're worried that something might go wrong with the dispersal of the will."

"Exactly." It was nice that he understood her concerns and didn't make her feel silly for having them.

"You have nothing to worry about," Logan told her. "J.D. set this will up in such a way that it would be almost impossible to contest it."

"Almost?"

He grinned. "Caught that, did you?"

"I did, and it's a little scary to think about. If someone contested the will, all of the bequests might be nullified, right?"

"It's possible, yes," he admitted, then leaned back in his oversize leather swivel chair. "But highly unlikely. J.D. was competent when he made his will. And it was his estate to divide how he saw fit. I know some of the family are upset with what that will said, but there's not much they can do about it. So to answer your question, I don't see any problems looming. Go ahead and sell your place. Buy the one you want."

Colleen released a breath she really hadn't been aware she was holding. Somehow she felt even more reassured than she had when talking to Walter. Maybe it was because the older lawyer tended to speak more in legal terms, and Logan made the process seem less confusing. "Thanks. I feel better."

"Happy to help," Logan said, rising to come around his desk. "I know this must be strange, suddenly coming into so much money. But it's all real, Colleen. You can trust it."

She stood up and offered her hand. This was what she'd needed to hear: the confirmation that her new life was about to begin. For some reason, she'd been half expecting someone to pull the rug out from under her and leave her sprawled, broken and bruised, on the floor. Metaphorically speaking, of course.

Now though, she would reach out and grab hold—with both hands—of the changes headed her way.

Logan walked her to his door and smiled. "Try to relax and enjoy all of this, Colleen. J.D. clearly wanted that for you."

"I think he did," Colleen agreed as she shook Logan's hand one last time. "I really appreciate your time."

"If you have any more worries, feel free to come back."

But she wouldn't be worried now. At least not about the bequest. Instead, she would worry about Sage Lassiter and how important he was becoming to her. When just the thought of his name sent an electrical charge buzzing through her, she knew she had *plenty* to worry about.

Seven

"**W**ow," Jenna chirped later that day. "According to Google, Sage Lassiter is worth about ten *billion* dollars." She glanced up from the laptop and fanned herself with one hand. "I mean I knew he was rich…but that is *seriously* rich."

The two of them were in Colleen's bedroom at her condo. The room was small but neat, with cream-colored walls, a bright quilt on the bed and dozens of jewel-toned pillows stacked against the headboard. Colleen looked at her friend, sitting cross-legged on her bed. "You're supposed to be checking real estate on the mountain for me."

"I am, on another webpage," Jenna said with a shrug. "But I can multitask. Besides, I had to look him up. You're going to stay at his ranch for a few days and I want to see what my friend's getting into. You know, I bet there are rich serial killers, too."

Laughing, Colleen said, "He's not a serial killer."

"No harm in checking," Jenna told her. "So, according to this website that is all gossip all the time, Sage made his first million by investing in some thingamajig for computers that his college roommate invented."

"Well, that tells me he believed in his friend, so that's nice."

"And made a boatload off that investment," Jenna continued, scrolling down the page, "which he then invested in several other inventors with great ideas."

"That's a good thing. He helped a lot of people get started and they all became successes." Colleen folded another T-shirt and dropped it into her suitcase. She would drive up to Sage's ranch in the morning and nerves were beginning to settle in. Three days at his house. God, she could hardly sit across from him in a restaurant without her body erupting in dangerous wants and needs. The next few days were going to be agonizing.

Unless, she thought wildly, something happened between them to release all this tension she felt building inside her. But if they did sleep together, then what? From everything she'd learned from J.D., she knew that Sage wasn't interested in a real relationship. And even if he were, he wouldn't want her, she knew that already.

So what would she gain by going to bed with him?

Lovely memories, her brain shrieked. *Orgasms galore,* her body chimed in.

She shivered again.

This had seemed like such a good idea, having Sage show her the mountains and how to avoid danger.

Which was really funny if you thought about it, because Sage himself was dangerous to her. He was becoming too important to her. While she planned her new life, looking forward to all the exciting things stretching out in front of her, Sage was in those mental images, too. He had become a part of the dream she'd nurtured for so long and she didn't know how to separate them now.

The only thing she *could* do was try to protect her heart from the inevitable crash that was headed her way.

"Hello?" Jenna demanded her attention. "Did you know he was that rich?"

In spite of everything, Colleen laughed. "It never crossed my mind to ask J.D. what Sage's bank account looked like."

"Well, it just doesn't seem fair, does it?" Jenna turned the laptop so that Colleen could see the screen, where an image of Sage stared out at her. "A man should not be allowed to be *that* amazing-looking *and* rich to boot. Just seems selfish somehow."

Colleen would have laughed, but she was staring at the image of Sage, drawn from some tabloid site. He looked impossibly handsome in a tux and was glaring at the camera even as the woman on his arm, last year's Oscar winner, beamed at the photographer as she draped herself against Sage's broad chest.

There it was, she told herself silently. Proof that whatever was between her and Sage wasn't permanent. Wasn't anything more than a temporary fantasy on her part, just a lot of chemistry that sizzled and flashed between them.

So, knowing it was all fleeting, what was she supposed to do? Stay home? Avoid Sage? Or should she accept the fact that this was all transitory and simply enjoy it for what it was? A swirl of expectation swam in her veins, side by side with a few slim threads of reality. It would be interesting to see which sensation finally won out.

"Anyway," Jenna was saying as she slapped the laptop lid down, shattering the spell Colleen had been under. "I found a couple of cabins for sale. One has a lot of land with it—like thirty acres—the other's close to a county road."

"Sounds great." She smiled appreciatively as Jenna handed over a piece of paper with the addresses. "I'll see if Sage can take me to look at them."

"We're depending on Sage a lot lately, aren't we?" Colleen quirked a smile. "Is that the royal *we?*"

"It's the *you* we," Jenna said, leaning back against the headboard of Colleen's bed and stretching out her legs to cross them at the ankle. "You've really been seeing a lot of him and now you're off to stay with him at his place."

"Not *with* him," Colleen corrected, though her body hummed at the idea. "Just at his house."

"Uh-huh." Jenna just looked at her for a second or two, then she huffed out a breath. "It's crazy, I know, but I'm worried he's going to break your heart."

"What?" Surprised, Colleen stared at her friend.

"Okay, sure, I was caught up in the whole billionaire-suddenly-wanting-to-date-my-friend thing, too. But honestly, now that he's stuck around for a while, I'm just... uneasy."

"Why?" Colleen knew why Jenna was uneasy, of course. Because she still couldn't quite bring herself to believe that Sage was actually interested in her. But she'd like to hear her friend's reasons.

"Because he's too damn solitary," Jenna blurted. "Anybody who's alone *that* much? There's probably a reason and I don't want to see you get caught up in whatever his issues are."

Colleen laughed shortly.

"What's so funny?" Jenna demanded.

"Nothing." Waving one hand, she said, "It's just, I thought you were going to say what I've been telling myself. That I'm not the kind of woman he usually goes for. Not sophisticated enough or beautiful enough or rich enough for him."

"Please." Clearly offended, Jenna sat straight up. "He'd be lucky to have you. You're plenty beautiful and way better than sophisticated or rich, you're *real*. You have a warm and generous heart. Maybe sometimes too generous."

Colleen reached over and hugged Jenna tight. When she let her go again, she said, "Thanks for that. But don't worry, okay? I'm pretty sure that whatever this is, it's short-lived. I'm not going to let my too-generous heart get all gooey and involved. Honestly."

"You know the too generous thing was a compliment, right?"

"Absolutely."

"Good." Jenna nodded. "So…back to mystery mountain man."

"He's not a mystery," Colleen insisted. "And this isn't some romantic getaway. Sage is going to show me around the mountain and probably try to scare me out of the idea of living alone up there."

"If only he could."

"Thank you for your support," Colleen said wryly.

"Oh, I support you, sweetie." Jenna sat up, grabbed a T-shirt and folded it as she continued, "But you forget, I've lived in Wyoming all my life. I know how dangerous the mountains can be. Beautiful, yes, but also deadly if you're not careful."

Colleen started to talk, but her friend cut her off.

"I don't like the idea of you living in the high country all on your own." She waved one hand as if to dismiss the argument she didn't give Colleen a chance to make. "Yeah, yeah, feminists, hear us roar, but just because you *can* do a thing doesn't mean you *should* do it, you know?"

Colleen dropped onto the edge of the bed, pushed the suitcase out of the way and faced her friend. "Fine. I'm a little anxious about being alone up there, I admit it, but I'll get used to it. And Jenna, I'm not helpless or stupid. I'll take care and I'll make sure to get help if I need it."

"I know." Jenna nodded and shrugged helplessly. "Maybe I just don't want you to move away."

Colleen leaned in and gave her friend another hug. "I'll miss you, too. But we'll still see each other."

"Oh, you bet we will. You're not going to get rid of me *that* easy." Jenna handed her the folded shirt. "But do me a favor. When you see the cabins, even if you fall in love…don't make a hasty decision. I don't want you to rush into something that you won't be able to get out of easily."

That was good advice. And not just about the cabins. She was about to head off to stay at the home of a man who turned her knees to mush. Was she already in way too deep for her own good? Would she get out now if she could?

No.

Colleen thought about it while she finished packing and realized that if it would be smart to stay far, far away from Sage Lassiter…she'd rather be stupid.

* * *

It had only been a week.

But in that week, Sage had spent a lot of time with Colleen and when he wasn't with her, she was filling his mind. He still wasn't sure how she'd managed it, but whenever they were together, she actually got him to talk. He'd opened up to her about his ranch, his plans, his life—something he hadn't done with anyone else. Not even Dylan or Angelica.

Colleen had slipped up on him. He hadn't expected to actually *like* her. Hadn't thought that he'd want her so badly that every night was a torture and every day was a lesson in self-control. Plus, he was no closer to finding out what he needed to know than he had been before this started.

Was this a deliberate maneuver on her part? Suck him in, distract him with her big blue eyes and then set the sexual tension bar so damn high that he couldn't think straight?

If that was her plan, it was a damn good one.

Hell, he hadn't even *kissed* her. How could he be this torn up and feel so out of control over a woman he hadn't even *kissed?*

"And why haven't you kissed her?" he asked himself in disgust. Because he knew that the moment he tasted her, took that luscious, amazing mouth with his, that there would be no stopping. He'd have to have *all* of her. And that had not been the plan. But then, he'd expected that he would have answers by now. Since this was going to take longer than he'd thought, the plan had to change.

As that thought settled into his mind, Sage took his first easy breath in a week. Talking to her wasn't working, so he would seduce any secrets she held out of her.

He'd use sex—crazed, hot, sweaty, incredible sex—to find out if she was withholding any information he might need to contest the will.

Then when he had what he needed, he would walk away.

She wasn't the kind of woman to go for a one-night stand, and once she discovered that was all he was willing to offer her, she'd *let* him walk.

But first, he would have her. Under him. Over him. And then he'd finally be able to get her out of his mind.

He scrubbed both hands over his face, then adjusted the fit of his jeans, hoping to ease the ache that had locked around his groin for the past week. It didn't help. Nothing would. The only way to ease that pain was to bury himself inside Colleen and thankfully, that was about to happen. He'd felt the chemistry between them. Knew that she was strung as tightly as he was. Seducing her wouldn't be difficult.

She was going to be here. Every day. Every night. He could hear her voice in his mind again: *Will you show me what I need to know?* Oh, there was plenty that he wanted to show her and very little of it had to do with survival.

What the hell had he been thinking, asking her to stay here? "Must be a closet masochist," he muttered darkly.

Or he *had* been, before he'd altered his plan. But things were different now. When Colleen finally showed up here at the house today, he was going to do what he should have done days ago: kiss the hell out of her. And then he'd get her into his bed as quickly as possible and scramble her mind so completely, she'd tell him whatever he needed to know.

Gritting his teeth against yet another wave of desire

thrumming inside him, he turned into the stable and headed down the long center aisle. The familiar scents of horses, straw and leather combined to welcome him and he sighed in gratitude. One thing he could count on was that being with the horses he bred and raised eased his mind. Here, he could push thoughts of Colleen aside—however briefly.

He paused long enough to greet one of the mares who poked her head through the half door to her stall.

"Belle, you're a beauty," he whispered. The chestnut mare butted his shoulder with her head as he stroked her jaw and neck, murmuring soft words that had the animal whickering in delight. It was this he lived for. Being around these animals that he loved. Caring for them, training them. Horses didn't lie. Didn't betray you. They were who they were and you accepted them at face value. You always knew where you stood with an animal.

It was people who let you down.

"Hey, boss!"

Frowning at the interruption, Sage gave the horse one last pat and turned to look back at one of the cowboys who lived on his ranch. "What is it, Pete?"

"Thought you'd like to know your sister just drove up."

Of course she did. Grimacing tightly, Sage muttered, "Okay, thanks."

So much for looking in on the newest foal born on the ranch. Instead, he gave the mare another long stroke over her neck, then headed back out of the stable. Pushing one hand through his hair, he told himself that it seemed women were destined to plague him lately. Wouldn't you know his sister would show up on the very day he was at last going to taste Colleen Falkner?

Sage couldn't even remember the last time Angie had come up the mountain to see him. Hell, usually she was living in L.A., but when she did come home, she stayed at Big Blue and visited her friends in Cheyenne.

But this visit was different, wasn't it? She'd lost her father, and then lost faith in him. She was upset about the will and having lost control of Lassiter Media, he knew. What he didn't know was what he could do about it. He and Dylan had talked this through several times and neither of them had come up with a way to challenge J.D.'s will.

So far, it had been made plain to them all that J.D. had definitely been in his right mind when he had the will drafted, and fighting his last wishes might very well invalidate the whole document. Until they could be sure of their next moves, he and Dylan at least had agreed to take this slowly.

Since J.D. was gone now, that made Sage the head of the family—and he had to consider everyone's inheritances, not just Angie's. He didn't want to risk Chance losing the ranch, or their aunt Marlene losing her bequest.

As much as it pained him, Sage couldn't make this any easier on the sister he loved. All he could really do was listen. A damned helpless feeling for a man more accustomed to having the answers than scrambling unsuccessfully for them. Scrubbing his hands over his face, he pushed those unsettling thoughts from his mind and headed for the main house.

The ranch yard was laid out a lot like Big Blue, he thought as he walked across it. But that wasn't a homage to J.D., he assured himself. It just made sense. The main house was set back at the end of a curving drive.

A landscaped sweep of greenery and flowers spread out in front of it in barely tamed splendor. The barn, stables and cabins for the cowhands who worked and lived on the ranch were set farther back and there was a pool that curved around a rock waterfall, with a stone patio surrounding it.

And from every spot on his property, the views were tremendous. He'd had his architect build the house to accommodate the beauty and become a part of the mountains itself. Acres of wood and glass and stone made the house look as though it had always been there, as if it had grown from the rocks and the forest. Trees were everywhere, and the scent of pine flavored every breath.

In Wyoming, winter held on, sometimes even into summer, especially this high up the mountain. An icy wind tore at Sage's hair as he walked toward his sister. Angelica was just climbing out of her car when he approached, and one look at her told Sage that she wasn't in much better shape than she had been when he'd seen her a couple nights ago.

True to their plan, he and Dylan had dropped in on their sister at Big Blue. It still wasn't easy walking into that house, cluttered with memories, but for his sister, he was willing to bite the bullet.

Evan had been there too, of course, but the tension between the formerly happy couple was unmistakable. Evan was doing his best to make this work, but Angie was so hurt and angry at her father that there wasn't a lot of give in her at the moment. How they were managing to work together through this was a mystery to Sage. Judging by the tight expression on Angie's face now, that tension hadn't eased up any either.

"Sorry to just drop in," she blurted, shrugging into

a navy blue sweater that dropped to midthigh. "I had to get out of the house."

"You're welcome here anytime," Sage told her, mentally letting go of his plans for Colleen—at least until his sister was on her way again. "What's going on now?"

"What *isn't?*" she snapped, then stopped, gave him a sheepish look and said, "I'm sorry, Sage. Seriously, I'm acting like queen bitch of the universe and I can't seem to stop myself."

"Hey," he said, dropping one arm around her shoulder and pulling her in for a hug, "that's my baby sister you're talking about."

Angie wrapped both arms around his waist and held on. Tenderness swamped Sage as he simply stood there holding her, knowing there was nothing he could say to make things better. Since she was a little girl, Sage had done everything he could to protect her. To take care of her. He hated not being able to help her now.

After a long minute or two, she pulled back and looked up at him. "You always steady me. How do you do that?"

"It's a gift," he quipped and gave her another squeeze. "Now, you want to fill me in on what's happening?"

She leaned into him. "It's just a rumor."

"Plenty of them to go around," Sage said, giving her a squeeze. "Tell me what you heard."

Tipping her head back, she looked up at him and bit her lip. Then she finally blurted, "The word is, Jack Reed is interested in Lassiter Media."

Jack Reed. Sage wasn't really surprised…how could he be? Jack Reed had the reputation of a great white shark. He bought up companies in trouble, then broke them down to the bare bones and sold off the pieces.

If Reed was interested, then it wouldn't be long before more sharks started circling the Lassiter family. They couldn't afford to be divided right now. They had to stand together against all comers. Which was just what he told Angie.

"We *are* together," she argued.

"What we are is pissed," he said flatly. "We all are. And we're spending too damn much time trying to figure out what was running through J.D.'s mind when he made that will."

"I know, I know." She stepped away from him, pulled the edges of her sweater tighter and wrapped her arms around her middle. "My first instinct, you know, was to contest the will."

"Yeah, I felt the same way," he said, "so did Dylan." He didn't add that he and their brother hadn't been able to come to a decision.

She took a deep breath and tossed her hair back from her face. "I don't know what the right thing to do is anymore, Sage. I want that company, but now I don't know how to get it. Do I fight my father's dying wishes? Do I try to accept this? How?"

"The whole situation's screwed up, that's for damn sure. But we'll figure something out," Sage said. He knew what J.D. had done had eaten away at her confidence, her self-assurance—hell, even her own image of herself. Their dad had spent a lifetime building her up and then with one stroke of the pen, he'd torn her down. *Why?*

She laughed shortly and threw both hands into the air. "I'm a mess, sorry. I shouldn't have just driven up here and thrown myself on you. But I really needed someone to talk to. Someone who would understand."

"You can drop in on me any damn time you want and you know that, Angie," he told her. "But just out of curiosity, where's Marlene?"

"Oh, she's at the ranch," she said, and started walking toward the wraparound porch on the main house. Sage matched his strides to her shorter ones. "And yes, she's always willing to listen, but she can't be objective about Dad...and I really wish Colleen were still at Big Blue. She was super easy to talk to."

Yeah, he thought. Colleen was easy to talk to. Easy to look at. She also made it easy for him to forget why he'd started all of this.

As if just thinking about her could make her appear, an old red Jeep pulled up the drive and everything in Sage quickened. Like a damn kid waiting for a date with the girl of his dreams, he felt his heartbeat thundering in his chest, and an all-too-familiar ache settled low in his gut and grabbed hold.

"Well," Angie said thoughtfully, with a pointed glance at him. "This is interesting."

Instantly, Sage tamped down the internal fires raging through him. He didn't need his sister making more of this than there was. "It's not what you're thinking, so dial it down."

"Really?" she asked as the car engine cut off and the driver's side door opened. "Because that looks like a suitcase she's pulling out of her car...."

His insides tightened even further. "Don't even start, Angie...."

Colleen wrangled her overnight bag out of the car and set it at her feet. She looked at the ranch house and quickly swept it in one thorough gaze. It was smaller than Big Blue, but not by much. Its windows gleamed in the afternoon sun and the long wraparound porch boasted plenty of chairs for sitting out and enjoying the view. The honey-colored logs looked warm and inviting, the scent of pine was pervasive, and the two people on the porch were both watching her.

She hadn't expected to find Sage's sister here, too, but maybe that was a good thing. All morning, Colleen's stomach had been twisting and turning in anticipation of her arrival here at Sage's ranch. For longer than she cared to think about she had been fascinated by him. And now that they'd actually been spending time together, that fascination had escalated into something that was as scary as it was thrilling. Having Angie as a buffer might make these first few minutes easier.

"Angie, hi." Though she spoke to his sister, Colleen's gaze went first to Sage, and even that one brief connection with his intense blue eyes sent goose bumps racing along her spine.

"Hi, yourself." Angelica walked out to meet her and gave Colleen a hug. "I've missed you since you moved out of Big Blue."

"I missed you, too." Focusing on his sister gave Colleen the chance to tear her gaze from Sage's. "How is everyone doing? Marlene?"

"She really misses Dad. A lot. We all do, of course, but…" Angie shrugged. "It's hard. And since the reading of the will, it's even harder." Taking a deep breath, she looked up at Sage. "Why don't you get Colleen's suitcase and I'll walk her in."

"Oh, that's okay, I can—"

Sage nudged her hand off the handle, and a now-familiar buzz of sensation hummed from her fingers, up her arm, to rocket around in the center of her chest.

He looked at her, and in his eyes, she saw the realization that he'd felt it, too. That electric spark that happened whenever they touched. As if a match had been held to a slow burning fuse that was about to reach the explosives it was attached to.

Then he picked up her suitcase as if it weighed nothing—and Colleen knew she hadn't packed light. For another long second, he looked at her and Colleen's heart beat began to race. Her mouth went dry, her knees went weak and if Angie hadn't been there, watching the two of them, she might have just thrown herself at Sage.

"Come on," Angie said then, splintering that happy little fantasy. Colleen followed her into the house and once she was there, she buried those feelings in the curiosity she had for Sage's ranch. She'd heard J.D. describe it, of course, but the reality was so much more.

Outside, it was set up much like the Big Blue. Outbuildings, barns, stables, though from what she'd seen at a quick glance, there was a much bigger corral for working horses than J.D.'s ranch provided. Obviously, that made sense, because she knew that Sage bred and raised racehorses. But it was the *inside* of the main house that had her captivated.

It, too, was constructed of hand-hewn logs, but there the similarity with Big Blue ended. Instead of the ironwork that made up much of the Lassiter home ranch, Sage's place was all wood and glass. Wood banisters on the wide staircase, intricately carved to look like vines climbing up posts. Bookcases that looked as though they'd been sculpted into the walls, boasted hundreds of leather-bound and paperback books.

The wide front windows afforded a view that was so spectacular it took her breath away. Despite the number of trees on the property, the view was wide-open and provided a glimpse of the valley and the city of Cheyenne that at night must be staggering. A stone fireplace dominated one wall and the hand-carved mantel displayed pictures of his brother and sister and a young couple who must have been his biological parents.

While Sage and Angie talked, their conversation veering from muted tones to half shouts, Colleen wandered around the great room. Oak floorboards shone in the sunlight slanting through the windows. Brightly colored rugs dotted the floor, adding more warmth to a room that rang with comfort. Overstuffed brown leather chairs and sofas were gathered in conversational knots and heavy oak tables were laden with yet more stacks of books. She loved it.

The house was perfect and she couldn't wait to explore the rest of it. It was just as she would like her own home to be—on a smaller scale, of course. A comfortable refuge.

"You don't understand," Angie was saying and had Colleen turning around to face the siblings. "Evan is acting as if this is nothing. He keeps offering to let me run the company. But he doesn't get that him *giving* me control isn't the same as *having* control. He's trying to take a step back for me at the office, but I don't want him doing that, so it's a vicious circle. He thinks I should have control, and I want it, but if Dad *didn't* want me to have it, how can I try to claim it? We're arguing all the time now, and I can't help wondering why Dad did this. Did he want Evan and I to break up? Or was he really that disappointed in me?"

Colleen saw the torment on Sage's face and when he reached for his sister, pulling her in tight and wrapping his arms around her, Colleen felt a pang in her tender heart. He was so kind. So loving. Yet when she'd told him just that, he'd denied it. Why couldn't he see it?

"Dad loved you," he said simply. "Something else is going on here, Angie, and we will find out what it is."

His gaze speared into Colleen's and she felt a quick bolt of ice that snaked along her spine and made her shiver. There was nothing tender in that look. But before she could really wonder what he was thinking, the expression dissolved once again into concern for his sister.

Angie pulled away, spun around and looked at Colleen. "You're the one who spent the most time with him toward the end. Did he tell you why he was doing this? Why he cut me out as if I were nothing?"

With both Lassiters staring at her, Colleen felt completely ill at ease. She didn't have answers for them, though she wished she had.

Shaking her head, she could only say, "No, Angie. He didn't talk about his will with me. I had no idea what he was going to bequeath to everyone."

"That's really not an answer though, is it?" Sage muttered and her gaze locked on his. The shutters were in place, but even with him closing her out, she felt the cold emanating from him. Only minutes ago, he'd given her a look filled with heat, and now it was as if he'd shut that part of himself down.

"He talked to you, Colleen," he prodded. "If not about his will, then about how he was feeling. What he was thinking. And you know what he said. So tell us."

She blinked at him. "What can I tell you that you don't already know? He loved you all. He talked about you with such warmth. So much pride…"

"Then why would he do this?" Angie demanded. *"Why?"*

"I just don't know." Colleen sighed heavily. "I wish I did."

Sage's features went very still, as if he were considering what she said and wondering if she was holding something back. Finally he muttered, "Angie, she doesn't know. No one does. *Yet.* We'll find out, though, I swear."

"For all the good it'll do," she said and forced a smile. "I'm really sorry. I don't mean to dump on you guys. I'm just so torn up about this and so...*confused.*"

"Your father loved you, Angie," Colleen said softly. "He was proud of you."

Her eyes glistened with tears, but she blinked them back and lifted her chin. "I want to believe you, Colleen. I really do."

"You can."

"I hope so." Nodding, she turned to her brother. "I'm gonna go. I promised Marlene I'd take her into town for a nice dinner, and if I'm going to make it, I've got to start back now."

"Okay," Sage said, dropping a kiss on her forehead. "Try not to worry. We'll work this out."

"Sure." She flashed a smile at Colleen. "And now, I can leave you two alone to do...whatever you were planning before I showed up."

Colleen flushed. "Oh, please don't get the wrong idea. I'm just here so Sage can show me what life in the mountains is like. I want to move up here and—"

"You're going to move here?" Angie interrupted.

"Not *here,* here," Colleen corrected with a fast glance at Sage to see what his reaction was to his sister's teasing. But it was as if he wasn't listening to Angie at all.

His gaze was locked with hers and the heat in his eyes warmed her all the way to her toes. Still, she added for Angie's benefit, "Just here in the mountains, here."

She was babbling and now felt like an idiot. Of course Angie hadn't meant anything by what she'd said. She knew that there was nothing between Colleen and Sage. Nothing but a lot of chemistry that neither of them had acted on.

"Right, so you have a place in mind?"

"I have the addresses of a couple of cabins that are for sale. I was hoping Sage could show me where they are."

"Oh, my big brother is so *helpful,* I'm sure he won't mind at all." She smiled at him. "Will you, Sage?"

"Don't you have somewhere to be?" he asked pointedly.

Brother and sister stared at each other for a long minute or two, then finally Angie said, "Yeah. I guess I do. After dinner with Marlene, I'm meeting Evan in town tonight. We both thought it would be better to talk away from the office. It's just too…hard when we're there. But we do have to talk about plans for the company."

"That's good, Angie."

"In theory," she said. "We'll have to see, now that he's my *boss.*"

Colleen winced and wished she knew why J.D. had done this to his daughter. She would love to be able to give Angie a reason. An explanation. Something. But she simply had no idea why he would turn his family on its head like he had. And she couldn't help but feel guilty every time she thought about what Angelica was going through. She'd been hurt by her father's will while Colleen had been given a gift for which she was immensely grateful.

"Anyway," Angie said, crossing the room to hug Colleen. "You guys have fun or whatever. Don't let him turn you into Dan'l Boone or something, okay?"

Colleen laughed. "I don't think that's going to be an issue."

"You never know when the hermit of the mountain's involved."

"'Bye, Angie," Sage said firmly.

"Uh-huh." Angie shifted a sly look between the two of them then flashed a knowing smile at Colleen. "I'm sure Sage will show you *everything* you'll ever need to know."

And with that loaded insinuation, she left, Sage walking her out. Alone in the great room, Colleen found herself suddenly wondering if the lessons she came to learn weren't going to be very different than what she'd expected.

Eight

Once his sister was gone, Sage went back into the house and stopped in the doorway of the great room. Colleen had her back to him as she stared out the windows at the wide, uninterrupted view of trees and sky. His gaze raked her up and down and his body roared into life in response.

Hell, he'd been with beautiful, glamorous women who spent hours in front of mirrors, and had their own fashion stylists, hair people, makeup artists, and he'd never felt the pulse-pounding desire for them that he did for Colleen. Her hair was loose, hanging over her shoulders in a windblown tousle of waves and curls. She wore jeans, sneakers and a red sweater over a white shirt. And she looked amazing.

As if sensing his presence, she turned to face him and their eyes locked.

"I feel really bad about all of this will business," she said, her soft voice barely discernible in the cavernous room.

A brief spark of suspicion rose up inside him. Was she going to confess to conspiring with J.D. to cheat Angie out of what was rightfully hers? Hell, he almost hoped not, because he *really* wanted to seduce it out of her. "Why should you?"

"I know how upset she is over the will…and yet for me, it was life changing."

"For her, too," Sage said wryly.

She winced. "I know. I wish I could help."

With the afternoon sunlight streaming in through the window behind her, Colleen looked as though the tips of her hair were dusted with gold. She seemed to shimmer in that soft light and damned if he didn't feel that lurch of something that was more than attraction. More than simple desire.

Shaking his head, he asked, "You actually mean that, don't you?"

"Of course I mean it," she said, clearly confused by the question. "Why wouldn't I?"

Why indeed. If she was hiding something, she was damn good at it. And if she was innocent—that didn't change anything. He still wanted her and he would still *have* her.

"Never mind," he said, walking toward her in long, easy strides. "Let me see the addresses of those cabins."

She dug the paper out of her pocket and handed it over. He knew both places. One wasn't far. The other was much higher up the mountain. "Okay, let's go take a look."

* * *

"This is Ed Jackson's place," Sage said as he steered Colleen down the rocky path toward the small one-bedroom cabin. The first address she'd given him was about two miles higher up the mountain from Sage's ranch. The roads were in good repair, but the sharp curves and the straight-down drop off the edge were enough to give even the best drivers nightmares.

And he hadn't missed the fact that Colleen had had a death grip on the armrest every time he maneuvered around one of those curves that had been carved out of the mountain. But now that they'd arrived, the look on her face told him that she was so entranced by the setting she'd already forgotten the treacherous ride to get there. He held on to her hand as they took the narrow path to the front door, relishing the buzz of sensation that simply touching her caused.

The flower beds had long ago gone to seed and now there were only monstrous weeds fighting each other for space. The cabin itself was well built, but the white paint on the wood-plank walls was cracked and peeling. The front porch still boasted two chairs, and he remembered coming up here as a kid to find Ed and his wife sitting side by side, talking and laughing together. But then Helen had died five years ago and Ed lived here alone, refusing to move to the city. Finally, though, age had conquered his stubbornness, forcing him to put the home he loved up for sale and move to an assisted-living apartment in Cheyenne.

"It's pretty," she said, stopping to take it all in. "I love all the trees standing like guarding sentries around it."

"Nice spot," he agreed, trying to keep his mind off the

fact that she was close enough to touch. Close enough to— "Come on. I'll show you the inside."

"We can get in?"

"Ed always left a key above the doorframe." He found it, unlocked the front door and stepped into the past. The furnishings were at least forty years old and the air smelled of neglect and loneliness.

He watched as Colleen walked through the small house, checking out the tiny bedroom, the single bath and then the functional but narrow kitchen. Every window sported a view of the surrounding forest and the deep ravine that tracked off to one side of the house. "Why's the owner selling?"

He told her Ed's story and watched as sympathy filled her eyes. She was intriguing. Always. He liked that she cared why a house was for sale and that she felt pity for the man forced by time to give up the house he loved. He felt a swift stab of something beyond the pulsing desire still throbbing inside him, but he ignored it and looked at the cabin through objective eyes.

"You'd have to get a generator," he said, scanning the interior. "Ed didn't care about losing power, but I'm thinking you would."

She smiled and his heart rate jumped into a gallop. "You're right."

"You've got a wood-burning stove, so that's good," he continued, slapping one hand down on the dusty cast-iron fireplace in one corner of the living room. "But those pines along the side of the house will have to be cut way back or down altogether. Too dangerous. A heavy snowfall or a high wind could bring them crashing down on your roof. Not to mention, you should have a clearing around the house in case of forest fires."

"But those trees have been there for *years.*"

"Yeah, Ed wasn't worried about the *what-ifs,* because he could patch a roof or get out there and hack out a clearing fast if he needed to." He paused meaningfully. "You couldn't."

She frowned slightly, walking through the room, running her fingertips across the backs of the chairs, straightening framed photographs on the walls.

"Structure's sound enough, I guess," he mused, looking around in an effort to keep from staring at her. "But you'd have to have an inspection to be sure. County road's at the end of the drive, so the snow would get cleared fairly quickly out there."

She glanced at him. "What about the drive itself?"

He looked at her then and shook his head. "The county's not going to clear your drive. You'd have to get a snowblower or hire someone to come in after a storm."

Colleen nodded and huffed out a breath as she considered everything he was saying. She was getting a hard lesson in what it meant to live so far from the city, and he almost felt sorry for her. Almost, but not quite, because he still didn't like the idea of her being up here on her own. There were women on this mountain capable of taking care of any kind of emergency, and he knew that. But Colleen was city through and through, and she had no idea of what she might be letting herself in for.

"You'll want the roof checked out, too," he added. "We had heavy snows last winter and Ed wasn't in shape to take care of things like that himself."

"Right. Another inspection," she murmured, looking around the room wistfully.

"This lot's on high ground, so you don't have to worry too much about spring runoff, but you should have the gullies cleared so melting snow won't get backed up and flood the house."

She laughed a little. "So I have to worry about the snowfall and then about when the snow melts."

"Pretty much." He leaned against one wall and watched as she peered through the kitchen window at the surrounding trees.

"How long did Ed and his wife live here?"

"About forty years," he said with a shrug. "After Helen died, Ed didn't visit much with anyone. They never had kids—it was always just the two of them. And without her, he kept to himself. Didn't really keep up with the cabin, either."

"He missed her." She turned to look at him.

Gaze locked with hers, he nodded. "Yeah, he did."

Which was yet another reason to keep to yourself. If you never let anyone in, you didn't miss them when they were gone. He'd learned that lesson as a kid—and then again later on, when he should have known better, but took a risk, only to be slammed for it.

"I want to look around outside," she said and he wondered if she could read minds. She was staring at him oddly and she'd suddenly gone quiet, and that just wasn't like Colleen.

But he followed her out, locked the door after them and returned the key to its resting place. She walked to the end of the porch, leaned on the railing and gazed out over the rocky ravine that dropped from the edge of the porch and ran down the side of the mountain. Her hair trailed over her shoulders and as she leaned out farther, her jeans tightened over her behind, making Sage's breathing a hell of a lot harder to control.

Then everything changed.

He heard a snap, then a squeak of alarm, and he was moving before he even realized it. In a blink, he reached out and caught her arm as the railing gave way. He heard the crash and rattle as the heavy wood barrier, rotted by time and weather, clattered and rolled down into the rocks below.

Pulling Colleen tight against him, he wrapped both arms around her and held on. He felt her trembling and knew that he was doing the same damn thing. "I told you he hadn't kept the place up." His voice came out in a harsh rasp of tension and what felt a lot like fear. "Never lean on a railing you're not sure about. Hell. Never lean on a railing no matter what."

"Good advice," she murmured, her voice muffled against his chest. When she lifted her head and looked up at him, Sage felt the last of his control snap as completely as that rotted-out railing had.

Her mouth was *right there*. Her breathing was fast and the pulse point in her throat throbbed. He knew she was shaken. So was he. If he hadn't grabbed her so quickly, she might now be at the bottom of that damned ravine. Broken. Bleeding. Hell, she'd have been lucky to survive the fall.

But she hadn't fallen. And now she was pressed close to him and when his control snapped, all he could think was *thank God*. He bent his head, covered her mouth with his and tasted her for the first time.

Heat slammed into him and Sage surrendered to it. His kiss was hard and fierce and desperate. No time for subtle seduction. This was need. Hot and thick and running through his body like lava. He ground his mouth over hers and felt her surrender when she lifted her arms to wrap them around his neck.

He groaned in response and flipped them around until her back was braced against the cabin wall. His tongue parted her lips and he delved deep, determined to taste all of her after waiting so long. Longer than he'd ever waited before to claim a woman he desired. And he'd never wanted a woman as he wanted Colleen.

Fire roared through his veins, blurring his mind, leaving only his body in charge, and the aching throb in his groin let him know he couldn't wait much longer. Need pounded inside him, feeding the flames threatening to consume him. Her breasts pressed to his chest, her fingers sliding up into his hair and all he could think was *too many clothes.*

The icy-cold wind sliding off the top of the mountain didn't deter him as he reached down and tugged the hem of her shirt up. She shivered, but continued kissing him, giving him everything she had, pouring her own need and desire into the melding of their mouths.

His hands cupped her breasts and she gasped, tearing her mouth from his to lean her head back against the cabin wall and arch her body into his touch. Even through the fragile lace of her bra, he thumbed her nipples until she was groaning, leaning into him, offering herself.

And he took. Lifting the bra up and out of his way, Sage looked his fill of the full, luscious breasts that he hadn't been able to stop thinking about since the first night he'd seen her in that red dress. Her dusky-rose nipples were hard and erect and he couldn't help himself. He dipped low and took first one, then the other into his mouth, rolling that sensitive tip between his lips and tongue, scraping the edges of his teeth across the pebbly surface until she was sobbing his name. She held his head to her tightly and when he suckled her she actually shrieked. That unfettered sound went straight to his groin and pushed him to take more. To give more.

To have it all.

He straightened up, dropped his hands to the waistband of her jeans and quickly undid the snap and zipper. Their eyes were locked on each other as he dipped one hand down, sliding across her abdomen, beneath the sliver of elastic of the panties she wore, and then delved deeper, cupping her hot, wet core. At his first touch, her so-expressive eyes glazed over and she rocked her hips into his hand, silently asking for more. But he held still, not moving, not stroking, torturing them both. He luxuriated in the feel of her hot, slick flesh beneath his hand and gritted his teeth as he fought for control. Then he slid the pad of his thumb across one particularly sensitive spot and her body jerked in response.

Her breath hissed in and out of her lungs, her eyes grew wide, her lips parted and her tongue swept out to lick them. He bent his head and kissed her briefly as he continued to tease her, stroking that bud of sensation, enjoying the tremors that continued to rack her body as she twisted and writhed in his grasp.

"Sage, please…" She tore her mouth from his to beg him for the release he continued to keep just out of her reach. "You have to," she murmured, her gaze imploring him, pleading with him to ease the coiled tension inside her. "Touch me. Take me."

He lost himself in her eyes and gave her what she needed. What they *both* needed. Sage dipped his fingers into her depths, stroking, caressing. Her movements quickened, her breath was strangled, and still she whispered his name as the cold air wrapped itself around them in an icy embrace. He felt the magic of her tight heat as she groaned and writhed wildly against him. She clung to his shoulders, widened her stance to give him more access and moved with him at every stroke of his hand.

He watched her. Couldn't take his eyes off of her. He'd never seen anything more beautiful than Colleen in the grip of passion. Small, breathless sounds escaped her throat. She chewed at her bottom lip and locked her gaze with his until all he could see of the world were her amazing, deep blue eyes.

Everything she felt shone clearly on her face, so he knew when her climax was hurtling toward her. Knew when she reached the precipice and fused his mouth to hers when she finally bolted over the edge, trembling and quaking in his arms with the force of her release.

And when it was done, he wanted more. He was hungrier for her now than he had been before he had touched her, and damned if he was going to wait any longer.

"Come with me," he blurted, hoping she could hear him through the sexual haze clouding her mind and her eyes.

He didn't bother doing up her jeans again. He'd only have to undo them in a second or two. Taking hold of her hand, he marched back to the front door, grabbed the key and unlocked it. Pulling her inside after him, he threw the bolt on the door, then grabbed her and held her tightly enough to him that she couldn't help but feel the hard thickness of his own arousal pushing into her. Still, she was a little nervous about going into someone else's home like this.

"Can we do this? In a stranger's house?"

"Ed's not a stranger to me," Sage whispered. "Trust me, he'd approve. So? What do you think?"

Colleen hoped he was right about what Ed would think because she really didn't want to waste this moment. He was staring down into her eyes and her sense of caution was washed away in a rising tide of desire.

"Yes," she whispered in answer to his unspoken question. "Yes, Sage. Now."

She licked her lips and then went up on her toes to kiss him as hungrily as he had kissed her the first time. He met that passion with all of his own. Tearing her sweater off, he then pulled up her shirt and whipped it over her head before tossing it to the nearest chair. She was pulling at his jacket, too, then ripping at his shirt. He heard a couple of buttons sail across the room and he didn't give a damn. Anything to have her skin against his. Now. This minute.

No more waiting.

He was blind to everything but her. Sage had never known such all-consuming desire before. Sex had always been fast and hot and no deeper than a puddle. This was more because *she* was more. But he didn't want to think about that now. Didn't want to consider just *why* he was so desperate to have her. It was enough that he needed. Wanted.

She pulled free of the kiss, reached for his belt buckle and undid it, her gaze on his, never shifting. *Nothing sexier than a woman who can look you in the eye while getting naked.* She unbuttoned his jeans and then reached inside to cup her hand around his aching, rock-hard erection.

At the first touch of her fingers, he damn near lost it and that was humiliating to admit, even to himself. But he was wound so tight, hurting so bad, it wasn't surprising. Her grip was strong and gentle, firm and soft, and the touch of her fingers on his sensitized skin was like putting a match to dry kindling.

"Don't." Gritting his teeth, he took hold of her hand and pulled it free as he gave her a half smile to take the sting out of his sharp warning. "You keep that up, and it's over before we get started."

"Okay then. Can't have that." She toed off her sneakers before taking hold of her jeans to drag them off.

"I'll do that," he said, stroking his hands across her breasts, cupping them in his palms, thumbing her nipples, until she swayed unsteadily on her feet. "I've been thinking of nothing but stripping you out of your jeans for the past few days. I want to enjoy the moment."

"Hope it's okay if I enjoy it, too," she whispered.

"Absolutely." Smiling, he dropped his hands to the waist of her jeans and slowly pushed them down over her generous, gorgeous hips. He took that tiny swatch of lace panties with him as he went, and going down on his knees, he left a trail of kisses along her flesh as it was exposed to his gaze. "You have an amazing body," he murmured.

She squirmed in his grasp and reached down to slide her fingers through his hair, dragging her nails across his scalp. "My boobs are too big," she argued in a quiet voice. "And so are my feet and my butt."

"You're wrong," he whispered and as if to prove a point, he slid his hands around to cup her behind, his fingers kneading her tender flesh until she whimpered and swayed unsteadily. "You have a great butt and your breasts…beautiful."

She held on to his shoulders to keep herself steady

and then stepped out of her jeans when he wanted her to. Then she was naked, standing there in a splash of watery sunlight, as glorious as he'd known she would be. He ran his hands over the line of her hips and all the way down her long, shapely legs to her narrow feet. "I love your curves. A man could get lost in your body and happily stay that way."

She cupped her hand under his chin and tipped his head back so she could look into his eyes. "You mean that," she asked after a long second or two, "don't you?"

"Babe," he assured her, "your body is a wonderland."

She had curves and he liked them. She had long legs and he wanted them wrapped around his hips, pulling him deeper into her body. And the dark blond curls at her center were at just the right height for him to do something he'd been dreaming of doing for far too long.

Still looking up at her, Sage reached out to brush those curls aside, clearing a path for his mouth, his tongue. She knew what he was about to do. Her eyes went wide and she sucked in a deep breath and held it. "Sage…"

"I want to taste all of you," he said and leaned in, covering her heat with his mouth.

She gasped and arched into him, her fingers digging into his shoulders, her short, neat nails scraping his skin. She wobbled unsteadily, but his hands on her butt kept her still, held her in place.

He licked and kissed and stroked and fed the frenzy leaping inside him. He sensed the tension in her body and tightened it with every slide of his tongue. His hands ran up and down her thighs, over her hips, and then dipped down so that he could invade her heat even while he tasted her.

The world shrank down until there was only Colleen. Her taste, her scent—she was all. She was everything. Every soft moan and gasp that escaped from her throat made him more frantic to feel her body bucking under his. He sensed she was close to another climax, and this time, he was going to be buried deep inside her when she came.

And suddenly he couldn't wait another second to bring them together in the only way that mattered. He pulled away, stripped off his jeans and laid her down on the threadbare rug with its pattern of faded pastel flowers. He levered himself over her as she reached for him, parting her legs, so ready, so eager, so—

"Damn it."

"What?" She shook her head, blindly blinking to bring him into focus. "What is it? Why'd you stop? Please, don't stop."

He dropped his forehead to hers and if he'd been strong enough, he would have jumped to his feet and kicked himself. But hell, he hadn't carried protection around with him in the hopes of getting lucky since he was a kid. "Have to stop. No condom."

"No problem."

He lifted his head, stared down into her eyes and asked, "You're covered?"

She licked her lips again, driving him further along the road of no return. "I am. I went on the pill a couple of months ago to regulate my period. As long as you're healthy, we're covered."

Relief flooded him along with a renewed pulse of desire that damn near strangled him. "I'm so healthy I should be two people."

She choked out a laugh. "I only need one of you at the moment."

He grinned. Hell, he'd never talked with a woman once he had her naked. He'd never joked with one, either. Colleen was different on so many levels from every other woman he'd ever known. There was another hard lurch in his chest as his heart thudded like a jackhammer. He wasn't going to examine anything here. Now wasn't the time for thinking—it was just about feeling.

"That's what you're gonna get, babe," he promised and moved to cover her body with his.

Finally, skin to skin. The soft smoothness of her flesh sang against his. Her breasts rose and fell with the quickness of her breath and she lifted one leg to stroke her foot along his calf. Sensations coursed through him, too fast and too many to count. And he didn't need to. Didn't need to worry about a damn thing but getting where he needed to be.

He eased back on his haunches, looked down at her and spread her wide. Stroking her core with his fingertips, he smiled as she twitched and writhed before him, as frantic, as desperate as he.

"Sage, don't make me wait anymore." She lifted her hips in invitation and offered a weak smile. "If you're not inside me soon, I may explode."

"Can't have that," he said, and leaned over her, pushing his body into hers in one swift, sure stroke.

"Sage!" She arched up off the floor at his invasion and he held perfectly still, though it cost him, until she began to adjust to the size of him. Once she had, she moved, lifting her hips, taking him deeper. That provocation was all he needed. He moved against her, his hips rocking, settling into a fast, hard rhythm that she matched. Breaths mingled, kisses lingered, as bodies raced along the line of tension stretched so tautly between them. Hands explored, whispered words lifted into the silence, and the sighs and groans of two bodies merging became a kind of music.

Sage felt surrounded by her, engulfed by her, and he'd never known anything quite like it. Her slick heat held him, her body welcomed him and her hands left trails of fire along his skin wherever she touched him.

Again and again, they parted and came together, each of them eager for the climax just out of reach. Each of them trying to draw out the moment. His mind raced, his heartbeat thrummed in his ears. She locked her incredible legs around his hips and called his name out as the first wave of tremors crashed down on her. He felt every one of them and took her mouth in a hard, deep kiss, swallowing her cries, her breath, everything he could, drawing her into him in every way possible.

And then he let himself follow. Finally surrendering his slippery grip on control, he tumbled off the edge of the world and felt her arms come around him to cushion his fall.

Colleen didn't want to move. Ever. She'd be happy here, forever, just like this, on the hard floor with Sage's muscular body covering hers. She felt alive in a way she never had before. It was as if her entire body had suddenly awakened from a deep sleep. Her heartbeat slowly returned to normal even as she still shook with the force of the release she'd found with Sage.

And already, one pesky corner of her mind was springing into life trying to quantify what had just happened. Trying to explain the unexplainable.

She wasn't a virgin. She'd had sex exactly twice before this time, and looking back, she had to admit that neither of those times had come even *close* to what she'd just experienced.

In fact, it wasn't very long ago that Colleen had decided she simply wasn't a very sexual person. That maybe she was one of those people who would *never* see fireworks or feel the earth move during sex.

Well, she told herself with a self-satisfied grin, so much for *that* theory.

Sage eased up onto one elbow, and instantly, she missed the feeling of him lying atop her. "You okay?"

"Oh, yeah," she said on a sigh. "I'm terrific. You?"

He laughed shortly. "I think so. Come on, that floor can't be too comfortable."

"I'd rather stay here until my legs work again, thanks."

He shook his head and gave her an all-too-brief smile. "I think that's the nicest thing any woman's ever said to me."

And there had no doubt been plenty of them, Colleen thought sadly. The sophisticates. The skinny women with tiny feet in designer shoes. Ah, yes. Well, that thought was enough to put a damper on the lovely residual heat spreading inside, and have her moving to sit up and grab for her clothes.

"So," Sage asked as he, too, got dressed, "what do you think of the cabin?"

She looked up at him and found his eyes unshuttered, filled with a warmth she hadn't seen before. "I like it. Well, everything except the railing." She grimaced. "I didn't even thank you for saving me from that drop."

"I think," he said, "we pretty much thanked each other."

How funny. He'd saved her but couldn't accept her gratitude. As if by keeping an emotional distance, he could compartmentalize what had just happened between them. Which was enough to have Colleen drawing her romantic notions to a quick close.

"Actually, I'm feeling pretty fond of that railing myself," he said, and stood up to tug on his jeans. "If it hadn't snapped..."

She shivered at the thought, remembering the view of the steep drop. Of that moment of sheer terror when she'd thought she was going to fall. Of feeling Sage grab her, pull her in tight and then...

"Hey, Colleen," he said softly. "You okay?"

"Oh, I'm better than okay," she assured him and hoped he didn't hear the tremor in her voice. She was so not okay. She was in turmoil. Because she had just realized that tumbling down a rocky ravine might have bruised and broken her body—but sex with Sage Lassiter just might break her heart.

Nine

He scowled a little. "You surprise me all the damn time."

"That's a bad thing?"

"I don't know yet," he said. He looked down at her as if trying to read her mind, see into her heart. And Colleen really hoped he couldn't. Because right now, he'd see too much. Know too much.

Frowning slightly, he turned his head, glanced out the window and abruptly said, "We have to go. It's snowing."

"Snowing?"

"A spring snow is nothing new, you know that." Sage turned to her and there was a grim expression on his face. "This high up, it's even more likely to happen."

Colleen looked, too, watching as huge white flakes drifted from a cloud-studded sky. An hour ago, it had been cold and clear. But weather in Wyoming was unpredictable at the best of times, as she already knew. When she and her mother had first moved here from California, the first thing they'd learned was, if you don't like the weather, wait five minutes. These few flakes could wink out of existence in minutes—or they could be the herald of a heavy storm. There was just no way to tell.

In a few minutes, they were dressed and leaving the cabin behind. They walked to the car in silence, and on the way down the wickedly winding road, that silence stretched on. Colleen's mind whirled with too many thoughts to sort through. Besides, the silence was deafening and she had to wonder if Sage was regretting what had happened. If he planned to just pretend it *hadn't* happened at all. Maybe it would be better if she pretended the same thing. Heck, if her body wasn't still alive with sensation, Colleen might have been able to believe it.

How could he shut down so completely? Moments ago, there had been heat and wonder and something… *more* between them. And now it was as if he'd already moved on. There was no closeness between them. No sense of extended intimacy.

There was only the softly falling snow.

And the quiet.

By the next morning, Sage had convinced himself that he had overreacted to what had happened the day before.

That long ride from the cabin back to his home ranch had been a tension-filled misery. He'd felt her waiting for him to say something, but what the hell could he say? He'd just thrown her down onto a dirty cabin floor and taken her so fast and so hard she'd probably have bruises. It had been damned humiliating to know how completely he'd lost control. To know that she'd taken him to the edge and then pushed him over. So what the hell could they possibly have talked about?

The storm had faded away soon after they returned to his ranch, leaving just a chill in the air and a few patchy spots of quickly melting snow. He'd needed some space. Some time to get his head together, so he'd ordered up an early dinner, showed Colleen to a room just down the hall from his and said good-night.

He'd seen the flash of surprise in her eyes when he walked away, but he'd had to. If he'd stayed another minute he'd have found a way to tip her back onto the guest-room bed and have her again. And he refused to lose control twice in the same damn day.

The hell of it was, rather than being satisfied by their encounter, he had been wound even tighter than he was before. It was as if the tension, once released, had instantly coiled inside him again. There was no relief. Only more hunger. That one climax with Colleen had taken him to a place he hadn't even guessed existed—and his instincts wanted to go back.

Always before, bedding a woman who'd gotten under his skin had eased that itch. That nagging pulse of desire.

But with Colleen, it was just the opposite. He wanted her even more, now that he knew what having her was like.

Of course, after practically dumping her in her room and leaving her to fend for herself last night, there wasn't much chance of having more of her. He'd seen that look of surprise on her face when he'd walked away. Surprise, mixed with something else. Hurt? Maybe. Hell, didn't she understand he'd left her alone for her own good? Probably not.

Everything about Colleen was different. Her openness. The innocent pleasure always shining in her eyes. Her smile. Her laugh. The way she consistently looked for the good in people—and didn't stop until she found it. He liked her, damn it, and that had *not* been a part of the plan.

Racked with guilt over that tense, awkward goodbye, he'd devoted several mind-numbing hours to paperwork and emails and going over new contracts his lawyers had sent on. He'd also looked into Jack Reed to see if there was any more information to be gathered—there hadn't been. There was bound to be trouble if Reed was interested in Lassiter Media and Sage just added that complication to the growing list in his mind.

He'd buried himself so completely in the mundane tasks of maintaining the empire he was creating, it was long after midnight before he finally closed his books and trudged upstairs to his bedroom suite. Not that it had done him any good. How the hell could he sleep, knowing she was just down the hall?

No, instead of sleeping, he'd spent all night long reliving those moments with her in the cabin. When he did close his eyes, even briefly, her face was there. In front of him. And even if he *had* been able to sleep, she would have been in his dreams. The scent of her, the warmth of her. The slick slide of her legs around his hips.

By dawn, he'd given up on any pretense of rest and gone to work. God knew there was enough to do on a working ranch to exhaust him enough that even thoughts of sex with Colleen wouldn't be able to keep him awake.

"Pitiful. Seriously pitiful." Disgusted with himself, Sage tossed the hammer and nails into the bucket at his side, then sat back on his heels and stared up at the late-morning sky. The view from the roof of the main stable was pretty damn impressive, yet all he could think about was her.

He could see her, lying beneath him, staring up at him from the floor in a dusty cabin. *Nice seduction moves, Sage.* Pull out all the romantic stops to get her to spill her secrets. Way to go. Of course, his mind argued, he hadn't been thinking of seduction. Only the need to claim her. To be a part of her.

And now he wanted to do it all again.

He shifted his gaze from the sky to the ranch yard. He saw the place he'd built, the men who worked for him, his dog—a big golden retriever—taking a nap in the shade. The sky was that deep, startling blue you only found in the mountains. Thick white clouds sailed in the wind that shook the trees and rattled their leaves. In the corral, two of the cowboys were working with a yearling mare, putting her through her paces.

Sage smiled, grateful for the distraction from his own thoughts. That mare was going to be a star one day. She was already faster than most of the horses in his stable and she was proud enough that she liked winning.

Still smiling, he started down the ladder propped against the side of the stable, thankful that he hadn't fallen off the roof and broken his neck due to lack of concentration. Colleen had affected him so much that she'd ruined his focus, and yet he couldn't seem to mind.

Shaking his head, he neared the bottom of the ladder and dropped the bucket holding shingles, a hammer and nails to the ground.

"What were you doing up there?"

He went completely still, amazed at the sensation of heat that snaked through him just at the sound of her voice. He could hardly believe she'd stayed after what had happened yesterday. But he was glad she had. What the hell was wrong with him? A few weeks ago at the rehearsal dinner, he'd been intrigued enough by the look of her that he'd wanted to talk. Maybe take a quick roll in the hay if she was interested.

Now he knew her. He understood that there wasn't a dishonest bone in her body. Hell, there was just no way Colleen would even think of tricking or deceiving a sick old man. She hadn't slicked her way into a fortune. Hadn't cheated the Lassiter family. He knew that now. Knew her mind, her sense of humor, her generosity, and he knew what touching her did to him. She was paving right over all the roadblocks he'd had set up around his mind and heart for years…and it was damned disconcerting.

Colleen stood not a foot from the ladder, watching him, and he wondered why he hadn't heard her walk up. Too busy thinking of her, he told himself wryly. Yeah, this seduction plan was working out nicely.

"Loose shingles on the stable roof," he said, hitting the ground, then bending over to snatch up the bucket before straightening to look into her eyes. Instantly, he felt that punch of something raw and elemental—and it was getting harder to ignore.

He'd missed her at breakfast, too. Deliberately. He'd grabbed a cup of coffee and one of his housekeeper's famous muffins and headed outside—where he'd stayed, keeping as busy as he could. "The wind kicked up last night, and after last winter a few of the shingles were ready to go."

She looked up, squinting into the late-morning sunlight, as if she could see where he'd been working. "You do the repairs yourself?"

"Sometimes," he admitted, and hefted the ladder across one shoulder. When he started walking toward the equipment shed where tools were stored, she followed him. "Why sound so surprised? It is my ranch."

The golden retriever rose lazily from his spot by the barn and stretched before trotting to Colleen's side. She stopped, dropped to one knee and smoothed both hands across the top of the lucky dog's head. A hell of a thing, Sage thought, when a man envied his dog.

"He's so sweet," she said, throwing a quick look up at Sage. "But I don't understand his name."

In spite of what he was feeling, Sage choked out a laugh. "You mean Beback?"

She scrubbed the dog's ears, then stood up, tucking her hands into the pockets of her jeans. "Yes. What kind of name is that?"

Shrugging, Sage said, "When he was a pup, he kept running off into the forest, but he was always running right back. One of the guys said it reminded him of a famous line in a movie...*I'll be back.*"

Colleen laughed and, God, he loved the sound of it. And as soon as that thought slid through his mind, he pushed it back out again. *Love?* What the hell?

"Beback. I like it," she said with a grin as she watched the dog race off after one of the cowboys. "I always wanted a dog. In fact, I'm going to get one as soon as I find my place."

"Not the Jackson cabin?"

She threw him a quick look and her eyes flared as if she were remembering their encounter. "I don't know yet. Maybe."

Nodding, Sage continued on to the shed and sensed rather than heard her follow him. And naturally, she was still talking.

"Going back to me being surprised at you doing the repairs to one of the buildings...I don't know, I guess I thought you would have one of the men who work for you do the minor repairs." She waved one hand to encompass the whole of the yard and the half dozen or so ranch hands working at different tasks.

His long strides never slowed, though he knew she had to be hurrying to keep up with him. "J.D. always said, 'Don't be afraid to do your own work. Men will respect you for it.'"

Frowning, he wondered where that had come from. He wasn't really in the habit of quoting his father. Yet it seemed that since J.D. died, Sage had thought more about him than he had in years. And the situation wasn't helped by Colleen's presence. After all, the only reason they were together at all was because of the old man.

"So you do have some good memories of J.D."

"Didn't say they were good ones," he muttered, leading the way into the shed. "Just memories."

Inside it was cool and dark. The walls were covered with hooks from which clean, cared-for tools hung neatly. One wall contained a long workbench with drawers beneath it and the rest of the place held everything from shovels to snowplows.

With her standing so close to him, it was hard to keep hold of his own self-control. Desire pulsed heavily inside him even while his brain kept shouting for caution. If he had any hope of keeping his mind clear, he needed some distance between them. Releasing a breath, Colleen glanced around the shed. "I won't need anywhere near this much equipment," she said as if to herself.

"You'll need plenty of it, though," he warned, taking the opportunity to spread a little more doubt in her mind. "Snowblower or plow. Shovels, pickaxes, and by the way, that old Jeep of yours isn't going to cut it up here, either."

"What?" She flashed him a stunned look. "Why not?"

"For one thing, it's too small. You'll need a truck."

At that, she laughed a little. "Why would I need a truck? My Jeep has been fine for me in the snow."

"The wheelbase is too short," he told her, and shook his head when he saw the blank confusion in her eyes. "Too easily tipped over. And in a high wind on the mountain road..."

She shivered as he'd meant her to—because the thought of her navigating those switchback curves alone in a storm gave him a damn heart attack.

"For another thing," he added, "you'll need the truck bed, because there's no trash collection here. You'll have to make trips to the dump yourself."

She chewed at her bottom lip and Sage felt a confusing mix of satisfaction and guilt. He didn't necessarily want to be the one to ruin her dream. But hell if he wanted her alone in a situation she wasn't prepared for either.

"Where's the dump?"

"I can show you." And that would serve as a negative, too. Once she got a whiff of the dump, she'd be less inclined to have to go there regularly.

"Okay..."

"There's no mail delivery up here either," he said

while he still held her attention. "You'll have to get a P.O. box in town."

She sighed. "I hadn't thought it would be so complicated." Turning in a slow circle, she let her gaze wander over the walls of tools as if she were trying to figure out how to use them. "All I want to do is live on the mountain, closer to where my patients will be."

"Most things generally are complicated," he said, emptying the work bucket he'd brought in with him. He opened drawers, returning the hammer, nails and leftover shingles to their proper places and when he was finished, he turned to find Colleen staring at him, a smile as bright as sunlight on her face. "And when you live up here—especially alone—you have to expect to take care of a lot of things most people don't worry about... what are you smiling at?"

"You." She shrugged. "It's funny, but I don't think I ever pictured you as being a fix-it kind of guy."

"Yeah, well." He closed the drawer and walked to set the bucket down in a corner of the shed. "J.D. had Dylan and I working all over Big Blue when we were kids. The two of us had a chores list that would make a grown man weep. We worked with the cattle and the horses, learned how to rebuild engines and shingle roofs when they needed it." He leaned one hip against the workbench, folded his arms across his chest and continued, "J.D. thought we should know the place from the ground up. Be familiar with everything so we were never at the mercy of anyone else. During school, we had plenty of time for homework, but during summer, he worked us both."

She tipped her head to one side and looked up at him. "Sounds like it was hard work."

"It was," he admitted, realizing he hadn't thought about those times in years. When they were kids, he and Dylan had hated all the chores. But they'd learned. Not that Dylan needed most of those lessons today, what with spearheading the Lassiter Grill Group. But Sage could admit, at least to himself, that everything he'd learned on the Big Blue had helped him run his own ranch better than he might have done otherwise. Sourly, he acknowledged that growing up as J.D. Lassiter's son had prepared him for the kind of life he had always wanted to live.

All those hot summers spent training horses, riding the range rounding up stray cattle. The long hours sweeping out the stable and the barn. The backbreaking task of clearing brush away from the main house. He and his younger brother had become part of the crew working Big Blue. The other wranglers and cowboys accepted them as equals, not the boss's adopted kids.

Shaking his head, Sage looked back on it all now and could see that J.D. had been helping them build their own places on Big Blue. To feel a part of the ranch. He'd been giving them a foundation. Roots to replace the ones they'd lost.

"Crafty old goat," he muttered, with just a touch of admiration for the father he had resented for so long.

"He really was, wasn't he?"

Sage caught the indulgent smile on her face and stiffened. But Colleen was unaware of the change in him, because she kept talking.

"He used to make me laugh," she was saying. "He couldn't get out much in his last couple of months, but he managed to steer everyone around him into doing just what he wanted them to do. He ran the ranch from his bed and his recliner. He even convinced me to accompany him to the rehearsal dinner," she added softly, "when I *knew* he wasn't well enough for the stress of the evening."

"That wasn't your fault," he said quickly.

"Wasn't it?" Her gaze locked with his. "I was his nurse. Supposed to guard his failing health, not give in to him when I knew it was dangerous." She reached up and pushed her hair back from her face, and suddenly Sage thought of how it had felt to have his own hands in that thick, silky mass.

Gritting his teeth, he pushed that thought aside and only said, "J.D. had a way of getting just what he wanted from folks. You shouldn't feel guilty about being one of them."

"He was a lovely man," she whispered. "Hard, but fair. Tough, but he loved his family. All of you. He talked about you all so much…"

Sage's ears perked up. "Did he?"

"Oh, yes." She walked closer to him, running her fingertips along the edge of the workbench. "He was so proud of Dylan's work with the grill. And he talked about Angie all the time—"

She broke off, as if remembering that J.D.'s will sort of belied that last statement.

"And you." She moved even closer and he caught her scent on the still, cool air. The scent that had haunted him all night long. Her eyes shone up at him with innocence and pleasure, as if she was really enjoying being able to share all of this with him. "He took so much pride in what you've built. He used to go on and on about how you made your first million while you were in school, and how he'd had to go to great lengths to convince you to stay at college when all you really wanted to do was build your own ranch—"

Sage's vision went red. And just like that, the seductive, sensual air between him and Colleen sizzled into an inferno that apparently only he could sense. His mind burned and thoughts chased each other through the darkness spreading through him. Years-old fury reawakened as if it had never gone to sleep, and he trembled with the force of the control required to keep from shouting out his rage.

Her voice was just a buzz of sound now, but even through the anger churning within, he could see that Colleen clearly believed that she'd scored a point. That she'd made Sage see his father as the *caring, thoughtful, generous* man she thought he was. That she'd found a way past the old angers and hurts. But instead, all she had done was relight the fuse that had been smoldering for years.

He took a breath and interrupted her stream of conversation. "Yeah. He was proud. Too damn proud. And he wasn't the kindhearted, feeble old gentleman you think you knew."

"What are you talking about?"

He threw a glance at the open shed door and the ranch yard beyond. Golden sunlight washed over his ranch, making the inside of the shed seem even darker in comparison. But damned if he'd have this talk out in public so that anyone could overhear. He strode across the straw-littered floor, slammed the door and threw the lock. Only then did he turn around to face Colleen again, and in the back of his mind, he noted that her eyes were wary.

"You met J.D. when he was old and tired and looking to find the fast track into heaven," Sage finally said and had the small satisfaction of seeing her blink in surprise. "I knew him back in the day and trust me, he wasn't a sweetheart. He was domineering, a know-it-all and damned arrogant with it."

One dark blond eyebrow lifted. "Remind you of anyone?"

He snorted in spite of the anger bubbling into an ugly brew in the pit of his stomach. "Okay, I can accept that maybe I picked up a few of his less pleasant traits along the way. But I never—" Damn. The words were stuck in his throat like bitter bile. He hadn't talked about this in years. And he'd *never* told anyone else about this. Not Dylan. Not Angie. The only person he had ever been open with about it was J.D. Because the old man himself was at the heart of it.

Shaking his head fiercely, as if he could dislodge the blackness wrapped around his memories, he muttered, "You said he wanted me to stay in college. That he told you he *talked* me into it."

"That's what he said, yes."

"Well, then, he had a really selective memory," Sage said flatly. "Because he didn't talk me into anything. He maneuvered me until he got his way. Just like he did everything else in his life."

"What do you mean, maneuvered?"

He hadn't meant to allow old memories to nearly choke him as they rushed up from the black bottom of his heart to spill through his mind like tar. But there they were, and he'd come too far to stop now.

"Unlike J.D., I never figured that I knew best how another man should live his life. I never made it my business to take something from a person just because I could."

"*What* are you talking about?"

"I was in college. My sophomore year. Twenty years old and I figured I had all the answers." He pushed one hand through his hair and tipped his head back to look up through the skylight at the cloud-scudded sky. Even with his age-old fury pushing his words, they caught in his throat and had to be forced out. But if he was going to say it, he was going to look into those oh-so-innocent eyes that saw only the good in people. That way he could be a witness when she finally had to admit that J.D. was nothing like she'd thought he was.

"What happened?" The concern in her voice was as real as the touch of her hand on his arm. The electrical whip of heat that sliced through him did battle with the anger and lost.

He snorted. "What happened? J.D. happened. I went home one night and told him that I was leaving school."

"Why?"

His gaze speared into hers. "I was in love. Or at least I thought I was. I told J.D. we were going to get married and start up my ranch."

Her voice was soft and uncertain as she asked, "What did he say?"

"Oh," Sage said on a sharp bark of laughter, "J.D. said all the right things. Told me he'd help me get into the inheritance my parents left me. Wasn't much," he added, "but it would've given me a start."

"That's good though, isn't it?" Her eyes were shimmering with hurt and he didn't know if it was for him or herself. "J.D. said he'd help you."

"Yeah, and then the next day, when I got to my girlfriend's place, her roommate told me she was gone and wouldn't be back." Amazing, Sage thought, that it could still hurt after all these years. That the betrayal was as sharp. The fury as thick.

"Why would she leave?"

He looked at her and quirked one eyebrow, inviting her to fill in the blanks. When she didn't, he did it for her. "She left me a note. Told me that it had been fun, but she was moving to Paris to paint. And she wasn't supposed to let me in on it, but apparently she didn't mind turning on J.D., either, because she told me in the note that he'd paid her two hundred thousand bucks to leave."

Colleen looked up at him, and for the first time in her life, didn't have the slightest clue what to say. This J.D. was not the man she had known. How could he have hurt his son so badly? And while her heart hurt for Sage, there was pain for herself, as well.

Sage had been in love. He'd wanted to get married. And though it was years ago, a part of her ached hearing the words.

He scrubbed both hands across his face. "I called him on it right away and he was furious that Megan had told me what he'd done." He shook his head and choked out another laugh. "He didn't see anything wrong with what he'd done, of course, but he was pissed as hell that I'd found out about it. Told me he'd done it for my sake. That Megan wasn't the kind of woman to stand by a man—"

She opened her mouth and he spoke quickly to cut her off.

"—before you can say it, yeah, he was right about Megan. If she had loved me, she never would have taken the money. But he should have let *me* find out the truth about her myself. Instead, he charged in, just like always, and rearranged the world to suit himself."

Megan was a fool. An idiot. She'd had this proud, strong, yes, *arrogant* man's love and she'd sold it. Colleen would never have betrayed him. She would have been proud to have his love, to work with him to build a ranch, a legacy for the family they would build and—

Colleen's throat closed up. All of a sudden she couldn't breathe. Couldn't stop the sting of tears in her eyes. What on earth was wrong with…

Oh, God. *She was in love.*

For the first time in her life, she was madly, completely, passionately in love with a man who probably would never return the feeling. The realization staggered her and if she hadn't had the workbench behind her as a brace, she might have just slumped to the floor. How was she going to get past this feeling? How could she possibly be in love with a man who wanted nothing to do with love and family? Who believed that love meant betrayal?

Sage was still talking and she forced herself to listen. He didn't need to know what she was feeling, that her heart was breaking. What he needed was to get past the old pain still gnawing on him. "Sage…"

"Forget it. You can't say anything, Colleen. J.D. was a bastard. End of story."

Her own feelings didn't matter right now, she told herself. What *did* matter was the pain Sage was still in. She couldn't bear seeing him cling to old injuries that were only hurting him, keeping him from moving on, and understanding that though his father had treated him badly, it wasn't because he hadn't loved him.

Colleen moved in closer, laid one hand on his chest

and said, "What he did was terrible, you're right. But he did it because he loved you."

"Hell of a way to prove it," he muttered. "He betrayed me, bottom line. And so did Megan, though in the long run, she did me a favor."

"Can't you say J.D. did, too?"

He snorted. "Don't know that I'm ready to thank him. But looking back, I can see that I mistook lust for love and I'm guessing J.D. saw that more clearly than I did back then." He blew out a breath and Colleen saw the anger fade from his eyes as he began to let go of the past. "I can say that if he hadn't stuck his nose in, I might not be standing here in front of a woman who turns my blood to fire with a look."

Instantly, Colleen's whole body lit up as if a sudden fever erupted inside her. She loved him. She wanted him. She stared into his eyes and knew that though he might not love her back, his desire was real and every bit as powerful as her own. "Sage…"

"I'm done talking about J.D. right now, Colleen," he murmured, dropping both hands to the workbench on either side of her, pinning her in place. "I've been trying to stay away from you—"

"I know," she said. "Why?"

"Because I want you too much. You're all I think about. All I give a flying damn about. You're in my blood, Colleen."

"You're in mine, too," she whispered, reaching up to cup his face between her palms. Her thumbs traced across his cheekbones and he held perfectly still as she went up on her toes, moved in and kissed him.

That soft brush of her lips against his was a benediction of sorts. A wiping away of the past and a welcome into the present—the future?

He fell into her kiss willingly, eagerly, and wrapped his arms around her. Colleen gave herself up to the moment, letting go of everything but the magic shimmering in the air between them.

But just as the kiss was deepening, spiraling out of control, Sage pulled back, looked down at her and muttered, "Damned if we're going to be together in an old cabin and then in an equipment shed where any one of my cowboys could glance in the window for a peek."

She flushed and laughed, burying her face briefly against his chest. "I forgot entirely where we were."

"Yeah, you have that effect on me, too," he confessed. "But today we're going to try an actual *bed.* Come with me."

He took her hand and led her out of the shed toward the main house and all Colleen could think was, she would go with him anywhere.

Ten

She woke up early in the master bedroom to find that Sage was already up and gone.

Colleen sighed and stretched languorously in the big bed she'd shared with him all night. Her mind filled with images of the night before and bubbles of residual heat slid through her bloodstream like champagne. She'd only managed about two hours' sleep all night, but she'd never felt more awake, more aware.

Who would have guessed that *love* could heighten every sense? Could make you both grateful and miserable with the kind of feelings that were so overwhelming? She couldn't stay, she knew she couldn't. She loved him and he didn't love her and never the twain would meet just like when it happened in those literary, depressing love stories.

But God, she didn't want to go. Her gaze fixed on

the wall of windows and French doors leading to a wood deck, beyond which she saw an amazing sweep of stormy sky that was punctuated by the tips of pine trees. It looked as though they would get another storm, and she knew she should go before that storm hit. Now all she needed was the courage to make the move. She was in love, but he wasn't. In fact, he would probably panic and run if he knew how she felt about him. But when she remembered the tenderness, the amazing heat that spiraled between them when they made love, it was hard not to dream that one day, he might love her back.

"Oh, God," she murmured, pulling her pillow out from under her head to drop it onto her face. "Try not to be a complete idiot, Colleen. Sex isn't love. Just because he's good at it doesn't mean he cares. He's just… thorough."

She threw one arm across that pillow so that her voice was muffled and she wouldn't have to listen to herself. Honestly, this was a serious mess. Falling in love was just—unavoidable, she thought. Now she had to work out what to do about it. Keep her mouth shut, obviously. And get off this mountain as quickly as possible. Because the longer she stayed, the harder it would be to eventually walk away.

Just as that depressing thought took up root in her mind, Colleen's cell phone rang and she rolled out of bed to grab her jeans off the floor. Fumbling through the pockets, she found her phone, saw the caller ID and winced. "Hi, Mom."

"Hi, sweetie, how's it going?"

"Great, really. Um…" She looked around for *something* to slip on. She couldn't just stand there naked and chat with her mother. Finally settling for a sheet, she snaked it off the bed and wrapped it around her.

"So." Laura's voice was bright and happy. "Did you find the house you want to buy?"

Memories of the cabin rose up in her mind and she smiled wistfully. "I think so," she said, "but I'm still looking."

Because she loved that cabin and thought it would be perfect for her. But the question was, would she be able to live with the memories of what she and Sage had done there once they weren't together anymore? Could she really face those memories every day?

"That's wonderful, honey. It's so nice of Sage to take the time to show you around."

"Yep, very nice." And so much more.

"I know it's early to call, but I had to tell you, your aunt Donna is coming for a visit next week."

"That's great." She could hear the excitement in her mother's voice and Colleen sent another silent thank-you to J.D. for making this possible. Even if her own life was teetering on the brink of despair, at least her mother was having fun.

"We're going to plan our trip together and get our passport photos taken together," Laura said in a tangled rush of words. She kept talking, outlining her plans and laughing more than Colleen had heard her laugh in years. Finally, though, her mom slowed down and said, "You're awfully quiet."

"What?" Damn. She should have been paying closer attention. Her mother always had been really good at picking up on Colleen's moods.

"Never mind trying to play it cool, kiddo. Spill it."

Colleen dropped onto the edge of the bed, stared out

at the view and took a deep breath before saying, "I screwed up."

"Impossible."

She laughed and a little of her depression lifted. "Thanks, Mom."

"Tell me what's wrong, sweetie."

"I'm in love with a man who likes me."

"But that's wonderful." Laura practically cheered.

Colleen shook her head and with one hand, pushed her hair back from her face. "I think you missed the most important part in that last sentence, Mom. He *likes* me. He doesn't love me."

"He will, though. How could he not?"

God bless mothers, Colleen thought with a sad smile. Though her mom would always support her, always believe in her, there was no way she could understand how Colleen was feeling right now. Her parents had fallen in love at first sight. They'd only known each other a month before they got married and they'd stayed deeply in love until the day Colleen's father died. So with that kind of background, her mother would never be able to see just how hopeless Colleen's situation was.

"It's not that easy." Not when his past held memories of a woman who had betrayed him.

"Who said it was supposed to be easy?" her mother asked, then added, "Okay, yes, your dad and I had it easy. We found each other and it all fell together. But Sage likes you. That's not so far from love."

Outside, the sky opened up and rain pelted the windows. They'd had sun, snow and now rain in just a few days. Colleen shivered a little and wondered if the storm was an omen. Then she dismissed that thought. No need to get crazy here.

"Have you told him how you feel?"

"Of course not," she said, horrified at the thought. She'd like to hang on to a little bit of dignity if she could. "I can't admit to that. How humiliating."

"Or," her mother said slyly, "how liberating. You risk nothing but a little pride. And honey, love is worth any price you have to pay."

A few minutes later she hung up, but her mother's words were still echoing through Colleen's mind. Was she right? Should she tell Sage what she was feeling? Or should she just pack up her heart before it got bruised and run back to reality?

An hour later, she was dressed and downstairs, looking for a cup of coffee. She was packed and would be leaving as soon as she spoke to Sage. She just still hadn't made up her mind what exactly to say to him and was hoping caffeine would help her think more clearly. When she heard Sage's voice, she followed the sound without even thinking about it. Walking down the long, gloomy hall, her sneakered footsteps were quiet on the wood floor. She tapped gently on his office door, then opened it.

He was sitting at his desk, holding the phone to his ear, which explained her hearing his voice. His back was to her, his gaze fixed on the raging storm beyond the wide glass window. Adrenaline pulsed through her as he started speaking again, as if her body was tuned to the timbre and richness of his voice. But before she could back out of the room and give him privacy for his call, *what* he was saying caught her attention.

"Dylan," he said, sounding bored and impatient as he talked to his brother, "dating Colleen was the only sure way to find out exactly what J.D. was up to before he died."

Her heart stopped and a thin sliver of air worked its way down her lungs. Blindly, she reached out one hand to the doorjamb and held on as if it meant her life.

"She was the closest to the old man and it's entirely possible that she knows something she's not even aware of," Sage continued.

Colleen felt sick. Her heartbeat was slow. Heavy. Like a movie played in extremely slow motion. Ice dropped into the pit of her churning stomach and the cold seemed to spread, snaking out tentacles that reached throughout her body until she shivered with reaction.

She should leave.

She knew she should turn and run. Hit the front door, race to her car and get off the mountain. But she couldn't move. It was as if her feet were nailed to the floor. She wanted to be struck deaf so she wouldn't have to hear any more. She wanted to have never come downstairs. To have never come here to this ranch at all.

Sage shook his head and laughed at whatever his brother was saying. "You're wrong, Dylan. Trust me, I'm not getting too close to Colleen. I don't *do* close. Besides, this isn't about what I *want*—it's about what I want to find out."

Did she make a sound? She might have. A tiny gasp. A small moan. Of course she did. How could her body contain so much pain without letting some of it escape? Whatever that sound was, he heard it, because he slowly swiveled around in his chair, spotted her across the room and said simply, "Colleen."

Funny. It was the look in his eyes that finally freed her enough to run. The shock. The surprise. The *guilt.* By the time he slammed the phone into its cradle, she was gone.

* * *

Panic roared into life in Sage's chest and had him bolting from his office, racing after her, determined to catch her. To explain. To— Hell. He didn't know what he'd do.

"Damn it, Colleen, *wait!*" He caught her at the front door and slammed one hand on the heavy oak panel so she couldn't yank it open no matter how hard she tried.

"Get away," she said and he heard tears choking her voice.

Pain lanced him as he called himself all kinds of vicious but accurate names.

"I mean it, Sage," she muttered thickly. "Let me go."

"It's raining, Colleen. You can't leave in a storm."

"I know how to drive in the rain—and I'm leaving."

"I can't let you do that." That panic was still bubbling up inside him and staring down into her damp eyes, it only got worse. She was trying to leave and he couldn't let her. Not like this.

"What you heard back there? It wasn't true." He hung his head and gave it a shake before finding the strength to meet those tear-filled blue eyes again. "I was just trying to get Dylan off my back, that's all."

"No," she said, her mouth twisting as if she were trying desperately to keep her bottom lip from quivering. "It was true. All of it. I'm only surprised I didn't see it sooner."

Seeing tears clouding her clear, beautiful eyes tore at him. Knowing he had caused it nearly killed him. The worst kind of bastard, he'd hurt a woman who didn't deserve it, all to cover his own ass and save his pride with his brother.

"Why else would you ever go for a woman like me?"

Shaking her head, she lifted her chin and he saw what that defiant, proud move cost her. "So don't tell me that conversation with your brother wasn't true. Recent behavior notwithstanding, I'm not an idiot, Sage. Now open this door and let me leave."

"You don't really want to go and I don't want you to," he said, gaze moving over her lovely features, searing her face into his mind. He drew her scent in deep and felt her permeate every cell in his body.

He should have locked the damn office door. Then this wouldn't be an issue. She never would have overheard him. They could have gone on as they were, and both of them would have been happy. Instead, he had to try to unravel the damage he'd done.

The thing was, he hadn't meant a damn thing he'd said to his brother. He just hadn't wanted to admit to himself, let alone Dylan, that he'd come to…care for Colleen. Oh, it might have started out differently, using her as a means to an end, but somewhere along the line, that had changed. Into what, he couldn't say. All he was sure of was that he hated seeing her in pain. Hated knowing he was the cause.

Bending his head, he kissed her and refused to allow her to turn her face from his. Wouldn't let her ignore the fire between them. And in seconds, in spite of the turmoil churning inside her, she was kissing him back. His heart gave one wild lurch as he realized that maybe, just maybe, he could still salvage what he had with her. He wrapped his arms around her and held her tightly, losing himself, as always, in the heat that engulfed him the moment they came together.

Seconds, minutes, it could have been hours that passed as they stood, wrapped up in each other, mouths fused, hearts beating in tandem. But when he tried to draw back, to lead her toward the stairs and his bedroom, Colleen said, "No."

He stared at her, confused by the refusal. "What?"

"No," she said again, pulling away from him, taking a step back to increase the space between them. "I won't go back upstairs with you, Sage. I can't."

He shoved one hand through his hair. "But you kissed me back just now. You believed me when I told you that I didn't mean any of what you heard."

"Didn't you?" Her eyes were wounded. There was no sign of tears now, but the cool detachment he saw in her expression worried Sage more than a flood of tears might have. "Why did you first come to see me, Sage? Why did you first want to spend time with me?"

Instead of answering, he asked a question of his own. "Why are you doing this?"

She laughed shortly, but the sound was harsh and strained. "I really don't want to, but I have no choice. So tell me why, Sage."

He wouldn't lie to her. Couldn't bring himself to look into those honest, oh-so-innocent eyes and lie just to save his own ass. He'd bring her more pain and it would rip him apart, but she deserved the damned truth.

"You know why." As his gaze locked with hers, he saw her eyes widen slightly and another slash of pain dart across their surfaces.

"So it's true."

"It's not true *now*," he countered and took a step toward her. He stopped when she backed away, maintaining the distance between them. "I didn't know you," he said, forcing himself to keep meeting her eyes, acknowledging the pain he was causing her even as it sliced at him, too. "All I knew was that J.D.'s will had been changed. He'd cheated my sister out of what should have been hers, and J.D.'s private nurse was suddenly a millionaire."

She sucked in a gulp of air and the gasping sound filled the quiet house. "You really believed I had somehow tricked J.D. into leaving me money and cheating your sister?"

"Don't you get it, Colleen? *Nothing* was making sense. J.D. turned on his daughter. Thinking you were somehow behind it all made as much sense as anything else." It sounded so stupid now, knowing her as he did. But in his own defense, hadn't he had his own experience with J.D. paying women off? "Can you blame me? You know what my father did to me once before. He betrayed me then…and now, from the damn *grave,* he's doing the same thing to Angie."

She shook her head sadly. "You've let that one horrible experience color your whole life, haven't you?"

"Why shouldn't I? It was a valuable lesson and I learned it well."

Her luscious mouth twisted into a parody of a smile that was almost harder to see than the single tear escaping her eye to roll along her cheek.

"Oh, Sage," she said, her voice aching with the hurt he'd just dealt her. "What you *didn't* learn was that J.D. didn't do that to hurt you. He did it to protect you. That's what we do for people we love."

"*Protect* me?" He laughed, astonished that she could still take J.D.'s side in this, in spite of everything. "How? By making me doubt myself, my judgment? By ensuring that I wouldn't trust another damn soul? Some help."

Shaking her head again, she looked at him with disappointment. "You chose that path, Sage. Your father didn't put you on it." Her voice was so quiet he had to strain to hear it over the thundering beat of his own heart. "He was trying to save you from more pain later on down the road." She paused, then hurried on before he could speak. "Sure, he made mistakes. But people do. Especially the people who love us."

What the hell was he supposed to do with a woman like her? She continually looked for the good in people—and had found it in J.D. Despite what he'd done to Sage so many years ago, the old man had done the best he could by *all* of his children, and maybe Sage was now willing to accept that. If he did, it just made the will that much more perplexing.

As confusing as the woman standing before him. He didn't want to examine those feelings. Didn't want to explore the wild explosion of thoughts and sensations churning in his mind. All he wanted was *her*.

And he couldn't have her.

A tight fist was squeezing his heart and lungs, making it almost impossible to draw an easy breath. Finally though, he said, "So can't you see that I made a mistake? About you? Can't you forgive that and let it go?"

That sad smile curved her mouth again as she murmured, "I can forgive it, but I'm still leaving."

"Why?" That one word was a demand.

"Because I love you, Sage," she said simply. "And I deserve better."

Staggered, he couldn't think of a single thing to say. She loved him? She *loved* him. And she was leaving anyway? She was opening the front door and the sound and scent of a driving rain sneaked across the threshold. She loved him. Those three words kept echoing in his mind, rattling his soul.

"Before I go, though, there is one thing J.D. told me that you should know."

His eyes narrowed on her as suspicion leaped up to the base of his throat. "What?"

"God. Even now you're still wondering if I betrayed you or not."

"No." He denied it. He knew she wasn't capable of betrayal. Knew that she was too intrinsically honest to be a part of any deception. Just as he knew that when she said she loved him, she meant every word.

"J.D. was proud of you. And he regretted that the two of you weren't close." She blew out a breath. "He was heartsick that his sons believed he didn't care."

He wished he could believe that she was lying about all of this. Because if it was all true, then he and J.D. had both been cheated of the relationship they might have had.

"He also told me," she said softly, "that he left you the Lassiter Media shares so that you would always remember that you're family. So you would realize that family is important and that *love* is all that matters."

Then she was gone.

And he was alone.

Two weeks crawled past.

Sage didn't see her. Didn't speak to her. Didn't do much of anything, really. In that first week, he couldn't give a damn about the ranch that had once been the most important thing in his life. He didn't care about stock prices or the phone calls and emails he kept getting from the various boards of the companies he sat on.

All he could think about was Colleen and the last words she'd said to him. Words that J.D. had often said when Sage was a kid. *Family. Love was everything.*

Love.

Sage hadn't really known what that was until Colleen had loved him and left him. As a younger man, he'd mistaken lust for love and just as Colleen said, he'd allowed that one poor choice to color the rest of his life. He'd cut himself off, in theory to protect himself, but in reality all he'd been doing was hiding.

Well, he was through hiding. That's why he spent the second week setting wheels in motion. There were things to do. Things to be said. A life to be lived.

When Sage walked through the front door of Big Blue, he looked around and for the first time in years, he didn't cringe from the memories rushing toward him. His heart was still heavy, but that had nothing to do with J.D. Not anymore. Sage had finally come to accept that his father was just a man, as capable of making mistakes as anyone. God knew Sage had made plenty. Especially lately.

"Sage! What're you doing here?" Angie came down the stairs, a smile on her face, and rushed toward her oldest brother for a hug. "I'm so glad to see you. And hey, *honored* that you left your ranch."

"Yeah, well," he told her, "a lot of things have changed." And how was she going to take what he had to say to her? He didn't want to hurt his sister. Hell, he'd do anything to avoid that. He just didn't see a way around it.

"No kidding," she said wryly and he knew that she was still thinking about the will and what J.D. had done to her.

It was the perfect opening for what he'd come to say. They had talked about this before, but at the time, he hadn't made the final decision that he now had to share with his sister.

"Angie, we can't fight the will."

"What?" Confused, she said, "Why not?"

He took both of her hands in his, glanced around the entry hall and felt the years of being a Lassiter settle down onto his shoulders. He was J.D.'s son and it was high time he started acting like it.

"Because if we do that and lose, a lot of people could be hurt. Marlene. Chance…" *Colleen,* he thought but didn't say.

"But you said we'd do something about this. That we'd figure it all out. I thought you were on *my* side."

His heart squeezed. "I am on your side, honey. You're my sister and I love you. But you know, too—hell, we *all* know, that J.D. loved you to death." He squeezed her hands. "So he had a reason for what he did no matter how crazy it seems to us. We're going to sit back and trust that our father did the right thing."

"That's easy for you to say." Angie yanked her hands from his and glared at him. "Dad didn't turn on you."

"Yeah, I know. Just like I know that J.D. had a *reason* for everything he ever did. We just have to find out the reason behind this."

"And that'll make it better?" The short laugh that shot from her throat told him how she felt about that.

"Didn't say that." Shaking his head, Sage looked at his sister and tried not to see the unshed tears glittering in her eyes. "We both know J.D. would never do anything to deliberately hurt you, so there's a reason for what he did. We're going to trust it's a good one."

"I can't believe this." There was hurt in her eyes, but mostly she was furious.

Well, he could deal with an angry sister. Anger he understood.

"Angie, I spent a lot of years mad at J.D. I wasted what I could have had." Disgusted with himself and sad that missed chances could never be recaptured, he said, "I'm through wasting time. I'm through holding a grudge against our father. I love you, Angie, but I won't support you if you try to fight the will."

"Sage—"

"You, me, Dylan," he said, cutting off whatever she might have said, "we're family. And love is all that matters."

She choked out a strained laugh. "You sound just like Dad."

Sage grinned. "About time, don't you think?"

Colleen hadn't expected love.

At thirty-one, she'd long ago given up on the whole Prince Charming thing and had made up her mind to enjoy her career and her life, and if love found her, then great. If not, that would be okay, too.

Well, love had found her. When she'd least expected it, love had arrived. "And lucky me, now I know exactly what it's like to try to live without it."

The past two weeks had been awful. Just awful. She was tired of putting on a happy face for her mother—but it was necessary because she didn't want her mom worrying. And it was a strain pretending everything would be great to Jenna—who wanted to drive up the mountain and kick Sage. The worst part of it all was trying to get by on fifteen minutes of sleep every night.

Sage was on her mind all the time. She couldn't sleep, couldn't eat—at least she'd lost six pounds—and just the thought of never being with him again made Colleen want to crawl into a hole and die. How was it possible, she wondered, for your whole world to change completely in just a matter of weeks?

Looking back, she could see how it had all happened. She'd been half in love with Sage from the moment J.D. had told her the first story about his oldest son. She was lost from the moment she'd seen him at the rehearsal dinner. And now she was just lost.

Sitting at the table in her condo kitchen, she looked over the sales papers and signed her name at every highlighted X. The condo was sold and she was now officially homeless. She still had to finish qualifying as a nurse practitioner, but most of that could be done online. And when she had to come to Cheyenne for classes, she was willing to drive down off the mountain to do it. She was ready for change. Ready to start living the rest of her life.

All she needed now was to find a place to live.

"Poor little rich girl," she murmured, flipping through the pages. Three million dollars and no home to call her own. She'd have to start over, looking for a place, because she couldn't buy that cabin. Not now. Not ever. She wouldn't be able to live there, remembering the passion, the incredible sense of rightness that she'd felt with Sage so briefly.

"It's okay," she told herself, signing her name with a flourish. "I'll find something else. There's more than one cabin in the mountains. I'll still—"

God, who was she trying to kid? Who was she being brave for? She was all alone here. No mom. No Jenna.

She could cry and wail and weep if she wanted to—for all the good it would do her. It had already been two weeks. Sage had forgotten all about her and it would really be a good thing if she could do the same.

Nodding, she picked up the sheaf of papers, slid them back into the envelope her real estate agent had dropped off and then sealed it. It was done. Her house was sold. Her new life was about to begin. She only wished she could be happy about that.

When the doorbell rang, she jumped up, eager for any distraction to take her mind off her depressing thoughts. To keep her too busy to think of Sage and everything that might have been.

She pulled the door open and there he was. For a second, his presence didn't really compute. It was as if she'd spent so much time thinking about him that her mind had actually conjured a vision of him just for her. But that silly thought was gone the moment he opened his mouth.

"We have to talk."

"No, we don't." Colleen shook her head and tried to close the door, but his booted foot kept it open. "I'm really not a masochist, Sage, so if you don't mind I'd appreciate you just going away. If you're here to apologize, thanks. You're forgiven. Happy trails and all of that."

God, what it cost her to tell him no. But how could she let him back in, even temporarily? *Salt, meet wound.* No. She just couldn't do it. Already she wasn't sleeping or eating and her eyes were constantly red from all the tears. She had nothing left.

"I'm not here to apologize," he muttered through the gap between her door and the wall.

"You're *not?*" She glared at him through that same gap. "You should be."

"You already forgave me, remember?"

Frowning, she was forced to admit he had a point. "Fine. Then there's no reason for you to be here at all. So go away."

"Beback misses you."

"That's just mean," she snapped. He knew how much she liked his dog. How much she wanted one of her own.

"I miss you."

"You miss the sex," she countered because she simply would not let herself believe anything else. She was through building castles in the air. Just because he was here didn't mean anything between them had changed.

"Sure I do. Don't you?"

She looked into his eyes, those really amazing, wonderful, soulful eyes and couldn't deny it. Naturally she missed the sex. "Yes."

"And you miss me," he said softly.

Oh, she did. She really did.

"I'll get over it," she told him and shoved harder on the door. But the man was just too strong for her.

"I don't want you to get over it. Or me."

"Sage…" She sighed, leaned her forehead against the door and murmured, *"Please* go away?"

He reached through the gap, covered her hand with one of his, and Colleen felt that so familiar zing of heat that whispered inside her, urging her to listen. To let him in. To remember how good they were together. But remembering wouldn't change anything, so why go there?

"Why are you here?" She pulled her hand free of his, though she missed the warmth of his touch.

"I have to show you something," he said softly. "Will you take one more trip with me up the mountain?"

"Why should I?"

"There's no reason in the world you should," he admitted and pulled his foot out of the doorway. "But I'm asking you to anyway."

If he'd tried to smooth talk her into it, she might have refused. Instead, he'd played a new game. Honesty. And frankly, she was tired of fighting him. She knew she'd regret it later, of course, but at the moment, going with him was just easier.

The ride was tense, neither of them talking much. Colleen's mind was whirling with possibilities and questions. Why had he come? Where were they going? Why?

She sneaked glances at him, and he was always the same. Stoic. Eyes focused on the road ahead, which should have relieved her, since this drive could be treacherous. But she wished that he would glance her way. Give her some indication of what was going on. Instead, he drove the narrow, winding road up the mountain in silence, passing his ranch gates, and she turned in her seat to look at them as they drove by. "I thought we were going to your house."

"No," he said, not looking at her, focusing instead on the road stretched out in front of them.

Her stomach swirled uneasily as she realized where they were probably headed. The cabin. Where else would he be taking her on this mountain road? But then, why would he take her to the cabin? It was the first question she asked when he pulled into the drive and parked.

"Like I said at your house," he told her, climbing out of the huge SUV, "there's something I want to show you."

He took her hand, just as he had the first time, as they headed along the path to the cabin. But it was different now. The flower beds were weeded and bursting with newly planted, bright spring blossoms. Their scent rose up into the air and twisted with the ever-present aroma of pines.

The path itself was covered in fresh gravel. The surrounding pines had been trimmed back, still providing shade for the cabin but no longer threatening to tip over in a storm. The walls were painted a crisp white with navy blue trim around the windows. The chairs on the front porch had brand-new, dark blue cushions and there was a sturdy iron railing snaking along the porch, replacing the rotted wooden one that had snapped on their last visit.

It was beautiful. It was perfect. But she still couldn't buy it. "I can't," she said, looking up at him. "I can't buy this cabin, Sage. I appreciate you fixing it up for me but—"

"The cabin's not for sale anymore."

"What?"

"I bought it last week." He closed in on her and Colleen's heartbeat sped up. "Went to see Ed at his new place and paid him for it on the spot."

"Why?" she asked and was lucky she'd managed to squeeze out that single word.

"Let's go inside. There are some things I want to say to you."

She walked the path, ran her fingertips over the heavy black wrought-iron railing. When he noticed, he said, "I had my guys over here every day this week, fixing this place up. But the railing I installed myself." He caught her hand in his. "It's sturdy enough that you could do handstands on it, but I'd take it as a favor if you wouldn't. I don't want to risk losing you again."

Pleasure slid through her heart, leaving a trail of eager

anticipation in its wake. Was he saying what she thought he was? Could she believe? Her logical mind told her emotional half to get a grip, but it wasn't listening.

He smiled at her and tugged her along after him. "Come on."

She followed and the minute she stepped into the cabin, she realized he'd been at work here, too. The wood floors were gleaming under a fresh coat of wax. Bright throw rugs added splashes of color. Bookcases stood on either side of the wood-burning stove and there was a scent of lemon polish still hovering in the air.

"Linda, my housekeeper," Sage was saying as she walked through the little cabin that was now as shiny as new pennies. "She handled most of the inside work, though my guys did the paint job."

"It's beautiful," she told him, walking back to stop just a foot from him. "But I still don't understand. Why did you buy it?"

"For us," he said simply. He stood there opposite her in his black jeans, black leather jacket and white shirt and looked more gorgeous than she remembered. Just looking at the man gave her chills, but what he said next had every sense reeling.

"I bought it for us, Colleen. I wanted us to have this place to come to, just the two of us. I want us to always remember that we started here. That what's between us grew from here."

Oh, God. Her heartbeat was hammering so quickly now she could hardly draw a breath. But she didn't need air, Colleen realized. All she needed was to know that he meant this. Because if he had done all of this for the two of them, that could only mean that he loved her, and that would be everything.

"See," he said, moving toward her, laying both hands on her shoulders so that she could feel the strong, steady warmth of him seeping into her body. "I know now that I wasted what time I had with my father. I don't want to waste another minute of my time with you."

"Sage…"

"You said you loved me," he reminded her and gave her a slow smile. "I hope that hasn't changed, because I love you, too, Colleen."

Her eyes filled with tears and her breath caught in her throat. It was everything she'd hoped for. Only better.

"I love your mind. Your humor. Your kindness. I love everything about you."

"I can't believe this," she murmured, wondering if somehow she had fallen asleep back at the condo and maybe this was all just a very real, very involved dream.

"Believe it," he said, bending low enough to kiss her forehead before drawing back to look at her again. "Remember what J.D. said? Family is important and love is all that matters?"

"I remember." His eyes were shining down on her. The shutters were gone. They were clear and beautiful and glittering with emotions so deep they stole her breath.

"Well, *you're* my family. And my love for you is everything." He pulled her in close to him, lifted both hands and cupped her face between his palms. "I'm asking you to marry me, Colleen. Marry me and make a family of our own. Kids. Dogs. Horses. We'll have it all if you'll just say yes."

She wanted to. More than anything in her life, she wanted what he was offering. But she had to say, "I still want to get my practitioner's license. I want to have that rural practice I told you about."

He grinned and her heart nearly leaped up her throat. Would he always have this effect on her? God, she hoped so.

"Not a problem, honey," he said. "When you have calls to make, I'll watch the kids."

"Kids," she repeated, because she loved the sound of it.

"At least five or six."

She laughed then and felt her whole world come right again.

"So, will you marry me, Colleen?" He kissed the tip of her nose, then brushed her mouth with his. "Trust me, love. I've learned enough to listen. To know that though I could make it through my life alone, I don't want to. I want you—I *need* you—by my side. Always."

"There's really nowhere else I'd rather be," she said as she leaned into him. Her heart was full, and she had everything she'd ever dreamed of, right there offering her his heart. His life. His love. "Sage, I love you so much, of course I'll marry you."

"Thank God," he whispered and kissed her there in the room where they had first begun. Where they would come when they wanted to remember. When they wanted to celebrate the fact that love really was the only thing that mattered.

Epilogue

The wedding was two weeks later.

Colleen was amazed at just how quickly everything could come together. But Sage hadn't wanted to wait, and really, neither had she. Why wait when you had at last found the one person in the world for you?

Sage's ranch was decorated with flowers everywhere. He'd arranged for both a florist and a gardener to come in and turn the yard into a rainbow of color. There was also a hastily constructed dance floor on the wide front yard, lit by miles of tiny white twinkling lights that in the dusk looked like stars being born. Music from a local country band had the dance floor crowded and the scent of barbecue tempted everyone there.

It had been perfect, Colleen thought. Even the weather had cooperated, blessing the ceremony with a cool, clear day and a starry night.

She'd been on her feet for hours now, but she wasn't the least bit tired. Joy filled her, keeping a smile on her face and a thrill in her heart. She took a sip of champagne and looked out across the ranch at the people who had come to celebrate with them. It had been a small ceremony, only friends and family, and somehow that had made the whole thing more special.

Marlene was dancing with Walter Drake, the older woman laughing at something he said. Angie and Evan looked to be involved in a heated discussion, and Colleen frowned slightly. She could only hope that the situation would be cleared up soon, before it destroyed what the couple shared. Dylan was supervising the barbecue station and Chance was talking to Sage's ranch manager. Jenna and her husband were dancing and Colleen's mother and Aunt Donna were huddled at a table, no doubt planning their upcoming cruise.

"You're looking way too thoughtful for a bride," Sage said, coming up behind her. "And did I tell you how beautiful you are?"

She felt beautiful in her floor-length, off-the-shoulder white dress that skimmed her curves and swirled at her feet. But then, Sage was handsome in a black suit that was so elegantly cut he took her breath away.

"You did," she assured him, "but feel free to repeat yourself."

He chuckled, slid his arms around her middle and held her close to him. Colleen laid her hands on his arms and leaned her head back against his broad chest. "It's just such a perfect day."

He bent his head briefly to kiss her neck. "Any day I can get Colleen Falkner to say 'I do' is a good day."

She looked up at him. "That's Colleen Lassiter to you, mister."

He grinned and her heart did a flip. "Sounds good, doesn't it?"

"Sounds wonderful," she agreed, then nodded toward her mother and aunt. "They're so excited about the house you're having built for them on the ranch."

He laughed a little. "I know. Between the two of them, they're about to drive the architect wild enough to jump out a window."

Colleen's gaze slid across to the other side of the wide, manicured lawn, where the foundation of a house had already been laid. Sage had surprised her, and thrilled her mother, with his plans to build a three-bedroom house on the property for Laura and Donna. They would have their own place but be close enough to the main house that they could come and go as they pleased. The two women hadn't stopped talking about it since.

"They've changed the layout of the downstairs three times already," Sage mused, humor evident in his tone.

"You realize that with this beautiful house, they probably won't want to move to Florida after all?" And really, the two women had only decided on Florida because Aunt Donna already lived there and it would have been the easiest solution. Now things were different.

"Why would they, when Wyoming has everything?" he asked, then, smiling gently he added, "They only wanted to live together. Now they don't have to be in Florida to do it. And if your mom gets sick of winter, we'll buy the two of them a condo in Florida and they can go as often as they like."

Her heart did the flippy thing again as she realized

just what an amazing man she'd fallen in love with. "You're incredible."

"Not really," he said wryly, "but I'm glad you think so."

"I really do," she told him, turning in his arms so that she could look at him. Colleen knew that every ounce of love she felt for him had to be shining from her eyes, because she felt lit from within, as if she was absolutely glowing with the happiness she'd found.

"Besides," he said on a low laugh, "once the two of them have their passports in hand, I have a feeling they're going to be taking lots of trips. They can't wait for that cruise you're sending them on. But home will always be here. Waiting for them."

She studied his features, wanting to be absolutely sure he was okay with this and not just doing it because he knew she'd love having her family close by. "Are you really positive, Sage? There aren't many men willing to have their mother-in-law, not to mention her sister, living right on his doorstep."

All trace of amusement left his face as he met her eyes. He lifted one hand to smooth a stray lock of her hair back behind her ear before saying, "J.D.'s not here today—and damned if I don't wish he was. But I know what he'd say and I feel the same way. Family is important. Love is all that matters."

Tears filled her eyes. "Oh, you really know how to touch my heart."

"You are my heart, Colleen." He bent to kiss her gently, briefly. "And your mom. Donna. They're nice women. Why shouldn't they be with their family?" He grinned. "Besides, when our babies start arriving, how great will it be to have two willing babysitters close by?"

They'd already started trying to make their family, and Colleen sighed with the thought. Babies. A husband who loved her. Her vision still blurred with a wash of tears she was too happy to shed, she went up on her toes and kissed him. "I love you, Sage Lassiter."

"Damn straight you do," he said, his half grin taking all of the arrogance out of the statement.

"You're impossible."

"And very lucky," he added.

"Oh, that too," she agreed, sliding her arms around his waist and cuddling in close. He held her tightly enough that she heard the steady thump of his heart beneath her ear. Closing her eyes, she smiled to herself and relished the sensation of having her life be everything she could ever have hoped for.

A beautiful, love-filled wedding on a gorgeous ranch that was now her home. Her family was close and happy. Soon, she would be on her way to getting her practitioner's license and she had the love of her life holding her so gently it was as if she were a fragile, priceless treasure.

"So," he whispered, "how much longer do you figure we have to stay at this party?"

She smiled up at him. They would be spending their wedding night in the cabin where this had all begun. Tomorrow they were off by private jet for a week in Paris. And then home again to start their lives together. She couldn't wait. Colleen was as anxious as Sage to be alone with him.

"I love that we'll be at the cabin tonight," she told him.

"Me, too. And just think," he said, drawing her close for a hard squeeze, "one day, we'll take our grandkids out there, show them the railing and tell 'em about the day Grandma almost fell off the mountain—but how their strong, brave grandpa saved her, carried her inside and—"

Playfully, she slapped his chest. "We can't tell them *that*."

He caught her hand in his and kissed her palm. "How about we just tell them that Grandma saved Grandpa that day, too?"

Her heart melted. How was it possible to love a man as much as she loved Sage? And how had she ever lived without that love?

"How about we give the party one more hour?" she asked.

He groaned. "Deal. One hour, then if I don't have you, you'll be married to a dead man."

Colleen hugged him tight and turned her face up to his. "One hour. You can make it."

"For you," he promised, *"anything."*

Then he drew her onto the dance floor, and as their family and friends cheered, they danced their way into the future.

* * * * *

FROM SINGLE MUM TO SECRET HEIRESS

BY
KRISTI GOLD

Kristi Gold has a fondness for beaches, baseball and bridal reality shows. She firmly believes that love has remarkable healing powers and feels very fortunate to be able to weave stories of love and commitment. As a bestselling author, a National Readers' Choice Award winner and a Romance Writers of America three-time RITA® Award finalist, Kristi has learned that although accolades are wonderful, the most cherished rewards come from networking with readers. She can be reached through her website at www.kristigold.com, or through Facebook.

To my fellow Lassiter authors, particularly
Kathie DeNosky, my good friend and brainstorming
buddy. I can always count on you to have my back,
as long as you've had your coffee.
Couldn't have done this one without you.

One

What a way to begin the end of April—with limited funds and leaky plumbing.

Yet Hannah Armstrong couldn't quite believe her sudden change in fortune. Twenty minutes after placing the 5:00 p.m. service call, and hearing the dispatcher's declaration that they would *try* to send someone out today, her doorbell sounded.

She left the flooded galley kitchen and carefully crossed the damp dining-room floor that was littered with towels. After entering the living room, she navigated another obstacle course comprised of a toy plastic convertible painted shocking pink, as well as a string of miniature outfits that would be the envy of the fashion-doll world. "Cassie, sweetie, you have to pick up your toys before you can spend the night with Michaela," she called on her way to answer the summons.

She immediately received the usual "In a minute, Mama," which came from the hallway to her right.

Hannah started to scold her daughter for procrastinating, but she was too anxious to greet her knight in shining tool belt. Yet when she yanked the front door open, she was completely taken aback by the man standing on her porch. The guy had to be the prettiest plumber in Boulder. Correction. All of Colorado.

She quickly catalogued the details—a six-foot-plus prime specimen of a man with neatly trimmed, near-black hair that gleamed in the sun and eyes that reminded her of a mocha cappuccino. He wore a navy sports coat that covered an open-collared white shirt, dark-wash jeans and a pair of tan polished cowboy boots, indicating she'd probably pulled him away from a family function. Or quite possibly a date since he didn't appear to be wearing a wedding band.

"Ms. Armstrong?" he asked as soon as she stepped onto the porch, his voice hinting at a slight drawl.

Considering her ragtag appearance—damp holey jeans, no shoes, hair piled into a disheveled ponytail and a faded blue T-shirt imprinted with Bring it On!—Hannah considered denying her identity. But leaky pipes took precedence over pride. "That's me, and I'm so glad to see you."

"You were expecting me?" Both his tone and expression conveyed his confusion.

Surely he was kidding. "Of course, although I am really surprised you got here so quickly. And since I've obviously interrupted your Friday-night plans, please know I truly appreciate your expediency. Just one question before you get started. What exactly do you charge after normal business hours?"

He looked decidedly uncomfortable, either from the question or her incessant rambling. "Anywhere from two-fifty to four hundred regardless of the hour."

"Dollars?"

"Yes."

Ridiculous. "Isn't that a bit exorbitant for a plumber?"

His initial surprise melted into a smile, revealing dimples that would make the most cynical single gal swoon. "Probably so, but I'm not a plumber."

Hannah's face heated over her utterly stupid assumption. Had she been thinking straight, she would have realized he wasn't a working-class kind of guy. "Then what are you? *Who* are you?"

He pulled a business card from his jacket pocket and offered it to her. "Logan Whittaker, attorney at law."

A slight sense of dread momentarily robbed Hannah of a response, until she realized she had no reason to be afraid of a lawyer. She gained enough presence of mind to take the card and study the text. Unfortunately, her questions as to why he was there remained unanswered. She'd never heard of the Drake, Alcott and Whittaker law firm, and she didn't know anyone in Cheyenne, Wyoming.

She looked up to find him studying her as intently as she had his card. "What's this about?"

"I'm helping settle the late J. D. Lassiter's estate," he said, then paused as if that should mean something to her.

"I'm sorry, but I don't know anyone named Lassiter, so there must be some mistake."

He frowned. "You are Hannah Lovell Armstrong, right?"

"Yes."

"And your mother's name is Ruth Lovell?"

The conversation was growing stranger by the minute. "Was. She passed away two years ago. Why?"

"Because she was named as secondary beneficiary should anything happen to you before you claimed your inheritance."

Inheritance. Surely it couldn't be true. Not after all the years of wondering and hoping that someday…

Then reality began to sink in, as well as the memory of her mother's warning.

You don't need to know anything about your worthless daddy or his cutthroat family. He never cared about you one whit from the moment you were born. You're better off not knowing….

So shell-shocked by the possibility that this had something to do with the man who'd given her life, Hannah simply couldn't speak. She could only stare at the card still clutched in her hand.

"Are you okay, Ms. Armstrong?"

The attorney's question finally snapped her out of the stupor. "I'm a little bit confused at the moment." To say the least.

"I understand," he said. "First of all, it's not my place to question you about your relationship with J. D. Lassiter, but I am charged with explaining the terms of your inheritance and the process for claiming it. Anything you reveal to me will be kept completely confidential."

When she realized what he might be implying, Hannah decided to immediately set him straight. "Mr. Whittaker, I don't have, nor have I ever had, a relationship with anyone named Lassiter. And if you're insinuating I might be some mistress he kept hidden away, you couldn't be more wrong."

"Again, I'm not assuming anything, Ms. Armstrong. I'm only here to honor Mr. Lassiter's last wishes." He glanced over his shoulder at Nancy, the eyes and ears of the neighborhood, who'd stopped watering her hedgerow to gawk, before turning his attention back to Hannah. "Due to confidentiality issues, I would prefer to lay out the terms of the inheritance somewhere aside from your front porch."

Although he seemed legitimate, Hannah wasn't comfortable with inviting a stranger into her home, not only for her sake, but also for her daughter's. "Look, I need some time to digest this information." As well as the opportunity to investigate Logan Whittaker and determine whether he might be some slick con artist. "Could we possibly meet this evening to discuss this?" Provided she didn't discover anything suspicious about him.

"I can be back here around seven-thirty."

"I'd prefer to meet in a public venue. I have a daughter and I wouldn't want her to overhear our conversation."

"No problem," he said. "And in the meantime, feel free to do an internet search or call my office and ask for Becky. You'll have all my pertinent information and proof that I am who I say I am."

The man must be a mind reader. "Thank you for recognizing my concerns."

"It's reasonable that you'd want to protect not only yourself, but your child." He sounded as if he truly understood, especially the part about protecting Cassie.

She leaned a shoulder against the support column.

"I suppose you've probably seen a lot of unimaginable things involving children during your career."

He shifted his weight slightly. "Fortunately I'm in corporate law, so I only have to deal with business transactions, estates and people with too much money to burn."

"My favorite kind of people." The sarcasm in her tone was unmistakable.

"Not too fond of the rich and infamous?" he asked, sounding somewhat amused.

"You could say that. It's a long story." One that wouldn't interest him in the least.

"I'm staying at Crest Lodge, not far from here," he said. "They have a decent restaurant where we can have a private conversation. Do you know the place?"

"I've been there once." Six years ago with her husband on their anniversary, not long before he was torn from her life due to a freak industrial accident. "It's fairly expensive."

He grinned. "That's why they invented expense accounts."

"Unfortunately I don't have one."

"But I do and it's my treat."

And what a treat it would be, sitting across from a man who was extremely easy on the eyes. A man she knew nothing about. Of course, this venue would be strictly business. "All right, if you're sure."

"Positive," he said. "My cell number's listed on the card. If your plans change, let me know. Otherwise I'll meet you there at seven-thirty."

That gave Hannah a little over two hours to get showered and dressed, provided the real plumber didn't show up, which seemed highly unlikely. "Speaking of calls, why didn't you handle this by phone?"

His expression turned solemn once more. "First of all, I had some business to attend to in Denver, so I decided to stop here on the way back to Cheyenne. Secondly, as soon as you hear the details, you'll know why I thought it was better to lay out the terms in person. I'll see you this evening."

With that, he strode down the walkway, climbed into a sleek black Mercedes and drove away, leaving Hannah suspended in a state of uncertainty.

After taking a few more moments to ponder the situation, she tore back into the house and immediately retreated to the computer in her bedroom. She began her search of Logan Whittaker and came upon a wealth of information, including several photos and numerous accolades. He graduated from the University of Texas law school, set up practice twelve years ago in Dallas, then moved to Cheyenne six years ago. He was also listed as single, not that it mattered to Hannah. Much.

Then it suddenly dawned on her to check out J. D. Lassiter, which she did. She came upon an article heralding his business acumen and his immeasurable wealth. The mogul was worth billions. And once again, she was subjected to shock when she recognized the face in the picture accompanying his story—the face that belonged to the same man who had been to her house over twenty years ago.

That particular day, she'd returned home from school and come upon him and her mother standing on the porch, engaged in a heated argument. She'd been too young to understand the content of the volatile conversation, and when she'd asked her mom about him,

Ruth had only said he wasn't anyone she should worry about. But she had worried…and now she wondered….

Hannah experienced a surprising bout of excitement mixed with regret. Even if she had solid proof J. D. Lassiter was in fact her father, she would never have the opportunity to meet him. It was as if someone had given her a special gift, then immediately yanked it away from her. It didn't matter. The man had clearly possessed more money than most, and he hadn't spent a dime to support her. That begged the question—why would he leave her a portion of his estate now? Perhaps a guilty conscience. An attempt at atonement. But it was much too late for that.

She would meet Logan Whittaker for dinner, hear him out and then promptly tell him that she wouldn't take one penny of the Lassiter fortune.

At fifteen minutes until eight, Logan began to believe Hannah Armstrong's plans had changed. But from his position at the corner table, he glanced up from checking his watch to see her standing in the restaurant's doorway.

He had to admit, he'd found her pretty damned attractive when he'd met her, from the top of her auburn ponytail to the bottom of her bare feet. She'd possessed a fresh-faced beauty that she hadn't concealed with a mask of makeup, and she had the greenest eyes he'd ever seen in his thirty-eight years.

But now…

She did have on a little makeup, yet it only enhanced her features. Her hair hung straight to her shoulders and she wore a sleeveless, above-the-knee black dress that molded to her curves. Man-slaying curves that reminded Logan of a modern version of those starlets from days gone by, before too-thin became all the rage.

When they made eye contact, Hannah started forward, giving Logan a good glimpse of her long legs. He considered her to be above average in height for a woman, but right then she seemed pretty damn tall. Maybe it was just the high heels, although they couldn't be more than two inches. Maybe it was the air of confidence she gave off as she crossed the room. Or maybe he should keep his eyes off her finer attributes; otherwise he could land himself in big trouble if he ignored the boundary between business and pleasure. Not that he had any reason to believe she'd be willing to take that step.

Logan came to his feet and rounded the table to pull out the chair across from his as soon as Hannah arrived. "Thanks," she said after she claimed her seat.

Once he settled in, Logan handed her a menu. "I thought for a minute there you were going to stand me up."

"My apologies for my tardiness," she said. "My daughter, Cassie, had to change clothes three times before I took her to my friend's house for a sleepover."

He smiled over the sudden bittersweet memories. "How old is she?"

"Gina is thirty. Same as me."

Logan bit back a laugh. "I meant your daughter."

A slight blush spread across Hannah's cheeks, making her look even prettier. "Of course you did. I admit I'm a little nervous about this whole inheritance thing."

So was Logan, for entirely different reasons. Every time she flashed those green eyes at him, he felt his pulse accelerate. "No need to be nervous. But I wouldn't blame you if you're curious."

"Not so curious that I can't wait for the details until after dinner, since I'm starving." She opened the menu and began scanning it while Logan did the same. "I'd forgotten how many choices they offer."

He'd almost forgotten how it felt to be seated at a dinner table across from a gorgeous woman. The past few years had included a few casual flings for the sake of convenience with a couple of women who didn't care to be wined and dined. Sex for the sake of sex. And that had suited him fine. "Yeah. It's hard to make a decision. By the way, did you get your plumbing fixed?"

She continued to scan the menu. "Unfortunately, no. They called and said it would be tomorrow afternoon. Apparently pipes are breaking all over Boulder."

With the way she looked tonight, she could break hearts all over Boulder. "Do you have any recommendations on the menu?"

"Have you had bison?" she asked as she looked up from the menu.

"No. I'm more of a beef-and-potatoes kind of guy."

"Your Texas roots are showing."

She'd apparently taken his advice. "Did you check me out on the internet?"

"I did. Does that bother you?"

Only if she'd discovered the part of his past he'd concealed from everyone in Wyoming. *Almost everyone.* "Hey, I don't blame you. In this day and time, it's advisable to determine if someone is legitimate before you agree to meet with them."

"I'm glad you understand, and you have quite the résumé."

He shrugged. "Just the usual credentials."

"They certainly impressed me."

She undeniably impressed him. "Have you eaten bison before?"

"Yes, I have, and I highly recommend it. Much leaner and healthier than beef."

"I think I'll just stick with what I know."

Her smile almost knocked his boots off. "Perhaps you should expand your horizons."

Perhaps he should quit sending covert looks at her cleavage. "Maybe I will at some point in time." Just not tonight.

A lanky college-aged waiter sauntered over to the table and aimed his smile on Hannah. "Hi. My name's Chuck. Can I get you folks something to drink? Maybe a cocktail before dinner?"

Bourbon, straight up, immediately came to Logan's mind before he realized booze and a beautiful woman wouldn't be a good mix in this case. "I'll have coffee. Black."

Hannah leveled her pretty smile on Chuck. "I'd like a glass of water."

The waiter responded with an adolescent grin. "Have you folks decided on your meal?"

She took another glance at the menu before closing it. "I'll take the petite bison filet, medium, with a side of sautéed mushrooms and the asparagus."

Logan cleared his throat to gain the jerk's attention. "Give me the New York strip, medium rare with a baked potato, everything on it."

Chuckie Boy jotted down the order but couldn't seem to stop staring at Hannah as he gathered the menus. "How about an appetizer? I highly recommend the Rocky Mountain oysters."

That nearly made Logan wince. "I believe I'll pass on that one, Chuck."

"I second that," Hannah said. "A salad with vinaigrette would be good."

Chuck finally tore his gaze away from Hannah and centered it on Logan. "Can I bring you a salad, too, sir?"

No, but you can get the hell out of Dodge. "Just the coffee and a glass of water."

The waiter backed away from the table, then said, "I'll have that right out."

"What an idiot," Logan muttered after the guy disappeared into the kitchen.

Hannah frowned. "I thought he was very accommodating."

"He definitely wanted to accommodate you and it didn't have a damn thing to do with dinner." Hell, he sounded like a jealous lover.

Hannah looked understandably confused. "Excuse me?"

"You didn't notice the way he was looking at you?"

"He was just being friendly."

She apparently didn't realize her appeal when it came to the opposite sex, and he personally found that intriguing. "Look, I don't blame the guy. You're an extremely attractive woman, but for all he knows, we're a couple. The fact that he kept eyeing you wasn't appropriate in my book."

Her gaze momentarily wandered away and the color returned to her cheeks. "But we're not a couple, and he wasn't *eyeing* me."

"Believe me, he was." And he sure couldn't blame the guy when it came right down to it.

She picked up the cloth napkin near her right hand, unfolded it and laid it in her lap. "If he was, I didn't notice. Then again, I haven't been out much in the past few years."

"Since your…" If he kept going, he'd be treading on shaky ground. The kind that covered a major loss from the past. He knew that concept all too well.

She raised a brow. "Since my husband's death? It's okay. I've been able to talk about it without falling apart for the past four years."

He definitely admired her for that. Even after nine years, he hadn't been able to discuss his loss without flying into a rage. "I admire your resiliency," he said, all the while thinking he wished he had half of her tenacity.

Chuck picked that moment to bring the drinks and Hannah's salad. "Here you go, folks. Dinner will be right out."

As bad as Logan hated to admit it, he was actually glad to see the jerk, if only to grab the opportunity to turn to a lighter topic. "Thank you kindly, Chuck."

"You're welcome, sir."

After the waiter left the area, Logan returned his attention to Hannah. "So it's my understanding you recently obtained your degree."

She took a quick sip of water and sent him a proud smile. "Yes, I did, and apparently you've done your homework on me, too."

"I had to in order to locate you." Thanks to J. D. Lassiter not providing much information when they discovered the annuity's existence.

She picked up a fork and began moving lettuce around on the plate. "That old internet is a great resource for checking people out."

He only wished she would thoroughly check him out, and not on the computer. And where in the hell had *that* come from?

He cleared his throat and shifted slightly in his seat. "I take it you're satisfied I'm not some reprobate posing as an attorney."

"Yes, but frankly, I'm curious as to why you relocated from Dallas to Cheyenne, Wyoming. That must have been quite a culture shock."

He didn't want to delve into his reasons for leaving his former life behind. "Not that much of a shock. You find cowboys in both places."

"Were you a cowboy in another life, or just trying to blend in now?"

"I've ridden my share of horses, if that's what you mean."

She smiled again. "Let me guess. You were born into an affluent ranching family."

"Nope. A not-quite-poor farming family. Three generations, as a matter of fact. My parents ran a peach orchard in East Texas and raised a few cattle. They're semiretired now and disappointed I didn't stick around to take over the business."

"What made you decide to be a lawyer?"

He grinned. "When I wore overalls, people kept mistaking me for a plumber, and since clogged drains aren't my thing, studying the law made sense."

Her soft laughter traveled all the way to her striking green eyes. "Something tells me you're not going to let me live that one down."

Something told him he could wind up in hot water if he didn't stop viewing her as a desirable woman. "I'll let you off the hook, seeing as how we just met."

"And I will let you off the hook for not giving me fair warning before you showed up on my doorstep."

He still had those great images of her branded in his brain. "You know, I'm really glad I didn't decide to handle this over the phone. Otherwise, I wouldn't have met you, and something tells me I would have regretted that."

Hannah set down the fork, braced her elbow on the edge of the table and rested her cheek in her palm. "And I would have missed the opportunity to get all dressed up for a change and have a free meal."

She looked prettier than a painted picture come to life. Yep. Trouble with a capital *T* if he didn't get his mind back on business. "After you learn the details of your share of the Lassiter fortune, you'll be able to buy me dinner next time." Next time? Man, he was getting way ahead of himself, and that was totally out of character for his normally cautious self.

Hannah looked about as surprised as he felt over the comment. "That all depends on if I actually agree to accept my share, and that's doubtful."

He couldn't fathom anyone in their right mind turning down that much money. But before he had a chance to toss out an opinion, or the amount of the annuity held in her name, Chuck showed up with their entrées.

Logan ate his food with the gusto of a field hand, while Hannah basically picked at hers, the same way she had with the salad. By the time they were finished, and the plates were cleared, he had half a mind to invite her into the nearby bar to discuss business. But dark and cozy wouldn't help rein in his libido.

Hannah tossed her napkin aside and folded her hands before her. "Okay, we've put this off long enough. Tell me the details."

Logan took a drink of water in an attempt to rid the dryness in his throat. "The funds are currently in an annuity. You have the option to leave it as is and take payments. Or you can claim the lump sum. Your choice."

"How much?" she said after a few moments.

He noticed she looked a little flushed and decided retiring to the bar might not be a bad idea after all. "Maybe we should go into the lounge so you can have a drink before I continue."

Frustration showed in her expression. "I don't need a drink."

He'd begun to think he might. "Just a glass of wine to take the edge off."

She leaned forward and nailed him with a glare. "How *much?*"

"Five million dollars."

"I believe I will have that drink now."

Two

She'd never been much of a drinker, but at the moment Hannah sat on a sofa in the corner of a dimly lit bar, a vodka and tonic tightly gripped in her hand. "Five million dollars? Are you insane?"

Logan leaned back in the club chair and leveled his dark gaze on hers. "Hey, it's not my money. I'm only the messenger."

She set the glass down on the small table separating them, slid her fingers through the sides of her hair and resisted pulling it out by the roots. "You're saying that I can just sign some papers and you're going to hand me a fortune."

"It's a little more complicated than that."

After having the five-million-dollar bombshell dropped on her head, nothing seemed easy, including deciding to refuse it. "Would I have to go before some probate court?"

"No, but there are some stipulations."

She dropped her hands into her lap and sat back on the cushions. "Such as?"

"You have to sign a nondisclosure waiver in order to claim the inheritance."

"Nondisclosure?"

"That means if you take the money, by law you can't disclose your connection to the Lassiters to anyone."

She barked out a cynical laugh. "I refuse to do that. Not after living my entire life in the shadow of shame, thanks to my biological father's refusal to acknowledge me."

"Then you have reason to believe J. D. Lassiter is your father?"

Good reason. "Yes, there is a chance, but I don't know for certain because I have no real proof. Regardless, I do know I won't take a penny of his hush money."

Logan downed the last of his coffee, sat back on the opposing sofa and remained quiet a few moments. "What does your future hold in terms of your career?"

A little hardship, but nothing she couldn't handle. "I'm going to teach high-school human physiology and probably health classes as well."

He released a rough sigh. "It takes a lot of guts to stand in front of a room full of teenage boys and talk about the facts of life, especially looking the way you do."

Hannah appreciated his skill at doling out the compliments, even if she didn't understand it or quite believe it. "I assure you I can handle whatever teenage boys want to throw at me."

"I don't doubt that," he said. "But it's not going to be easy. I know because I was one once."

She imagined a very cute one at that. "Most men still retain some of those prepubescent qualities, don't you agree?"

He grinned, giving her another premiere dimple show. "Probably so. Do you have a job lined up?"

That caused her to glance away. "Not yet, but I've had my degree for less than two weeks, and that's when I immediately started the search. I expect to find something any day now."

"And if you don't?"

She'd harbored those same concerns due to the lack of prospects. "I'll manage fine, just as I've been managing since my husband died."

He sent her a sympathetic look. "That must have been a struggle, raising a child and going to school."

She'd been lucky enough to have help. Begrudging help. "My mother looked after my daughter when necessary until Cassie turned two. I lived off the settlement from my husband's work accident and that, coupled with Social Security benefits, allowed me to pay for day care and the bills while studying full-time. I obtained grants and student loans to finance my tuition."

"If you don't mind me asking, do you have any of the settlement left?"

She didn't exactly mind, but she felt certain she knew where he was heading—back into inheritance land. "Actually, the payments will end in October, so I still have six months."

He streaked a hand over the back of his neck. "You

do realize that if you accept this money, you'll be set for life. No worries financially for you or your daughter."

If Cassie's future played a role, she might reconsider taking the inheritance. "My daughter will be well provided for when she turns eighteen, thanks to my in-laws, who've established a million-dollar-plus trust fund in her name. Of course, I'm sure that will come with conditions, as those with fortunes exceeding the national debt are prone to do."

"Guess that explains your aversion to wealthy people."

Her aversion was limited to only the entitled wealthy, including Theresa and Marvin Armstrong. "Daniel's parents didn't exactly approve of my marriage to their son. Actually, they didn't approve of me. It was that whole illegitimate thing. They had no way of knowing if I had the appropriate breeding to contribute to the stellar Armstrong gene pool. Of course, when I became pregnant with Cassie, they had no say in the matter."

He seemed unaffected by her cynicism. "Are they involved in your daughter's life at all?"

"Theresa sends Cassie money on her birthday and collector dolls at Christmas that carry instructions not to remove them from the box so they'll retain their value. What good is a doll you can't play with?"

"Have they ever seen her?"

"Only once." And once had been quite enough. "When Cassie was two, they flew us out to North Carolina for a visit. It didn't take long to realize that my mother-in-law and active toddlers don't mix. After Theresa accused me of raising a wild animal, I told her

I'd find a good kennel where I could board Cassie next time. Fortunately, there wasn't a next time."

Logan released a deep, sexy laugh. "You're hell on wheels, aren't you?"

She took another sip of the cocktail to clear the bitter taste in her mouth. "After growing up a poor fatherless child, I learned to be. Also, my mother was extremely unsocial and rather unhappy over raising a daughter alone, to say the least. I took an opposite path and made it my goal to be upbeat and sociable."

He grinned. "I bet you were a cheerleader."

She returned his smile. "Yes, I was, and I could do a mean backflip."

"Think you could still do it?"

"I don't know. It's been a while, but I suppose I could don my cheerleading skirt, though it's probably a little tight, and give it the old college try."

He winked, sending a succession of pleasant chills down Hannah's body. "I'd like to see that."

"If you're like most men, you just want to see up my skirt." Had she really said that?

He sent her a sly grin. "I do admire limber women."

A brief span of silence passed, a few indefinable moments following unmistakable innuendo. Hannah couldn't recall the last time she'd actually flirted with someone aside from her husband. And she'd been flirting with a virtual stranger. An extremely handsome, successful stranger.

A very young, very peppy blonde waitress sauntered over and flashed a grin. "Can I get you anything, sir?"

"Bring me a cola," Logan said without cracking a smile.

She glanced at Hannah. "What about you, ma'am?"

"No, thank you."

"Are you sure?" Logan asked. "You wouldn't like one more round?"

She was sorely tempted, but too sensible to give in. "I'm driving, remember?"

"I could drive you home if you change your mind."

"That would be too much trouble," she said, knowing that if he came anywhere near her empty house, she might make a colossal mistake.

"It's not a problem."

It could be if she didn't proceed with caution. "I'm fine for now. But thanks."

Once the waitress left, Hannah opted for a subject change. "Now that you know quite a bit about me, what about you?"

He pushed his empty coffee cup aside. "What do you want to know?"

Plenty. "I saw on your profile you're single. Have you ever been married?"

His expression went suddenly somber. "Once. I've been divorced for eight years."

She couldn't imagine a man of his caliber remaining unattached all that time. "Any relationships since?"

"Nothing serious."

She tapped her chin and pretended to think. "Let me guess. You have a woman in every court."

His smile returned, but only halfway. "Not even close. I work a lot of hours so I don't have much time for a social life."

"Did you take a vow of celibacy?" Heaven help her, the vodka had completely destroyed her verbal filter.

When the waitress returned with the cola, Logan pulled out his wallet and handed her a platinum card to close out the tab, or so Hannah assumed. "Keep it open for the time being," he said, shattering her assumptions.

Once the waitress retreated, Hannah attempted to backtrack. "Forget I asked that last question. It's really none of my business."

"It's okay," he said. "I've had a few relationships based solely on convenience. What about you?"

He'd presented a good case of turnabout being fair play, but she simply had little to tell when it came to the dating game. "Like you, I haven't had time to seriously consider the social scene. I have had a couple of coffee dates in the past year, but they were disastrous. One guy still lived at his mother's house in the basement, and the other's only goal was to stay in school as long as possible. He already had three graduate degrees."

"Apparently the last guy was fairly smart," he said.

"True, but both made it quite clear they weren't particularly fond of children, and that's a deal breaker. Not to mention I'm not going to subject my child to a man unless he's earned my trust."

He traced the rim of the glass with his thumb. "It's logical that you would have major concerns in that department."

"Very true. And I have to admit I'm fairly protective of her. Some might even say overprotective." Including her best friend, Gina.

Logan downed the last of his drink and set it aside. "I'm not sure there is such a thing in this day and time."

"But I've been known to take it to extremes. I've even considered encasing her in bubble wrap every day before I send her off to school."

Her attempt at humor seemed to fall flat for Logan.

"You really can't protect them from everything, and that's a damn shame."

His solemn tone spurred Hannah's curiosity. "Do you have children from your previous marriage?"

He momentarily looked away. "No."

Definitely a story there. "Was that a mutual decision between you and your wife?" Realizing she'd become the ultimate Nosy Nellie, she raised her hands, palms forward. "I'm so sorry. I'm not normally this intrusive."

"My wife was an attorney, too," he continued, as if her prying didn't bother him. "Having kids wasn't in the cards for us, and that was probably just as well."

"How long were you married?"

"A little over seven years."

She started to ask if he'd been plagued with the legendary itch but didn't want to destroy her honorable-man image. "I'm sorry to hear that. I'm sure the divorce process can be tough."

"Ours was pretty contentious. But it wasn't anything compared to losing someone to death."

He almost sounded as if he'd had experience with that as well. "They're both losses, and they both require navigating the grief process. I was somewhat lucky in that respect. I had Cassie to see me through the rough times."

"How old was she when your husband died?" he asked.

"I was five months pregnant, so he never saw her." She was somewhat amazed she'd gotten through that revelation without falling apart. Maybe her grief cycle was finally nearing completion.

"At least you were left with a part of him," Logan

said gruffly. "I assume that did provide some consolation."

A good-looking and intuitive man, a rare combination in Hannah's limited experience. "I'm very surprised by your accurate perception, Mr. Whittaker. Most of the time people look at me with pity when they learn the details. I appreciate their sympathy, but I'm not a lost cause."

"It's Logan," he told her. "And you're not remotely a lost cause or someone who deserves pity. You deserve respect and congratulations for moving on with your life, Hannah."

Somewhat self-conscious over the compliment, and oddly excited over hearing her name on his lips, she began to fold the corner of the cocktail napkin back and forth. "Believe me, the first two years weren't pretty. I cried a lot and I had a few serious bouts of self-pity. But then Cassie would reach a milestone, like her first steps and the first time she said 'Mama,' and I realized I had to be strong for her. I began to look at every day as a chance for new opportunities. A new beginning, so to speak."

The waitress came back to the table and eyed Hannah's empty glass. "Sure I can't get you another?"

She glanced at the clock hanging over the bar and after noticing it was nearly 10:00 p.m., she couldn't believe how quickly the time had flown by. "Actually, it's getting late. I should probably be going."

"It's not that late," Logan said. "Like I told you before, I'll make sure you get home safely if you want to live a little and have another vodka and tonic."

Hannah mulled over the offer for a few moments. Her daughter was at a sleepover, she had no desire to watch TV, and she was in the company of a very attractive and attentive man who promised to keep her safe. What would be the harm in having one more drink?

"I should never have ordered that second drink."

Logan regarded Hannah across the truck's cab as he pulled to a stop at the curb near her driveway. "It's my fault for encouraging you."

She lifted her face from her hands and attempted a smile. "You didn't force me at gunpoint. And you had no idea I'm such a lightweight when it comes to alcohol."

Funny, she seemed perfectly coherent to him, both back in the bar and now. "Are you feeling okay?"

"Just a little fuzzy and worried about my car. It's not much, but it's all that I have."

He'd noticed the sedan had seen better days. "It's been secured in the valet garage, and I'll make certain it's delivered to you first thing in the morning."

"You've done too much already," she said. "I really could have called a cab."

In reality, he hadn't been ready to say good-night, although he couldn't quite understand why. Or maybe he understood it and didn't want to admit it. "Like I told you, it's not a problem. You don't know who you can trust these days, especially when you're an attractive woman."

She gave him a winning grin. "I bet you say that to all the women who refuse a five-million-dollar inheritance."

"You happen to be the first in that regard." Absolutely the first woman in a long, long time to completely capture his interest on a first meeting. A business meeting to boot. "I'm hoping you haven't totally ruled out taking the money."

"Yes, I have. I know you probably think I've lost my mind, but I do have my reasons."

Yeah, and he'd figured them out—she was refusing on the basis of principle. He sure as hell didn't see that often in his line of work. "Well, I'm not going to pressure you, but I will check back with you tomorrow after you've slept on it."

She blinked and hid a yawn behind her hand. "Speaking of sleeping, I'm suddenly very tired. I guess it's time to bid you adieu."

When Hannah reached for the door handle, Logan touched her arm to gain her attention. "I'll get that for you."

"Whaddya know," she said. "Looks like chivalry is still alive and well after all." She followed the comment with a soft, breathless laugh that sent his imagination into overdrive.

Before he acted on impulse, Logan quickly slid out of the driver's seat, rounded the hood and opened the door for Hannah. She had a little trouble climbing out, which led him to take her hand to assist her. Weird thing was, he didn't exactly want to let go of her hand, but he did, with effort.

He followed behind her as they traveled the path to the entry, trying hard to keep his gaze focused on that silky auburn hair that swayed slightly with each step she took, not her butt that did a little swaying, too.

Right before they reached the front porch, Hannah glanced back and smiled. "At least I'm not falling-down drunk." Then she immediately tripped on the first step.

Logan caught her elbow before she landed on that butt he'd been trying to ignore. "Careful."

"I'm just clumsy," she said as he guided her up the remaining steps.

Once they reached the door, he released her arm and she sent him another sleepy smile. "I really enjoyed the evening, Logan. And if you'll just send me what I need to sign to relinquish the money, I'll mail it back to you immediately."

He still wasn't convinced she was doing the right thing in that regard. "We'll talk about that later. Right now getting you to bed is more important." Dammit, that sounded like a freaking proposition.

"Do you want to come in?" she asked, taking him totally by surprise.

"I don't think that's a good idea." Actually, it sounded like a great idea, but he was too keyed up to honestly believe he could control his libido.

She clutched her bag to her chest. "Oh, I get it. You're afraid you're going to be accosted by the poor, single mom who hasn't had sex in almost seven years."

Oh, hell. "That's not it at all. I just respect you enough not to put us in the position where we might do something we regret, because, lady, being alone with you could lead to all sorts of things."

She leaned a shoulder against the support column and inclined her head. "Really?"

"Really. In case you haven't noticed, I've had a hard time keeping my eyes off you tonight." He was having a real *hard* time right now.

She barked out a laugh. "I'm sorry, but I'm having a difficult time believing you would be interested in me."

She couldn't be more wrong. "Why wouldn't I be?

You're smart and savvy and pretty damn brave to raise a child on your own and finish college at the same time."

"Keep going."

He could…all night. "You're a survivor and very beautiful, although you don't seem to know that. And that's not only hard to find in a beautiful woman, it's appealing."

"And?"

"Right now I'd like to kiss you," he blurted out before his brain caught up with his mouth. "But I'm not going to."

"Why not?" she asked, looking thoroughly disappointed.

"Because if I kissed you, I might not want to stop there. And as I've said, I respect you too much to—"

Hannah cut off his words by circling one hand around his neck and landing her lips on his, giving him the kiss he'd been halfheartedly trying to avoid.

Logan was mildly aware she'd dropped her purse, and very aware she kissed him like she hadn't been kissed in a long, long time—with the soft glide of her tongue against his, bringing on a strong stirring south of his belt buckle. He grazed his hand up her side until his palm rested close to her breast, and he heard her breath catch as she moved flush against him. He considered telling her they should take it inside the house before someone called the cops, but then she pulled abruptly away from him and took a step back.

Hannah touched her fingertips to her lips, her face flushed, her emerald eyes wide with shock. "I cannot believe I just did that. And I can't imagine what you must be thinking about me right now."

He was thinking he wanted her. Badly. "Hey, it's chemistry. It happens. Couple that with a few cocktails—"

"And you get some thirty-year-old woman acting totally foolish."

He tucked a strand of hair behind her ear. "You don't have to feel foolish or ashamed, Hannah. I'm personally flattered that you kissed me."

She snatched her bag from the cement floor and hugged it tightly again. "I didn't give you a whole lot of choice."

"You only did what I wanted to do." Trouble was, he wanted to do it again, and more. "For the record, I think you're one helluva sexy woman and I'd really like to get to know you better."

"But we've just met," she said. "We don't really know anything about each other."

He knew enough to want to move forward and see where it might lead. "That's the get-to-know-each-other-better part."

"We don't live in the same town."

"True, but it's only a ninety-mile drive."

"You're busy and I have a five-year-old child who is currently in school, plus I'm looking for a job."

He remembered another search she should be conducting, and this could be the key to spending more time with her. "There's something I've been meaning to ask you all night."

"Have I taken total leave of my senses?"

He appreciated her wit, too. "This is about your biological father."

That seemed to sober her up. "What about him?"

"Just wondering if you have any details about his life."

She sighed. "I only know that my mother hooked up with some guy who left her high and dry when she became pregnant with me. According to her, he was both ruthless and worthless."

Some people might describe J. D. Lassiter that way. "Did she ever offer to give you a name?"

"No, and I didn't ask. I figured that if he wanted nothing to do with me, then I wanted nothing to do with him." Her tone was laced with false bravado.

He did have a hard time believing J.D. would be so cold and uncaring that he would ignore his own flesh and blood no matter what the circumstances. "Maybe there were underlying issues that prevented him from being involved in your life."

"Do you mean the part about him being an absolute bastard, or that he was married?"

Finally, a little more to go on. "Do you know that to be a fact? The married part."

"My mother hinted at that, but again, I can't be certain."

"Then maybe it's time you try to find out the truth. You owe it to yourself and to your daughter. Because if J.D. is actually your father, you have siblings."

Hannah seemed to mull that over for a time before she spoke again. "How do you propose I do that?"

"With my help."

She frowned. "Why would you even want to help me?"

"Because I can't imagine what it would be like to have more questions than answers." In some ways he did know that. Intimately. "And since I'm an attorney, and I know the Lassiters personally, I could do some subtle investigating without looking suspicious."

"It seems to me you would be too busy to take this on."

"Actually, I have a light caseload this week." Or he would as soon as he asked his assistant to postpone a few follow-up appointments. "But I would definitely want you to be actively involved in the search."

"How do you suggest I do that from here?"

Here came the part that would probably have her questioning his motives. "Not here. In Cheyenne. You could stay with me for a few days and I'll show you the sights and introduce you to a few people. You could so some research during the day while I'm at work."

Hannah's mouth opened slightly before she snapped it shut. "Stay with you?"

He definitely understood why that part of the plan might get her hackles up. "Look, I have a forty-five-hundred-square-foot house with five bedrooms and seven baths. You'd have your own space. In fact, the master bedroom is downstairs and the guest rooms are all upstairs. We could go for days and not even see each other." Like he intended for that to happen.

"Good heavens, why would a confirmed bachelor need a house that size?"

"I got a good deal on the place when the couple had to transfer out of state. And I like to entertain."

"Do you have a harem?"

He couldn't help but laugh for the second time tonight, something he'd rarely done over the past few years. "No harem. But I have five acres and a couple of horses, as well as a gourmet kitchen. My housekeeper comes by twice a week and makes meals in advance if I don't want to cook."

"You know how to cook?" she asked, sounding doubtful.

"Yeah. I know my way around the stove."

She smiled. "Mac and cheese? BLT sandwiches? Or maybe when you're feeling adventurous, you actually tackle scrambled eggs?"

"My favorite adventurous meal will always be Italian. You'd like my mostaccioli."

She loosened her grip on her bag and slipped the strap on her shoulder. "As tempting as that sounds, I can't just take off for Cheyenne without my daughter. She won't be out of school for five weeks."

"Is there someone who could watch her for a few days?" Damn, he almost sounded desperate.

"Possibly, but I've never left Cassie alone for more than a night," she said. "I don't know how she would handle it. I don't know how *I* would handle it. Besides, I'm not sure I could accomplish that much in a few days even if I did decide to go."

He might be losing the battle, but he intended to win the war. "You could drive up for day trips, but that would require a lot of driving. If you stayed with me a couple of days, that would give us time to get to know each other better."

"Residing in a stranger's house would require a huge leap of faith."

He closed the space between them and cupped her face in his palm. "We're not strangers anymore. Not after you did this."

He kissed her softly, thoroughly, with just enough exploration to tempt her to take him up on his offer.

And once he was done, he moved away but kept his gaze locked on hers. "There could be more of that if you decide you want it. Again, no pressure. I'm just asking you to think about it. You might have the answers you need about your heritage, and we might find out we enjoy each other's company. Unless you're afraid to explore the possibilities…"

Logan realized he'd hit a home run when he saw a hint of defiance in Hannah's eyes. "I'm not the cowardly type, but I am cautious because I have to be. However, I will consider your suggestion and give you my answer tomorrow."

"Do you mind giving me your number? So I can call and let you know when your car's on its way." And in case he needed to further plead his case.

She dug through her purse for a pen and paper and scribbled down the information on the back of a receipt. "That's my home and cell number," she said as she handed it over. "Feel free to send me a text."

As Logan pocketed the paper, Hannah withdrew her keys, turned around and unlocked the door with a little effort, then walked inside without another word.

Logan was left alone on the porch to ponder why being with her again seemed so damn important. He had his choice of beautiful women back in Cheyenne, although most hadn't come close to capturing his interest like Hannah Armstrong.

He could chalk it up to chemistry, but he inherently knew that was only part of it. He did appreciate her keen sense of humor, knock-'em-dead body and those expressive green eyes that could drop a man in his tracks. He appreciated her all-fire independence and that she had the temperament of a mother bear when it came to her kid. In some ways, that attracted him more than anything else. But above all, she'd experienced the loss of a loved one. Their true common ground.

Hannah might understand his grief because she'd lived it, but if he told her his story, would she see him in the same light? Or would she turn away when she learned the truth?

Only time would tell if he'd find the courage to confess his greatest sin—he'd been partially to blame for the death of his only child.

Three

Her car was back, and so was the man who'd been foremost on her mind all morning long. All night, too.

Hannah peered out the window and watched Logan emerge from her aged blue sedan dressed in a long-sleeved black shirt, faded jeans secured by a belt with a shiny buckle and dark boots. Her heart immediately went on a marathon, the direct effect of an undeniable attraction she'd experienced all too well last night. That attraction had given her the courage to kiss him, something she normally wouldn't have the audacity to do. But by golly she had, and she'd liked it. A lot.

Hormones. That had to be it. Those pesky freaks of nature that made people act on impulse. She made a point to banish them as soon as she climbed out of bed. Granted, when he'd called to say he was bringing the car back, she'd made certain she looked more presentable than she had during their first meeting. She'd dressed in simple, understated clothing—white capri pants, light green, short-sleeved shirt and rhine-stone-embellished flip-flops. Of course, she had put on a little makeup and pulled her hair back in a sleek, low ponytail. The silver hoop earrings might be a little much, but it was too late to take them off unless she ripped them out of her earlobes.

When the bell rang, Hannah automatically smoothed her palms over the sides of her hair and the front of the blouse. She measured her steps to avoid looking too eager, even though she wanted to hurl herself onto the porch and launch into his arms. Instead, she gave herself a mental pep talk on the virtues of subtlety before she slowly opened the door.

He greeted her with a dimpled grin and surprisingly stuck out his hand. "Mornin'. I'm Logan Whittaker, in case you've forgotten."

Hannah didn't know whether to kick him in the shin or kiss that sexy look off his face. She chose option three—play along for now—and accepted his offered handshake. She noticed the calluses and the width of his palm as he gave her hand a slight squeeze before he released her. "Good morning, Mr. Whittaker, and thank you for returning my car."

"You're welcome, but after last night, you should call me Logan."

Cue the blush. "I'm trying to forget about last night."

"Good luck with that because I sure can't forget it. In fact, it kept me tossing and turning most of the night."

She'd experienced the same restlessness, not that she'd admit it to him. "Do I need to drive you back to the lodge?"

"Nope," he said. "One of the valet guys will be here in about ten minutes."

Must be nice to have people at your beck and call, but she supposed that perk came with money. "Are you sure I can't drop you off? It's the least I can do."

"I'm sure, but I'm not leaving until we discuss your inheritance and my proposal."

No amount of money would ever convince her to agree to sign a nondisclosure form, even if she had no intention of aligning herself with the Lassiters. And that's the way it would stay. "I haven't changed my mind about the money, and the jury's still out on the other, to coin a legal phrase."

"Well, since you haven't ruled it out, I think you should let me in to argue my case. I'm housebroken and I won't destroy the furniture."

The sexy dog. "I suppose that's okay, but I have to warn you, the place is a mess, thanks to my child and the plumbing problems."

He had the gall to grin again, revealing those damnable dimples and perfectly straight, white teeth. "I promise you won't regret hearing me out."

She already did when he brushed past her and she caught the subtle scent of his cologne. Even more when once they moved inside, he turned and asked, "Where do you want me?"

An unexpected barrage of questionable images assaulted Hannah, sending her mind in the direction of unadvisable possibilities. Clearly those inherent female desires she'd tried to bury in everyday life weren't completely dead. That was okay, as long as she didn't act on them. Again.

She swallowed hard and bumped the door closed

with her bottom. "Let's go in the dining room." A safe place to interact with Mr. Charisma. "Actually, the floor's wet in there, so we can stay in here." First, she had to clear the worn floral couch of kid debris.

Before she could do that, Logan presented a frown that didn't detract from his good looks one iota. "Leaky pipe?"

"You could definitely say that. I managed to cut off the water under the sink, but this morning I got up only to discover the valve is leaking, too. Now the flood waters are trying to take over my kitchen."

"Tough break."

When Logan began rolling up his sleeves, Hannah's mouth dropped open. "What are you doing?"

"I'm pretty handy when it comes to pipe problems."

"That's not what you said yesterday."

"I've learned not to reveal my skills. Otherwise I'll be hounded every time someone has a plumbing issue. But for you, I'm willing to take a look."

She'd already taken a look. A covert look at his toned forearms threaded with veins, and the opening in his collar that revealed tanned skin and a slight shading of hair she'd tried not to notice last night. "Now I get it. You're really a repressed plumber masquerading as a lawyer."

His reappearing smile had the impact of a jackhammer. "No, but I am good with my hands."

She'd bet her last buck on that. "Thanks for offering to help, but it's not necessary. A real plumber should be here today."

Now he looked plain cynical. "Good luck with that, too. They don't get in a big hurry on a Saturday." He winked. "Besides, I'll save you that weekend rate and check it out for free."

He did have a valid argument, and she really liked the free part. What would be the harm in letting him peruse her pipes, or anything else of hers he'd like to peruse? She seriously needed to get a hold on her self-control. "Fine, but you're going to get wet. I did."

"Not a problem. Getting wet isn't always a bad thing."

Logan's suggestive tone wasn't lost on her. "Since you insist, be my guest." She pointed toward the opening to the dining room. "Just swim through there and keep going. You can't miss the kitchen sink."

Hannah followed behind Logan, covertly sizing up his butt on the way. A really nice butt, not that she was surprised. He happened to be one major male specimen, and she'd have to be in a coma not to notice. Still, she refused to let a sexy, dark-eyed, dimpled cowboy attorney muddle her mind. She'd let him fix her sink and say his piece before sending him packing back to Cheyenne without her.

Logan grabbed a wrench from the counter, lowered to his knees and stuck his head into the cabinet beneath the sink. Hannah leaned back against the counter to watch, unable to suppress a laugh over the string of oaths coming out of the lawyer's mouth.

"Sorry," he muttered without looking back. "I need to tighten a fitting and it's not cooperating."

"Is that the reason for the leak?"

"Yeah. It's a little corroded and probably should be replaced eventually. But I think I can get it to hold."

At least that would save her an after-business-hours service call. "That's a relief."

"Don't be relieved until I say it's repaired."

A few minutes passed, filled with a little more cursing and the occasional groan, until Logan finally emerged from beneath the cabinet and turned on the sink. Seemingly satisfied, he set the wrench aside and sent Hannah another devastating smile. "All done for the time being. Again, it needs to be replaced. Actually, all the pipes should be replaced."

Hannah sighed. "So I've been told. The house was built over forty years ago and it's systematically falling apart. I just paid for a new furnace. That pretty much ate up my reserves and blew my budget."

He wiped his hands on the towel beside the sink. "If you claim the inheritance, you'd never have to worry about a tight budget."

She couldn't deny the concept appealed to her greatly, but the cost to her principles was simply too high. "As I've said, I have no intention of taking my share." Even if J. D. Lassiter did owe her that much. But money could never make up for the years she'd spent in a constant state of wondering where she had come from.

Logan leaned back against the counter opposite Hannah. "And what *are* your intentions when it comes to my invitation?"

"I just don't see the wisdom in running off to Cheyenne on what will probably be a wild-goose chase."

"But it might not be at all. And you would also have the opportunity to meet some of the Lassiters, in case you decide you'd like to connect with your relatives since you wouldn't be bound by the nondisclosure."

"I'm not interested in connecting with the Lassiters."

He studied her for a few moments, questions in his eyes. "Aside from your in-laws, do you have any family?"

Hannah shook her head. "No. I'm an only child and so was my mother. My grandparents have been gone for many years."

"Then wouldn't it be good to get to know the family you never knew existed?" he asked.

She shrugged. "I've gone all these years without knowing, so I'm sure I'll survive if I never meet them."

"What about your daughter? Don't you think she deserves to know she has another family?"

The sound of rapid footsteps signaled the arrival of said daughter. Hannah's attention turned to her right to see the feisty five-year-old twirling through the dining area wearing a pink boa and matching tutu that covered her aqua shirt and shorts, with a fake diamond tiara planted atop her head. She waved around the star wand that she gripped in her fist and shouted, "I'm queen of the frog fairies!"

Cassie stopped turning circles when she spotted the strange man in the kitchen, yet she didn't stop her forward progress. Instead, she charged up to Logan, where she paused to give him a partially toothless grin. "Are you a frog or a prince?"

Possibly a toad in prince clothing, Hannah decided, but that remained to be seen. "This is Mr. Whittaker, Cassie, and he's a lawyer. Do you know what that is, sweetie?"

Her daughter glanced back and rolled her eyes. "I'm not a baby, Mama. I'm almost six and I watch the law shows on TV with Shelly. That's how I learned about lawyers. They look mad all the time and yell 'I object.'"

Hannah made a mental note to have a long talk with the sitter about appropriate television programs for a kindergartner. When Cassie began twirling again, she caught her daughter by the shoulders and turned her to face Logan. "What do you say to Mr. Whittaker?"

Cassie curtsied and grinned. "It's nice to meet you, Mr. Whittaker."

Logan attempted a smile but it didn't make its way to his eyes. In fact, he almost looked sad. "It's nice to meet you, too, Your Highness."

Being addressed as royalty seemed to please Cassie greatly. "Do you have a little girl?"

His gaze wandered away for a moment before he returned it to Cassie. "No, I don't."

"A little boy?" Cassie topped off the comment with a sour look.

"Nope. No kids."

Hannah sensed Logan's discomfort and chalked it up to someone who hadn't been around children, and maybe didn't care to be around them. "Now that the introductions are over, go pick up your toys, Cassandra Jane, and start deciding what you'll be wearing to school on Monday since that takes you at least two days."

That statement earned a frown from her daughter. "Can I just wear this?"

"I think you should save that outfit for playtime. Now scoot."

Cassie backed toward the dining room, keeping her smile trained on Logan. "I think you're a prince," she said, then turned and sprinted away.

Once her daughter had vacated the premises, Hannah returned her attention to Logan. "I'm sorry. She's really into fairy tales these days, and she doesn't seem to know a stranger. Frankly, that worries me sometimes. I'm afraid someday she'll encounter someone with questionable intentions. I've cautioned her time and again, but I'm not sure she understands the risk in that behavior."

"I understand why that would worry you," he said. "But I guess you have to trust that she'll remember your warnings if the situation presents itself."

Hannah sighed. "I hope so. She's everything to me and sometimes I'd like to keep her locked in her room until she's eighteen."

He grinned. "Encased in bubble wrap, right?"

She was pleasantly surprised he remembered that from the night before. "Bubble wrap with rhinestones. Now what were you saying before we were interrupted by the queen?"

"Mama! Where's my purple shorts?"

Hannah gritted her teeth and spoke through them. "Just a minute, Cassie."

"Look, maybe this isn't a good time to discuss this…." Logan said.

She was beginning to wonder that same thing. "You're probably right. And it's probably best if I say thanks, but no thanks, to your proposal, although I sincerely appreciate your offer."

When Logan's phone beeped, he took the cell out of his back pocket and swiped the screen. "The driver's here."

"Then I guess you better go." She sounded disappointed, even to her own ears.

He pocketed his wallet then unrolled his sleeves. "Do you have a pen and paper handy so I can give you my info?"

Hannah withdrew a pencil from the tin container on the counter and tore a piece of paper from the nearby notepad. "Here you go, but don't forget, I already have your card."

He turned his back and began jotting something down. "Yeah, but you don't have my home address."

She swallowed hard. "Why would I need that?"

He faced her again, caught her hand and placed the card in her palm. "In case you change your mind and decide to spend a few days as my guest in Cheyenne."

Oh, how tempting that would be. But… "I would have to ask my friend Gina if Cassie could stay with her. And I'd have to suspend my job search, even though that's not going anywhere right now." Funny, she sounded as if she was actually considering it.

He took a brief look around before he leaned over and brushed a kiss across her lips. "If you do decide to come, don't worry about calling. Just surprise me and show up."

With that, he strode through the living room and out the door, leaving Hannah standing in the kitchen in a semi-stupor until reality finally set in. Then she snatched up the cordless phone and pounded out a number on her way to the bedroom, where she closed the door. As soon as she heard the familiar hello, she said the only thing she could think to say.

"Help!"

"He wants you to do *what?*"

Sitting in a high-back stool at the granite island in her best friend's kitchen, Hannah was taken aback by Gina Romero's strong reaction to her declaration. Normally the woman rode her mercilessly about finding a man. "I'll speak more slowly this time. He wants me to go to Cheyenne for a few days and investigate the possibility that the man I'm inheriting from might be my biological father." She sure as heck wasn't going to reveal that inheritance was basically a fortune.

Gina swept one hand through her bobbed blond hair and narrowed her blue eyes. "Is that all he wants to investigate?"

Hannah would swear her face had morphed into a furnace. "Don't be ridiculous, Gina."

"Don't be naive, Hannah."

"I'm not being naive." Even if she wasn't being completely truthful. "He really is trying to help me."

Gina handed her eight-month-old son, Trey, another cracker when he began to squirm in the nearby high chair. "So tell me what's so special about this mystery attorney who wants to *help* you."

That could take hours. "Well, he's fairly tall, has dark hair and light brown eyes. Oh, and he has incredible dimples."

Gina gave her a good eye-rolling, the second Hannah had received today. "Okay. So he's a hunk, but does he have anything else to back that up?"

"As a matter of fact, he does. He's a full partner in a very prestigious law firm in Cheyenne."

"How's his butt?" she asked in a conspiratorial whisper.

The memory brought about Hannah's smile. "Stellar."

"Well, then, why aren't you home packing?"

"You'd think that would be enough, but I still have quite a few reservations."

"Unless you're lying and he's really in his eighties and drives a Studebaker, you should go for it."

"He's thirty-eight and drives a Mercedes. But he's also childless and divorced."

"Not everyone who's divorced is an ogre, Hannah," Gina said. "You can't judge him by your experience with that Henry what's-his-name you went out with for a while."

Gina could have gone all year without mentioning that jerk. "I only went out with him twice. But you know I worry when I meet a man who couldn't make his marriage work."

Gina frowned. "There are all sorts of reasons why marriages don't work, and it might not have even been his fault."

She couldn't argue that point since she had no details about Logan's divorce. "But what if it was his fault? What if he has some horrible habits that can't be overlooked?" Or worse, what if he cheated on his wife?

When the baby began to fuss, Gina rifled through the box of crackers and handed another one to her son. "Tell me, did this attorney do anything weird at dinner like that Henry guy you dated? Did he pick his teeth and belch? Or did he try to unsnap your bra when you hugged him good-night?"

"I didn't hug him good-night."

"Too bad."

"But I did kiss him."

Gina slapped her palm on the table, sending the baby into a fit of giggles. "You've been sitting here for ten minutes and you're just now telling me this?"

"It was a mistake." A huge one. "I had a couple of drinks and I guess it stripped me of all my inhibitions."

Gina sent her a sly look. "Question is, did you strip following the kiss?"

Heaven forbid. "Of course not. I just met the guy and I'm not that stupid."

"Yet you're considering going away with him," Gina said, adding a suspicious stare.

"I wouldn't be going away with him. I'd be staying at his house, which is very big, according to Logan."

"Wonder if his house is the only thing that's big."

Hannah playfully slapped at Gina's arm. "Stop it. This has to do with filling in the missing pieces of my family history, not getting friendly with Logan."

"Sure it does, Hannah. Just keep telling yourself that and you might start to believe it."

Leave it to Gina to see right through her ruse. "So what if I am attracted to him? Is there anything wrong with that?"

Gina made a one-handed catch of Trey's cracker when he tossed it at her. "There's absolutely nothing wrong with that. In fact, it's about time you start living again, girlfriend."

Same song, fiftieth verse. "I have been living, *girlfriend*. I've finished school and raised my daughter and I'm about to start a new career."

"Don't forget you cared for your ungrateful mother during the final months of her illness." Gina reached across the island and laid a palm on Hannah's forearm. "What you've done for your family since Danny's death is admirable. Heck, I'm not sure I could do the same thing if something happened to Frank. But now you need to do something for yourself."

Hannah still harbored several concerns. "What if I make this trip, decide that he's someone I want to spend a lot more time with and end up getting hurt?"

"That will happen only if you let him hurt you."

"True, but you have no idea how I felt being around him last night. I could barely think."

"Chemistry will cloud your mind every time."

Chemistry she could handle. "I'm worried it's more than that, Gina. I wish I could explain it." How could she when she couldn't explain it to herself? "I sense he really is a compassionate person, and maybe he's had some hard times during his life, too."

Gina took Trey from the high chair, placed him in the playpen and then signaled Hannah to join her in the adjacent den. She sat on the sofa and patted the space beside her. "Come here and let's have a heart-to-heart."

Hannah claimed her spot on the couch and prepared for a friendly lecture. "Bestow me with your sage advice, oh, wise one."

Gina sent her a smile. "Look, while we were growing up, you always walked the straight and narrow, always striving to be the best cheerleader, best student and an all-around good girl."

She bristled over her friend's words. "And what was wrong with that?"

"Because you did all those things to please your mother, and it never seemed to matter. Then you married Danny at the ripe old age of twenty. You worked hard to please him by quitting college so he could go to trade school when his parents cut him off because he married you."

She could feel her blood pressure begin to rise. "I loved Danny with all my heart and he loved me."

"Yes, he did, and he appreciated your efforts, unlike Ruth. But don't you think it's time you have a little adventure?"

Adventure had been a word sorely missing from

her vocabulary. "Maybe you're right, but what do I do about Cassie?"

Gina looked at her as if she'd lost her mind. "I can't count the times you've kept Michaela when Frank and I went out of town for a long weekend, including the one when I got pregnant with Trey. It's way past time for me to return the favor and watch Cassie for however long it takes for you to thoroughly investigate the attorney."

Hannah couldn't stop the flow of sexy, forbidden thoughts streaming through her imagination, until reality came calling once more. "But you're going to be saddled with two giggling girls and a baby. That doesn't seem fair."

Gina stood and began picking up the toys bouncing across the hardwood floors while Trey kept hurling more over the side of the playpen. "I'm used to this little guy's antics, and the girls will be in school during the day. Unless you plan to be gone until they reach puberty, it shouldn't be a problem."

"If I do go—" and that was a major *if* "—I only plan to stay a couple of days. A week, tops. But you're still going to have to deal with them at night, not to mention you have a husband to care for and—"

Gina held up a finger to silence her. "Frank has been trained well. And besides, he's been talking about trying for another kid next year. I might as well get in some practice before he knocks me up a third time."

The sound of those giggling girls grew closer and reached a crescendo as one red-headed ball of fire and one petite, brown-haired follower rushed into the room dressed in too-big formal attire, their faces showing the signs of a makeup attack.

"Aren't we pretty, Mama?" Cassie asked as she spun around in the red sequined strapless grown.

"Very," Hannah lied when she caught sight of the charcoal smudges outlining her daughter's eyes. "But did you have permission to raid Gina's closet?"

"Those came out of my cedar chest, Hannah," Gina said. "Cassie's wearing my prom dress and Michaela's wearing yours, in case you didn't recognize it."

Hannah did recognize the black silk gown all right, but she didn't remember giving it to her friend. "What are you doing with it?"

Gina looked somewhat chagrined. "I borrowed it and forgot to give it back."

Michaela's grin looked as lopsided as her high pony-tail, thanks to the scarlet lipstick running askew from her mouth. "Can I keep it, Hannah?"

"Yes, honey, you most certainly can." The terrible memories of her part-octopus prom date, Ryan, were still attached to the gown, so no great loss.

"Do you have something you'd like to ask your daughter, Hannah?" Gina inquired.

Hannah supposed it wouldn't hurt to get Cassie's reaction to the possibility of her traveling to Cheyenne. "Sweetie, if I decided to take a trip out of town for a few days, would you mind staying here with Michaela and Gina?"

Cassie ran right out of her oversized high heels and practically tackled Hannah with a voracious hug. "I want to stay, Mama! When are you going?"

Good question. She pulled Cassie into her lap and planted a kiss on her makeup-caked cheek. "I'm not sure yet. Maybe tonight, but probably tomorrow."

Cassie looked crestfallen. "Go tonight, please. Me

and Mickey want to have a wedding. Gina said we could use her dress."

Hannah glanced at Gina. "You said that?"

"Yes, I did. But they've been forewarned that the groom will either be a stuffed animal or the baby brother, no boys from the neighborhood."

Cassie came to her feet and gave Hannah a hopeful look. "So can I stay, Mama? I'll be good and I'll help Mickey clean her room and I'll go to bed when I'm told."

Hannah couldn't in good conscience make a promise she might not keep. "We'll see. Right now you need to wash that purple eye shadow off your lids and go for something a little more subtle, like a nice beige. But before you do that, I want to take a picture."

While she fished her cell phone from her pocket, the girls struck a pose and put on their best grins. And as soon as she snapped the photo, the pair took off down the hall, sounds of sheer excitement echoing throughout the house.

She then noticed the blinking blue light indicating she'd received a text. And she couldn't be more surprised when she noted the message's sender. "Speak of the sexy devil."

Gina moved close to her side. "Devil as in the attorney?"

"Yes."

"What does it say?"

"'Dinner should be ready around seven. Italian. I also have a good bottle of wine. The only thing missing is you.'"

"Now I'm worried," Gina said.

Hannah pocketed the phone and stared at her friend. "You have something against Italian food?"

"I'm part Italian, silly. No, I'm worried because the devil didn't mention good sex."

She elbowed Gina in the side. "Would you please get off the sex thing? We have two impressionable, minor children in the house and they hear everything within a fifty-mile radius."

Gina pushed off the sofa and picked up the whimpering baby. "Come on, Hannah. Put on your big-girl panties and get with the program."

Something suddenly dawned on her. "Oh, my gosh, all I have are big-girl panties. Not a sexy pair in the drawer."

Her friend claimed the rocker across from the sofa and positioned the baby on her shoulder. "It's not even close to noon yet, so you have a few hours left to remedy that. Have you used the department-store gift card I gave you on your birthday?"

She was somewhat ashamed she'd held on to it for three months. "No, but before you get *your* big-girl panties in a wad, I've been too busy to shop."

"You better get busy if you want to be in Cheyenne by sundown," Gina said as she set the rocker in motion and rubbed her sleepy son's back.

A barrage of memories assaulted Hannah, recollections of a time when she'd rocked her baby girl, plagued with emotions that ran the gamut from bliss to utter sadness that her daughter's father would never know those precious moments. She secretly longed to have another child someday, and to be able to share that with a special someone. She suspected Logan Whittaker might not be the one to fulfill that dream.

"What's wrong now, Hannah?"

She looked at Gina through misty eyes. "Nothing really. Just remembering when Cassie was a baby, I guess. Time has a way of zipping by before you even realize it's gone."

"True, and time's a wastin' for you," Gina said. "Go shopping and buy those sexy panties along with a few nice outfits. Then go home and pack and get thee to Cheyenne."

If only it were that easy. "Do you really think this is the right thing to do?"

Gina sighed. "I think you'll never know unless you try, so just stop thinking and do it."

Her best friend was right. Nothing ventured, nothing gained, and all that jazz.

She might live to regret the decision, but darned if she wasn't actually going to do it.

Four

Never in a million years had Logan believed she'd actually do it. But there Hannah stood on his threshold, wearing a fitted, long-sleeved blue silk blouse covering tapered jeans, a small silver purse clutched in her hands. Talk about feeling underdressed in his faded navy T-shirt, tattered jeans and rough-out work boots. She'd parked her car beneath the portico and set two bags at her feet, which sported some deadly black heels, causing Logan to think questionable thoughts he shouldn't be thinking before she even made it into the house.

"You're here," he said, slight shock in his tone.

"I guess I should have called," she replied, clear concern in her voice.

"I told you to surprise me."

"Yes, but you looked absolutely stunned when you opened the door."

He grinned. "I thought you were the maid."

Fortunately she returned his smile. "I suppose we're going to have to work on that mistaken identity thing."

He personally would have to work on resisting the urge to kiss her at every turn. "We can do that after dinner."

"As long as I don't have to cook, it's a deal."

After grabbing Hannah's bags, Logan stepped aside and nodded toward the open door. "Come inside and make yourself at home."

The minute she entered the house, Hannah's gaze traveled upward toward the two-story foyer flanked by twin staircases with modern black banisters. "Wow. This is amazing."

He'd pretty much taken the view for granted and enjoyed seeing it through her eyes. "Yeah, it's impressive. But overall the place is more comfortable than elaborate."

She shot him a cynical look. "It's practically a mansion."

He started up the wood-covered stairs to the right. "I'll show you to your room before I give you the grand tour."

Hannah followed behind him to the second floor, where Logan stopped at the landing, allowing her to move in front of him for a purely selfish, and very male reason—to check out her butt. "Just go right and keeping walking until you reach the end of the hall."

She paused to peer inside the first of the three spare bedrooms. "Very nicely appointed. I really like the navy stripes mixed with yellows."

A color pallet he wouldn't have personally chosen, but if it worked for her, it worked for him. "The house was basically move-in ready. You can thank my decorator for the finishing touches. That's definitely not my thing."

"She's very good at what she does. I'm sure she has clients lined up for her services."

"Actually, she doesn't decorate for a living. She's a good friend of mine."

"A really good friend?"

When he heard the mild suspicion in Hannah's tone, he knew exactly what she was thinking. "Her name is Marlene and she's sixty years old. I'll introduce you in the near future." He decided to withhold the fact the woman was the late J. D. Lassiter's sister-in-law.

She passed the bathroom and peeked inside, then did the same with the next guest room, and pulled up short when she came to the closed door. "What's in here?"

A room he hadn't had the heart to touch, even if it did unearth bittersweet memories he'd just as soon forget. "It's a kid's bedroom that I haven't redone yet. I figured since I have three more guest rooms, I'm not in any hurry."

When she glanced back at him, Logan could tell she wasn't buying it. "Are you sure it's not your secret man-cave?"

"That's downstairs," he said, relieved she wasn't as suspicious as he'd assumed.

"Mind if I take a look?" she asked.

"Knock yourself out."

When Hannah opened the door and stepped inside, her expression said it all. The place was a little girl's fairy tale come to life, from the four princesses painted on the walls, to the pink cushioned seat built in beneath a ceiling-high window overlooking the courtyard at the front of the house.

"Cassie would absolutely love this," Hannah said as she looked around in awe. "That was one lucky little girl."

At least someone's little girl had been that lucky. "It's not exactly my taste, but then as a kid I preferred all things rodeo and baseball."

She turned and smiled. "Is that the décor you chose for your man-cave?"

His presumed "man-cave" would suit both genders. "You can see for yourself after we get you settled in, so keep going because we're almost there."

She turned and bowed. "My wish is your command, captain."

Grinning, he headed back into the hall and strode to the door he'd intentionally kept closed just so he could enjoy her reaction when he opened it. As expected, Hannah looked completely awed when he revealed the orange-tinted skies and the Rocky Mountain backdrop in clear view through the floor-to-ceiling windows.

"That is unbelievable," she said.

So was Logan's immediate physical reaction to the breathless quality of her voice. Keeping a firm grip on his control, he set her bags on the bench at the end of the king-size bed. "I have to agree with you there. It's better than the view from my bedroom, but you'll see that for yourself." When he noticed the trepidation in Hannah's eyes, he decided to backtrack for the second time in the past five minutes. "It's included on the tour, unless you want me to leave it off."

She shook her head. "No. Since we're both grown-ups, I can go into your bedroom without the fear of being grounded."

He wouldn't mind keeping her there for an indeterminate amount of time, a fact he'd keep to himself for now. "The bathroom's to your left."

She breezed through the bedroom, opened the double doors and then looked back with a smile. "Is this where you hold all your parties?"

He wouldn't mind holding a party there for the two of them. "Nope, but I probably could fit six people in the steam shower, and at least four in the jetted bathtub."

Hannah moved inside and ran her hand over one of the two granite-topped vanities. "I feel like I've died and gone to five-star-hotel heaven."

He thought he might die if he didn't get a little lip action real soon. "It's yours to enjoy for the duration."

She turned and leaned back against the vanity. "I could use a good soak in the tub."

And he'd gladly soak with her. "If you can wait until after dinner, that would be preferable. And speaking of that, it won't be too long before it's ready."

Hannah straightened and smiled. "Great, because I'm starving."

Man, so was he—for her undivided attention. "Then let's get going with the tour." Before he suggested they say to hell with dinner and take advantage of that tub. He definitely didn't want her to believe he intended to take advantage of her.

Logan showed Hannah to the upstairs den and then escorted her downstairs. He did a quick pass through the great room, pointed out his office and the game room, pausing as he arrived at the last stop before he led her to kitchen. "And this is my favorite place, the media room," he said as he opened the heavy double doors.

Her gaze traveled over the dark gray soundproof walls as she strolled down the black-carpeted, declining aisle. She paused to run her hand along the arm of one beige leather chair before facing him again. "Media room? This is more like an honest-to-goodness movie theater. All that's missing is a popcorn machine."

He nodded to his left. "In the corner behind that curtain, next to the soda fountain."

"Of course."

Hannah sounded almost disapproving, which sent Logan into defense mode. "Hey, the whole setup was here when I bought the house, including a huge collection of movies." Most of which he'd never watched because he didn't like watching alone. He planned to remedy that…and soon.

After folding her arms beneath her breasts, she slowly approached him. "I'd love to check out your collection."

"Not a problem, but right now I better check on dinner before I burn everything to a crisp and we have to call out for pizza."

She made a sweeping gesture toward the exit. "After you."

She followed quietly behind him as he led the way back through the great room and into the kitchen. As she'd done in the media room, Hannah took a visual trek through the area, her eyes wide with wonder. "State-of-the-art appliances, enough cabinets to store supplies for an army and a stainless island that I would sell my soul to have. Are you sure you don't have a robot hidden away somewhere to prepare your food?"

At least she'd said it with a smile, and that relieved him. He'd never been one to seek approval, but for some reason her opinion mattered. "No robot. Just me and sometimes the maid. I learned to cook after the divorce. It was either that or starve."

Hannah claimed the chrome-and-black bar stool across from the oven and folded her hands before her. "I hope it tastes as good as it smells."

He rounded the island, rested his elbows on the silver counter and angled his lower body away. "The recipe's never failed me before." He couldn't say the same for his self-control because he was having one hell of a fantasy involving her and that bar stool.

"What are we having?" she asked.

He personally was having a major desire to kiss her. "The mostaccioli I told you about."

"Fantastic. I've never had it before, but it's always good to try something new."

"And it's great to share something new with someone who's never experienced it before."

"I'm looking forward to a lot of new experiences while I'm here."

As their gazes remained connected, tension as apparent as the smell of the pasta hung in the air, until Hannah broke their visual contact by leaning around him. "According to your timer, we still have five minutes."

He straightened and glanced behind him before regarding her again. "True, and it needs to rest for another ten." Now what to talk about during those few minutes that would keep him from taking an inadvisable risk. "How did your daughter feel about you coming here?"

Hannah frowned. "She couldn't get me out of town fast enough. I can't compete with best friends and their baby brothers."

"I guess sometimes kids need a break from their parents."

She sighed softly. "I agree, but this is the longest break from each other we've ever had. I am glad to know she's in good hands, and that she's going to have a great time in my absence dressing up like a teenage harlot."

"Oh, yeah?"

Hannah pulled her cell phone from her pocket, hit an app and turned it around. "I took this photo this morning of my kiddo and her best friend, Michaela."

Logan started to laugh but the urge died when he homed in on the little girl standing next to Hannah's daughter. The resemblance might be slight, but the memories overwhelmed him. Recollections of his black-haired baby girl they'd appropriately named Grace.

He swallowed hard before handing Hannah the phone. "Gotta love their imaginations."

"Yes, but I don't like the fact she's trying to grow up too fast."

He'd give up everything he owned for the opportunity to watch his daughter grow up, but she'd been torn from his life after only four brief years. Now might be a good time to tell Hannah about her, but he wasn't ready yet. He wasn't sure he would ever be ready to make that revelation. "While we're waiting on dinner, do you want a glass of wine?"

"Sure," she said with a soft smile. "As long as you're also partaking tonight. I've decided it's best I not drink alone."

He'd learned that lesson all too well. "I'm not much of a wine drinker, but I do like a beer now and then."

"Whatever works for you."

Everything about Hannah Armstrong worked for him, and he'd just have to take out that thought and analyze it later. At the moment he needed to play the good host.

Logan crossed the room to a small bar where he'd set out an expensive bottle of red and poured a glass. Then he bent down and pulled out his favorite lager from the beverage refrigerator.

He returned to his place across from Hannah and slid the wine toward her. "Let me know if this meets your standards."

"I'm sure it will since I can only afford the cheap stuff," she said. "And before you mention that I can afford the best if I take the millions, don't waste your breath. I still haven't changed my mind."

"That's fine by me." And it was, to a point. "If you do refuse the inheritance, the funds will be merged into the Lassiter Foundation and given to charity."

She looked slightly amazed. "I didn't think J.D. would have a charitable bone in his body after the way he apparently treated my mother."

"And you," Logan said. "But he always has been somewhat of a philanthropist, and a good parent, which is why I'm surprised he would ignore his child."

"Perhaps he did have his reasons, and chances are I won't know. Maybe I don't want to know."

He didn't want to spoil the evening by being bogged

down by emotional chains from the past. "Let's concentrate on the present and worry about the rest later."

Hannah grinned and lifted her glass. "Here's to procrastination."

This time Logan did laugh as he touched his beer to her wine. "And to good food, new friends and more good food."

She took a sip of her wine and set the glass down. "Just don't feed me too well. If I put on an extra five pounds that means I'll have to lose fifteen instead of ten."

"You don't need to lose weight," he said, and he meant it. "You look great."

She lowered her gaze for a moment. "Thank you, but I really need to get back in shape so I can comfortably do those backflips."

That made him grin again. "I've got quite a few acres if you want to practice after dinner."

"Do you really think that's a good idea in the dark?"

No, but he could think of several things he'd like to do with her in the dark. Or the daylight. "You're right. I have another place to show you anyway."

She bent her elbow and supported her jaw with her palm. "Where do you plan to take me?"

Places she hadn't been before, but he didn't want to jump the gun, or get his hopes up...yet. "It's my second favorite place."

She narrowed her eyes. "You aren't referring to your bedroom since you left it off the tour, are you?"

He'd done that intentionally in an effort not to move too fast. "Not even close."

"Can you give me a hint?"

Without regard to the taking-it-slowly plan, he

reached over and brushed a strand of silky auburn hair from her cheek. "You surprised me tonight. Now it's time for me to surprise you."

Hannah had to admit she was a bit surprised when Logan suggested an after-dinner walk. She was even more shocked by his skill as a chef. Never before had she sampled such great food at the hands of a culinary hobbyist, who also happened to be a man.

She imagined his skills went far beyond the kitchen, particularly when it came to the bedroom. And although she'd been curious to see his sleeping quarters, she appreciated that he hadn't presented her with that possible temptation. Of course, she had no reason to believe he actually wanted to get her in his bed. She could hear Gina laughing at her naiveté the minute that thought vaulted into her brain.

According to Logan, the temperature had dropped quite a bit and now hovered around forty-five degrees, sending Hannah upstairs to change right after they cleaned the kitchen together. Hopefully the weather would begin to warm up in the next few days with the arrival of May. She rifled through her unpacked bag and withdrew a sweatshirt. After putting that on, she exchanged her heels for a pair of sneakers, did a quick makeup check, brushed her hair and then sprinted back down the stairs.

She found Logan waiting for her at the back door right off the mudroom adjacent to the kitchen, exactly where he'd told her to be. "I'm ready to walk off all that delicious food."

He inclined his head and studied her. "You really thought it was that good?"

Men. Always looking to have their egos stroked, among other things. She would actually be game for both…and obviously she was turning into a bad, bad girl. "I believe I said that at least five times during dinner, when I wasn't making the yummy noises."

His beautiful smile lit up his intriguing brown eyes. "Just making sure."

After Logan opened the door, Hannah stepped in front of him and exited the house. She was totally stunned, and extremely thrilled, when he rested his palm on the small of her back as he guided her toward a somewhat visible rock path illuminated by a three-quarter moon.

Unfortunately he dropped his hand as they began their walk toward a large expanse of land, but the Rocky Mountains silhouetted against the star-laden sky proved to be a great distraction. "It's really nice outside, even if it's a little cold."

"Feels good to me," he said.

She glanced at him briefly before turning her focus straight ahead to prevent tripping. "I can't believe you're not freezing since you're only wearing a lightweight jacket."

"The wind's not nearly as bad as it usually is around here. And I'm also pretty hot-blooded."

She had no doubt about that. He was hot, period. "What's that building in the distance?"

"A barn."

"Is that where you're taking me?"

"Nope."

She didn't quite understand why he seemed bent on being evasive. "Are you purposefully trying to keep me in suspense?"

"Yeah, but it'll be worth it."

A roll in the hay in the barn would be well worth it to her, and she'd best keep her questionable opinions to herself.

They continued to walk in silence until a smooth-wire fence stopped their forward progress. "This is my second favorite place," Logan said as he propped one boot on the bottom rail and rested his elbow on the top.

Hannah moved beside him and waited for her vision to adjust to the dark before taking in the panorama. The lush pasture traveled at an incline to what appeared to be a stream lined by a few trees. Not far away, she noticed two shadowy animals with their heads bent to graze on the grass. "Are those your horses?"

"Yeah. Harry and Lucy."

"Didn't they star in a fifties sitcom?"

Logan's laughter cut through the quiet. "I'm not sure about that, but they both came to me already named."

After she turned toward him and leaned against a post, his profile drew her attention. It was utterly perfect, from forehead to chin. "How long have you had them?"

"I bought Harry when I turned eighteen. He was a year-old gelding. I broke him and trained him to be a pretty good cutting horse. He's twenty now."

She had no idea what a cutting horse was, but she didn't want to show her ignorance. "What about Lucy?"

He went suddenly silent for a few seconds before speaking again. "I've had her about ten years, I guess. She's a retired pleasure horse and pretty kid-proof."

"That sounds about my speed."

He lowered his foot and faced her. "You've never ridden a horse?"

She internally cringed at the thought. "Twice. The first time I was sixteen and I went on a trail ride with friends. A controlled environment is a good place to start, or so they told me. They didn't, however, tell Flint, my ride. He decided to take off ahead of the pack and it took every ounce of my strength to get him to stop. After that, the trail master tied him to his horse to make sure he behaved."

"But you still got on a horse again?"

"On a beach in Mexico. I rode a really sweet mare and by the end of the ride, I'd trusted her enough to actually gallop." She closed her eyes and immersed herself in the memories. "The wind was blowing through my hair and the sun was on my face and I remember feeling the ocean spray on my feet. It was incredible."

"You're incredible."

She opened her eyes to find him staring at her. "Why?"

"Most people aren't brave enough to get back on a horse after a bad experience. I'm starting to wonder if anything scares you."

She was scared by the way she felt around him—ready to jump headfirst into possible heartache. "Believe me, I have fears like everyone else. I've just tried not to let them paralyze me."

Logan inched closer and streamed a fingertip along her jaw. "Would you be afraid if I kissed you again?"

She might die if he didn't. "Not really."

He bent and brushed a soft kiss across her cheek. "Would it scare you if I told you that you're all I've thought about for the past two days?"

"Would it scare you if I said I've been thinking about you, too?"

"I'm glad, because I can't get thoughts of us, being really close, off my mind." When he laced their fingers together, the implications weren't lost on Hannah.

"It's been a long time, Logan. I don't take intimacy lightly."

"I respect that," he said, not sounding the least bit disappointed. "That's why I only want to kiss you. Tonight."

After he said it, he did it, and he did it very well. The first time she'd kissed him, she'd fumbled through the motions. The first time he'd kissed her, he'd been quick about it. But not now.

He explored her mouth with care, with the gentle stroke of his tongue, allowing her to capture all the sensations. She responded with a soft moan and a certain need to be closer to him. On that thought, she wrapped her hands around his waist while he wound one hand through her hair and planted the other on her back.

When Logan tugged her flush against him, the cold all but disappeared, replaced by a searing heat that shot the length of Hannah's body and came to rest in unseen places, leaving dampness in its wake.

Too long since she'd been kissed this way, felt this way. Too long since she'd experienced a desire so strong that if Logan laid her down on the hard ground beneath their feet and offered to remove her clothes, she'd let him.

Clearly Logan had other ideas, she realized, when he broke the kiss and tipped his forehead against hers. "I need you so damn bad I hurt."

She'd noticed that need when she'd been pelvis-to-pelvis with him. "Chemistry definitely can commandeer your body."

He pulled back and studied her eyes. "But I don't want to screw this up, Hannah, so we're going to take this slowly. Get to know each other better. But sweetheart, before you leave, I plan to make love to you in ways you won't forget."

Hannah trembled at the thought. "You're mighty confident, Mr. Whittaker."

"I just know what I want when I want it, and I want you." He ran the tip of his tongue over the shell of her ear and whispered, "I think you want me just as badly. So let's go before I change my mind and take you down on the ground and get you naked."

Her body reacted with another surge of heat and dampness over Logan's declaration. Yet they walked back to the house, hand in hand, like innocent young lovers who'd just discovered each other, not mature adults who were approaching the point of no return.

Hannah knew better than to cross that line too soon. She knew better than to lead with her heart and not her head. Yet when Logan said goodbye to her at the bedroom door, she almost tossed wisdom out the window for a night of wild abandon. Instead, she let him go and sought out the place where she would spend the night alone longing for things she shouldn't. Wanting, needing, Logan's words echoing through her cluttered mind…

But sweetheart, before you leave, I plan to make love to you in ways you won't forget…

Deep down she had no doubt he was a man of his word. But if she took that leap into lovemaking, would her heart suffer another devastating blow?

Five

"What do you mean you didn't do it?"

That was the last thing Hannah wanted to hear first thing in the morning, especially from her best friend.

After turning the cell on speaker and setting it on the bed beside her, she slid a sneaker onto her foot and began lacing it. "He happens to be a gentleman, Gina. And I didn't call to talk about my sex life. I called to talk to my daughter."

"You don't have a sex life, and you can't talk to Cassie because she's not here right now."

She tightened the shoestrings just a little too tight. "Where is she?"

"Out with bikers she met bar-hopping last night."

Infuriating woman. "I'm serious, Regina Gertrude Romero."

"You know how I hate it when you use my middle name."

"Yes, I do," she said as she pulled on the remaining shoe. "Now tell me my daughter's actual whereabouts before I tell everyone in your book club that you want to be a pole dancer when you finally grow up."

Gina let out an exaggerated sigh. "She's with Frank at his sister's house. Since it's going to be close to eighty degrees today, and we don't know how long this heat wave is going to last, the kids are going to swim."

Hannah was poised to hit the panic button. "Are you sure it's warm enough there because it's not nearly that warm here."

"I checked the weather, Hannah. And don't forget, you're almost a hundred miles away."

She hadn't forgotten that at all, and now the distance between her and her child really worried her. "I hope the adults pay close attention because Cassie—"

"Can swim better than you and me," Gina said. "Stop being such a worrywart."

Her patience was starting to unravel. "Did you pack sunscreen? You know how easily she burns."

"Yes, I did, and I put the fire department on alert, just in case."

One more acerbic comment and she might very well come completely unglued. "Real funny, Regina. And why are you home?"

"Trey kept me up a good part of the night, so Frank let me sleep in while the baby is sleeping. I'll be heading out in an hour or so. By the way, where is your attorney now?"

He wasn't *her* attorney, but Hannah saw no reason to debate that point. "I'm not sure. I just got out of the shower and I haven't left the bedroom yet."

"I could see where you'd still be in the bedroom if

he was in there with you, but it's almost ten o'clock. Don't you think he might be wondering if you've flown the coop, leaving the rooster all alone?"

Hannah had thought about that, but so far she hadn't heard a thing coming from downstairs. "Maybe he's sleeping in, too. But I won't know until I get off the phone."

"Hint taken. Call me this evening and I'll put your daughter on the phone, unless, of course, you're engaged in some serious cross-examination."

"I'm hanging up now, Gina." As soon as she ended the call, Hannah hopped to her feet, ready to face the day—and Logan.

After a quick makeup application and hair brushing, she sprinted down the stairs, tugging at her plain light blue T-shirt and wishing she'd worn a better pair of jeans. But casual seemed to suit Logan. Very well.

She wound her way through the cowboy palace, following the scent of coffee in hopes of locating the master of the manor. When she arrived in the kitchen, there he was in all his glory, sitting with his back to her at the island. He wore a navy plaid flannel shirt and a cowboy hat, which almost sent Hannah completely into a female frenzy over her Wild West fantasy coming to life.

She stood in the kitchen opening just long enough to take a good look at his broad back before she slid onto the stool across from him. "Good morning."

He lifted his gaze from his coffee cup and smiled, but only halfway. "Mornin', ma'am. How did you sleep?"

Like a woman who couldn't get his kisses off her

blasted mind. "Pretty darn well, thank you. That mattress is as soft as a cloud."

"I'm glad you found the accommodations satisfactory." He nodded at the counter behind her. "There's some coffee left if you want me to get you a cup."

"I'll get some in a minute," she said when she noticed the keys resting near his right hand. "Have you been out already this morning?"

"Not yet, but unfortunately I'm going to have to get a move on. I got a call from Chance Lassiter. He's Marlene's son and the ranch manager at the Big Blue. He needs some extra help herding a few calves that got out of a break in the fence last night."

It figured her plans would be foiled by a Lassiter. So much for spending a relaxing Sunday getting to know him better. "How long will that take?"

"Hard to say, but it could be quite a while since we'll need to cover a lot of land. And the ranch is about thirty minutes north of here. Feel free to turn on the TV while I'm gone, or use the computer if you want to do some research on the Lassiters. If you need supplies, they're in the desk drawer."

She wondered why he would invite her—a virtual stranger—into his private domain. "You're absolutely sure you don't mind me hanging out in your office?"

He sent her a sexy-as-sin grin. "I don't have anything to hide. All my professional files are password protected, but if you have a hankerin' to hack into those, knock yourself out. The legal jargon on mergers and acquisitions is pretty damn riveting. Just be forewarned you're going to need a nap afterward."

She wouldn't mind taking a nap with him. "Do you want me to whip something up for dinner?"

"Don't worry about me. As far as you're concerned, there's quite a bit of food in the refrigerator, so help yourself."

Hannah admittedly was a bit disappointed he hadn't asked her to join him on the day trip. "Thanks."

"I really hate having to leave you, but—"

"I'm a big girl, Logan. I can entertain myself until you return."

He reached over the counter and ran a fingertip along her jaw. "When I get back, I have some entertainment in mind for you."

She shivered like a schoolgirl at the thought. "And what will that entail?"

After he stood, Logan rounded the island, came up behind her and brought his mouth to her ear. "You'll just have to wait and see, but it will be worth the wait."

After Hannah shifted toward him, Logan gave her a steamy kiss that made her want to initiate his kitchen counter. Or the floor. But he pulled away before she could act on impulse.

He snatched up his keys and winked. "I'll let you know when I'm heading home."

"I'll be here." And she couldn't think of any place she would rather be at the moment, aside from home with her daughter. Or in bed with him.

Naughty, naughty, Hannah.

After Logan left out the back door, she hurried to the great room to peer out the picture window facing the front drive. She waited until he guided the massive black dual-wheel truck and silver horse trailer onto the main road before she returned to the kitchen for coffee. She poured a cup and doctored it with lots of sugar and cream, then ate the apple set out in a fruit bowl.

Now what? TV watching seemed about as appealing as contemplating the cosmos. She did bring a book, but she wasn't in the mood to read. Doing a little research on Logan's computer called to her curiosity. After finishing off the coffee, she went in search of his office and retraced her steps from when Logan showed her around. Following a few wrong turns, she finally located the room beyond the formal dining room.

The French doors were closed, but not locked, allowing Hannah easy entry into the attorney's inner sanctum. A state-of-the-art PC sat in the center of a modern black desk that looked remarkably neat. Two walls of matching bookshelves housed several law manuals, as well as quite a few true-crime novels.

She dropped into the rolling black leather chair and scooted close to the computer, ready to start looking for more info on the Lassiters. Yet something else immediately drew her attention.

In Hannah's opinion, a man's desk drawer was equivalent to a medicine cabinet—worthy of investigation. But did she dare poke around? That would undeniably be considered an invasion of privacy. Sort of. Hadn't he said to help herself to any supplies? Of course, she didn't need any paper or pens yet, but she did have a strong need to satisfy her nosiness.

With that in mind, Hannah slid the drawer open slowly, and like the desk, the thing was immaculate. She took a quick inventory after she didn't notice anything out of the ordinary on first glance. A few pens in a plastic divider, along with some binder clips. A box of staples. A stack of stationery stamped with his name, along with coordinating envelopes.

Not quite satisfied, Hannah pulled the drawer open

as far as she could, and glimpsed the corner of something shiny. She lifted the brown address book to find a small silver frame etched with teddy bears and balloons, the bottom stamped with a date—February 15, twelve years ago. She withdrew the photo of a pretty newborn with a dark cap of hair, a round face, precious puckered lips and what looked to be a tiny dimple imprinted on its right cheek. Unfortunately, she couldn't quite determine the gender due to the neutral yellow gown, but she would guess this baby happened to be a little girl. The question was, *whose* little girl?

Logan had been adamant he had no children, leaving Hannah to assume the infant could be a sibling's child, if he had any siblings. She could clear up the mystery when he came home, but since the frame had been tucked away out of sight, she would have to admit she'd been snooping.

Right now she had another mystery that needed her focus, namely trying to find any clues indicating John Douglas Lassiter was her mother's sperm donor.

With that in mind, Hannah booted the computer and brought up her favorite search engine. She decided to dig a little deeper this time, expand her inquiries, and learn as much about the Lassiter family as possible, beginning with where it had all begun. She read articles about the self-made billionaire and his various ventures, from newspapers to cattle to his media corporation in California. He'd married a woman named Ellie, adopted her two nephews and lived through the loss of his wife, who sadly died at forty-two just days after giving birth to a daughter.

She took a few moments to study a recent publicity photo of that daughter, Angelica Lassiter, who could possibly be her sister. The sophisticated-looking woman was tall and slimly built, with dark hair and eyes—nothing that physically indicated Hannah might be kin to the reported "brains" behind Lassiter Media. Apparently Angelica had broken off her engagement to Evan McCain, interim chairman and CEO of the company, after a reported dispute over the terms in her father's will. High drama indeed.

Hannah surfed a little longer, trying to establish some connection between J.D. and her mother, yet she found nothing whatsoever to prove that theory.

Stiff-necked and bleary-eyed, Hannah noticed the time and realized a good part of the day had already passed her by. And as far as she knew, Logan hadn't returned home yet. She sat back in the chair and closed her eyes, remembering his lips fused with hers, his body pressed flush against her body, how badly she had wanted him last night. How badly she wanted him still, though she shouldn't…

The phone shrilled, startling Hannah so badly, she nearly vaulted from the rolling chair as she fumbled the cell from her pocket. Disappointment washed over her when Gina's name—not Logan's—displayed on the screen. "No, we haven't done it yet."

"Done what, Mama?"

Great. This was not the way she wanted to introduce her child to human sexuality. "Hi, sweetie. I miss you. Do you miss me?"

"Uh-huh, a little."

That stung Hannah like a hornet. "Are you back at Gina's?"

"Nope. We're still at Aunt Linda's house and we're swimming a lot."

Funny how Cassie had adopted the Romero family's relatives. But then she had very few relatives aside from Danny's parents. For the most part, they didn't count. "Are you sunburned?"

"A little on my nose. I'm gonna get more freckles, right?"

She was somewhat surprised that her daughter sounded almost happy about it. "If you continue to stay in the sun, yes, you probably will."

"Or if I swallow a nickel and break out in pennies."

"Where did you hear that, Cassie?"

"Frank told me. I like Frank. I wish he was my daddy. I mean, I love my daddy in heaven, but I want a real one. Mickey said she'd share him."

Hannah's heart took a little dip in her chest when she recalled how difficult it had been to grow up without a father. At least Cassie knew who her dad was, even if she'd never known him. She also had many pictures of Danny available to look at any time she desired. "Well, honey, maybe someday that might happen."

"Are you gonna marry your prince?"

Cassie sounded so hopeful Hannah hated to burst her fairy-tale bubble. "If you mean Mr. Whittaker, he's a lawyer, not a prince, and he's only my friend."

"But he's really cute and he doesn't have a kid. Everyone should have a kid."

From the mouth of her matchmaking babe.

Hannah heard a background voice calling for Cassie to come on, followed by her daughter saying, "Gotta go, Mama. We're eating pizza!"

"Okay, sweetie, tell Gina that—"

When she heard a click, Hannah checked to see if the call had ended, which it had. The conversation had been too brief for her liking, and too telling, yet she understood Cassie's excitement over being a part of a complete family.

At some point in time, perhaps she could provide that family for her daughter, but she didn't believe it would happen in the foreseeable future. And definitely not with Prince Logan. Though she didn't know the details of his divorce, she sensed he wasn't willing to travel that road again. Regardless, she would enjoy their time together and let whatever happened, happen. Now that she knew Cassie was faring well without her, she wasn't in a rush to head home.

"What is the rush to leave, Logan Whittaker?"

If he answered the question, it would require explaining his houseguest to Marlene Lassiter. And although she was as good as gold, she had a penchant for trying to direct his private life. "I'm just ready to take a shower and prepare for work tomorrow." And get home to a woman who'd weighed on his mind all day long.

She patted her short brown hair before pulling out a chair for him at the dining table in the corner of the kitchen area. "You've got time to eat. I made my famous meat loaf and cornbread."

Logan hadn't realized he was hungry until she'd said the magic words. Nothing like good old country cooking. He hadn't checked in with Hannah yet, so she wasn't expecting him. That didn't discount the fact he was still in a hurry to get home to her. "Do you mind fixing me a plate to go?"

That earned him Marlene's frown as she hovered above him. "Do you have a meeting of some sort?"

"Not exactly."

"Could—wonder of wonders—you have a date?"

If he didn't throw her a bone, she'd keep hounding him. "I have a friend staying with me and I'd like to get in a visit before I go to bed." Among other things.

Marlene smoothed a hand down her full-length apron. "Well then, I'll just make up two plates since I wouldn't want *him* to go hungry."

Damn. He might as well correct the gender issue. "I'm sure *she'll* appreciate it."

Marlene pointed a finger at him. "Aha! I suspected you're harboring a woman."

That sounded like he was holding Hannah against her will. He turned the chair around backward and straddled it. "Before you start getting any wrong notions, she's just a friend."

Marlene walked into the nearby pantry, returned with two paper plates and began dishing out food from the stove. "Are you sure about that friend designation? One of the hands said you seemed distracted, and nothing distracts a man more than a woman."

Double damn. "Just because I temporarily lost one of the heifers that left the herd doesn't mean I was distracted. It happens."

She shot him a backward glance. "It doesn't happen to you. But I'm glad you're finally getting back into the dating scene."

He could set her straight, or let her think what she would. He chose the first option. "Look, I'm handling a legal matter for her. That's why she's here."

After covering the plates with foil, Marlene turned and leaned back against the counter. "Is there potential for it being more than a client-attorney relationship?"

"It might, but I'm not in the market for anything permanent at this point in time." If ever.

"Does she know this, or are you leading her on?"

She had an uncanny knack for seeing right through him. "I'm not going to do anything to hurt her, if that's what's worrying you. Besides, she doesn't strike me as the kind of woman who's looking to nab a husband. Not only is she widowed, she also has a five-year-old daughter to consider."

Marlene frowned. "Have you told her about Grace?"

He should've seen that coming. "You know I don't talk about that with anyone but you, and that's only because you prodded me about my past." After he'd had a few too many during a party she'd hosted that happened to have fallen on Grace's birthday. He'd spent the night on her couch and woken the next morning with a hangover and more than a handful of regrets over baring his soul.

"Maybe you should talk to someone else about her, Logan," she said. "Keeping all that guilt and grief bottled up isn't doing you any good. You can't move forward if you stay stuck in the past."

"I'm not stuck." He tempered his tone, which sounded way too defensive. "I like to keep my private life completely private."

"And if you keep that attitude, you're never going to be happy." She took the chair next to his. "Honey, you're a good man. You have a whole lot to offer the right woman. You can't let yourself get bogged down in mistakes you think you might have made. One day you're going to have to forgive yourself, go on with your life and take a chance on love again."

He *had* made mistakes. Unforgivable mistakes.

"Isn't that the pot-and-kettle thing, Marlene? You never remarried after Charles died."

Marlene turned her wedding band round and round her finger. "No, I didn't. But that doesn't mean I cut myself off from love."

Exactly what he'd assumed, along with everyone else in town. "You mean you and J.D."

"I didn't say that."

She didn't have to. Logan saw the truth in her hazel eyes. He'd also seen something else in her at J.D.'s funeral, that soul-binding sorrow that he'd known all too well. "Come on, Marlene. You lived here with J.D. all those years after you both lost your spouses. No one would fault the two of you for being close."

"He was totally devoted to the kids and Ellie's memory." She sighed. "His wife meant everything to him and he never really got over her."

Which meant Marlene's love could have been one-sided. "Are you going to deny he cared for you, too?"

She shook her head. "No, I'm not, because he did care. But I couldn't compete with his cherished ghost. Regardless, we had some very good times."

That led Logan to believe the pair had been lovers, not that he'd ever request verification. "I tell you what, when you decide to have a serious relationship again, then I'll consider it, too." He figured he was pretty safe with that pact.

Marlene smiled sagely. "You never know what the future holds."

After checking the clock on the wall, Logan came to his feet. "I better get back to the house, otherwise Hannah might not speak to me again."

"Hannah?" she asked, more concern than curiosity in her voice.

"Yeah. Hannah Armstrong. Why?"

She attempted another smile but it fell flat. "Nothing. I've always thought it's a lovely name for a girl."

Logan wasn't buying that explanation, but he didn't have the energy to question her further tonight. He'd set aside some time later and have a long talk with her. Marlene Lassiter's relationship with her brother-in-law could be the key to solving the mystery of Hannah's past.

Yeah, he'd wait a little while before he sought more information from Marlene. If she did hold the answers, then Hannah would no longer have any reason to stay. And he damn sure wasn't ready for her to leave.

She wasn't quite ready to leave the heavenly bath, but when Hannah heard sounds coming from downstairs, she realized the dashing attorney was finally home.

After extracting herself from the jetted tub, she hurriedly dried off and prepared to get ready to greet him. And since she'd had headphones stuck on her ears until a few minutes before, and she hadn't checked her cell for messages in the past hour, she had no idea when Logan had returned.

She quickly dressed in a white tank with built-in bra and black jeans, then had a crisis of confidence and covered the top with a coral-colored, button-down blouse. She brushed her teeth, applied subtle makeup and opted to leave her hair in the loose twist atop her head. Danny had often told her she looked sexy with her hair up…and she really shouldn't be thinking about him while in the home of another man. An undeniably sexy man who'd commandeered her common sense from the moment she'd met him. And that lack of common sense had her slipping the first three buttons on the blouse to reveal the lace-edged tank beneath. An obvious indication of a woman bent on seduction.

Bracing her palms on the vanity, Hannah leaned forward and studied the face in the mirror. The same face that looked back at her every morning. Yep, she looked the same, but she felt very different. Her nerves sang like a canary and she felt as if her skin might take a vacation without her.

What was she thinking? It took a good three months for her and Danny to consummate their relationship. She'd only known Logan for three days. Yet she was older, and wiser, and lonely. She wanted to be in the arms of a man she was beginning to trust. Why she trusted him, she couldn't say. Intuition? Or maybe she was simply so foggy from lust that she wasn't thinking straight at all. That didn't keep her from sliding her feet into a pair of silver sandals and dabbing on perfume when she thought she heard him calling her name.

After rushing out of the bathroom and jogging through the bedroom, Hannah stopped in the hall to catch her breath. Seeming too enthusiastic might lead to misunderstanding. She might be happy to see him. She might be game for a little more serious necking. But she didn't know if she had the courage to go any farther than that.

She took her sweet time walking down the stairs and basically strolled to the great room. When she didn't find Logan there, she entered the kitchen to find it deserted as well. She did discover a pair of boots in the mudroom and his keys hanging on the peg, and detected the sound of the dryer in the adjacent utility room that was about as large as her den back in Boulder. At least she hadn't imagined he'd returned, but maybe she *had* imagined he'd called her.

Determined to locate the missing lawyer, she explored all the rooms he'd shown her, to no avail. That left her with only one uncharted location—his bedroom. She didn't dare go there. If he needed to speak with her, he could come and get her.

Two hours had passed since she'd eaten the ham sandwich, so she retrieved a bottle of water from the fridge and then perused the pantry for some sort of snack. She targeted the bananas hanging on the bronze holder and snapped off the best of the bunch.

Hannah had barely made herself at home on the bar stool when she heard heavy footfalls heading in her direction. The thought of seeing Logan gave her a serious case of goose bumps. When he walked into the kitchen, dressed in only a low-slung navy towel, she thought she'd been thrust into some nighttime soap opera starring a half-naked Hollywood hunk. He had a twelve-pack's worth of ridges defining his torso, a slight shading of hair between his pecs and another thin strip pointing downward to ground zero. Broad shoulders, toned biceps. Oh, boy. Oh, man.

While she sat there like a mime, appropriately clutching a phallic piece of fruit, Logan flashed her his dimpled grin. "You're here."

"You're wearing a towel." Brilliant, Hannah.

He pointed behind her. "I've got clothes in the dryer. I thought maybe you'd gone to bed already."

She noticed what looked to be a red tattoo on his upper right arm, but she couldn't see the details unless she asked him to turn toward her. Right now speaking at all was an effort, and the frontal view couldn't be beat. "It's not even six o'clock. I never go to bed that early."

"Maybe that theory was a stretch, but you didn't answer when I called you. And you didn't respond to my text."

She was surely responding to him now. All over. "I was taking a bath. The jets in the tub were going and I was listening to my MP3 player."

He cocked a hip against a cabinet and crossed his arms over his extremely manly chest. "Did you enjoy the bath?"

Not as much as she was enjoying the view right now. "Yes. Very relaxing. You should try it."

"I've got a big tub in my bathroom, but I'm not a bath kind of guy."

Maybe not, but he was one gorgeous guy. "Most men aren't into taking baths."

"True," he said. "Showers have always suited me better. A lot less effort. Easy in, easy out."

That conjured up images Hannah shouldn't be having. "I prefer showers, too, but I like a good bath now and then."

When he pushed away from the counter, she held her breath. She released it when he started toward the laundry room. "My clothes are probably dry now, so I better get dressed."

Please don't, she wanted to say, but stopped the comment threatening to burst out of her mouth. "Good idea."

The dryer door opened, followed by Logan calling, "If you're hungry, there's a plate of food in the refrigerator Marlene sent with me."

Hannah unpeeled the banana she still had in a death grip. "Thanks, but I've already eaten." She took a large bite of the fruit. Probably too large.

"Did you do any online research today?" he said over the sound of shuffling clothes.

"Yes, I did," she replied, her words muffled due to banana mouth.

"Find anything interesting?"

She swallowed this time before speaking. "Not much other than business articles." And a photo in his drawer that had piqued her interest.

While Hannah finished the fruit fest, Logan returned a few minutes later, fully dressed in beige T-shirt and old jeans. "I have an idea on how we might get some information on J.D.," he said.

She slid off the stool, opened the walk-in pantry and tossed the peel into the trash before facing him again. "What would that be?"

He leaned over the island using his elbows for support. "I'll let you know after I investigate further. It could end up being a dead end."

The man was nothing if not covert in his dealings. Must be the attorney thing—confidentiality at all costs. "Fine. Just let me know if you turn something up."

"I will." He straightened and smiled. "Are you in the mood for a little entertainment?"

She'd already been quite entertained by his recent show of bare flesh. "Sure. What do you suggest we do?"

"Watch a movie in the media room."

Not exactly what she had in mind, but what she'd been envisioning wouldn't be wise. "I'm all for a movie. Lead the way."

Six

Logan had chosen the lone theater chair built for two, along with a shoot-'em-up suspense film. But he hadn't bargained for the racy sex scene that came during the movie's first fifteen minutes.

He glanced to his right at Hannah, who had a piece of popcorn poised halfway to her mouth, her eyes wide as wagon wheels. "Wow. What is this rated?"

"R, but I thought that was due to the violence factor."

She popped a kernel into her mouth and swallowed. "I can't believe he didn't take off the shoulder holster when he dropped his pants. What if the gun goes off?"

"It does give a whole new meaning to 'cocked and ready.'" And he might have gone a bit too far with the crudeness.

Surprisingly, she released a soft, sultry laugh. "Ha, ha. It's hard for me to imagine a man taking a woman in an alley in broad daylight, gun or no gun."

That didn't exactly surprise him. "Anything's possible when you want someone bad enough." Exactly how he felt at the moment.

She tipped the red-striped box toward him. "Want some of this?"

His current appetite didn't include popcorn. "No thanks."

As the on-screen bumping and grinding continued, Logan draped his arm over the back of the seat, his hand resting on Hannah's shoulder. When he rubbed slow circles on her upper arm, she shifted closer to his side and laid her palm on his thigh. If she knew what was happening a little north of her hand, she might think twice about leaving it there. And if the damn movie didn't return to the run-and-gun scenes real soon, no telling what he might do.

No telling what *Hannah* might do was his immediate thought when she briefly nuzzled his neck, then brushed a kiss across his cheek. His second thought... the cheek kiss wasn't enough.

Logan tipped Hannah's face toward him and brought her mouth to his, intending only to kiss her once before going back to the film that fortunately now focused on the suspense plot. But the lengthy sex scene had obviously ignited the sparks between them, and from that point forward, everything began to move at an accelerated pace.

They made out like two teenagers on a curfew to the sounds of gunfire and cursing. He couldn't seem to get close enough to Hannah and that prompted him to pull her up onto his lap. He wound his hands through her hair and continued to kiss her like there was no tomorrow.

With Hannah's legs straddling his thighs, the contact was way too intimate for Logan to ignore. Every time she moved, he grew as hard as a hammer. To make matters worse, she broke the kiss, rose up and pulled away the band securing her lopsided ponytail. Obviously she was testing his sanity when she unbuttoned her blouse, slipped it off and tossed it aside, leaving her dressed in a thin tank top that left little to the imagination.

Seeing her sitting there with her tousled auburn hair falling to her shoulders, her lips slightly swollen and her green eyes centered on his, Logan's strength went the way of the popcorn that had somehow ended up on the floor. And just when he'd thought she was done with the surprises, she slid the straps off her shoulders and lowered the top.

He'd dimmed the lights before he'd cued the movie, but he could still make out the details. Incredible details. Unbelievable, in fact. Too tempting to not touch. That's exactly what he did—touched both her breasts lightly while watching her reaction. When Hannah tipped her head back and exhaled a shaky breath, Logan personally found it hard to breathe at all, and even harder not to take it further.

Pressing his left palm against her back, he nudged her forward and replaced his right hand with his mouth. Logan circled his tongue around one pale pink nipple, drawing out Hannah's soft groan. When he paid equal attention to her other breast, she shifted restlessly against his fly. If she didn't stop soon, it would be all over but the moaning. He damn sure didn't want to stop completely. He had a perfectly good bed at their disposal…and a perfectly good reason to halt the insanity before he couldn't. She deserved better than a quick roll in a chair, and he had no condoms available.

On that thought, he returned Hannah to the seat beside him and leaned back to stare at the soundproof ceiling while his respiration returned to normal.

"What was that?" Hannah asked, her voice somewhat hoarse.

Logan straightened to find her perched on the edge of the seat. Fortunately she'd pulled her top back into place, otherwise he wouldn't be able to concentrate. "That was uncontrollable lust."

"And, might I add, two adults acting like oversexed sixteen-year-olds," she said. "All we need now is to climb into the backseat of your car and have at it."

He didn't need to entertain that notion, but damned if he wasn't. "Hey, it happens."

"Not to me," she said. "I have never, ever been that bold."

He liked her boldness. A lot. "Not even with your husband?"

"Not really. We were both young when we met, and not very adventurous."

Interesting. "What about the men before him?"

Her gazed faltered for a moment. "Danny was my first. There wasn't anyone before him and there hasn't been anyone since."

Man, he hadn't predicted that. She kissed like someone who'd been around the block. Apparently she was a natural, even if she was somewhat of a novice. "Had I known that, I would've stopped sooner."

She frowned. "Why?"

"Because I don't want to do anything you don't want to do."

This time she released a cynical laugh. "I would think it's fairly obvious I wanted to do what I did, or I wouldn't have done it."

"Neither of us was thinking clearly." But he sure was now.

"Probably not, but since we're both consenting adults, I certainly don't consider our behavior shameful by any stretch of the imagination."

"I'm not sure I'm ready for this." He'd heard those words before, but never coming out of his own mouth.

Hannah looked perplexed. "Excuse me?"

He leaned forward, draped his elbows on his parted knees and focused on the popcorn-riddled carpet. "I'm not sure this is the right thing for either of us. More important, I don't want to hurt you, Hannah."

She touched his shoulder, garnering his attention. "I'm a big girl, Logan. I don't have any wild expectations of happily-ever-after. I want to feel desired by a man I can trust to treat me well. I know that man is you."

Yet she didn't know what he'd been concealing from her. She didn't know the demons still chasing after him. And she had no idea that his feelings for her were going beyond animal attraction.

He needed time to think. He needed to get away from her in order to keep his libido from prevailing over logic. Being the second man in her life would be a big burden to bear. He'd gained skill as a lover through experience, but he sucked when it came to the possible emotional fallout. If they continued on this course, they would only grow closer, and she might begin to have expectations he couldn't meet, regardless of what she'd said about not having any.

For that reason, he grabbed the remote from the adjacent chair, turned off the movie and stood. "I have an early day tomorrow and I'm pretty tired. We'll continue this discussion later."

Hannah stood and propped both hands on her hip. "That's it? You're going to run out on me without explaining why you've suddenly gone from hot to cold?"

He couldn't explain unless he made a few revelations that he wasn't prepared to make at this point. "I have some thinking to do, Hannah, and I can't do it with you in the same room."

"Suit yourself," she said as she moved past him and headed toward the exit.

He couldn't let her leave without telling her one important fact. "Hannah."

She turned at the door, anger glimmering in her eyes. "What?"

"I just don't want you to have any regrets."

"I don't," she said. "But I'm beginning to think you do."

Logan only regretted he might not be the man she needed. The man she deserved. And he had to take that out and examine it later before he made one huge error in judgment.

For the past two days, Hannah had barely seen Logan. He'd left for work before she'd awakened, and returned well after she'd retired to her room. She'd whiled away the lonely hours researching her possible family until she was certain her eyes might be permanently crossed. Her only human contact had come in the form of Logan's fiftysomething housekeeper,

Molly, who'd been extremely accommodating, right down to preparing meals in advance.

Of course, on several occasions she had spoken to Cassie, who had reinforced that she was having the time of her life with her best friend. Out of sight, out of mind, Hannah realized, at least when it came to her daughter and the attorney. And that hurt.

But after spending the morning in the public library perusing archived newspapers, Hannah had the perfect excuse to seek out Logan. She'd intentionally dressed in her professional best—a white sleeveless silk blouse, charcoal-colored skirt and black three-inch heeled sandals that Gina had fondly termed "do-me shoes." Hopefully she wasn't wasting those on a possible lost cause named Logan.

She didn't bother to call ahead before she arrived at the Drake, Alcott and Whittaker law firm located not far from the library. After playing tug-of-war with the strong Wyoming wind for control of the heavy wood door, she simply marched up to the very young, very pretty brunette receptionist and presented her best smile. "I need to see Mr. Whittaker please."

The young woman eyed Hannah suspiciously. "Do you have an appointment?"

She finger-combed her gale-blown hair back into place as best she could without a brush. "No, I don't. But I'm sure if you'll give him my name, he'll see me." If luck prevailed.

"What *is* your name?" the receptionist asked, sounding as if she believed Hannah might be some crazed stalker.

"It's Ms. Armstrong. Hannah Armstrong."

"Just a moment please." She picked up the phone and

pressed a button. "Mr. Whittaker, there's a Ms. Armstrong here and she... Of course. I'll send her right in." She replaced the phone and finally put on a pleasant demeanor. "His office is down the hall to your right, the second door on the left."

"Thank you."

Hannah traveled down the corridor with a spring in her step, feeling somewhat vindicated, until she realized she probably looked a whole lot disheveled. She paused long enough to open her bag for the appropriate tools, then brushed her hair and applied some lip gloss before continuing on to Logan's office. A brass plate etched with his name hung on the closed door, but the raised blinds covering the glass windows lining the hallway gave her a prime view of Logan, who happened to be on the phone.

She wasn't sure whether to wait until he hung up, or barge in. She opted to wait, until Logan caught her glance and gestured at her to come in.

Hannah stepped into the office, closed the door behind her and chose the chair across from the large mahogany desk. In an attempt not to appear to be eavesdropping, she surveyed the office while Logan continued his conversation. She had three immediate impressions—massive, masculine and minimalist. Neutral colors with dark blue accents, including the sofa and matching visitors' chairs. Blue-and-white-tiled fireplace with a barren mantel. A few modern Western paintings. Overall, a nice place to visit, but she wouldn't care to work there. The whole area could use some warming up.

Hannah couldn't say the same for herself. Seeing the sexy attorney dressed in coat and tie, his dark hair combed to perfection, his large hand gripping the phone, she had grown quite warm.

He seemed to be listening more than speaking until he finally said, "I understand, Mom, and I promise to do better with the calls. Tell Dad to stop giving you grief, and I'll talk to you next week. I love you, too." He then hung up and sent her a somewhat sheepish grin. "Sorry about that."

"I think it's nice you're close to your mother." The kind of relationship she'd wanted with hers, but never really had. "Are you an only child?"

"Actually, no," he said. "I have an older sister. She and her husband are both geologists living in Alaska with their five kids."

That could explain the picture in his desk drawer. "Wow. Five kids, huh?"

He grabbed a pen and began to turn it over and over. "Yeah. All boys."

She could have sworn that the baby in the photo she'd found in the desk had been a girl. "I suppose when you live somewhere as cold as Alaska, you have to find creative ways to keep warm."

"True, but constant procreating seems pretty extreme to me."

Hannah let out a laugh, but it died on her lips when she noticed his obvious uneasiness. "I was hoping you might introduce me to some more Lassiters."

He loosened his tie, a sure sign of discomfort. "It's been crazy busy around here."

Like she really believed that after he'd told her his schedule happened to be light this week. "Are you sure you haven't been avoiding me?"

He turned his attention back to the pen. "Not intentionally. I'm sorry that I haven't spent much time with you."

So was she. "Anyway, that's not exactly why I'm here. I came upon something at the library this morning that I found interesting." She dug through her bag and withdrew the copy of the archived article, then slid it across the desk. "This is a picture of J.D. and his brother, Charles, at a rodeo here in Cheyenne over thirty years ago. Charles won the roping competition."

Logan studied it a few moments before regarding Hannah again. "And?"

She reached across the desk and pointed at the text below the photo. "Look at the list of winners."

Logan scanned the text before looking up, sheer surprise in his expression. "Your mother was a barrel racer?"

"Yes, she was, but she gave it up after I was born." Only one more thing Ruth had blamed on her daughter. "Now I'm wondering if she met J.D. through his brother during one of these competitions."

Logan seemed to mull that over for a moment. "I planned to question Marlene Lassiter about J.D.'s past. They were very close, so she might know something about an affair."

"I'd appreciate that, Logan." She would also appreciate a better explanation for his behavior the other night in the media room. "Now that we've settled this matter, we do need to move on to our other issue."

"What issue would that be?"

She refused to let him play dumb. "The one involving our attraction to each other, and your concerns that I don't know my own mind."

"Hannah, I'm worried that—"

"I'll have regrets…I know. You're worried I'm going to get hurt. But as I told you during our last conversation, I don't have any expectations. I don't need poetry or candy or any promises. I only want to enjoy your company while I'm here, whatever that might involve."

"I don't want to do anything to hurt you."

Time to set him straight. "I'm not some fragile little flower who needs to be sheltered from life, both the good and the bad."

"I never thought of you as fragile, Hannah. But you have to know that I'm not in the market to settle down and have a family."

How well she understood that. "Fine. I get that. I'll hold off on picking out the engagement ring. Now I have a question for you."

"Shoot."

She scooted to the edge of her chair and stared at him straight on. "Do you still want me?"

He tossed the pen aside. "You really have to ask that?"

"Yes, and I want an answer."

When he rolled the chair back and stood, Hannah expected one of two things—Logan was going to kiss her, or show her to the door. Instead, he walked to a control panel mounted on the wall, pushed a button and lowered the electronic blinds, securing their complete privacy. Then he moved in front of her chair, clasped her wrists to pull her into his arms and delivered a kiss so soft and sensual, she thought her knees might not hold her. As if he sensed her dilemma, he turned her around and lifted her onto the desk.

Her skirt rode up too high to be considered ladylike, but frankly she didn't care. She was too focused on the feel of Logan's palms on her thighs, the strokes of his thumbs on the inside of her legs that seemed timed with the silken glide of his tongue against hers. *Higher,* she wanted to tell him. *Please,* she almost pleaded. But before she could voice her requests, he broke the kiss.

"Are you convinced I still want you, Hannah?"

This time she decided to play dumb in hopes he'd make more attempts at persuading her. "Almost."

"Maybe this will help." He took her palm and pressed it against his erection, showing her clear evidence of his need.

"I'm convinced." And veritably panting.

He placed her hand back into her lap. "Do you know what I really want right now?"

Hopefully the same thing she wanted—for him to have his very wicked way with her on top of his desk. "Do tell."

"Lunch."

Clearly the man was bent on driving her straight into oblivion. "Are you serious?"

Logan lifted her off the desk and set her on her feet. "Dead serious. There's a café right down the street that serves great burgers where we can eat and talk. I've been meaning to take you there."

Hannah wanted him to just take her. Now. But a talk was definitely warranted. She sent a pointed look in the direction of his fly. "Are you sure you're up to it? Oh, wait. Obviously you are."

He let go a boisterous laugh. "You'll need to walk in front of me for a few minutes. Just don't shake your butt."

Oh, how tempting to do that very thing. Instead, she picked up her purse and took her time applying more lip gloss. After she popped the cap back on and dropped the tube into her bag, she smiled. "Are you recovered now?"

"Enough to retain my dignity, so let's get out of here before I change my mind, lock the door and tell Priscilla to hold all calls while I hold you captive for a few more hours."

"Promises, promises," Hannah teased as they walked into the hall and started toward the lobby.

When they rounded the corner, an attractive sixty-something, brown-haired woman wearing a tasteful red tailored coat dress, nearly ran head-on into Hannah. "I'm so sorry, honey," she said. "I shouldn't be in such a hurry."

"You're always in a hurry, Marlene."

She patted Logan's cheek and smiled. "Not any more than you are, young man. Particularly the other evening when you rushed out of my house like your hair was on fire."

Hannah sent a quick glance at Logan, then returned her attention to the first Lassiter she'd encountered thus far.

Logan moved behind Hannah and braced his palms on her shoulders. "Hannah, this is Marlene Lassiter. Marlene, Hannah Armstrong."

The woman gave her an odd look before she formed a tentative smile and offered her hand. "It's nice to finally meet you."

Hannah accepted the brief shake, but she couldn't quite accept that the woman found the situation nice at all. "And it's a pleasure to finally meet you, too. Logan has told me a lot of good things about you."

"Well, you can't believe everything he says," Marlene added with a sincere smile directed at Logan.

"Were you here to see me, Marlene?" Logan asked.

"No," she said. "I'm having lunch with Walter, provided he's ready to go. The man still works like a field hand when he should be considering retirement."

The sparkle in Marlene's eyes, and the telling comment, led Hannah to believe the couple must know each other beyond any business arrangements. "I suppose that comes with the territory."

Marlene fiddled with the diamond necklace at her throat. "Yes, I suppose it does. And I better see if I can hurry him along."

"Again, it's nice to meet you," Hannah said as Marlene hurried past them.

"You, too, Hannah," she said over one shoulder before disappearing into the office at the end of the hall.

Hannah and Logan remained silent until they exited and stepped foot onto the sidewalk, where Logan turned to Hannah. "I suspect there's a story there with Walter and Marlene."

Considering Marlene's uneasy expression when they met, Hannah wondered if the woman might actually know the story of her life.

Before Logan could open the glass door to the Wild Grouse Café, a brown-haired man walked out, blocking the path. At first he didn't recognize him, until he realized the guy happened to be a client, a premiere chef, and the second Lassiter he'd encountered that day. "Are you checking out the competition, Dylan?"

"Hey, Logan," he said with a smile as he shook Logan's offered hand. "Actually, I grabbed a bite here because it's still one of the best eateries in town, at least until the grand opening of our newest restaurant. I've barely had time to eat since I've been working on grabbing some good press for this venture to circumvent the bad press over the will dispute."

Bad press compliments of Dylan's sister, Angelica. "I hear you on the bad press, and finding time to eat. I'm actually going to have lunch for a change."

"So they do let you out of the law cage?"

"It happens now and then." When he remembered Hannah was behind him, he caught her arm and drew her forward. "Dylan, this is Hannah Armstrong. Hannah, this is Dylan Lassiter, CEO of the Lassiter Grill Corporation, a veritable restaurant empire."

Dylan grinned. "Pleased to meet you. And where have you been hiding her out, Whittaker?"

"I'm his maid," Hannah said as she returned his smile.

Dylan frowned. "Seriously?"

Leave it to Hannah to throw out a comeback, but then he'd really begun to appreciate her easy wit. "She's a teacher during the day."

"And Logan actually moonlights as a plumber," she said.

They exchanged a smile and a look over their inside joke, interrupted by Dylan clearing his throat. "Logan, as a word of warning, I just had lunch with my sister. She's still loaded for bear over the will, in case you want to reconsider and find somewhere else to dine."

Great. Another Lassiter, and this one wasn't going to be pleasant. "I can handle Angelica." As long as he used kid gloves. He just hoped she wasn't wearing boxing gloves.

Dylan slapped him on the back. "Good luck, Whittaker. And it was damn good to see you again. Nice to meet you, too, Hannah."

After Dylan rushed away, Logan escorted Hannah into the restaurant and walked up to the hostess stand to request a table. He glanced across the crowded dining room and immediately spotted Angelica Lassiter sitting alone, wearing a white tailored business suit and a major scowl. Unfortunately, she spotted him as well. Too late to turn tail and run, he realized, when she slid out of the booth and approached him at a fast clip.

She bore down on him like a Texas tornado, her dark hair swaying and brown eyes flashing. "Logan Whittaker, you didn't return my last call."

An intentional oversight, not that he'd tell her. "I've been busy, Angelica, and you should address all questions regarding the will to Walter."

"Walter won't listen to me," she said. "He keeps saying there's nothing I can do to change the paltry percentage of Lassiter Media I inherited and I should learn to live with the fact Evan controls the majority of the shares, and the voting power that affords him. I still can't believe Daddy did this to me."

Frankly, neither could Logan. Nor could he believe how Angelica, a strong, independent businesswoman, reportedly the spitting image of her mother, could sound so much like a lost little girl. "I'm sure he had his reasons, and I know they don't seem logical or fair. All I can say is hang in there."

This time Hannah stepped forward on her own volition. "Hi, I'm Hannah Armstrong, a friend of Logan's."

Angelica gave Hannah's offered hand a gentle shake and presented a pleasant smile. "It's truly a pleasure to meet one of Logan's friends. Perhaps we can have dinner at some point in time."

"I'd like that." And she would, for reasons she

couldn't even reveal—namely this woman could actually be her sister.

Angelica turned back to Logan. "I'm asking you as a friend to talk to Walter and see if I can somehow contest the will. That company should be mine, not Evan's." And with that she was gone as quickly as she'd come, fortunately for Logan and for Hannah.

Once they were seated across from each other in the booth Angelica had just vacated, Hannah folded her hands on the table before her. "What were the odds I'd meet two of J.D.'s offspring in one day?"

Slim to none. "Now that you have met them, what do you think?"

She seemed to mull over that query for a minute. "Well, Dylan seemed nice enough, and so did Angelica, although she did seem pretty angry. I assume it had something to do with the breakup and that will dispute that I came across in a newspaper article. Am I right?"

He wasn't at liberty to hand her all the dirty details. "That's part of it. But just so you know, she's actually a very nice woman. Smart and savvy and she spends a lot of time involved in charity work."

"Don't forget she's very pretty," Hannah added.

"Yeah, you could say that." And he'd probably said too much.

"Have you dated her?" Hannah asked, confirming his conjecture.

"No. She's ten years younger and not my type."

She braced her bent elbow on the table and propped her cheek on her palm, reminding him of that first night they'd had dinner together. "Exactly what is your type?"

Hard to say, other than she seemed to be fitting the

bill just fine. "Keen intelligence, a nice smile. Green eyes. And most important, a smart-ass sense of humor."

Hannah leaned back and laid a dramatic hand above her heart. "I do declare, Mr. Whittaker. You sure have high standards."

He narrowed his eyes. "And you're getting a Texas accent."

"I wonder why." She went from smiling to serious in less than a heartbeat. "It's really hard for me to believe the people I met today could be my half siblings. And it makes me angry that my mother withheld vital information years ago, preventing me from making my own decision whether or not to connect with them."

If she only knew the vital information he'd been withholding from her, she wouldn't be too thrilled with him, either. But little by little, he'd begun to think he could trust her enough to tell her about his own sorry past. Eventually. "If you did decide to sign the nondisclosure, you'd never have a chance to get to know them. And since you're determined not to sign it, you really should give getting to know them a shot."

Hannah pondered that statement for a few moments before speaking again. "That's an option I'm not ready to explore. And signing the nondisclosure waiver would be the price I'd pay if I claimed my inheritance."

He wondered if she'd come to her senses and changed her mind. "Are you reconsidering taking the money?"

She shook her head. "No. Although it's tempting, I still don't feel I can claim it in good conscience, or sign the nondisclosure. Knowing the annuity will be turned over to charity does make my decision much easier."

She didn't sound all that convincing to Logan. "You

still have some time to think it through before you have to leave." And he wasn't looking forward to her leaving, though he had no right whatsoever to ask her to stay.

After finishing their food, they engaged in casual conversation, covering movies and music they liked, before their discussion turned to Hannah's child. Logan listened intently while Hannah verbally demonstrated her devotion to her daughter. Not a day had gone by when he hadn't thought about his own daughter, Gracie, and what she would look like now at age twelve. If she'd be chasing boys, or chasing cows with her grandpa. If she'd be smart as a whip like her mom, and love all things horses like him. The signs had pointed to that equine love, but he'd never known for sure, and never would. Gracie had only ridden Lucy one time, and that was a shame on many counts. A mare that willing and able and gentle should be ridden more often....

"Did I lose you somewhere, Logan?"

His thoughts scattered and disappeared after Hannah made the inquiry. "Sorry. I just came up with a really good idea." And he had. A banner idea.

"What would that be?" she asked.

He stood, held out his hand and helped her out of the booth. "I'm going to take the rest of the day off and we're going to have some fun."

"What, pray tell, do you have in mind, Mr. Whittaker?"

"Sweetheart, we're going to take a long, long ride."

Seven

This wasn't at all what Hannah expected when Logan mentioned going for a ride. She'd envisioned satin sheets and afternoon delight in his bedroom that she had yet to see. She *hadn't* expected to be sitting atop a plodding mare that kept stopping to graze as they headed toward the creek.

"You're doing fairly well for someone who hasn't been on a horse for a while."

She shot him a withering look. "Remind me of that when I have a sore butt for the next few days."

Logan's rich, deep laugh echoed across the pastureland. "Nothing a good soak in the tub won't cure. Or a massage."

"Know a good massage therapist?"

That question brought a frown to Logan's face. "Why would you need one when you have me?"

Her day suddenly brightened significantly, along with the sun. "Are you good at giving massages?"

"So I've been told."

She didn't care to ask who had told him. "That's nice to know in case I do need your services."

He winked. "Oh, you're going to need them all right. And I promise you're going to enjoy them."

"I'm counting on you to make good on that promise." And counting on herself not to let her heart get tangled up in him. Of course, that would be easier said than done.

They continued to ride in companionable silence, and after traveling over most the surrounding land, Logan finally dismounted in one smooth move a little farther away from where they'd stood the other night. Hannah did the same with much less poise, grabbed the reins and tugged a single-minded Lucy in Logan's direction before the mare launched into another grass attack. "Why did we stop?"

Logan guided the gelding to the gate opening up to the pasture that led to the creek. "I want to show you another special place."

"Good," Hannah replied. "My bottom was just about to give out."

After leading the horses through the gate, Logan turned and closed it, then said, "Let Lucy go for now."

As predicted, the mare went to the nearest clump of grass. "She's a regular chow hound."

"She needs to be ridden more often," Logan said as he detached a rolled blanket from the back of his saddle and tucked it beneath his left arm. "We can take another ride this weekend on my nearest neighbor's property. He has a larger spread and he told me to feel free to use it anytime."

Hannah's spirits plummeted when she realized she was set to leave in three days. "I plan to go home on Saturday."

He clasped her hand in his and gave it a gentle squeeze. "You can stay until Sunday."

She just might at that. One more day wouldn't matter to Cassie. If anything, her daughter might be disappointed to see her if it meant going back to her normal routine. "We'll see."

Logan guided her down the incline a hundred yards or so from the fence and stopped beneath a cottonwood tree not far from the narrow creek. He released her hand to spread the blanket over the ground. "I've been known to come here to think."

Hannah looked around the area, amazed at the absolute quiet. "It does seem to be a good place to clear your head."

"Among other things."

She turned to see Logan had already planted himself on the blanket, removed his boots and reserved a space beside him. "Take off your shoes and take a load off," he said.

She really wanted to remove more than her shoes. More like her clothes. And his. It had now been confirmed—she could star in her own made-for-TV movie about a very bad girl titled *Hannah and Her Outrageous Hormones*.

After she toed out of her sneakers, she dropped down next to Logan as a little flurry of butterfly nerves flitted around in her belly. "So are we going to meditate now?"

Logan's eyes appeared to grow darker in the shade, and undeniably more intense. "That's up to you."

With that, he brought her down onto the blanket in his arms, where she rested her head on his chest. They stayed that way for a time, the sound of his heart beating softly in Hannah's ear, his arm stroking her shoulder back and forth in a soothing rhythm.

She lifted her head to find him staring at the overhead branches. "Dollar for your thoughts. To account for inflation."

His smile made a short-lived appearance before he turned sullen again. "I was thinking how quickly life can change in one moment."

Hannah returned her head to his chest. "I know that all too well. One day you're sending the man you married off to work, the next you learn you'll never see him again."

"What exactly happened to him?" he asked. "If you don't mind talking about it."

She didn't mind, at least not now. "He was rewiring a commercial building that was under renovation and something went wrong. After the electrocution, they rushed him to the hospital and tried everything they could to save him, but it was too late."

"Does anyone know what went wrong now?"

"At first the insurance company claimed Danny was at fault, but his coworkers said he did everything he should have been doing in accordance with the wiring diagram. So they offered me a two-hundred-thousand-dollar settlement and I took it."

"You should have sued them."

Spoken like an attorney. "With a baby on the way and a new mortgage, I couldn't afford to ride it out, possibly for years, or risk losing the suit and ending up with nothing. Danny had a small insurance policy, but it barely covered funeral expenses, let alone any hospital bills I incurred after having Cassie."

"And your mother couldn't help out financially?"

A cynical laugh slipped out before she could stop it. "She always acted as if she didn't have a dime. However, she gifted us the down payment on our house out of the blue. I was able to repay her in a manner of speaking when I took care of her after her cancer diagnosis."

"You did that and attended school?" he asked, his voice somewhat incredulous.

"She only lasted two more months during the summer, so I wasn't in school." Hannah thought back to that time and the bittersweet memories. "Funny, I always felt as if I'd been a burden to her because she was so unhappy and bitter. Yet the day before she died, she told me thank you, and said she loved me. I don't recall her telling me that the entire time I was growing up. She was never the demonstrative type."

He released a rough sigh. "I can't imagine a parent not telling a child they loved them. But maybe she was so consumed by anger over being jilted by your father, she couldn't see what a gift she had in you."

Hannah's heart panged in her chest. "I don't know about being a gift, but I tried my best to be a good girl so I could win her approval. Unfortunately it never seemed to be enough."

He gave her a gentle squeeze. "As hard as it was, her attitude probably made you a stronger person. Definitely a good person. One of the best I've met in a long time."

He was saying all the right things, and he'd said

them with sincerity. "You're kind of remarkable yourself."

"Don't kid yourself, Hannah. I'm just an average guy who's made more than my share of mistakes."

Those mystery mistakes he had yet to reveal, leaving Hannah's imagination wide open. "Haven't we all screwed up a time or two, Logan? You just have to learn from those mistakes and move on. And eventually you have to stop blaming yourself for your shortcomings. That was fairly hard for me."

"Why were you blaming yourself?"

She truly hated to drudge that up, but soul-cleansing seemed to be the order of the day. "The morning Danny died, I got on him about leaving his shoes on the living room floor and missing the clothes hamper. I should have said I loved him, but the last words he heard from me had to do with cleanliness. I can count on one hand the times I didn't say I loved him before he left for work."

He brushed a kiss over her forehead. "You had no way of knowing he wouldn't be coming home."

If only she had known. "I finally acknowledged that, but it didn't lessen the guilt for a long time. If it hadn't been for Gina verbally kicking my butt, I might still not be over it."

"She's a good friend, huh?"

The very best and one of the few people she'd trust with her child. "Yes, she is. Granted, she does like to throw out advice whether I ask or not."

"How does she feel about you being here with me?"

She thought it best to hand him the abridged version. "Oh, she's all for it. In fact, if she'd had her way, we would've been having wild monkey sex from the minute I walked through your door."

"That would've worked for me."

She looked up to see his grin and poked him in the side. "That's rich coming from the guy who left me high and dry in his home theater."

"Believe me, that wasn't an easy decision."

Revelation time. "Just so you know, the way you make me feel…well…I thought I might never feel that way again."

He tipped her chin up and said, "That's my goal right now, to make you—" he kissed her forehead "—feel—" he kissed her cheek "—real good."

When Logan finally moved to her mouth, all Hannah's pent-up desire seemed to come out in that kiss, a hot meeting of tastes and tongues and mingled breath. Soon they were not only lip-to-lip, but also facing each other body-to-body until Logan nudged Hannah onto her back. He kissed the side of her neck as he slid his calloused hand beneath her T-shirt, at first breezing up her rib cage until he found her breasts. When he kissed her thoroughly again, he also circled her nipple with his fingertip through the lacy bra, and she reacted with an involuntary movement of her hips. Dampness began to gather in a place too long neglected, and she felt as if she might spontaneously combust due to the heat his touch was generating.

Her breathing, as well as her pulse, sped up as he skimmed his palm down her belly. She would swear her respiration stopped when he slipped the button on her jeans and then slid the zipper down.

Logan left her lips and softly said, "Lift up," and when Hannah answered his command, he pushed her pants down to her thighs, leaving her brand-new, leopard-skin panties intact.

For a few minutes, he seemed determined to keep her in suspended animation, toying with the lace band below her navel without sliding his hand inside the silk, no matter how badly Hannah wanted it. He finally streamed a fingertip between her thighs and sent it in a back-and-forth motion. He knew exactly how and where to touch her, but he only continued a brief time before he took his hand away. She responded with a somewhat embarrassing groan of protest, yet she soon discovered she had nothing to complain about when Logan worked her panties down to join her jeans.

From that moment forward, every bit of her surroundings seemed to disappear. The only sound she heard happened to be Logan whispering sensual words in her ear about what he wanted to do to her, what she was doing to him right then. Some of the comments could be considered crude, but she regarded them as the sexiest phrases she'd ever heard. He knew all the right buttons to push and, boy, did he push them well. The pressure began to mount, bringing with it pure pleasure on the heels of an impending climax, compliments of Logan's gentle, right-on-target strokes. And when the orgasm hit all too soon, Hannah inadvertently dug her nails into his upper arm and battled a scream bubbling up from her throat.

She'd never been a screamer. She'd never been in a pasture with her pants down around her knees either, being tended to by one outrageously gorgeous, sexy guy who knew exactly how to treat a woman.

Hannah was suddenly consumed by the overwhelming need to have him inside her. Yet when she reached for his fly, he clasped her wrist to stop her. "Not here," he said. "Not now. This was all for you."

She focused on his beautiful face, the deep indentations framing his mouth. "But—"

"It's okay, sweetheart. I'm going to be fine until we get back to the house."

She lifted her head slightly, with effort, to look at him. "What are we going to do when we get there?"

"I'm going to show you my bed." He favored her with a grin. "That is, if you want to see it."

Who was he kidding? "I seriously thought you would never ask."

Logan could have gone with spontaneity, but he wanted this first time between them to be special. More importantly, he needed Hannah to know she meant more to him than a quick roll on the ground, instant gratification, then over and out. She'd begun to mean more to him than she probably should.

Taking her by the hand, he led her into the master bedroom and closed the door behind them, determined to shut out the world and any lingering reservations.

Hannah remained silent when he tossed back the covers then guided her to the side of the bed. "Take off your shoes." And that would be the last thing she'd remove by herself if he had any say in the matter, which he did.

While she sat on the edge of the bed and took off her sneakers, he sat in the adjacent chair to pull off his boots. Once that was done, he lifted her from the bed and back onto her bare feet. He saw absolute trust in her eyes after he pulled the T-shirt over her head and tossed it aside. He noticed some self-consciousness in her expression as he removed her bra, and unmistakable heat when he slid her jeans and panties to the floor. She braced one hand on his shoulder for balance as she stepped out of the remaining clothes, a slight blush on her cheeks when he swept her up and laid her on the bed.

The sun streamed in from the open curtains covering the windows facing the pasture, casting Hannah's beautiful body in a golden glow. He needed to touch her. Had to touch her. But first things first.

Her gaze didn't waver as Logan stripped off his shirt, but she did home in on the ink etched in his upper arm. He'd have to explain that later. Right then he had more pressing issues. After shoving down his jeans and boxer-briefs, he opened the nightstand drawer, withdrew a packet and tossed it onto his side of the bed. He returned his attention to Hannah, who looked more than a little interested in his erection, her eyes wide with wonder.

She caught his glance and smiled. "I didn't realize you were that happy to see me."

Happier than he'd been in a long, long time. "I'm ecstatic to be here."

"So am I."

Relieved to hear that confirmation, Logan claimed the empty space beside Hannah and remained on his knees to allow better access. As he slid his fingertip between her breasts, pausing to circle each nipple, then moved down her torso, Hannah's breath caught. And when he replaced his hand with his mouth to retrace his path, he would swear she stopped breathing altogether.

When it came to sex, the advantage always went to women—they required little to no recovery time. And although his own body screamed for release, he was bent on proving that fact.

Logan nudged her legs apart to make a place for himself, then planted a kiss right below her navel. He didn't linger there long because he had somewhere more interesting to go. An intimate place that needed tending. When his mouth hit home, Hannah jerked from the impact. But he didn't let up, using his tongue to tease her into another climax. And as far as he could tell, this one was stronger than the last, apparent when she dug her nails even deeper into his shoulder.

He'd waited as long as physically possible to make love to her completely, and that sent him onto his back to reach for the condom. In a real big hurry, he tore the packet open with his teeth and had it in place in record time. He moved over her, eased inside her and called up every ounce of control to savor the feel of her surrounding him.

He'd learned long ago how to take a woman to the limits, but he also learned how to shelter his emotions in recent years. His sexual partners—and they'd been very few and far between—had been a means to an end. No commitments. No promises. Only mutual physical satisfaction. Up to that moment, he hadn't realized how empty his life had become. Until Hannah.

He minimized his movements as he held her closely. He wanted it to last, if not forever, at least a little while longer. But nature had other ideas, and the orgasm crashed down on him with the force of a hurricane.

Logan couldn't remember the last time he'd shaken so hard, or the last time his heart had beaten so fast. He sure as hell couldn't recall wanting to remain that way for the rest of the day, in the arms of someone he'd known for such a short while. But at times, he'd felt as if he'd known Hannah for years.

When she moved slightly beneath him and sighed, he took that as a cue his weight might be getting to her. But after he shifted over onto his back, she asked, "Where are you going?"

He slid his arm beneath her and brought her against his side. "I'm still here, Hannah."

She rose up and traced one half of the broken-heart tattoo on his upper arm, etched with an *A* on one side, and a *G* on the other. "Are these your ex-wife's initials?"

He'd expected that question, and he decided on a half-truth. "No. They belong to a girl I used to know." His baby girl.

She rested her cheek on his chest, right above his heart, which was pounding for a different reason now. "She must have been very special, and I'm sorry she broke your heart."

After another span of silence passed, Logan thought she'd fallen asleep. She proved him wrong when she asked, "You've never really considered having children of your own?"

Alarm bells rang in his head. "I'm not cut out for fatherhood."

She raised her head again and stared at him. "How could you possibly know that if you haven't even tried it? Or do you just not like kids?"

"I like kids a lot. They're way the hell more honest than adults. But it takes more than liking a child to raise them right."

She settled back on the pillow. "I personally think you'd be good at it, for what it's worth."

In a moment of clarity, Logan realized Hannah deserved the truth. She had to know the real man behind the facade. It pained him to think about reliving those details. He'd be tearing open an old wound that still refused to heal. He also could be inviting her scorn, and that would be even worse. Still, he felt he had no choice but to be open and honest.

"Hannah?"

"Hmmm…" she murmured as she softly stroked his belly.

"There's something I need to tell you, and it's not going to be pretty."

Hannah sensed he'd been concealing a secret all along, but was she prepared to hear it? She certainly better be, she realized, when Logan handed her the T-shirt and panties, then told her to put them on with a strange detachment that belied the sadness in his brown eyes.

While she dressed, Logan pulled on his jeans before sitting on the bed's edge and turning his back to her. A long period of silence passed and for a minute she wondered if he'd reconsidered confessing whatever it was he felt the need to confess.

"I had a daughter at one time."

Hannah bit back an audible gasp. She'd expected an affair, a business deal gone bad. Maybe even bankruptcy, although that didn't make much sense considering he'd purchased a million-dollar home. But she could not have predicated he'd lied about being a father. Then again, that could explain the framed photo she'd found in his desk drawer. "Did you lose custody?"

"I lost her because she died."

And Hannah only thought she couldn't be more stunned. "When did this happen, Logan?"

"Almost eight years ago," he said in a weary tone. "She was only four years old."

She swallowed around her shock right before her

ability to relate to his loss drew her to his side. She laid a hand on his shoulder. "I'm so sorry, Logan." It was all she could think to say at a moment like this. Now she understood why so many people had been at a loss for words following Danny's death.

He leaned forward, hands clasped over his parted knees as he kept his eyes trained on the dark hardwood floor beneath his feet. "Her name was Grace Ann. I called her Gracie."

The truth behind the tattoo. Devastating loss had broken his heart. Not a woman, but a precious child. "I know how badly it hurts to lose a husband, but I can't even begin to imagine how difficult it would be to lose a child."

"That's because it's unimaginable until it happens to you." His rough sigh echoed in the deathly quiet room. "When Jana got pregnant, we'd barely been out of law school. We were both ambitious and career-minded. A kid hadn't been a part of the plan. But when Gracie was born, and they put that tiny baby girl in my arms, I thought I'd be terrified. Instead, I was totally blown away by how much I loved her at that moment. How I would've moved mountains to keep her safe. And I failed to do that."

Hannah desperately wanted to ask for details, but she didn't want to push him. "Things happen, Logan. Horrible things that we can't predict or prevent."

"I could have prevented it."

Once more Hannah didn't know how to respond, so she waited until he spoke again. *If* he spoke again.

A few more seconds passed before he broke the pain-filled silence. "I bought her one of those little bikes for her fourth birthday. The kind that still had training wheels. She loved that bike." He paused as if lost in the memories before he continued. "A couple of days later, I was supposed to be home early to help her learn to ride it. I'd just made junior partner, and I was assigned the case of a lifetime that would've netted the firm a windfall. The pretrial hearing went on longer than expected that afternoon, so I wasn't going to make it home before dark. My job took precedence over my daughter."

The guilt in his tone was instantly recognizable to Hannah. "You're not the first man to put work over family when the situation calls for it. Danny missed dinner many times because he had to put in overtime to secure our future."

"But I had earned plenty of money by then, and so had my wife. I could have turned the hearing over to the associate working the case with me, but I was so damn driven to prove the senior partners had been justified in choosing me over two other candidates. And that drive cost my child her life."

She truly needed to know what had happened, but did she dare ask? "Logan, I'm really trying to understand why you feel you're to blame, but I'm having some problems with that with so little information to go on."

Logan glanced at her again before returning his focus to the floor. "When I drove up that night, I saw the ambulance and police cruiser parked in front of the house. I tried to tell myself one of the neighborhood teens had been driving too fast and had an accident. But my gut told me something inconceivable had happened, and it turned out I was right." He drew in a ragged breath and exhaled slowly. "I pulled up to the curb, got out of the car and started toward the ambulance, only to be met by an officer who told me not to go any farther. He said Grace had ridden the bike into the street and a woman driving by didn't see her, and she didn't even have time to put on her brakes."

Hannah felt his anguish as keenly as if it were her own. "Oh, Logan, I don't know what to say." And she honestly didn't. Again.

"Her death was instant, they told me," he said, as if he couldn't stop the flow of words. "She didn't suffer. But we all suffered. My marriage definitely suffered. Jana screamed at me that night and told me she'd never forgive me."

That threw Hannah for a mental loop. "She blamed you?"

He forked both hands through his hair. "We blamed each other. She blamed me for the bike and not being at a home on time. I blamed her for not watching Gracie closely enough. We both blamed the nanny for leaving early."

While Hannah pondered all she had learned, Logan went silent for a few more seconds before he released a ragged breath. "We had an alarm on the pool," he said. "We bought a top-rate security system and had every inch of the house child-proofed. But it wasn't enough. It came down to one unlocked door to the garage and Gracie climbing on a step stool to open the garage door, and she'd never been a climber."

Hannah had one burning question she had to ask. "Where was your wife at the time Gracie left the house?"

"Checking her email. She said Gracie was watching a DVD in the den only minutes before she went into the home office, and I had no reason not to believe her. Jana had always been a good mother, even if she had the same drive to succeed as I did. Basically, a few minutes of inattentiveness on Jana's part, and blind ambition on my part, irreparably changed our lives forever."

To Hannah, Logan's wife seemed more at fault than he did. But then she really couldn't completely blame her when she had been guilty of the same inattentiveness. "Children can be natural-born escape artists, no matter how vigilant the parent. Cassie got away from me in the grocery store once when I wasn't paying attention to her. It took a half hour and a security guard to find her. I was lucky someone didn't kidnap her when it would have been so easy."

"Gracie knew better than to leave the house without an adult," he said. "Until that night, she never had. I should have suspected she might pull something with the bike when I talked to her that afternoon."

"You spoke to Gracie?"

He smiled a sad smile that shot straight to Hannah's heart. "Yeah. I called Jana to say I was going to be late and she put Gracie on the phone so I could explain. When I told her I couldn't help her ride the bike that night, she was mad as a wet hen and told me she'd do it herself. I said that wasn't allowed and if she tried it, I'd take the bike away. She pouted for a few minutes but when I promised to help her the next day, and take her to the zoo that weekend, she seemed happy enough. Her last words to me were 'I love you, Daddy Bear.' She had a thing for Goldilocks."

Hannah's eyes began to mist like morning fog. "I know it's not the same thing as having her in your life, but at least you'll always have Gracie's wonderful last words to keep in your memory bank."

"But it's never been enough," he said, his voice

hoarse with emotion. "I finally did forgive Jana, but it was too little, too late. And when it came right down to it, she'd been right. I never should have bought Gracie the damn bike."

A solid stretch of logic, but logic didn't count for much when it came to guilt and grief. "When are you going to forgive yourself, Logan?"

He looked at her as if she'd presented a totally foreign concept. "Forgiveness is earned, Hannah. I'm not there yet."

She wanted to inquire as to how long it might take before he reached that point, but he looked completely drained. "I can tell you're tired." Of the conversation and the pain.

He swept both hands over his face. "I'm exhausted."

Hannah stretched out on her back on the bed and opened her arms to him. "Come lie down with me for a little while."

For a split second she thought he might ignore her request, but instead he shrugged out of his jeans and surprisingly accepted the solace she offered.

Curled up together, they slept for a while, until the sun had been replaced by darkness. Logan made love to her again, at first slowly, gently, completely, before a certain desperation seemed to take over. "I can't get close enough," he said, even though they were as close as two people could be.

"It's okay," she kept telling him, until his body went rigid and he released a low moan.

In the aftermath, he brought his lips to her ear and whispered, "Stay with me, sweetheart."

She caressed his shadowed jaw and almost started to cry over the tenderness in his request. "I'm not going anywhere, Logan."

"I meant don't leave on Saturday. Stay another week."

Temptation came calling, but wisdom won out. "I need to get home to Cassie."

"I know I don't have any right to ask, but I need you to be here for a little longer."

I need you....

Those three powerful words shattered Hannah's resolve. Cassie would be fine without her for another week, perhaps even happy to have the extra time with her best friend, that much she knew. Gina would be okay with her extended stay as well.

Logan needed her, and it felt so good to be needed. She instinctively knew she couldn't save him, but maybe if she loved him enough...

Loved him? If she wasn't completely there, she was well on her way, perhaps to her own detriment. She might regret giving in to that emotion, but she would never regret knowing him or what they had shared. What they would share.

"All right, Logan. I'll stay."

Eight

"Logan Whittaker, what brings you all the way out here in the middle of the week and the middle of the day?"

A quest for information he sensed Marlene held. He'd revealed his sorry secrets to Hannah several days ago, and now he wanted Marlene to do the same. "I'm taking a late lunch. Guess I should have called first."

"Don't be silly," she said as she held open the door. "You're practically family."

After he stepped through the door, Marlene pointed to the doors leading to the outdoor entertainment area. "Since it's such a lovely day, let's talk outside," she said as she showed Logan onto the flagstone deck adjacent to the massive great room. He settled on a rattan chair while she took the one to his left.

The 30,000 acres comprising the Big Blue ranch

spread out before them as far as the eye could see. The original homestead where J.D. and Ellie Lassiter had raised their family, now occupied by Marlene's son, Chance, sat in the distance beneath the blue sky that inspired the ranch's name. He'd learned the history early on, but it had never impacted him like it did today. "I'd like to build a house on a place like this in the future. Far away from everything with no signs whatsoever of the city." No suburban streets where playing kids could get hurt, or worse, and that unexpected thought gave him pause. He didn't intend to have any more kids. Not now. Not ever.

"It is peaceful," Marlene said. "All the Lassiter children enjoyed living here."

Speaking of Lassiter children...

Logan glanced back and peered inside through the uncovered floor-to-ceiling windows, looking for signs of other life—namely J.D.'s only daughter. "Is Angelica staying here right now?" Not only did he not want a repeat of their last conversation, but he also didn't want to risk her accidentally overhearing that her own father had taken a mistress, and produced a child. That would categorically send her over the edge. Of course, that would only happen if Marlene came clean.

"Angelica is back in L.A. for a couple of days," she said. "And quite honestly, that's a good thing. That girl has been in a constant tizzy lately. She needs a break. *I* need a break."

"I totally understand. J.D.'s decisions on who inherits his millions have created a lot of questions." Especially for Hannah.

Marlene reached over and patted his arm. "Now why are you here, honey?"

A perfect lead-in to the reason for his impromptu visit. "It's actually about those aforementioned questions. I'm pretty sure you have information about Hannah Armstrong's parentage, namely her connection to J.D. And if you do know anything about that, tell me now because she has a right to know."

She began to wring her hands like an old-time washer. "It's probably past time Hannah learns the truth, and I do know the details. But I wouldn't feel right discussing those particulars with you before I speak with her."

His suspicions had been upheld, and the answers were within Hannah's grasp. A good thing for Hannah because she would know the truth. A bad thing for him because she'd have no reason not to return to Boulder immediately. But delaying the revelation would be selfish on his part. "If I bring her by, will you tell her the whole truth?"

Marlene raised a brow. "She's still here?"

"Yeah. I asked her to stay another week." An unforgettable week of lovemaking and conversation and making a connection with a woman who'd become very special to him. A week that had passed way too fast. But since he had so little to offer her, he would be forced to let her go eventually.

"What makes this one so different from the rest, Logan?" Marlene asked, cutting into his thoughts.

He could recite every one of Hannah's attributes, but that would take hours, so he chose to list only a few. "She's funny and kind but also damn tough. Not many people could handle losing a husband, raising a child on their own, caring for an ill parent and finishing college in the process. Without even trying, she also has the means to make a person want to tell their life story." Much like the woman sitting next to him.

She raised a brow. "Did you tell her yours?"

He streaked a palm over his neck. "Yeah. She knows about Grace." And it had almost killed him to tell her.

Marlene smiled a mother's smile. "I am so glad, Logan. And since she's still sticking around, I assume that she holds the opinion you're not to blame, like I do. Am I right?"

"Yeah, you are." Even if he still didn't agree with that lack of blame assumption. "But she's also compassionate."

"She's a woman who understands loss," Marlene said. "I do as well. We're all unwitting members of a club drawn together by that loss, and sadly that also includes you, too. Hannah intimately understands your pain, and you're very lucky to have found her."

"Don't read too much into this relationship. On Saturday, she's going back to her life and I'll go back to mine."

"Your currently lonely life?" She topped off the question with a frown. "You'd be a fool to let her go, Logan, when she could be a part of your future."

Here we go again. "We had this conversation last week."

"And we'll continue to have it until you listen to reason."

If that's the way she wanted to play it, he'd reiterate all the reasons why a permanent relationship wouldn't work with anyone, especially Hannah. "Marlene, my job doesn't allow for a personal life, and I don't intend to quit for another twenty years, if then."

"Work isn't everything," she said. "Family is."

His profession had indirectly destroyed one family. He wasn't going to risk that possibility again. "Look, I enjoy being with Hannah, but I'm not sure I'll ever be able to make a serious commitment again. I've already been through one divorce and I don't want a repeat. And most important, Hannah's a single mom. She's going to have expectations I might not be able to meet."

Marlene narrowed her eyes and studied him for a few moments. "Part of your reluctance has to do with her daughter, doesn't it?"

Only someone as astute as Marlene would figure that out. "Could you blame me for being concerned? What if I became close with Cassie and my relationship with Hannah doesn't work out? That would be like—"

"Losing Grace all over again?"

She'd hit that nail on the head. "It wouldn't be fair to either one of them."

Marlene leaned forward, keeping her gaze on his. "Honey, life is about balance and a certain amount of chance-taking when it comes to matters of the heart. But life without the possibility of love isn't really living at all. We aren't meant to be alone. Just keep that in mind before you dismiss Hannah due to your fears."

"I'm only afraid of hurting her, Marlene." Afraid he might fail Hannah the way he'd failed his former wife and daughter.

"Maybe you should let her decide if she wants to take a chance on you."

Needing a quick escape, Logan checked his watch and stood. "I have an appointment in less than an hour, so I better get back to the office. When do you want to have that talk with Hannah?"

Marlene came to her feet. "Bring her over for lunch

on Saturday. I'll take her aside after that and speak with her privately. Better still, why don't you bring her daughter, Cassie, too? You could surprise her as a Mother's Day gesture, and give yourself some extra time with her as well."

He'd totally forgotten about the holiday. Marlene's suggestion would buy him more time with Hannah, and he knew she would appreciate the gesture. "I'd have to figure out how I could manage that without her knowing."

Marlene patted his cheek. "You're a smart man, Logan. You'll come up with a plan."

And that plan suddenly began to formulate in his mind. Marlene's suggestion just might work after all. But could he deal with being around a little girl so close in age to Grace when he'd lost her? He wouldn't know unless he tried, and this time he needed to consider Hannah, not himself.

Logan gave Marlene a quick hug. "Thanks for doing this for Hannah. She really needs to know how she came to be."

"You're welcome, honey. And once she learns the whole truth, she's going to need you to lean on."

Being there for her, like she had been there for him, was pretty much a no-brainer. "She's already figured out J.D. was her father. You'll only ease her mind if you confirm it."

Marlene sighed. "On second thought, maybe it's better I provide you with some information first so you'll be prepared. As long as you promise not to say anything to her before I do."

He just wished she would make up her mind. "Fine,

as long as you tell me everything, down to the last detail."

"J.D. didn't father Hannah."

Apparently they'd been traveling straight down the wrong-information path. "Then who was it?"

"My husband, Charles."

She'd spent the day doing laundry and packing her clothes—her final day in Cheyenne.

When Logan sent her a text saying he'd be home by 3:00 p.m., Hannah waited for him on the great-room sofa, wearing only his white tailored button-down shirt. She felt somewhat foolish, but what better way to greet him on their last night together? Even after days of nonstop searching, tomorrow she would return home with no answers about her father and no idea if she would ever see Logan again.

He'd seemed somewhat distant the past two days, or at the very least distracted. She couldn't help but believe he'd been planning his goodbye, and she should be preparing for it now. As soon as she implemented her current and somewhat questionable plan, she would. In the meantime, she refused to think about the impending heartache brought on because she'd been naive enough to fall in love with a man who might never love her back.

Ten minutes later, when she heard the front door open, Hannah stretched out on the cushions on her side and struck what she hoped would be deemed a sexy pose. Logan strode into the room, tossed his briefcase aside and stopped dead in his tracks when he caught sight of her. "Howdy, ma'am."

She brushed her hair back with one hand and smiled. "Howdy yourself."

He walked up to the couch and hovered above her. "I have never said this to a woman before, but you're going to have to get dressed."

She pretended to pout. "You don't like what I'm wearing?"

"Oh, yeah," he said. "But I have a surprise for you and it requires that you put on some clothes."

She straightened and lowered her feet to the floor. "I have a surprise for you, too. I'm not wearing any panties."

He hesitated a moment, his eyes growing dark with that familiar desire. "We don't have a whole lot of time, and I need to take a shower."

Hannah slipped two buttons on the shirt, giving him a bird's-eye view of her breasts. "Imagine that. So do I. We could go green and do it together."

His resistance dissolved right before her eyes, and he proved he was no match for their chemistry when he clasped her hands and tugged her off the sofa. "Then let's go conserve some water."

They rushed through the house, pausing to kiss on the way to Logan's bedroom. Once there, they began to shed their clothes article by article, until they reached the bathroom, completely naked and needy.

He pressed a series of buttons on the nearby chrome panel, sending several showerheads set into the stone walls into watery motion.

While the digital thermostat adjusted the temperature, Hannah stood behind Logan, her arms wrapped around his bare waist. "If I use your soap and shampoo, I'm going to smell like a guy."

He turned her into his arms and grinned. "Better than me smelling like a girl. Of course, you could go get your stuff, but that would take time we don't have." He punctuated the comment by placing a palm on her bottom and nudging her against his erection.

What a man. A sexy, incredible man. "I get the point. Now don't just stand there, take me in the shower."

"That's precisely what I plan to do."

All talk ceased as they took turns washing each other with soap and shampoo that smelled like Logan— clean, not cologne-like. For all intents and purposes, Hannah didn't care if she carried the trace scent of him on her flesh all night, or back home with her tomorrow for that matter. She rejected all thoughts of leaving, and fortunately for her, Logan aided in that cause with his gentle caresses and persuasive kisses that he feathered down her body. He kneeled before her and brought her to the brink of climax with his mouth, then suddenly straightened and pressed the control that cut off the sprays.

His rapid breathing echoed in the large stone shower before he groaned the single word, "Condom."

Hannah did a mental calculation and realized it would be the worst time to take a chance. "We absolutely have to have one before we go any further."

"I know. Getting you pregnant is the last thing I need."

She couldn't deny that his firm tone stung a little, but she also acknowledged he had his reasons for being so resolute—he wanted no more children, period. "Should we take this to the bedroom?"

"Good idea."

They had barely dried off before Logan gathered her

up in his arms, carried her to the bedroom and didn't even bother to turn down the covers. He simply deposited her on the navy comforter and put the condom in place in record time, then faced her on the mattress, one arm draped over her hip.

"I want to really see you when we make love," he said, followed by a brief yet stimulating kiss.

With the room bathed in sunlight, Hannah didn't view that as an issue. "It's still daytime."

"I want you to be in charge."

She gave him an intentionally furtive grin. "You want me on top."

"You got it."

Not a problem, she thought, as she rose up and straddled his thighs. Quite an extraordinary fit, she realized after he lifted her up and guided himself inside her. From that moment on, instinct took over as Hannah took the lead. She suddenly felt as if she'd become someone else—a truly sensual being with the capacity to be completely in control. Yet that control began to wane as Logan touched her again and again, and didn't let up until the last pulse of her orgasm subsided. Only then did she realize he was fairly close to losing it, and she took supreme advantage, using the movement of her hips to send him over the edge. She watched in wonder as the climax began to take hold. His respiration increased, his jaw locked tight and he hissed out a long breath as his body tensed beneath her, yet he never took his gaze from hers.

Feeling physically drained, Hannah collapsed against Logan's chest and rested her head against his pounding heart. He gently rubbed her back with one hand and stroked her hair with the other, lulling her into a total sense of peace.

After a time, he rolled her over onto her back, remained above her and touched her face with a reverence that almost brought tears to her eyes. "You're phenomenal, sweetheart."

But not phenomenal enough to figure into his future. "You're not so bad yourself, sexy guy."

She took his ensuing smile to memory to bring back out on a rainy day. "I wish…" His words trailed off, along with his gaze.

"You wish what?"

"I wish I'd met you years ago, back when we were both young and unattached."

Before his life had taken a terrible turn, she assumed. "Well, since you're eight years older, and I married at the ripe old age of twenty, that would have made me jailbait if you'd dated me before I met Danny."

"I guess you're right about that, and from what I gather, you loved your husband very much."

"I did," she said without hesitation. "But I also know he'd want me to be happy and go on with my life."

He turned onto his back and draped an arm over his forehead. "You deserve to be happy, Hannah. And someday you're going to find someone who will do that for you."

Clearly he believed he didn't qualify, when in truth he did. Not exactly goodbye, but pretty darn close.

She sat up and scooted to the edge of the bed so he wouldn't see the tears starting to form in her eyes.

"Hannah, are you okay?"

No, she wasn't. Not in the least. But she would be because she was a survivor. "I'm fine. I just thought

I'd get dressed since I do believe you mentioned we have some place to be."

When she started to stand, Logan caught her wrist before she could come to her feet. "Believe me, if things were different, if I were the right man for you—"

She pivoted around to face him and faked a smile. "It's all right, Logan. I told you before this thing started between us I had no expectations where we're concerned." And, boy, had she lied without even realizing it.

"You're one in a million, Hannah, and never forget that."

One thing she knew to be true, she would never forget him.

An hour later, Hannah climbed into Logan's Mercedes and they set out for who knew where. She dozed off for a bit and awoke to find they were close to Fort Collins in Colorado, heading in the direction of Boulder.

She hid a yawn behind her hand before shooting a glance at Logan. "If you wanted me to go home, all you had to do was ask."

He gave her a quick grin before concentrating on the road. "That's not where we're going."

"Do you mind telling me were we *are* we going?"

"You'll see real soon."

Five minutes later, he exited the interstate and pulled into a rest stop, leading Hannah to believe Logan needed a break. He shut off the ignition, slid out of the sedan without saying a word, rounded the hood and then opened her door. "Time to get out and take a walk."

"I don't need a walk."

"You'll want to take this one whether you need it or not."

She tapped her chin and pretended to think. "Let me guess. You've arranged for an intimate dinner to be catered at a roadside park."

"Not hardly."

"A picnic beneath the halogen light set to the sights and sounds of eighteen-wheelers, complete with the smell of diesel fuel?"

He braced a hand on the top of the door. "You can sit there and crack jokes, or you can come and see your surprise."

She saluted like a practiced soldier. "Whatever you say, Your Excellency."

Hannah exited the car with Logan's assistance and followed behind him, completely confused over where he could be taking her. Then she saw the familiar silver SUV, the sweet, recognizable face pressed against the back window, and it all began to make sense.

Gina came around from the driver's side, opened the door and released a squealing redhead dressed in white sneakers, floral blue shorts and matching shirt, and of course the tiara planted on her head. "Mama!"

Hannah kneeled down and nearly fell over backward due to her daughter's voracious hug. "I missed you so much, sweetie!" she said as she showered Cassie's cheeks with kisses. "But what are you doing here?"

The little girl reared back, wiped her wet face and displayed her snaggletoothed grin. "It's an early Mother's Day gift. Gina told me I'm gonna spend the weekend with you and the prince!"

"And it was all His Royal Hotness's idea," her best

friend said as she approached carrying Cassie's suit-case and booster seat.

Hannah straightened and turned to Logan. "How did you manage to make this happen without my knowl-edge?"

He streaked a hand over his nape. "It took some work and some sneaking around. I had to steal your phone when you weren't looking so I could get Gina's number."

"Then he called and asked me to bring Cassie half-way," she added. "Now here we are and Frank's at home with a crying son and a pouting daughter who's mourning the temporary loss of her best gal pal."

Only a short while ago, Logan had claimed he couldn't be the kind of man she needed, and then he did something so wonderfully considerate and totally unselfish to prove himself wrong, wrong, wrong. "This is a very welcome surprise, Mr. Whittaker. Thank you very much."

He took the bag and seat from Gina. "You're very welcome."

Cassie tugged on Logan's shirt sleeve to garner his attention. "I'm hungry, Prince Logan."

"Then we should probably get on the road so we can get the queen something to eat." His follow-up bow brought back Cassie's vibrant grin.

Hannah took the suitcase from Logan's grasp. "If you don't mind getting her settled into the car, I'll be along in a minute right after I receive a full report from Gina." She then set her attention on her daughter. "And Cassie, stay close to Logan when you're crossing the parking lot."

"You can count on that," he said with all the determination of a man who believed he'd failed to protect his own little girl.

When Cassie slid her hand into Logan's hand, Hannah saw the flash of emotion in his eyes and she could picture how many memories had assaulted him in that moment. After they walked away—the cowboy attorney with the slow, easy gait, and the bouncing queen wannabe—she turned back to her friend. "*Your Hotness?* Really?"

Gina shrugged. "Seemed pretty appropriate to me."

"You know, I'd be mad at you over that comment if I didn't so appreciate everything you've done. Not only this evening, but over the past two weeks."

"The question is, Hannah, was it worth it? Did you finally find what you were looking for?"

She shook her head. "I still don't know who my father might be, and I've accepted the fact I might never know."

Gina rolled her eyes. "I don't mean only the thing with your long-lost dad. I'm referring to you and the lawyer. Do you see a future with him in it?"

Sadly, she didn't. "He's not the kind to settle down, Gina. He's a remarkable man who's been through a lot, but he's closed himself off emotionally. And that's okay. I didn't expect anything to come of it anyway."

Her friend nailed her with a glare. "You did it, didn't you?"

This time Hannah rolled her eyes. "We had this discussion at least three times last week and once this week. Yes, we did it. Often."

"I'm not talking about the sex," Gina said. "You've gone and fallen in love with him, haven't you? And don't hand me any bull because I can read it all over your face, you ninny."

Hannah's hackles came to attention. "I am not a ninny, and I didn't fall in love with him." Much.

"You lie like a cheap rug."

"You're too meddlesome for my own good." Hannah hooked a thumb over her shoulder. "My daughter is waiting for me."

Gina held up both hands, palms forward, as if in surrender. "Fine. Go with your daughter and the hunk. But when you get home tomorrow, we're going to have a long talk about the virtues of emotionally safe sex."

That worked for Hannah, and after that talk, she could very well need to have a long, long cry.

By the time they arrived home, Logan had been steeped in so many recollections, he'd begun to feel the burn of regret. Watching Cassie at the café ordering a kid's meal and coloring on the menu, he remembered Gracie at every turn. And he missed her. God, did he miss her.

The ache grew worse when he carried a sleeping Cassie up the stairs and to the second surprise of the evening.

"You can put her in my bed," Hannah said from behind him.

That wasn't a part of the plan. "She'll sleep better in here." He opened the door to the room he'd kept as a tribute to his own daughter.

Hannah gaped when she saw the double bed covered by a white comforter imprinted with pink slippers to match the décor. "When did you do this?" she whispered as she turned down the covers.

He laid Cassie carefully on the sheets, her thumb planted firmly in her mouth, her eyes still closed against the light coming from the lamp on the nightstand. "I'll tell you in a minute."

After Hannah pulled off her daughter's shoes, then gave her a kiss on the cheek, they walked back into the hall.

Logan closed the door and turned to her. "The owner of a furniture store in town happens to be a client. I arranged to have the bed delivered right after we got on the road tonight."

"And the bedspread?"

"I bought it yesterday during lunch." Another gesture that had rocked him to the core.

Hannah folded her arms beneath her breasts. "I don't mean to seem ungrateful, because I do appreciate your consideration. But my question is, why would you buy a bed when we're only going to be here one night?"

"I thought maybe you'd agree to stay another night."

She sighed. "I need to get home and resume my job search."

He started to grasp at hopeless straws. "Maybe you and Cassie could visit now and then when you have the chance. I could teach her to ride Lucy."

"What would be the point in that, Logan? You've already established this relationship isn't going to go anywhere. So why would I get my daughter's hopes up and lead her to believe there could be more between us?"

She evidently wanted him to say there could be more, and he couldn't in good conscience promise her that. "I guess you're right."

"Yes, I am right. Now that we've cleared that up,

I'm going to get ready for bed and I'll see you in the morning."

He shouldn't be surprised by her curt dismissal, since he'd made it perfectly clear earlier that he couldn't be the man in her life, but he hadn't expected this rejection to twist his gut in knots. However, despite his wounded male pride, he still could provide the information she'd sought from the beginning. "Marlene Lassiter wants us to have lunch at the Big Blue ranch tomorrow."

She frowned. "I really planned to get on the road early."

"Can you wait to leave until later?" he asked, trying hard not to sound like a desperate idiot. "The ranch is a great place for a kid to play. Cassie would enjoy it." He'd learned long ago if you wanted to melt a good mom's heart, you only had to mention her kids.

He realized the ploy had worked when she said, "I guess a few extra hours won't matter. Besides, I might grab the opportunity to ask Marlene a few questions about J.D., if you don't think I'd be overstepping my bounds."

She had no idea that's exactly what Marlene intended to do—answer all her questions—and he couldn't help but feel guilty over not being forthcoming with what he knew. "Actually, it's a real good idea. Since you haven't signed the nondisclosure, I'm sure she'd be willing to tell you what she knows."

"Provided she actually knows something."

Little did she know, tomorrow she would not only learn about her real father, she would also discover she had a brother. "You might be surprised."

"Probably not," she said. "But I guess I'll find out."

When she started away, he caught her hand and pulled her into his arms. She allowed it for only a moment before she tugged out of his hold and said, "Sleep well, Logan."

For the first time in several days, Hannah retired to her own bedroom, and Logan left for his, without even a kiss good-night.

Sleep well? No way. Not with the prospect of letting her go hanging over his head. But he still had another day in her presence. He would make it his goal to show her and her daughter a good time, and try one more time to convince himself why he didn't deserve her.

Nine

When Marlene Lassiter showed her into a private study at the main house for an after-lunch chat, Hannah could barely contain her curiosity. She wondered if perhaps the woman might hand her the third degree about her relationship with Logan. If so, Marlene would be encountering a major dead end with that one. Truth was, after today, the relationship would be null and void.

"Have a seat, dear," Marlene said as she gestured to one of two brown leather chairs before she crossed the room, nervously tugging at the back hem of her white cotton blouse that covered her black slacks.

After Marlene paused at what appeared to be a bar, Hannah took a seat and conducted a quick visual search of the room. The office was rustic and large, like the rest of the Lassiter family homestead, with bookcases flanking another stone fireplace. That fireplace was much smaller in scale than the one in the great room, where they'd left Logan watching some animated film with Cassie, who'd adhered herself to his side like kid glue. He'd spent most of the morning keeping her entertained by letting her climb up to her castle—in this case, huge round bales of hay—under his watchful eye. If he'd minded the make-believe, or the recollections the interaction had most surely produced, he hadn't let on. He'd just patiently played the knight to the imaginary queen, wielding an invisible sword while sporting a sadness in his eyes that couldn't be concealed, at least not from Hannah.

"How big is this place?" she asked when Marlene bent down and opened the door to the built-in beverage refrigerator.

"Eight bedrooms, at least ten baths, I think because I always lose count, and around 11,000 square feet."

She'd known the glorified log cabin was huge when they'd driven through the gates of the Big Blue, but not that huge. "You have enough room to establish your own commune."

Marlene smiled over one shoulder. "Would you like a glass of wine, dear?"

Hannah normally didn't drink in the middle of the day, but it was well after noon, so what the heck? "Sure, but just a little. I have to head home this evening."

"I'll pour just enough to take the edge off."

Hannah wanted to ask why on earth she should be edgy, yet when Marlene returned with the drinks, looking as solemn as a preacher, she assumed she would soon find out.

She accepted the wine and said, "Thanks," then took

a quick sip. The stuff was so dry it did little to wet her parched throat.

Marlene took a larger drink then held the glass's stem in a tight-fisted grasp, looking as if she could snap it in two. "You might be wondering why I asked you in here, Hannah."

That was a colossal understatement. "I assume it has something to do with Logan."

"Actually, no, it doesn't. It has to do with—"

"Mom, are you in there?"

Marlene sent her an apologetic look before responding to the summons. "Yes, Chance, I'm here."

The door opened wide to a six-foot-plus, brown-haired, athletically built man wearing a chambray shirt with the sleeves rolled up to his elbows, worn leather boots and faded jeans. "Just wondering if the coals are still hot on the grill."

"Yes, they are," Marlene said. "And Chance, this is Logan's new girl, Hannah. Hannah, this is my son, Chance, and if he doesn't learn to wipe his boots better at the back door, I'm going to ban him from the house."

Hannah wanted to correct her on the "Logan's girl" thing, but when Chance Lassiter turned his gaze on her, she was practically struck mute. She met eyes the exact same color of green as hers, and although his hair was a light shade of brown, the resemblance was uncanny. Not proof positive she could be a Lassiter, but pretty darn close.

She had enough wherewithal to set the glass down on the coffee table and offer her hand. "It's nice to meet you, Chance."

He leaned over and gave her hand a hearty shake.

"Pleasure's all mine," he said before regarding his mother again. "Did you have burgers or steak?"

Marlene shrugged. "Steaks, of course. What I always have when we have guests. I saved you one in the fridge to cook to your liking. Two flips on the grill and it's done." She turned her attention back to Hannah. "Chance owns and runs the whole ranching operation, including developing the cattle breeding program. He raises the best Black Angus in the country, but I hope you know that after sampling our steaks."

Fortunately she hadn't been formally introduced to the cows before she'd literally had them for lunch. "Unequivocally the best."

Chance grinned with pride. "We aim to please. So now I'm going to leave you ladies to your girl talk while I go grab a bite. I take it that little redheaded girl napping on the sofa beside Logan belongs to you, Hannah."

Clearly Cassie had finally wound down, a very good thing for the poor lawyer. "Yes, she's all mine, and she's quite a live wire."

"She's as pretty as her mama," he said. "Logan is one lucky guy. Think I'll go tell him that before I grab a bite and get back to riding the range."

Chance Lassiter could talk until he was blue in the face, but luck had nothing to do with their inevitable parting a few hours from now.

After Chance closed the door behind him, Hannah smiled at Marlene. "He seems to be a great guy. Is he your only child?"

"Yes, he is. And he's done very well considering he lost his father when he was only eight. I believe you were around six years old at the time."

How would she possibly know that? Unless… "Marlene, has Logan mentioned anything to you about why I'm here in Cheyenne?"

She momentarily looked away. "Yes, he has, but don't hold that against him because he was only trying to help."

Logan's determination to come to her aid only impressed Hannah more. "Then you know about the annuity J.D. bequeathed to me?"

"I do, although no one else in the family knows about it."

"And the nondisclosure I have to sign to accept it?"

"J.D. added that clause to protect me."

And that made no sense to Hannah. "Why would he feel the need to protect you?"

Marlene downed the rest of her wine and set the glass aside on the end table positioned between the chairs. "Because my husband, Charles, was your father."

Hannah's mind reeled from the shocking revelation, jarring loose a host of unanswered questions. "And you knew about this for how long?"

"Charles came to me and told me about his brief affair with Ruth a few days after he ended it," she said. "Both of us learned about the pregnancy two weeks after you were born."

She didn't know whether to apologize to Marlene for her mother's transgressions, or scold her for not saying something sooner. "And you're absolutely sure Charles was my father?"

"I demanded a paternity test, and when it confirmed he was without a doubt your dad, Charles insisted on being a part of your life."

Hannah took a moment to let that sink in. "Apparently that never happened since I don't remember any man claiming to be my father spending time with me."

Marlene fished a photo from the pocket of her slacks and handed it to her. "You were two years old when this was taken."

She could only stare at the lanky yet handsome cowboy seated on a park bench, a smiling little girl on his lap. She didn't recognize him, but she positively recognized herself. "I have no memories of this or him." And she hated that fact with a passion.

"That's because your mother quit allowing visits when Charles refused to leave me for her."

Her fury returned with the force of an exploding grenade. "She used me as a pawn?"

"Unfortunately, yes," Marlene said. "If Charles wouldn't give in to her demands, then she wouldn't let him see his daughter."

Hannah wasn't sure she could emotionally handle much more, but she had to ask. "And he didn't think to fight for me?"

"No, dear, that's not the case at all. Charles consulted several lawyers on several occasions through the years. Ironically, he even spoke with one family law attorney who used to work at Logan's firm. They all basically told him the same thing. A mother's rights, especially a mother who'd conceived a child and was essentially *dumped* by a married man, would trump the biological father's rights."

She couldn't fathom the time she'd lost getting to know her father, all because of the law. "That's archaic."

"That's the way it was in that day and time." Marlene laid a hand on Hannah's arm. "But Charles never stopped hoping that might change, and he never stopped sending you money up until his death. I took over the payments after that."

Hannah was rapidly approaching information overload. "My mother claimed my father never gave her a penny of support."

Marlene sent her a sympathetic look. "I am so sorry you're learning this now, but Ruth received a monthly check every month from the day you were born, until J.D. learned you'd left college and married, which she failed to tell him."

Obviously all-consuming bitterness had turned her mother into the consummate liar. "She failed to tell me any of this." And now for another pertinent question. "Do you happen to know why J.D. came to our house when I was in the first grade? I remembered him when Logan first approached me about the annuity and I did an internet search."

"He went to tell her about Charles's death in my stead," she said. "Ruth only wanted to know who was going to sign the check. J.D. insisted on contributing the full amount and then some, but I refused to let him. That's when he established the annuity in your name."

"But why on earth would he list my mother as the secondary beneficiary?"

"I assume he believed it would allow him control over the situation. I honestly believe he didn't want to create a scandal for me, since he didn't know Charles had confessed to me about the affair and you. Regardless of what my husband had done, Charles and J.D. were always thick as thieves."

And that left one very important consideration—

the wronged wife. "Marlene, I can't imagine what you went through all those years, knowing your husband created a baby with another woman. And then you were charitable enough to see to that child's welfare." Even if the child had never known. And how horrible to learn her own mother had betrayed her. At least now she knew how Ruth had come by the down payment for the house. A weak gesture in light of the lies.

"Believe me, Hannah," Marlene continued, "I'm no saint. It took me years to forgive Charles, and I resented the hell out of your mother. I also resented you in many ways, and for that I am greatly ashamed."

Hannah set the photo next to her wineglass and clasped Marlene's hand. "I don't blame you at all. I *do* blame my mother for the deceit. Although it does explain why she never seemed happy, especially not with me. No matter what I did, I never felt it was good enough."

"Yet somehow you turned out so well, dear," she said. "I can tell you're a wonderful mother and a genuinely good person. Believe me, Logan knows that, too."

Regardless, that wasn't going to be enough to keep him in her life. "Logan is a very good man with a wounded soul. I hope someday he realizes he deserves to be happy again."

"With your help, I'm sure he will."

If only that were true. "I hate to burst your bubble, Marlene, but when I leave here, I doubt I'll be coming back anytime soon."

Marlene frowned. "I was hoping you'd return now and then to get to know your brother."

Her brother. She'd been so embroiled in the details she hadn't given Chance a second thought. "Does he know about me?"

"No, but I plan to tell him in the very near future. And I hope you'll tell Logan how you really feel about him before you go."

Time to admit the agonizing truth. "He's only going to be a special man I had the pleasure of meeting, and that's all he'll ever be."

Marlene had the skeptical look down to a science. "Don't try to fool an old fool, Hannah. I can spot a woman in love at fifty paces."

Hannah fixed her gaze on the almost-full glass next to the photo, but she had no desire to drink, only sob. "It doesn't matter how I feel about him. Logan has all but given up on love. And that's sad when he needs it so very much."

"I'm asking you not to give up on him," Marlene said. "Men have been known to come around, once the woman of their dreams has flown the love nest. But before you do that, you need to tell him how the cow ate the cabbage and convince him that you're worth fighting for. Then make sure you turn around and leave so he'll have time to chew on it awhile."

"I suppose I could give that a shot."

"You'd be surprised how effective it can be."

Hannah could only hope. That's about all she had left to hold on to. Actually, that wasn't exactly the case. She picked up the photo and studied it again. "Do you mind if I keep this?"

"Not at all, dear." Marlene stood and smiled. "Now let's go find that hardheaded attorney so you can have the last word."

Hannah had the strongest feeling it could very well be her last stand.

* * *

"Looks like it's going to rain."

In response to Logan's observation, Hannah looked up. The overcast skies reflected her gloomy mood, but she needed to snap out of the funk in order to tell Logan exactly what had been brewing in her mind, with a little help from Marlene.

She kicked at a random stone as the two of them walked a path leading away from the house. "Hopefully it won't be more than a spring shower. Just enough rain that lasts long enough for Cassie to get in a good nap."

"Chance is hoping for a deluge."

"You mean my *half brother,* Chance?" she asked, as she took a glimpse to her right to gauge Logan's reaction.

"I figured Marlene told you everything."

His poker face and even tone told Hannah he'd been privy to that knowledge. "How long have you known Charles Lassiter was my father?"

"Since Wednesday."

"And you went three days without telling me?" She'd thought she'd meant more to him than that. Obviously she'd been wrong.

"Now before you get all worked up," he said, "Marlene made me promise I wouldn't say anything to you before she could explain. It was damn hard keeping you in the dark, but I had to respect her wishes."

She shrugged. "What's three days when compared to thirty years? I still cannot believe my own mother never told me about him, or the fact that she received checks from Charles and then Marlene during my formative years and beyond."

Finally, Logan showed something more than detachment to her disclosures. "That part I didn't know, Hannah. I'm sorry you had to find out after the fact."

She was sorry she couldn't change his mind about settling down. Or having children. Yet expecting someone to alter their ideals made little sense. "It's done, and I'm over it. I have a great daughter, own my home and a degree. Now I just need to find a job and my life will be complete." That rang false, even to Hannah's ears.

"You know, you could look for a job here," Logan said.

The suggestion took her aback, and gave her hope. "Why would I do that when my life is in Boulder?"

"So you can get to know your new family since you're not going to take the inheritance."

So much for hoping he might actually see a future with her. "That really only includes Chance, since I have no idea how my cousins will take the news." And who was to say her brother would even want to have a relationship with her?

"I still think that if you moved closer, we could get together every now and then."

Not at all what she wanted to hear. "For the occasional booty call?"

He scowled. "You know me well enough to know I respect you more than that. I just thought we could see where it goes."

She knew exactly where it would go. Nowhere. "Let's review, shall we? I eventually want to marry again and have at least one more child. You, on the other hand, would prefer to live your life alone, moving from one casual conquest to another with no commitment, in typical confirmed-bachelor fashion. And since I don't intend to follow in my mother's footsteps and wind up as someone's mistress, that puts us directly at odds. Do you not agree?"

He stopped in his tracks to stare at her, anger glinting in his dark eyes. "I've never seen you as some kind of conquest and definitely not as a potential mistress. I only thought that if we spent more time together—"

"You'd suddenly decide by some miracle to become a family man again?"

"I told you why—"

"You don't want to settle down. I know. You're too wrapped in guilt and grief to give me what I need. But what about *your* needs?"

He shifted his weight from one leg to the other. "What do you think I need?"

He'd asked for it, and she was glad to give it to him. "You need to get over yourself. You're not the only one who's lost someone they loved more than life itself. But life does go on unless you say it doesn't. And that's what you've been saying for the past eight years. Do you think keeping yourself closed off to all possibilities is honoring your daughter's memory? Believe me, it's doing just the opposite."

His eyes now reflected pent-up fury. "Leave Grace out of this."

"I can't, Logan, because deep down you know I'm right. And if I never see you again, it's going to be tough, and it's going to break my heart just like that memorial tattoo on your arm. But I'm not a quitter, and I didn't peg you as one, either, when I stupidly fell in love with you."

He looked astonished over her spontaneous admission. "You what?"

No need to stop when she was on a roll. "I love you.

Oh, I fought it with everything in me. I chalked it up
to lust and liking your home theater. And of course
my appreciation of your plumbing skills. What woman
wouldn't want a man who could fix her leaky pipes?
And I really valued your determination to make sure
I found out the truth about my heritage." She hitched
in a breath. "But do you know when I quit questioning my feelings?"

"No."

"Today, when I watched you playing with my daughter, and I saw this longing in your eyes that took my
breath away. Whether you believe it or not, you're
meant to be a father, and somewhere beneath that
damned armor you've build around your heart, you
want to be one again. But that will never happen unless you stop beating yourself up and being afraid of
making a mistake."

Tension and silence hung between them despite the
whistling wind. Hannah allowed the quiet for a few
moments before she finished her diatribe. "Logan, I
only want what's best for you, believe it or not. And
I hate it that I hurt you by laying out the truth. I also
pray you find the strength to love again. Maybe I'm
not the woman you need, but you do need someone."

For the first time ever, he appeared to be rendered
speechless. Either that, or he was simply too irate to
speak.

When he failed to respond, Hannah decided to give
up, though that went against her nature. But she wasn't
too stubborn to recognize when it was time to throw
in that towel. "If it's not too much of a bother, I'd like
to go back to your place, collect my things and my car,
and get back to Boulder before dark."

This time she didn't bother to wait for his answer. She simply spun around and headed back to the house to gather her child in order to go home and lick her wounds.

Yet as she afforded a glance over her shoulder, and she saw him standing there in the rain, looking forlorn instead of furious, she wondered if maybe she'd expected too much from Logan too soon. Given up on him too quickly. She wanted desperately to believe he might eventually come around to her side.

And that possibly could be too much to ask.

Yesterday afternoon, Logan had told Hannah goodbye after giving her and Cassie a brief hug, not once giving away the sorry state of his heart. Since then, he'd been carrying around a brand-new bushel full of regrets that kept running over and over in his head. He wound up spending the night seated on the floor in the now-vacant child's room, alone and lonely. He dozed off now and then, always awakening with a strong sense that he'd made the biggest mistake of his life when he let Hannah go without putting up a fight.

He'd blamed her for treading on his pride, when all she'd done was shine a light on the hard truth. In many ways, he had stopped living. But he hadn't stopped loving, because he was—without a doubt—in love with her. He loved her wit and her gentle ways. He loved the way she made love to him. He loved the fact she could melt his heart with only a smile. He hated that he hadn't uttered one word of that to her before she'd driven away, and now it might be too late.

Although he was dog-tired, that didn't keep him from sprinting down the stairs when he heard the doorbell chime. He hoped to see Hannah on his doorstep, but instead he peered through the peephole and found Chance Lassiter. As much as he liked and respected the guy, he wasn't in the mood for company. But when he noticed the wind had begun to push the rain beneath the portico, he decided he should probably let him in.

Logan opened the door and before he could mutter a greeting, Chance said, "You look like hell, Whittaker."

He ran a hand over his unshaven jaw and figured he looked like he'd wrestled a bear and lost. "Good to see you, too, Lassiter."

Chance stepped inside without an invite, shrugged off the heavy weatherproof jacket and shook it out, sprinkling drops of water all over the travertine tile. He then dug a pair of tiny blue socks from his jeans pocket and offered them to Logan. "Mom told me Cassie left these at the house. Is Hannah still here?"

He wished that were the case. "She went home yesterday afternoon."

"Damn. I really wanted to talk to her. When's she going to be back?"

"I don't think she'll be coming back anytime soon." Voicing it made the concept all too real. "At least not to see me."

"Trouble in paradise?"

Paradise had disappeared the minute she'd walked out his door. "Guess some things aren't meant to be."

"That's really too bad," Chance said. "I was hoping maybe you'd be my brother-in-law in the near future, that way I wouldn't hesitate to call you when I need help with the cows."

Chance's attempt at humor sounded forced to Logan, and with good reason. Suddenly learning you have a sister because your late father was a philanderer would be a damn bitter pill to swallow. "You don't hesitate to call me for help now, and I take it Marlene told you the whole story about your father and Hannah's mother."

"Yeah, the whole sorry story." Chance let go a caustic laugh. "You spend your life idolizing your dad, only to learn the guy was a good-for-nothing cheater. But at least I got a sibling out of the deal. That's if she wants to acknowledge me as her brother. Had I known the facts before she took off, I would've spoken with her yesterday while she was still at the ranch."

Had Logan known how bad he would hurt, he might not have let her take off. "I've got her phone number and address if you want to get in touch with her."

"I'll do that," he said. "Question is, what are you going to do about her?"

"I'm not sure what you mean."

Chance shook his head. "For a man with a whole lot of smarts, you're not real good at pretending to be stupid."

He didn't much care for the stupid designation, even if it might ring true in this instance. "Didn't know you planned to deliver insults along with the socks."

"Well, if the shoe fits, as Mom would say."

Logan also didn't appreciate the pun. "Look, Hannah and I had a good thing going, but now it's over."

Chance narrowed his eyes, looking like he was prepared to take his best shot, or throw a punch. "You do realize you're talking about my sister. If you used her and then threw her away like garbage, that's grounds to kick your ass."

"I don't use women and I sure as hell didn't use

Hannah, so simmer down. In fact, I stayed awake all night thinking about her."

Chance seemed satisfied by that response, at least satisfied enough to unclench his fists. He also looked a little too smug. "Man, do you have it bad for her."

Dammit, he'd walked right into that trap. "That's one hell of a major assumption, Lassiter."

"Are you going to tell me I'm wrong?"

Not unless he wanted to hand Chance one super-sized lie. "No, you're not wrong."

"Well, hell, that sure explains why you look like something the mountain lion dragged in that the blood-hound couldn't stomach."

He really should have checked a mirror on his way downstairs. "Are you done deriding me now?"

"Nope. Not until you admit how you really feel about Hannah."

"I love her, dammit." There, he'd said it, and a hole in the tiled entry hadn't opened up and swallowed him. "Are you happy now?"

"As happy as a squirrel in the summer with a sur-plus of nuts. Do you still want to be with her?"

More than he could express. "Yeah, I do."

"Now what are you going to do about it?"

Logan didn't have a clue. "I'm sure you're itching to tell me."

"I don't even begin to understand what makes a woman tick," Chance began, "but I do know if you want her back, you've got to do it soon, before she has time to think about how you've wronged her."

"I'll call her as soon as I call my mom." Talk about serious avoidance.

Chance glared at him like he'd just proposed a plot

to commit murder. "Man, you can't do this over the phone. You have to go see her. Today."

"But—"

He pointed a finger in Logan's face. "You're going to show up at her house with something that will force her to forgive you."

"Flowers?"

"Yeah. Flowers are good, especially since it's Mother's Day. Do you have any planted in some garden?"

"Hell no. I'll have to buy them somewhere." Fortunately he had a connection who could accommodate him.

"What about one of those fancy silk suits?"

Logan's patience was wearing thin. "I'm an attorney, Chance. I have a damn suit."

"Sorry, but I had to ask because I've never seen you wear an entire suit, bud. Anyway, you'll show up in your suit with flowers—"

"For a die-hard bachelor, you're sure quick to dole out the advice."

"I just want my sister to be happy," Chance said in a surprisingly serious tone.

So did Logan. But would all the frills be enough to persuade Hannah to give them another chance? "What if she throws me out before I have my say?"

Chance slapped his back with the force of a steamroller. "Whittaker, according to Mom, Hannah loves you something awful, too. If you play your cards right, she'll let you come crawling back to her. Now I'm not saying you need to propose marriage because you've known each other a short time. My mom and dad only knew each other a month before they tied the knot and we now know how that one worked out."

Funny, Marlene hadn't mentioned that to Logan during their many conversations. "No kidding? Only a month?"

"No kidding," he said. "And then he cheated on his wife, not that I think you'd do that to Hannah."

"Not on your life." She was all he needed. All he would ever need.

"And to top it off," Chance continued, "Mom told me yesterday that in spite of my father's faults and weakness, she never doubted his love for her. It's just hard for me to believe love that strong exists."

Logan was beginning to believe it existed between him and Hannah, provided she hadn't fallen out of love with him overnight. "I hope you eventually forgive Marlene. She was just trying to protect you from the ugly truth."

"I'll forgive her eventually," Chance said. "As far as my dad's concerned, I'm not sure that will ever happen."

Logan knew all about that inability to forgive, and he could only hope Chance eventually came around like he had. But Hannah… "I hope like hell Hannah forgives me for taking so long to realize we need to be together."

"She'll forgive you the minute you show up at her door wearing your heart on your sleeve."

"Guess that's better than eating crow."

"You'll be doing that, too, Whittaker, so pack some salt. And groveling couldn't hurt. Hope that suit isn't too expensive in case you have to get down on your knees when you beg."

The suit didn't mean as much to him as Hannah. His pride no longer mattered much where she was concerned, either. "Are you sure you don't want to go with me, Lassiter? In case you want to talk with her after I do."

Chance grinned, grabbed his coat and backed toward the door. "You're on your own with this one, bud. Now go get a shower and shave, then go get your girl. Who knows? She might even be waiting for you."

Ten

Hannah walked out the door to meet Gina for their traditional Mother's Day brunch, only to stop short of the sidewalk when she caught sight of the black Mercedes parked at the curb. And leaning against that sedan's driver's door was the beautiful, wounded, brown-eyed man who'd invaded her thoughts the majority of the night. He wore a beige silk suit with matching tie and a white tailored shirt, a bouquet of roses in one hand, a piece of white paper in the other. If not for the dress cowboy boots, she might believe this was Logan Whittaker's clone. Yet when he grinned, showing those dimples to supreme advantage, that was all the confirmation she needed. But why was he here? She aimed to find out.

Hannah stepped across the yard, her three-inch heels digging into the grass made moist by the deluge that had arrived during the night. Fortunately the clouds had begun to break up, allowing the sun to peek through.

When she reached Logan, she shored up her courage and attempted a smile. "What are you doing here, Mr. Whittaker?"

"Thought you might need a plumber."

"My pipes appear to be holding, so no more water in the floor." On the other hand, her heart was flooded with a love for him that just wouldn't leave her be. "Since you're wearing a suit, I thought maybe you got lost on your way to some wedding."

"Nope, but I was pretty lost until I found you."

Her flooded heart did a little flip-flop in her chest. But she wasn't ready to give in to his pretty words and patent charms. Yet. "Who are the flowers for?"

"You," he said as he handed them off to her. "Happy Mother's Day."

She brought the roses to her nose and drew in the scent. "Thank you."

He leaned around her. "Where's Cassie?"

"Two houses down at the Romeros'. She's going to spend a few hours there while Gina and I have lunch together."

"Who's going to be watching her?"

His protective tone both surprised and pleased Hannah. "Gina's husband, Frank. He's used to watching their baby and the girls when Gina and I have plans."

"That sounds like a damn daunting job."

"He's a great dad, but he's had lots of practice."
And you would be a great dad, too, she wanted to say.

Amazingly the familiar sadness didn't show in his eyes. "I guess practice makes perfect."

He still had a lot to learn. "Not perfect, Logan. No parent is ever perfect."

"I'm starting to realize that."

Oh, how she wanted to believe him. Yet she continued to resist the notion he had finally seen the light.

Hannah pointed at the document now clenched in his fist. "What's that?"

"The annuity terms that include the nondisclosure clause." He unfolded the paper, tore it in half and then tossed the remains into the open back window. "And according to your wishes, it's no longer valid."

Hannah couldn't resist teasing him a little. "Darn. I decided last night to sign it and take the money."

"Are you serious?"

She stifled a laugh. "No, I'm not serious. I could always use that kind of money, but I have everything I need without it, especially since Cassie's future is secure, thanks to my in-laws."

He inclined his head and looked at her as if he could see right through her phony assertion. "Everything?"

Except for those things money couldn't buy—like his love. "Enough to get by until I find a job. And mark my words, I will find a job even if I have to flip burgers."

"Marlene told me there's an opening at one of the rural high schools between my place and the Big Blue. They need a biology teacher. You should go for it."

"You're saying I should just uproot my child, sell my house and move to the middle of nowhere?"

"As I mentioned earlier, you'd have the opportunity to get to know your brother. We can continue to get to know each other better, too."

And he would have to do better than that. "We've already had this discussion, Logan. I want—"

"A man who can promise you a solid future and more kids."

"Exactly."

Some unnamed emotion reflected in his eyes. "I can be that man, Hannah. God knows I want to be."

The declaration tossed her into an emotional tailspin. "If that's true, then what made you suddenly change your mind?"

"What you told me about not honoring Grace's memory. I sat up all night in that room with the princesses on the wall and had a long talk with my daughter, as crazy as it seems."

How many times had she had those conversations with Danny in the distant past? "It's not crazy at all. It's long overdue."

"Anyway, for the first time since the funeral, I cried like a baby. But that meltdown didn't occur last night only because of Gracie. It had a lot to do with losing you."

Hannah could tell the admission was costing him as much as it was costing her. She wanted to throw her arms around him, tell him it would be okay, but she wasn't quite ready to do that yet. "Are you sure you're prepared to make a commitment to me and Cassie if and when the time comes?"

"I'm all in, Hannah," he said adamantly. "I also know I can be a good dad to Cassie. And do you want to know how I figured that one out?"

"Yes, I would."

He looked down and toed a random clump of grass before bringing his gaze back to hers. "When I was playing with Cassie yesterday on the hay bales, she slipped a few times and I caught her. Once I couldn't reach her, but she managed to pick herself back up after she tumbled to the bottom. Granted, it scared the hell out of me for a few minutes, but it also made me acknowledge that kids are actually pretty resilient, and the truth is, you can't logically be there for your children all the time." He exhaled roughly. "You can only do the best you can to protect them, and sadly sometimes that isn't enough, but you can't spend your life being paralyzed by a fear of failure."

A lesson everyone should learn. Unfortunately, he'd learned it the hard way. "Cassie's completely enamored of you, Logan. She told me on the drive home that you would make a good daddy, and she's right. But I've known that all along. I'm just glad you finally realized it."

His smile was soft and sincere. "She still thinks I'm some kind of prince."

"So do I. Or maybe I should say a prince in progress. You still need some work, but the flowers helped your cause."

He reached over and clasped her hand. "If I tell you I can't imagine my life without you, would that help, too?"

Hannah held back the tears, with great effort. "Immensely."

He brought her closer. "How about if I tell you I love you?"

So much for keeping those tears at bay. "Really?"

He gently kissed her cheek. "Really. I didn't expect to fall so hard and so fast for someone, because I never have. Hell, I didn't expect you at all. And although neither of us knows what the future will bring, I do know what I want."

Hannah sniffed and hoped she didn't look like a raccoon. "For me to buy waterproof mascara from now on?"

He responded with that smile she had so grown to

adore. "No. I want to give us a fighting chance. I promise to do everything in my power to make it work."

"I promise that, too." And she did, with all her heart and soul. "I love you, Logan."

"I love you, too, sweetheart."

Then he kissed her, softly, slowly, sealing the vow they'd made at that moment, and those vows Hannah believed were yet to come.

"I guess this means brunch is off."

She broke the kiss to find Gina standing in the middle of the sidewalk, gawking. "I suppose we'll have to postpone until next year."

Gina shrugged. "That's probably for the best. Frank's been complaining of a cold all morning and Trey's teething. I'd feel guilty if I left him with three kids, and even more guilty if I spoiled this wonderful little reunion. However, it does pain me to break a long-standing tradition."

"Tell you what, Gina," Logan said as he kept his arms around Hannah. "If you'll let me take my lady to lunch, I'll give you and your husband a night on the town, my treat. We'll even keep the kids."

Gina's eyes went as wide as saucers. "How about tonight? That would so cure Frank of what ails him."

He returned his attention back to Hannah. "Works for me, if it works for you."

With one exception. "Sure, as long as we have a few hours alone before we're left in charge of the troops."

"It's a deal," Gina said as she backed up a few steps. "Have a good lunch, and have some of that wild monkey sex for dessert, too."

As soon as her friend left the immediate premises, Hannah gave Logan another quick kiss. "You're mighty brave, taking on three kids."

He responded with a grin. "Hey, I've got to get into practice for when we have our three. Or maybe four."

Sweet, welcome music to Hannah's ears. "Don't get ahead of yourself, buster. You'll have to marry me first, Logan Whittaker, my repressed plumber."

"You know, Hannah Armstrong, my maid-in-waiting, I just might do that sooner than you think."

The past six weeks had whirled by in a flurry of changes. She'd sold the house, moved into the Big Blue for the sake of her minor child, spent every day with Logan, and even a few nights alone with him, thanks to Marlene's generosity. Aside from that, the saintly woman hadn't even flinched when Cassie had begun to call her Grandma.

Best of all, Hannah had learned that morning she'd been awarded the high school biology teaching job and would begin in the fall. Things couldn't be going any better, and tonight she and Logan planned to celebrate with a night on the town and a hotel stay in Denver. But she'd better hurry up with the preparations, otherwise Logan might leave without her.

On that thought, she inserted the diamond earrings he'd given her two weeks ago on the one-month anniversary of their meeting. Admittedly, and ridiculously, she'd secretly hoped for jewelry that fit on her left ring finger, but she had no doubt that would eventually come. She had no doubts whatsoever about their future.

After a quick dab of lipstick and a mirror check to make sure the white satin dress was properly fitted, Hannah grabbed her clutch in one hand and slipped the overnight bag's strap over one bare shoulder. She then rushed out of the bedroom and down the hall of the wing she shared with Marlene.

She was somewhat winded when she reached the staircase, and her breath deserted her completely when she saw Logan standing at the bottom landing. He'd donned a black tuxedo with a silver tie, and he was actually wearing Italian loafers, not the usual Western boots.

She couldn't help but smile as she floated down the stairs and took his extended hand when she reached the bottom. "Okay, what did you do with my cowboy lawyer?"

"According to your daughter, tonight I'm supposed to be a prince. This is as close as I could get because I refuse to wear those damn tights and a codpiece."

She reached up and kissed his neck. "I'd buy tickets to see you in tights."

He sent her a champion scowl. "Save your money 'cause it ain't happenin'."

"That's too bad."

He grinned. "You like bad, especially when it comes to me."

Oh, yeah. "I won't argue with that."

He crooked his arm for her to take. "Are you ready, Ms. Armstrong?"

"I am, Prince Logan. Take me away."

Instead of heading toward the front door, Logan guided Hannah down the corridor and into the great room, where an unexpected crowd had gathered. A crowd consisting of Marlene wearing a beautiful white chiffon dress, Chance dressed in a navy shirt and dark jeans, Cassie decked out in her pink princess gown, complete with pretty coat and feather boa, and of all people, senior law partner, Walter Drake, who had debonair down pat. Hannah had to wonder if they were going to pile all these people into a car caravan and head to Denver together.

"Did you plan a party without me knowing?" she asked when Logan positioned her next to the floor-to-ceiling stone fireplace.

"That's somewhat accurate," Logan said. "And you're the guest of honor."

A frenzy of applause rang out, accompanied by a few ear-piercing whistles, compliments of Chance. Her half brother had become very special to her, and he'd proven to be a stellar uncle to Cassie, evidenced by the fact he'd picked up his niece and held her in his arms.

"First, thank you all for being here," Logan began, sounding every bit the attorney, with a little Texas accent thrown in. "But before we get to the celebration, I have something important to ask a very special lady."

Surely he wasn't going to… Hannah held her breath so long she thought her chest might explode, until Logan said, "Cassie, come here."

While Logan took a seat on the raised heart, Chance lowered Cassie to the ground. She ran over as fast as her little pink patent leather shoes allowed. She then came to a sliding stop, plopped herself down in Logan's lap and draped her tiny arms around his neck.

"Darlin'," Logan began, "you know I love your mama, and I love you, right?"

She nodded emphatically, causing her red ringlets to bounce. "Uh-huh."

"And you know that I'm never going to try to take your daddy's place."

"My Heaven daddy."

"That's right. But I sure would like to be your daddy here on earth, if that's okay."

"I'd like you to be my earth daddy, too," Cassie said.

Hannah placed a hand over her mouth to stifle a sob when she saw the look of sheer love in both Cassie's and Logan's eyes.

Logan kissed her daughter's forehead before setting her back on her feet. "Now I have to ask your mom a few questions."

Cassie responded with a grin. "You betcha." She then looked up at Hannah, who could barely see due to the moisture clouding her eyes. "I told you so, Mama. Logan is your prince."

Cassie ran back to her uncle while Logan came to his feet. He moved right in front of Hannah, his gaze unwavering. "Sweetheart, I want to wake up with you every morning and go to bed with you every night. I want to find a good balance between work and family. I don't want to replace Cassie's real dad, but I want to be the best father I can be to her. And I want, God willing, for your face to be the last one I see before I'm gone from this earth. Therefore, if you'll have me, Hannah Armstrong, I want more than anything for you to be my wife."

The room had grown so silent, Hannah would swear everyone could hear her pounding heart. This was no time for smart remarks. For questions or doubts. This precious request Logan had made only required one answer. "Yes, I will be your wife."

Following a kiss, and more applause, Logan pulled a black velvet box from his inner pocket and opened it to a brilliant, emerald-cut diamond ring flanked by more diamonds. "This should seal the deal," he said as he removed it from the holder, pocketed the box again, then placed it on her left finger.

Hannah held it up to the light. "Heavens, Logan Whittaker, this could rival the Rocky Mountains. I might have to wear a sling to hold it up."

Logan leaned over and whispered, "Always the smart-ass, and I love it. I love you."

She sent him a wily grin. "I love you, too, and I really and truly love the ring."

The pop of the cork signaled the party had begun as Marlene started doling out champagne to everyone of legal age. When Cassie asked, "Can I have some?" Logan and Hannah barked out, "No!" simultaneously.

She turned to Logan and smiled. "You're going to come in handy when she turns sixteen and the boys come calling."

"She's not going to date until she's twenty-one," he said in a gruff tone.

"And I'm the Princess of Romania," she replied, although tonight she did feel like a princess. A happy, beloved princess, thanks to her unpredictable prince.

Following a few toasts, many congratulations and a lot of hugs and kisses, Logan finally escorted Hannah out the door and into the awaiting black limousine, just one more surprise in her husband-to-be's repertoire. Then again, everything about her relationship with Logan had been one gigantic surprise.

After they were seated side by side, and the partition dividing the front and back of the car had been raised, Logan kissed her with all the passion they'd come to know in each other's arms.

"How did you enjoy that proposal?" he asked once they'd come up for air.

"It was okay. I really hoped you would have dressed like a plumber and presented the ring on a wrench."

He grinned. "Would you have worn a maid's uniform?"

"Sure. And I'd even pack a feather duster."

The levity seemed to subside when Logan's expression turned serious. "I've set up a trust fund in Cassie's name, in case you want to tell your former in-laws thanks, but no thanks."

"I'd be glad to tell them to take their trust fund and control and go to Hades. And if I did, frankly I don't think they'd care. But if they do decide they want to see her again, it wouldn't be fair to keep her from them." The same way she'd been kept from her father.

"We'll deal with it when and if the time comes. Together." Logan pulled an open bottle of champagne from the onboard ice bucket, then filled the two available glasses. "To our future and our family."

Hannah tipped her crystal flute against his. "And to weddings. Which reminds me, when are we going to do it?"

He laid his free hand on her thigh. "The seat back here is pretty big, so I say let's do it now."

Spoken like a man who'd spent a lot of time with a wise-cracker. She gave him an elbow in the side for good measure. "I meant, as if you didn't know, when are we going to get married?"

He faked a disappointed look that melted into an endearing smile. "I'm thinking maybe on July Fourth."

That allowed Hannah very little time to plan. But since this would be both their second marriages, it wouldn't require anything elaborate. "You know something? People will speculate I'm pregnant if we have the ceremony that soon."

He nuzzled her neck and blew softly in her ear. "Let's just give them all something to talk about."

Lovely. More rumors, as if the Lassiter family hadn't had enough of that lately. Oh, well. It certainly kept things interesting. So did Logan's talented mouth. "Then July Fourth it is. We can even have fireworks."

He winked. "Fireworks on Independence Day for my beautiful independent woman works well for me."

An independent woman and single mom, and a onetime secret heiress, who'd had the good fortune to fall in love with a man who had given her an incredible sense of freedom.

Now, as Hannah gazed at her gorgeous new fiancé, this onetime secret heiress was more than ready for the lifetime celebration to begin. Starting now.

* * * * *

EXPECTING THE CEO'S CHILD

BY
YVONNE LINDSAY

New Zealand born, to Dutch immigrant parents, **Yvonne Lindsay** became an avid romance reader at the age of thirteen. Now, married to her "blind date" and with two fabulous children, she remains a firm believer in the power of romance. Yvonne feels privileged to be able to bring to her readers the stories of her heart. In her spare time, when not writing, she can be found with her nose firmly in a book, reliving the power of love in all walks of life. She can be contacted via her website, www.yvonnelindsay.com.

To my dear friend Rose-Marie, who has known me since we were both teenagers—thank you for always being my friend and an especial thank you for calling florists in Wyoming for me! :) I owe you, Smithy!

One

Jenna puzzled over the complex wreath design a family had requested for their grandmother's funeral the coming Wednesday. She just about had it nailed; all she needed to confirm with the wholesale suppliers was that she'd be able to get the right shade of lilacs that had been the grandmother's favorite.

The sound of the door buzzer alerted her to a customer out front. She listened to see if her new Saturday part-time assistant would attend to the client, but the subsequent ding of the counter bell told her that Millie was likely in the cool room out back, or, unfortunately more likely, outside on the phone to her boyfriend again.

Making a mental note to discuss with the girl the importance of actually *working* during work hours, Jenna pushed herself up from her desk, pasted a smile on her face and walked out into the showroom. Only to feel the smile freeze in place as she recognized Dylan Lassiter, in all his decadent glory, standing with his back to her, his attention apparently captured by the ready-made bouquets she kept in the refrigerated unit along one wall.

Her reaction was instantaneous; heat, desire and shock flooded her in turn. The last time she'd seen him had been in the coat closet where they'd impulsively sought refuge—to release the sexual energy that had ignited so dangerously and suddenly between them. They'd struck sparks off one another so bright and so fierce it had almost been a relief when he'd returned to his base in Los Angeles. Almost.

Jenna fought the urge to place a hand protectively across her belly—to hide the evidence of that uncharacteristic and spontaneous act. She'd known from the day her pregnancy was confirmed that she'd have to tell him at some stage. She hadn't planned for it to be right now. At first she'd been a little piqued that he'd made no effort to contact her since that one incredible encounter. She had half understood he'd been too busy to call her in the aftermath of his father's sudden death during Dylan's sister's wedding rehearsal dinner. But afterward? When everything had begun to settle down again?

She gave herself a mental shake. No, she'd successfully convinced herself that she didn't need or want the complication of a relationship. Especially not now and especially not with someone as high profile as Dylan Lassiter. Not after all the years of work she'd put into rebuilding her reputation. She'd made a conscious choice to put off contacting him, too, and despite the slight wound to her feminine ego that he'd obviously done the same, she would just have to get over it because she sure as heck had plenty else to keep her mind occupied now.

"Can I help you?" she said, feigning a lack of recognition right up until the moment he turned around and impaled her with those cerulean-blue eyes of his.

Air fled from her lungs and her throat closed up. A perfectly tailored blue-gray suit emphasized the width of his shoulders, while his white shirt and pale blue tie emphasized the California tan that warmed his skin. Her mouth dried. It was a crime against nature that any man could look so beautiful and so masculine at the same time.

A hank of softly curling hair fell across his high forehead, making her hand itch to smooth it back, then trace the stubbled line of his jaw. She clenched her fingers into a tight fist, embedding her nails in her palms as she reminded herself exactly where such an action would inevitably lead.

He was like a drug to her. An instant high that, once taken, created a craving like no other. She'd spent the past two and a half months in a state of disbelief at her actions. She, who'd strived to be so careful—to keep her nose clean and to fly under the radar—was now carrying the child of a man she'd met the day it was conceived. A man she'd barely known, yet knew so much about. Certainly enough not to have succumbed the way she had.

It had literally been a one-night *stand,* she reminded herself cynically. The coat closet hadn't allowed for anything else. But as close as the confines had been, her body still remembered every second of how he'd made her feel—and it reacted in kind again.

"Jenna," Dylan said with a slow nod of his head, his gaze not moving from her face for so much as a second.

"Dylan," she replied, taking a deep breath and feigning surprise. "What brings you back to Cheyenne?"

The instant she said the words she silently groaned. The opening. Of course he was here for that. The local chamber of commerce—heck, the whole town—was abuzz with the news. She'd tried to ignore anything Lassiter-related for weeks now, but there was no ignoring the man in front of her.

The father of her unborn child.

A noise from the back of the store made both of them

turn around. Oh, thank God. Millie had finally deigned to show up and do her job.

"Ah," Jenna said, fighting to hide her relief. "Here's Millie. She'll be able to assist you with any requirements you might have. Millie, this is Mr. Lassiter, he's opening the Lassiter Grill in town. Please make sure you give him our best service."

She sent Dylan a distracted smile and turned to go, only to feel him snag her wrist with warm strong fingers. Fingers that had done unmentionably wicked things to her and whose touch now sent a spiral of need to clench deep inside her.

"Not so fast," Dylan said, spinning her gently back to face him again. "As capable as I'm sure Millie is," he continued, flashing a smile that had the impressionable teen virtually melting on the spot, "I'd prefer to deal with you directly."

"I'm sure you would," Jenna answered as quellingly as she could. "But Millie is available to help you with your inquiry. I am not."

Her heart rate skipped up a beat as a hint of annoyance dulled his eyes.

"Scared, Jenna?"

His low tones were laced with challenge. Jenna stiffened her spine.

"Not at all, just very busy."

"Not too busy, I'm sure, to catch up with an old *friend*."

Hot color stained her cheeks. They weren't anything near approaching friends. She barely knew him any better now than she had the day they'd met—the day they were so drawn to one another that flirtation had turned to touching, and touching had turned to impassioned, frenzied lovemaking in the nearest available private space.

A butterfly whisper of movement rippled across her lower belly, shocking her into gasping aloud. Of course—the moment she'd been awaiting for weeks, her baby's first perceptible motion, would have to happen with its father standing right here in front of her.

Dylan's fingers tightened on her wrist. "Are you okay?"

"I'm fine," she said hurriedly. "Just very busy."

"Then I'll only take a few minutes of your time." He gave her a searching look. "Your office?"

Her body wilted in defeat. "Through here."

He released her wrist and she felt the cool air of the showroom swirl around her sensitized skin, as if her body instantly mourned the loss of contact, his touch. She found herself rubbing at the spot where he'd held her, as if she could somehow rub away the invisible imprint he'd left upon her.

Stop being ridiculous, she growled silently. *He was nothing to you before, aside from an out of character dalliance, and he's nothing to you now.* Logically she knew she couldn't avoid him forever. Despite the fact he was based in L.A., with the new restaurant opening here in town they were bound to cross paths again sometime. It might as well be now.

The tiny fluttering sensation rippled through her belly again, reminding her that there was a great deal more to consider than just her own feelings about seeing Dylan Lassiter. Thankfully, he hadn't noticed that her petite frame carried a new softness about it now. That her figure, rather than being taut and flat, was gently rounded as the baby's presence had suddenly become more visible at thirteen weeks.

She hadn't shared news of her pregnancy with anyone yet, and had no plans to start right now. Instead, she'd sought to hide it by changing from her usual style of figure-hugging attire to longer, more flowing lines.

As they entered the tiny office she used for administration, she gestured to the chair opposite her desk and sank, gratefully, into her own on the other side. Instead of taking the seat offered to him, Dylan sat on the edge of her desk. She couldn't help but notice the way the fine wool of his trousers skimmed his long powerful thighs, or how the fabric now stretched across his groin.

Her mouth suddenly felt parched and she turned to reach for the water jug and glasses that she kept on a credenza behind her desk.

"Water?" she offered with a croak.

"No, I'm fine, thank you."

She hastily splashed a measure of clear liquid into a glass for herself and lifted it to her lips, relishing the cooling and hydrating sensation as the drink slid over her tongue. After putting the glass down on the desk, she pulled a pad toward her and picked up a pen.

"So," she said, looking up at him. "What is it you want?"

He reached out and took the pen from her hand, laying it very deliberately down on the notepad. "I thought we could talk. You know, reminisce about old times."

Heat pooled at the apex of her thighs and she pushed her chair back from her desk. Anything to increase the distance between them.

"Look, you said a few minutes, and frankly, that's all I had. Your time's up. If there's nothing business related you need to discuss…?" She hesitated a moment, her temper snapping now at the humor reflected in his eyes. "Then you'll have to excuse me so I can attend to my work."

Dylan's sinfully sensuous lips curved into a half smile.

"You're different, Jenna. I can't quite put my finger on it, but I'll figure it out."

She fought back a groan. The man was all about detail. She knew that intimately. If she didn't get him out of here soon he was bound to notice exactly what it was that was different about her. She wasn't ready for that, not right now, anyway. She needed more time.

Before she could respond, he continued, "I want you to do the flowers for the opening. Wildflowers, grasses, rustic—that kind of thing. Can you do it?"

"I'll get my staff on to preparing some samples for you on Monday. I take it you'll be around?"

His smile widened. "Oh, yes, I'll be around. And your staff won't be handling this for me. You will."

"My staff are well trained and efficient—"

"But they're not you—and I *want* you."

His words hung in the air between them. She could feel them as if he'd actually reached out and touched her.

"You can't have me," she whispered.

"Can't I? Hmm, that's a darn shame," he said. "Because then I'd have to take my business elsewhere."

His words, so gently spoken, sent a spear of ice straight through her. It would take only a day for the news that she'd turned his business away to get through town. Less than that again before more people would follow his cue and take their business to other florists, as well. She'd fought long and hard to get a reputation as the leading florist in town and she wasn't going to lose it just like that.

She bit the inside of her cheek as she swiftly considered her options. Well, option. She really had no other choice but to take his business. Refusing it, with the associated fallout when word got around that she'd turned down a Lassiter—well, it didn't bear thinking about. However, the benefits would roll in pretty quickly when it was known that she'd done the flowers for the opening. There was nothing some of the better-heeled members of Cheyenne society loved more than following a trend set by the Lassiter family.

"I may be able to carve out a little time," she hedged, not wanting him to see how easily he'd forced her to capitulate. "Do you have particular designs in mind?"

"Tell you what. Why don't we discuss this further over dinner tonight."

"I'm sorry, I have plans for tonight." Plans that included a long soak with her feet in a tub filled with warm water and Epsom salts, followed by a home pedicure while she could still bend down and reach her toes. "Perhaps you could give me your contact number for while you're here. I'll call you when I'm free."

He gave her a narrow-eyed glance, then lazily got to his feet, reached into his back pocket for his wallet and slid out a card. She went to take it, but he didn't immediately let it go. Instead, he tugged it closer to his body, thereby tugging her a little closer, too.

"You'll call me?"

"Of course. We're closed tomorrow, but I'll check my schedule on Monday and call you then."

"I'll look forward to it," he said with a lazy wink and released the card.

She followed him from the office into the showroom. Even though she'd worked here since she was a teenager, she was still attuned to the sweet, luscious fragrance of the blooms she had on display. The various layers of scent filled the air with a strong feminine presence. A complete contrast to the powerful masculinity that was Dylan Lassiter.

Jenna held the front door to the store open for him.

"Thanks for stopping by," she said as he stepped past her and onto the sidewalk.

Just as he did, a large delivery truck passed on the street. The subsequent whoosh of warm air hit her full on, the gust plastering her short-sleeved tunic against her body. Dylan didn't miss a trick. His eyes drifted over the new fullness of her breasts, then lower, to where her waist had thickened, and to the gentle roundness of her tummy. He stared at her for what felt like an aeon before his eyes flicked upward to her face.

What she saw reflected back at her had the ability to nail her feet to the ground, right where she stood. She'd read about his convivial side, his laissez-faire attitude to life and his ability to continually land on his feet even as he eschewed traditional choices. Conversely, it was widely known that he was a perfectionist in the kitchen, which took a keen mind and grim determination.

The expression that he presented to her belonged to a different man entirely. This was the face of the CEO of the Lassiter Grill Corporation, not the playboy, not the one-time lover. No, this was the face of a man who had a question and, she thought with a shiver, would do whatever it took to get his answer.

"Looks like we have a bit more than just flowers to discuss. I think we'd best be having that dinner mighty soon, don't you?"

He turned on the heel of his hand-tooled boot and strode toward a dark SUV parked a few spaces down the street. She couldn't help but watch the lithe way his body moved. Jenna closed her eyes for a second but still his image burned there as if imprinted on her retinas. And she knew, without a shadow of a doubt, that her time for keeping this baby a secret had well and truly passed.

Two

Dylan swung his SUV into the traffic and fought to control the anger that roiled inside him like a building head of thunderclouds.

She was pregnant. No wonder she'd been as skittish as one of Sage's newborn foals when he'd arrived. He was probably the last person on earth she either expected, or wanted, to see.

His baby? The timing would be about right—unless she was the type of woman who indulged in casual assignations with just about any man she met. The thought made her stomach pitch uneasily. He needed to know for sure if their encounter had resulted in pregnancy. God, pregnancy. A kid of his own. And with her.

It wasn't hard to recall how his eye had been drawn to her that cool March Friday. He'd wanted her, right there, right then.

He remembered his first sight of her as she flitted about like some exotic bird, her attention solely on the flower arrangements she'd designed for his sister, Angelica's, wedding rehearsal dinner—a dinner that had ended before it began when his adoptive father, J.D., had collapsed with a fatal heart attack—for a wedding that had been called off, permanently now it seemed.

The building had been full of people doing what they did best, but Jenna stood out among them all in her jewel bright colors. An effervescent energy simply vibrated off her. Their initial banter had been fun and she'd given as good as she got. But the real craziness had started the moment he caught her hand in his and pulled her into an alcove where he kissed her, so he could see for himself if she tasted as intoxicating as he'd imagined.

She'd spun out of his arms the instant he'd loosened his hold on her but the imprint of her slight frame against his body had stayed with him through the course of the next hour, until he'd known that one kiss was definitely not enough. Satisfied the catering team in the kitchen knew what they were doing, he'd hunted Jenna down as she'd applied the finishing touches to the floral design she'd created for the entrance to the Cheyenne Depot—a historic railroad station that had been converted into a popular reception hall. Hunted her down and entrapped her in his arms for what he'd planned to be just one more kiss.

One more kiss had turned into a frenzy of need and they'd found their way into the coat closet at the front of the building. In its dark recesses, they'd discovered just what level of delight they could bring each other to.

He'd never been the kind of guy who waited for anything to come to him. No, he always went out and got it. And he'd certainly gone out and gotten her—both of them swept along on a tide of attraction that still left him breathless whenever he thought about it. He'd had casual encounters before, but this had been so very different. But then his father had died and his world had changed.

By the time the formalities here in Cheyenne had been taken care of, he'd had to race back to L.A. to continue his duties as CEO of the Lassiter Grill Corporation. Hassling Angelica for the contact details of the florist she'd used for that night—a night from which repercussions continued to cause his sister pain—had seemed a cruel and unnecessary thing to do. Besides, he'd had enough on his plate with work. Now, it seemed, he had a great deal more.

His inattention to the road forced him to jam on his brakes when the traffic ahead slowed suddenly. He swore softly. Two hours. He'd give her two hours to call him about dinner—max. If she hadn't phoned by then, he'd sure as heck be calling her.

In the end it was fifty-eight minutes exactly before his cell phone began vibrating in his pocket. He took it out, a smile curving his lips as he saw the name of her store come up on the screen.

"I was thinking we could make it tonight," he said without preamble. "My place, seven o'clock."

"Y-your place?"

He rattled off the address. "You know where it is?"

"Sure. I'll find it," she answered, her voice a little breathless.

"Maybe I ought to pick you up. Don't want you changing your mind at the last minute."

"I won't, I promise. I'll see you at seven."

She hung up before he could say another thing. His mouth firmed into a grim line as he slid his phone back into his pocket. It was a rare thing indeed to find a woman of so few words. Even when they'd first met they'd been bigger on action than conversation.

That was certainly going to change. He had a list of questions as long as his arm and he wasn't letting her go until she'd answered every last one.

One thing was certain. If she was carrying his child, he was going to be a part of that baby's life. Losing his own parents when he was young, then being raised by his aunt Ellie and her husband, J. D. Lassiter, Dylan knew just how important family was. He'd been too young to remember his mom and dad properly, too young to mourn more than the sense of security he'd taken for granted from birth. After his parents died, however, that all changed, until Aunt Ellie and J.D. stepped in and ensured that he, his brother, Sage, and sister, Angelica, never wanted for a thing. Even after Ellie Lassiter passed away, her sister-in-law, Marlene, had become a surrogate mom to them. It had been family that had gotten them through.

Now, with J.D. gone, too, the whole concept of family was even more important to him than ever. His brother thought he was nuts putting so much store by it. At constant loggerheads with J.D. and determined to make his own place in the world, Sage had always insisted that the only family he needed was Dylan. As close as they were, Dylan had always wanted more. And, if Jenna Montgomery's baby was his, it looked like he might be getting it.

Jenna reluctantly got ready to go out to Dylan's place. He was a complication she would rather ignore right now, but clearly, he wasn't about to let that happen. She quickly showered, then took her time rubbing scented moisturizer into her skin. So what if she had just shaved her legs— they needed it. She certainly hadn't done it for *his* benefit.

Nor had she applied the makeup she barely ever wore anymore for him, either. She was doing this all for herself. Pure and simple. If it made her feel good, feel stronger, then she was doing it. The same principle applied to the clothes she'd chosen to wear tonight. The royal purple stretch lace dress flattered her figure, even with the additional curves that now showed. It empowered her, as did the black spike-heeled pumps she teetered on.

She paused for a moment to assess herself in the mirror. Too much? Her eyes scanned from her dark brown hair, worn loose and flat-ironed dead straight, to her shiny patent leather shoes. She swiveled sideways. This was a total contrast to the kind of thing she'd worn in recent weeks. And, yes, it was definitely too much—which was why she wasn't going to change a thing.

She grabbed her purse from the bed and told herself she was not nervous about this meeting. That's all it was. A meeting. She'd tell Dylan what she'd been planning to tell him all along, and that would be that.

She wouldn't be swayed by the depth of his blue eyes, or the careless fall of his hair, which always looked as if he'd just tumbled from bed. She knew he was handsome; she'd fallen prey to that so easily. She also knew he was successful and intelligent and had a charm that could melt a polar ice cap. But she'd be immune to all that now, too. At least she hoped she would be.

She'd had weeks to think about this. Weeks in which to decide that while Dylan should know about his baby, she was most definitely bringing it up on her own. She knew full well what not to do when raising a child. Her own parents had been the prime example of that. No, her baby would want for nothing. He or she would grow up secure in the knowledge of Jenna's love and protection.

A man like Dylan Lassiter, with his cavalier lifestyle, a girl for every day of the week, every week of the year, not to mention his celebrity status, which ensured he traveled constantly, did not fit into the picture at all. She'd taken a walk on that wild side of his and yes, she had enjoyed every precious second. But life, real life, had to be lived in a far more stable and measured way. She owned her own home and had a business that was doing well…. With a few economies she could and would do this all on her own.

With those thoughts to arm her, she locked up and

walked out to her car. Checking the map one more time, she headed north to the address he'd given her, on the outskirts of town.

Doubts began to assail Jenna as she pulled in between the massive gated pillars, each adorned with a wrought-iron, stylized *L,* at the entrance to the driveway. The drive itself had to be several football fields long. She knew the family was wealthy, but seriously, who did this? Who kept a property this immense when they spent only about two months of every year living here? The Lassiters, that's who. It was a stark and somewhat intimidating reminder of the differences between herself and Dylan, and it struck a nervous chime deep inside her.

What if he used his money and his position to make things difficult for her? She had no idea what he was really like, although she remembered, without the slightest hesitation, how he'd felt and how he'd tasted. He was forbidden fruit. The kind of man every woman, no matter her age, turned her head to watch go past. The kind of man every woman deserved to savor—as Jenna had—at least once in her lifetime. But he wasn't a forever kind of guy. She'd been thankful he hadn't contacted her after their…their…*tryst,* she reminded herself again. She definitely wasn't looking for the roller coaster ride or the intrusive media publicity a relationship with him would offer.

Almost everything she knew about Dylan Lassiter she'd gleaned from social media and word of mouth around town—of which there was plenty. He'd basically gone wherever whim had taken him, spurning the opportunities and advantages afforded him by his adoptive father, and refusing to go into the family business or even attend college. Jenna sighed. What would it have been like, she wondered, to be able to be so carefree? She knew he'd traveled widely, eventually training in Europe as a chef and then coming back to L.A. and building a solid name for his skills, together with a certain celebrity notoriety at the same time. His life, to her, just seemed so…*indulgent*.

Her upbringing had been as different from Dylan's as a bridal bouquet was from a sizzling steak platter. And from her perspective, while there was plenty about Dylan Lassiter to recommend him to anyone who liked to run fast and loose, there was very little to recommend him as father material.

That said, this baby was *their* creation. Dylan had rights—and she had no plans to stand in the way of those. But she also wanted her child to grow up secure, in one place, with a stable and loving parent. Not used in a tug-of-war between parents, as she had been. Not dragged from pillar to post as her father moved from country to country, then state to state in pursuit of some unattainable happily-ever-after. And certainly not implicated by her father's fraudulent schemes or left abandoned at the age of fifteen because her sole surviving parent was doing time in jail.

No, Jenna's baby was going to have everything she hadn't.

She gently applied the brake and her car came to a stop outside the impressive portico. She rested a hand on the slight mound of her belly, determined not to be totally overwhelmed by the obvious wealth on display before her. This baby had rights, too, and yes, he or she was entitled to be a part of what stood before Jenna. But right now she was the baby's only advocate, and she knew what was best for him or her. And she'd fight to her very last breath to ensure her child got exactly that.

She grabbed her bag and got out of the car. The front

door opened as she walked toward it, and Dylan stood on the threshold. Jenna's heart did that little double skip, just as it had the very first time she saw him. It was hard to remain objective when the man stood before her. He'd tamed his hair slightly, giving him a more refined look, and he'd changed his suit for a pale blue cotton shirt that made his eyes seem even bluer than before.

"You found the place okay?" he asked unnecessarily as she ascended the wide steps.

"Hard to miss it, don't you think?" she replied, not even bothering to keep the note of acerbity from her tone.

She didn't want him to think even for a minute that he had the upper hand in this meeting. He inclined his head slightly, as if acknowledging she'd scored a valid point.

"Come on in," he invited, opening the door wide. "You must be ready to put your feet up after working all day. Can I get you something to drink?"

"Just mineral water, if you have it, thanks."

She hadn't drunk alcohol since she'd known she might be pregnant. In fact, there were a lot of things she didn't eat or drink as a result of the changes happening deep inside her body.

"Sure, take a seat," he said, gesturing to the large and comfortable-looking furniture that dominated the living room off the main entrance. "I'll be right back."

He was as good as his word. She'd barely settled herself against the butter-soft leather of a sofa big enough to sleep on before he was back with two drinks. An ice-cold beer for himself and a tall glass of sparkling water for her.

"Thank you," she said stiffly, taking the glass from his hand and studiously avoiding making eye contact.

But she couldn't avoid the slight brush of fingers, nor could she ignore the zing of awareness that speared through her at that faint touch. She rapidly lifted the glass to her lips to mask her reaction. The bubbles leaping from the water's surface tickled her nose, further irritating her. She swallowed carefully and put the glass on the coaster on the table in front of her.

Dylan sprawled in the seat opposite, his large, rangy frame filling the chair. His gaze never left her face and an increasingly uncomfortable silence stretched out between them. Jenna cleared her throat nervously. Obviously, she was going to have to start this conversation.

"I—I wanted to say how sorry I was about your father's passing."

"Thank you."

"He was much respected and I'm sure you must miss him very much," she persisted.

"I do," Dylan acknowledged, then took a long draw of his beer.

Damn him, he wasn't making this easy for her. But then again, what had she expected?

"He'd have been proud of the new restaurant opening here in town," she continued valiantly.

"That he would."

"And you? You must be pleased with everything being on time."

"I am."

A muscle tugged at the edge of his mouth, pulling his lips into a half smile that was as cynical as it was appealing. Jenna suddenly had the overwhelming sense that she shouldn't have come here. That perhaps she should have waited a day or two before calling him. Hard on its heels came the contradictory but certain knowledge that she definitely should have been in touch with him long before now.

Was this how a mouse felt, she wondered, just before a cat pounced? Did it feel helpless, confused and frightened, with nowhere to look but straight into a maw of dread?

She watched, mesmerized, as Dylan leaned forward and carefully put his beer on the table. He rested his elbows on his knees, those sinfully dexterous hands of his loosely clasped between them. Warmth unfurled from her core like a slowly opening bud, and she forced her eyes to lift upward, to meet the challenge in his.

She fought to suppress a shudder when she saw the determination that reflected back at her. She reached for her water and took another sip, shocked to discover that her hand shook ever so slightly. She dug deep for the last ounce of courage she possessed. Since he was determined to make this so awkward, she'd find some inane way to carry the conversation even if it killed her.

"Thank you for asking me to dinner tonight. It's not every day I'm catered to by a European-trained celebrity chef."

She was surprised to hear Dylan sigh, as if he was disappointed in something. In her?

"Jenna, stop dancing around the issue and cut to the chase. Are you pregnant with my baby?"

Three

Dylan cursed inwardly. He'd been determined to be charming. He could do charming with his eyes closed and both hands behind his back. So why, then, had he so hamfistedly screwed up what he'd planned to be a relaxing evening of fact-finding with a woman he'd been fiercely attracted to from the second he'd first laid eyes on her?

It was too late now. The words were out and he couldn't drag them back no matter how much he wanted to. He huffed out a breath of frustration. Jenna looked about as stunned by his question as he was at actually blurting it out that way. Damage control. He desperately needed to go into damage control mode, but try as he might, he couldn't think of the words to say. What he wanted was the answer. An answer that only Jenna Montgomery could provide.

Beneath his gaze she appeared to shrink a little into the voluminous furniture. She was already a dainty thing—her small body perfectly formed—but right now she was dwarfed by her surroundings and, no doubt, daunted by the conversation they were about to have.

Dylan knew he should try and put her at ease, but the second she'd alighted from her car he had felt the shields she'd erected between them. It had aroused a side of him he hadn't displayed in years, made him deliberately uncooperative as she'd tried to observe the niceties of polite conversation. It had driven him to ask the question that had been plaguing him since that gust of wind off the road had revealed changes in her slender form that were too obvious to someone who knew that form as intimately, even if fleetingly, as he had.

"Well?" he prompted.

"Yes," she said in a strangled whisper.

Dylan didn't know what to say. Inside he felt as if he'd just scored a touchdown at the Super Bowl, but he also had this weird feeling of detachment, as if he was looking in on some other guy's life. As if what she'd just said wasn't real—didn't involve him. But he was involved, very much so. Or at least he *would* be, whether she liked it or not.

"Were you going to tell me sometime, or did you just hope that I'd never know?"

As much as he fought to keep the hard note of anger from his voice, he could feel it lacing every word. It left a bitter taste in his mouth and he struggled to pull himself under control. He didn't want to antagonize her or scare her away, and it wasn't as if he'd made an effort to get in touch with her again before today. This was way too important, and at the crux of it all an innocent child's future depended on the outcome of tonight.

"I meant to tell you, and I was going to—in my own time. I've been busy and I had a bit of a struggle coming to terms with it myself. Getting my head around how I'm going to cope."

Jenna's voice shook, but even though she was upset, he sensed the shields she'd erected earlier growing even thicker, her defense even stronger.

"And you didn't think I should have known about this earlier?"

"What difference would it have made?"

Her words shocked him. What difference? Did she think that knowing he was going to be a father made no discernible difference to his life, to how he felt about *everything?* Hell, he'd lost his own father only a couple months ago. Didn't she think he at least deserved a light in the darkness of mourning? Something to get him through the responsibility of having to get up every day and keep putting one foot in front of the other, all because so many other people depended on him to not only do exactly that, but to do it brilliantly—even when he wanted to wallow in grief?

"Trust me." He fought to keep his tone even. "It would have made a difference. When did you know?"

"About three weeks after we—" Her voice broke off and she appeared to gather up her courage before she spoke again. "I began to suspect I might be pregnant, and waited another week before going to my doctor."

Dylan sucked in a breath between his teeth. So, by his reckoning, she'd had confirmation that their encounter had resulted in conception for plenty of time. She could have shared the news—no matter how busy she was.

Damn it, he'd used a condom; they should have been safe. But nothing was 100 percent effective, except maybe abstinence. And there was one thing that was guaranteed, when it came to Jenna: abstinence was the last thing on Dylan's mind.

Even now, as quietly irate as he was right this second, she still had a power over him. His skin felt too tight for his body, as if he was itching to burst out and lose himself in her. His flesh stirred to life even as the idea took flight. Desire uncoiled from the pit of his belly and sent snaking tendrils in a heated path throughout him.

No one had had that power over him before. Ever.

Yet this diminutive woman had once driven him to a sexual frenzy that had tipped over into sheer madness. She still could.

A ringing sound penetrated Dylan's consciousness, a much needed reminder of the here and now and the fact that Jenna sat opposite him, quite a different woman from the one he'd so quickly but thoroughly made love to two and a half months ago.

"I'll be right back," he said, surreptitiously adjusting himself as he rose from the seat. "I need to check on something in the kitchen."

After a quick examination of the beef bourguignonne simmering on the stovetop, and checking that the rice in the cooker was fluffy and ready, he grunted with satisfaction. They would continue this discussion at the table, where, hopefully, he'd find his manners again and stand a better chance of hiding the effect she had on him.

He returned to the living room and painted a smile on his face.

"Dinner's ready. Would you like to come through to the kitchen? I thought we could eat in there, if you're comfortable with that."

"Since I usually eat standing up at the store or off a tray on my lap when I'm home, just sitting at a table sounds lovely."

She stood and smoothed her clothes, her hand lingering on the tiny bump that revealed a child of his now existed. It hit Dylan like a fist to the chest. His child. Someone of his blood. Everything else in his life right now faded into the background as that knowledge took precedence. Now there was another generation to think about, to protect and to teach.

The thought filled him with a new sense of purpose, of hope. The past five years had been challenging, the past couple of months even more so. But this baby was a new beginning. A reason for Dylan to ground himself in what was good, and to put some much needed balance back in his life, balance that was sadly lacking. This baby, his son or daughter, was a lifeline out of a spiral of work and hard play that had threatened to consume him. One way or another he would be a part of his child's world— every single day if he could, although that would take some engineering with him based in L.A. and Jenna here in Cheyenne. Whatever the logistics, he was prepared to work this situation out. He just needed to be certain that Jenna felt the same way.

She crossed the room to where he stood, and he put his hand at the small of her back and guided her through to the kitchen. He felt her stiffen slightly beneath his touch, and heard her breath hitch just a little. Knowing she wasn't as unaffected by him as she pretended went a long way toward making him feel better about the semi-erection he was constantly battling to keep in control.

He seated her at the square wooden table in the kitchen and gestured to the vase containing a handful of wild-flowers he'd found on his four-acre property when he'd gone to walk off some steam this afternoon.

"They could probably have done with your touch," he said as he turned to the oven to take warmed plates out and lay them on the table.

"They look fine just the way they are," Jenna commented.

But as if she couldn't resist, he saw her reach out and tweak a few stems. Before he knew it, the bouquet looked a hundred times better.

"How do you do that?" he asked, bringing the Dutch oven filled with the deliciously fragrant beef across from the stove.

"Do what?"

"Make a jumble of weeds look so good."

She shrugged. "It's a knack I picked up, I guess."

"What made you decide to work with flowers?"

"I didn't, really." She sighed. "They kind of picked me."

"Not a family business, then?" he probed, curious to discover just how she had ended up under Mrs. Connell's roof.

Jenna gave a rueful laugh. "No, not a family business at all, although once I started working at the store it felt like home to me."

There was a wistful note in her voice, one he wanted to explore further, but found himself reluctant to. There was time enough to find out all her secrets, he told himself.

He spooned rice from the cooker onto the warmed plates, and put them on the table.

"This looks great," Jenna commented, leaning forward to inhale deeply. "And smells even better. To be honest, I think your skills with food far outweigh mine with flowers. I can barely reheat a TV dinner without burning something."

Dylan feigned horror. "Wash your mouth out. TV dinners? You're going to have to do much better than that for the baby."

He reached for a ladle and spooned a generous portion of the beef onto her plate before serving himself. When she didn't immediately pick up her fork, he sat back and looked at her. Her lips had firmed into a mutinous line and there was a frown of annoyance on her forehead.

"What did I say?"

"I didn't come here to be told what to do. Maybe it's better if I go."

She pushed back her chair a little, but before she could go any farther he reached out and grabbed her hand.

"Okay, truce. I will try not to tell you what to eat, but you have to admit, for me it comes with the territory. It's what I do. It's in my nature to want to feed people well."

It was also in his nature to want to lift her from her chair, march her to the nearest accommodatingly soft surface and relive some of the passion they'd shared. She looked down at where his fingers were curled around her wrist, and he slowly eased his grip and let her go.

"As long as we're clear on that," she muttered, scooting her chair closer to the table again and lifting her fork.

She scooped up a mouthful and brought it to her lips. His brain ceased to function as she closed her eyes and moaned in pleasure. Other body parts had no such difficulty.

"That's so good," she said, opening her eyes again.

For a second Dylan allowed himself to be lost in their chocolate-brown depths. Just a second. Then he forced himself to look away and apply himself to his own meal.

"Thanks, I aim to please," he said with a nonchalance he was far from feeling.

It didn't seem to matter what he did or what he said, or even how she reacted to any of it—he was drawn to her on a level he'd never experienced before. Sure, that could play to his advantage, but he had the sneaking suspicion that Jenna Montgomery was a great deal more hardheaded than her feminine presence at his table suggested.

"Home grown?" she asked, spearing some beef and popping it into her mouth.

For a second he was distracted by her lips closing around the fork, then the enticing half smile they curved into as she tasted and chewed.

"Yeah, from the Big Blue. Nothing but the best."

"Your cousin runs it, doesn't he? Chance Lassiter?"

"And very well, too. It's in his blood."

And therein lay the rub. While he and Sage had been raised Lassiters, they weren't Lassiter by birth. Not like Chance, not like their sister, Angelica. It was one of the reasons why this baby meant so much more to Dylan than he had ever imagined. This child was a part of his legacy, his mark on the world. It was all very well gaining fame and fortune for doing something you excelled at and loved, but raising a child and setting him or her on a path for life—nothing compared to that.

"Have you thought about what you're going to do when the baby is born?" he asked, deliberately changing the subject.

"Do?"

"About work."

"I'll manage. I figure that in the early stages I should be able to keep the baby at work with me."

He nodded, turning the idea over in his mind. "Yes, sure—initially. I think that would be a good idea."

"I'm sorry?"

He looked at her in puzzlement. But his confusion didn't last long.

"What you think should matter to me, why, exactly?"

He let his fork clatter onto his plate. "Well, it is my baby, too. I have some say in what happens to him or her."

Even though he'd tried to keep his voice neutral, some of his frustration must have leaked through.

"Dylan, as far as I'm concerned, while you have rights to be a part of this baby's life, it doesn't mean you have a say in how I bring it up."

"Oh? And how do you see that working? Just let me jet in every now and then, have a visit and then jet out again?"

"Pretty much. After all, you live most of the time in L.A., or wherever else in the world you're flying off to—not here where the baby and I will be. Obviously, I won't stand in your way when you want to see him or her, though, as long as it's clear I'm the one raising the child."

That was not how things were going to happen. Dylan's hands curled into fists on the table and took in a deep, steadying breath. "That's good of you," he said, as evenly as he could. "Although I have another suggestion, one that I find far more palatable, and which will be better for all of us."

She looked at him in surprise. "Oh? What's that?"

"That we get married and raise the baby together."

To his chagrin she laughed. Not just laughed but snorted and snuffled with it as if she couldn't contain her mirth.

"It's not so impossible to think of, is it?" he demanded.

"Impossible? It's ridiculous, Dylan. We barely know one another."

He nodded in agreement. "True. That's something easily rectified."

All humor fled from her face. "You're serious, aren't you?"

"Never more so."

"No. It would never work. Not in a million years."

"Why not? We already know we're..." he paused a moment for effect, his eyes skimming her face, her throat and lower "...compatible."

"Great sex isn't the sole basis for a compatible marriage," she protested.

"It's a start," he said, his voice deepening.

Hot color danced in her cheeks—due to anger or something else? he wondered. Something like desire, perhaps?

"Not for me it isn't. Look, can we agree to disagree on

the subject of marriage? I've already said I won't stand in your way when it comes to seeing the child. Can we leave it at that for now?"

"Sure, for now. But, Jenna, one thing you will learn about me is that I never give up. Especially not on something this important."

Four

Jenna's heart hammered a steady drumbeat in her chest. He looked deadly serious. This wasn't how she had imagined their meal together going, not at all. She certainly hadn't imagined that he'd spring an offer of marriage on her like that.

Sure, there was probably a list as long as her arm of women who would jump at the opportunity. But she wasn't like that. And she'd meant it when she'd said his life was in L.A. and not here, because it *was*. While it was true that he'd been in Wyoming more often lately, it was only because of the new Grill opening in town. Once that was up and running he'd be straight back to the West Coast. Back to his high life and being featured in the celebrity news with his beautiful women.

No, marriage to Dylan Lassiter didn't even bear thinking of, she decided as she forced herself to take another bite of the melt-in-your-mouth perfection of the meal he'd prepared. He might be spending more time in the boardroom these days, she mused, but he hadn't lost his knack in the kitchen.

Maybe it would be worth marrying him just to have meals like this every day, she thought flippantly. An image of him barefoot and in the kitchen, wearing an apron and not much else, hovered in her mind, sending a pull of longing through her.

No, get a grip on yourself, she chided silently. She'd never settled for anything less than perfection when it came to a relationship. It was why she so rarely dated. That was why her behavior with Dylan back in March was such an aberration.

Once people began to notice her pregnancy, she had no doubt there'd be a whole ton of questions asked. Uncomfortable questions. Her hard-fought-for privacy would be invaded—her reputation open for all of Cheyenne to discuss. It shouldn't bother her, but it did. She knew what it was like to be the focus of unwanted attention, and she'd worked hard to stay out of the public eye ever since.

"I'm glad you acknowledge that our child is important. I happen to agree, which is why I'm not going to rush into anything or make any decisions today," she finally stated.

"You're important, too, Jenna," he answered softly.

For a second she felt a swelling in her chest—a glimmer of something ephemeral, an intangible dream emerging on the periphery of her thoughts. Then reality intruded. She shook her head.

"Don't lie to me, Dylan. We both know that since March neither of us has made any attempt to contact or see one another, until today. In fact, if you didn't have the restaurant opening coming up, we probably wouldn't even be here right now."

"I don't know about you, but I've thought about that evening a lot."

Jenna couldn't stop the warm tingling sensation that spread from the pit of her belly at his words.

"Don't!" she blurted.

"Don't what? Don't admit that we were blisteringly good together? Tell me you haven't thought about us, about what we did—and haven't wanted to try again. Even just to see if it wasn't some kind of weird fluke."

"I—"

Her throat closed up, blocked by a swell of need so fierce it overwhelmed her. She forced herself to erase the visual image that now burned in the back of her mind. An image he'd put there without so much as a speck of effort because it was always there, always waiting to be brought out into the light and examined, relived. She squirmed on her seat, suddenly uncomfortable, aching. For him. For more.

"Fine," she muttered curtly. "We were good together, but that's no basis for a future. We are two totally different people. Our lives barely intersect."

"That's not to say that they couldn't. Don't you want to just try it?"

He looked so earnest, sitting there opposite her at the table. It would be all too easy to give in, but she'd worked too hard for too damn long to even consider giving up her hard-won freedom, not to mention her hard-earned respect from the community.

She herself had been the product of a hurried marriage, one that hadn't worked on any level and had led to hardship and unhappiness for all concerned. She would not inflict that on her baby. No matter how enticing that baby's father was. No matter how much she wanted him.

What did he know of marriage, of commitment? Their own liaison was a perfect example of the impulsive life he led. See something? Want it? Have it, then just walk away without a backward glance. She couldn't risk that he'd do that with their child, let alone her. Not now, not ever.

"No," she said firmly. "I don't. Please don't push me on this issue, Dylan."

"Okay," he acceded.

She felt her shoulders relax.

"For today," he amended.

And the tension was right back again. He cracked a smile and she was struck again by his male beauty. There was not a thing about him, physically at least, that didn't set her body on fire. As to his morals, well, that was something else entirely. But her behavior didn't reflect so well on her, either, she reminded herself.

"Don't look so serious, Jenna. We'll declare a truce for this evening, all right?"

His voice was coaxing, warm. And almost her very undoing.

"Truce, then," she agreed, and applied herself again to her meal.

It truly was too good to ignore and, much as she hated to admit it, he was right that she should be eating better. Weariness had been quite an issue for her, and while prenatal vitamins and supplements were helping, nothing really substituted for a healthy diet and plenty of rest.

"More?" Dylan asked when her plate was empty.

"I'm stuffed," she said, leaning back in her chair with a smile on her face. "That was excellent, thank you."

"Just part of the package," he said with a smile. "So, are you too stuffed to think about dessert? Can I tempt you with some raspberry and white chocolate cheese-cake?"

"Tempt me? Are you kidding? Of course I want dessert."

When he took the dish from the refrigerator she almost dissolved into a puddle of delight.

"You made that, too?" she asked as he sliced a piece for her. She reached out and nabbed a white chocolate curl from off the top, laughing as he went to slap her hand away and missed.

"Not me personally this time. It's one of the desserts

we're trialing for the steak house," he said, sliding her plate toward her. "I picked it up this afternoon."

She spooned up a taste and then another.

"Good?" Dylan asked.

"Divine. Don't talk to me, you're messing with my concentration."

He laughed aloud and the sound traveled straight to her heart and gave it a fierce tug. *Oh, yeah, it was all too easy to think you could fall in love with a man like Dylan Lassiter,* she told herself. He was the whole package. Not just tall, dark and handsome, but wealthy, entertaining to be with and bloody good in bed. Well, in a coat closet, anyway. And then there was the near orgasmic cooking.

Don't go there, she warned herself. But it was too late. Arousal spread through her like a wildfire. Licking and teasing at her until she felt her breasts grow full and achy, her nipples tightening and becoming almost unbearably sensitive against the sheer fabric of her bra. She knew the very second Dylan's line of vision moved, the precise moment he became aware of her reaction.

"Remind me to feed you cheesecake more often," he said, his voice slightly choked. "I'm going to make coffee. Can I offer you some, or a cup of something else, maybe?"

"Hot tea, please," Jenna answered, fighting to get her wayward hormones back under control.

Dylan stood and turned away from the table, but not before she noticed he wasn't exactly unaffected himself. So it seemed the crazy attraction between them showed no sign of abating. What on earth was she going to do about it?

Nothing. Abso-freaking-lutely nothing at all. They'd get through the rest of this evening. They might even discuss the baby a little more. But they were not going to do a single thing about this undeniable magnetism between them. After all, look where it had led them the last time.

Dylan ground fresh coffee beans and measured them into his coffeemaker, taking his time over the task. This was getting ridiculous. Why couldn't she see just how suited they were to one another? Why wouldn't anyone want to take that further? Her physical attraction to him was painstakingly obvious. Not that he needed any help in that department, but it was a natural trigger for his own.

There was a lot to be said for being a caveman, he thought as he switched on the electric kettle and heated the water for her tea. He'd never before felt so inclined to drag a woman by her hair into his lair and keep her there—making love to her until she no longer wanted to leave. He gave himself a mental shake. No, that image was completely unacceptable. He liked his women willing. He'd never used force or coercion before and he wouldn't start now—no matter how tempting Ms. Jenna Montgomery made the idea seem. Somehow, he had to make her see that they'd be good together. Good enough for marriage and raising a kid.

He heard the scrape of her spoon on the plate as she finished her cheesecake, and he returned to the table with their hot drinks on a tray.

"Shall we take these back through to the living room?" he suggested.

"Sure."

She got up to follow him and his eyes drifted again to her belly, to where his baby lay safely nestled. It roused something feral in him. Something he'd never experienced before today. Something he knew, deep in his heart, would never go away. He knew it was possible to love another person's child—knew it from firsthand experience, from *being* that child, from being loved. For some reason, though, knowing it was his son or daughter she carried made Dylan feel as if he could give a certain superhero a decent run for his money in the leaping tall buildings department.

He also knew he'd do anything, lay down his life if necessary, to provide the best for his kid.

Jenna returned to her seat on the sofa and Dylan sat next to her, a sense of satisfaction spreading inside when she didn't scoot away from him.

"When's the baby due?" he asked, after taking a sip of his coffee.

"First week in December, all going well."

"A baby by Christmas," he mused aloud, struck by how much his life could change in a year.

"Life will be different, that's for sure."

"So what have you planned so far?"

Suddenly he needed to know everything she'd already done, and what she wanted to do for the rest of her pregnancy. This should involve him.

"Well, I've started getting a few things for the spare room in my house, you know, to turn it into a nursery. I found a bassinet at a yard sale last weekend. I'm going to reline it and get a collapsible stand. That way I'll be able to use it in my office at the store as well as at home, until the baby gets a little bigger."

Dylan suppressed the shudder that threatened to run through him at the thought that his child would have secondhand anything. Did that make him a snob? Probably. He and his brother had shared things as they grew up, and there'd been nothing wrong with that. It didn't stop him from wanting to race out to the nearest store and buy all new equipment for his child, though.

Jenna, sensitive already, obviously picked up on his thoughts. "What's wrong? You think our baby is too good for a secondhand bassinet?"

"Actually," he started, thinking he needed to tread very carefully, "I was thinking more along the lines of what I could do to help out financially."

If she was scouring yard sales, maybe she was a bit stretched when it came to money. She had the store, but also had her own home. Financing both took a lot of hard work and determination. And dollars and cents.

"I can manage, you know," she said defensively.

"The point is you don't have to *manage,*" he said. "I meant what I said when I told you I'm going to be a part of this baby's life, and I don't just mean the occasional visit. I'm happy to support you both."

She looked as if she was about to bristle and reject his words, but then she slumped a little, as though a load had been lifted from her slender shoulders.

"Thank you." She sighed softly. "It won't be necessary, but I do appreciate the offer."

"Hey," he said, taking one of her hands in his and mentally comparing how small and dainty it felt in his much larger palm. It roused a fierce sense of protection inside him. One he knew would be smacked straight into next week if he showed her even an inkling of how she made him feel. "We got into this together, and that's how it's going to stay."

She looked up at him, her dark eyes awash with moisture. "Do you think we can do that? Stay friends through this?"

"Of course we can."

"It's not going to be easy."

"Nothing worthwhile ever is," he commented.

At the same time he promised himself that no matter

what, she would not be doing this on her own. And one way or another, he'd get her to change her mind about marrying him. Now that he had her back in his life, he didn't want to let her go again. There was a damn fine reason why he hadn't been able to shake her image from his thoughts every single day. Now he had every incentive to find out exactly what that reason was.

Five

By the time Jenna rose to leave, weariness pulled at every muscle in her body. She was grateful tomorrow was Sunday. A blessed day of rest, with time to weigh up everything that had happened since Dylan Lassiter had walked back into her life. Maybe she'd get to work in the garden for a while, too—she always found that restful. Or even a lazy stroll around the Cheyenne Botanic Gardens might be nice.

"It's late," she said, stifling a yawn. "I'd better get home. Thank you for tonight. I mean that."

"You're welcome," Dylan replied, getting to his feet and putting his hand at the small of her back again.

Despite her exhaustion, her body responded instantly. It would be so easy to give in. To turn toward him, press her body against his large hard frame and sink into the attraction between them. To allow him back behind the barriers she'd erected when the reality of their encounter had hit home. Instead, she put one foot in front of the other and headed for the door.

"Are you okay to drive?" he asked, a small frown of concern causing parallel lines to form between his brows. "I don't mind dropping you home. I can always bring your car to you tomorrow."

"No, I'll be all right. Thank you."

"You know, independence is fine and all that, but accepting help every now and then is okay, too."

"I know, and when I need help, I'll ask for it," she answered firmly.

She could feel the heat rolling gently from his body, bringing with it the leather and spicy wood scent of his cologne. It made her want to do something crazy, like nibble on the hard line of his jaw, or bury her nose in the hollow at the base of his throat. Man, she really needed to get out of here before she acted on those irrational thoughts.

"Thanks again for tonight," she said.

"You're welcome. We still have plenty more to discuss. Okay if I get in touch?"

She hesitated, wishing she could say no, and knowing she needed to say yes. Given the way he tugged at her, emotionally and mentally, she knew it wasn't going to be easy sharing a baby with him. Jenna settled for a quick nod and all but fled down the stairs. But he was right at her side, so that when she got to her car it was his hand that opened the door for her. He leaned down once she was settled inside.

"Red fluffy dice?" he asked with a chuckle when he saw the things dangling from the rearview mirror of her ever-so-practical station wagon.

"I have dreams of owning a red convertible one day. *Had* dreams," she corrected.

With the baby on the way, that was one dream that would have to be shelved for a while. Maybe even forever.

"Classic or new?" Dylan persisted.

"Classic, of course."

He gave her a wink. "That's my girl."

She felt an almost ridiculous sense of pride in his obvious approval, and forced herself to quash it. It didn't matter whether he approved of her dreams or not. They weren't going to happen, not now. She was doing her best to hold everything else together. Luxury items were exactly that: luxury. An extravagance that was definitely not in her current budget.

"Well, good night," she said, staring pointedly at his hand on the door.

To her surprise he leaned down and reached for her chin, turning her head to face him, before capturing her lips in an all too short, entirely too sweet kiss.

"Good night. Drive safe," he instructed as he swung her door closed.

Her hands were shaking as she started the car and then placed them on the wheel. As she drove around the turning loop to head down the driveway, she sought refuge in anger. He'd done it on purpose, just to prove his point about compatibility. The thing was, she *knew* they were compatible sexually. Now they had to be compatible as parents. Seemed to her they'd definitely missed a few steps along the way, and now there was no going back.

His proposal of marriage was preposterous. She sneaked a glance in her rearview mirror at the two-story house, fully lit up from the outside and looking as unattainable as she knew a long-term relationship with a man like Dylan Lassiter was, too. Jenna forced her eyes forward, to focus on the road ahead, and her future. One where she'd have to fight to keep Dylan Lassiter on the periphery if she hoped to keep her sanity.

By the time she rolled her car into her garage and hit the remote to make the door close behind her, she felt no better. Seeing Dylan again had just put her well-ordered world into turmoil. She'd had enough chaos to last a lifetime. It was why, when she'd been placed with Margaret Connell after her father was jailed, she'd put her head down and worked her butt off to fit in and to do things right. Mrs. Connell's firm but steady presence had been a rock to a fifteen-year-old teetering on the rails of a very unsteady life.

Mrs. Connell had not only provided a home for her, she'd provided a compass—one Jenna could live by for the rest of her life. The woman had also provided a sense of accountability, paying Jenna a wage for the hours she spent cleaning up in the florist shop after school and learning how to put together basic bouquets for people who came in off the street and wanted something quick and simple.

By the time Jenna had finished high school, she'd known exactly what she wanted to do. She'd put herself through business school, spending every spare hour she wasn't studying working in the flower store, which she'd eventually bought and made her own. Mrs. Connell was now enjoying a well-earned retirement in Palm Springs, secure in the knowledge that all her hard work, both with Jenna and the business, hadn't been in vain.

Jenna calculated the time difference between here and Palm Springs. It probably still wasn't too late to call Mrs. Connell, and she so desperately needed the guidance of someone else right now. Someone older and wiser. Someone stronger than she was. But that would mean disclosing how she'd gotten herself into this situation. Telling someone else about behavior that she wasn't terribly proud of. The last thing Jenna wanted to hear in her mentor's voice was disappointment.

She climbed out of her car, went inside the house and got ready for bed. For all that Dylan had said about wanting to be a part of everything, she'd never felt so alone in her life, nor so confused.

Would he be so keen, she wondered, if he knew exactly who she was and what her life had been like? It was hardly the stuff of Disney movies. Her father had come home from work one day when she was nine, to find Jenna alone after school—her mother having abandoned them to sail, from New Zealand and her family, with the outgoing tide and pursue her dream of being a singer on a cruise ship. He'd pulled up stakes by the time Jenna was ten, and taken her to his native U.S.A., where he'd told her again and again that they'd strike it lucky any time, and that happily-ever-after was just around the corner for them both.

Unfortunately, his idea of luck had been inextricably linked to fleecing older, vulnerable women of their wealth, and using his looks and charm to get away with it. Until one day he'd gone a step too far.

Jenna pushed the memory to the back of her mind, where it belonged. She'd learned the hard way what it meant to be an unwitting public figure, and how cruel the media could be. Given the Lassiter family profile, any relationship between her and Dylan would be bound to garner attention—attention she didn't want or need. For her own sake, and that of her unborn baby, she would do whatever it took to keep a low profile.

She slid between the 800-thread-count bed linens she'd happily picked up in a clearance sale, and smoothed her feet and legs over the silky soft surface. She might not be in his league financially, but she didn't do so badly. She could provide for her baby, who certainly wouldn't want for anything. So what if some of their possessions were a little care-worn or threadbare or—Jenna grimaced in the dark, remembering Dylan's reaction—secondhand. She would manage, and her private life would remain that way: private.

* * *

Dylan whistled cheerfully as he drove away from the classic car dealer, relishing the sensation of the wind ruffling his hair. The thrum of the V8 engine under the shiny red hood before him set up an answering beat in his blood. Today was a perfect day for a picnic and he had just the partner in mind to share it.

After swinging by the Grill to make sure everything was running smoothly, he put together some food and drink, checked the GPS on his phone and headed toward Jenna's address, which he'd happily plucked from a phone book. He was curious to see where she lived—where she'd planned to raise their baby. *Planned* being in the past tense, because now that he was on the scene, he didn't intend for them to live apart. All he needed to do was convince Jenna.

When he turned into her driveway he had to admit he was surprised at where she lived: it was a new neighborhood, the streets lined with modern homes. Skateboards, bikes and balls littered the front yards. He could see why she'd be comfortable here. Even though he hadn't seen anyone yet, there was a sense of community and projected longevity about the area.

He saw curtains in windows on either side of her house twitch as he turned off the ignition and sat a moment in the car. A smile played at his lips. Neighborhood watch, no doubt. It was good to know Jenna had people looking out for her when he wouldn't be.

Dylan got out of the car. He couldn't wait to see her face. He strode up the path that led to the front door and pressed the doorbell. Nothing. He waited a minute and tried again.

"You looking for someone?" A woman's voice came

from over the well-trimmed hedge on one side of Jenna's property.

"Yes, ma'am," he answered with a smile that wiped the distrustful look off her face in an instant. "Is Jenna home?"

The woman blushed prettily. "She's gardening out back. Just follow the path around the side of the house and you'll find her."

"Thank you."

Clearly, he'd passed muster. He jangled the car keys in his hand as he made his way around to the rear of the house. It only took a minute to find her. She knelt by a raised bed of roses, pulling vigorously at the weeds and dumping them in a bucket beside her.

"That looks suspiciously like hard work. Need a break?"

Jenna jumped at his voice and looked up, using the back of her hand to push a few loose strands of hair from her eyes.

"No, thank you. This job isn't going to do itself."

"Why don't you get someone else in to help?"

"Because first, I don't have money to throw around like that, and second, I enjoy it."

His eyes swept across her face, taking in the smear of dirt on her flushed cheek and the dark shadows that were painted beneath her eyes.

"If you tell me what to do, will you let me help for a while so I can take you out to play after we're done?"

She looked startled for a minute. "Seriously?"

"Yeah, of course I'm serious."

She pursed her lips a second, making him wish he could taste them again. Last night's chaste kiss had done nothing but ignite a desire for more.

"You don't really want to garden, do you."

It was a statement, not a question. He shrugged. "I'd be lying if I said I did. But I'll do what's necessary to achieve my objective."

Jenna narrowed her eyes. "And your objective is…?"

"Taking you out to lunch."

"I'm not dressed for lunch."

"That's okay, I prepared a picnic."

A wistful expression replaced the wariness in her eyes. "A picnic? I've never been on one of those."

He couldn't hide his shock. "Never?"

She shook her head.

"Then let me be the one to remedy that for you." He stepped closer and took her hand in his, stripping off her gardening glove before doing the same with the other hand. "The weeds will still be here when we get back."

"Unfortunately."

"Then worry about them later. Come with me," he coaxed. "Now."

For a second she chewed at her lower lip, her gaze fixed on her hand still held in his.

"Shouldn't you be at work? The grand opening's not all that far away now, is it?"

"No, it's not. I've already been by the Grill today. Everything's under control. Besides, I'm the boss—when I say I need a bit of time out, I take it. So, are you coming?"

"Okay. But let me freshen up first."

"No problem. I'll meet you out front."

As much as he was itching to step inside her small home, to see what things she'd chosen to surround herself with, he sensed he'd pushed enough for one day. That she'd agreed to come out on the picnic with him was a coup in itself, and he'd take that victory before reaching for the next one.

"Give me ten minutes, then," she said, already walking toward the screened back door.

"No problem. Take all the time you need."

The door slammed behind her and he took a moment to look around the garden. Here and there were splashes of color, interspersed among some midsize trees. It was a good backyard, as backyards went. But it wasn't where his kid would grow up playing. Kids needed space—and he'd be providing it. Eventually.

Inside Jenna quickly changed from her tattered and dirty gardening gear into a T-shirt and jeans. To her surprise, she couldn't fasten the top button on her jeans, which was something she'd been able to manage, barely, last week. That was one thing pregnancy definitely guaranteed—change, and plenty of it.

She washed her face and smoothed on some tinted moisturizer. It would probably be too much to apply her usual makeup, but she wasn't going out with Dylan without feeling at least a little in control. She attempted a quick brush of her hair, but it was impossible to smooth the tangles that a sleepless night had wrought, so instead she carelessly swept it up and secured it with a few pins, then tied a scarf around her head.

Surveying the results in the mirror, she allowed herself a grin of approval. Her T-shirt was long and loose-fitting, her bra made of sturdier material than last night's. She'd be fine.

It took only a few seconds to lock up and head out the front door, but the instant her feet hit the porch she came to an abrupt halt. There, in her driveway, sat the car that had featured in all her fantasies. It was as if Dylan had reached into her mind and extracted the information himself, she thought, as she surveyed the fire-engine-red Cadillac convertible with whitewall tires and the top down. It was her dream car—right down to the red fluffy dice, twins to her own, hanging in front.

Dylan straightened from where he leaned against the passenger door, and flashed her a smile.

"You like it?"

Jenna forced herself to walk toward him, still locked in a state of disbelief.

"I love it. What…? How…?" She shook her head. "Did you hire it for the day or something?"

"No," he said. "After you mentioned it last night I thought I'd look around online. I saw it this morning and bought it."

"You *bought* it? Just like that?"

He lifted the keys and dangled them in front of her face. "You want to drive?"

"Do I!" She snatched the set from his hand and tossed her bag in the back before racing around to the driver's side. She threw herself into the seat and ran her hands over the steering wheel and the dash. "I can't believe it. You really bought this today?"

Dylan seated himself next to her with another one of those smiles that made her insides melt. "Sure did. Shall we give her a run? I was thinking we could head out to the Crystal Lake Reservoir, find a nice spot and have our picnic."

It was at least a forty-minute drive to get there. She'd love every second of it.

"Let's get going then," she said, smiling back at him.

He stared at her, the smile on his face changing, his expression becoming more serious. He lifted a hand and touched her cheek with one finger.

"You're so beautiful, you know that?"

Jenna didn't know what to say. Her stomach clenched

in reaction to his touch, to his softly spoken words. She wanted to refute it, but at the same time wanted to hold those words in a safe place in the corner of her heart, forever.

Dylan let his hand drop, breaking the spell. "C'mon," he said, "let's get this show on the road."

The engine's powerful roar when it turned over sent a shiver of happiness up her spine.

"I still can't believe you bought this," she said as she backed out the drive and onto the street. "That's just so impulsive."

"Why shouldn't I?" He shrugged. "I bought it for you."

Six

Dylan watched as her expression turned from one of sheer glee to one of horror. She jammed on the brakes, throwing him slightly forward.

"Whoa, there. Easy on the brakes, sweetheart."

"Tell me you didn't do that."

"Didn't do what?"

"Buy me this car."

"If I did, I'd be lying."

"I can't accept it." She shook her head vehemently. "That's just crazy."

"It is what it is."

But he was walking on thin air. She was out of the car—leaving the engine still running, the driver's door open—and standing on the sidewalk, her arms wrapped around herself in protection as if warding off some terrible pain.

Dylan shot out of the car and closed in on her, but she put up her hands, halting him in his tracks. What had he done? He could see her shaking from here.

"What is it? What's wrong?"

"You're trying to buy me, aren't you?" Her voice quavered and her face was pale. "Trying to make me do what you want."

"Jenna, the car's a gift."

"Some bloody gift!" she snapped, her eyes now burning as she looked at him squarely. "I know what a car like that is worth. You don't just buy one in the morning and give it away by the afternoon."

"Jenna, I'm hardly a poor man. I want to see you have nice things."

"Why?"

He was confused. *"Why?"*

"Yes, why? Why me? Why now? As I said last night, we hardly know each other. We had sex *once.* We're having a baby. That's it. That's all there is to us, and now you're buying me a Cadillac?"

"Maybe I'm buying it just because I can. Maybe I need to prove to you that I can provide for you, that you don't need to do all this on your own, that you don't need to keep pushing me away. Yes, we're having a baby—*together.* I know we're doing this all back to front, but I want to get to know the mother of my kid. I want to see if we can be a couple."

Jenna's eyes flicked away from his, but not before he saw the sheen of tears reflected there. Before he could close the distance between them, the first drop spilled off a lash and tracked down her cheek. She lifted a hand and furiously scrubbed it, and those that followed, away.

"I don't want the car," she said adamantly, through clenched teeth. "I will not be bought."

"Fine. I'll take it back tomorrow. But can't we just enjoy today? Take it for a spin. Enjoy it while we can?"

He tentatively put his arms around her, pulling her closer. She lifted her chin and blinked away the moisture in her eyes. She was one tough chick, that was for sure.

"Just for today?" she asked, her voice tight.

"Sure, if that's what you want."

"So it's not mine anymore?"

"Nope."

He felt a pang of regret that he'd have to say goodbye to the big red beast, but if that's what it took to begin to win her trust, then that's what he'd do. Jenna looked past him at the car and he could see the longing in her gaze. Even though she wanted it, she would still refuse it. Her moral ground remained solid, even in the face of a desire so hungry she was almost salivating with it.

"Jen?" he said, noticing that he wasn't the only one with eyes on her right now. In fact, not only were curtains twitching, but there were faces appearing at windows, too.

"What?"

"I don't want to rush you, but shall we go? We're providing a bit of a show here."

"Oh, God," she groaned. Her lips firmed and she drew in a breath. "Fine, let's go then. But you can drive."

He didn't argue. Instead he guided her around to the passenger side of the car and helped her into her seat before closing the door and heading to the driver's side.

"You okay?" he said, reaching across the car to squeeze her hand.

"I'm fine. Just go, will you?"

"Whatever the lady wants."

The trip to the reservoir was accomplished in silence. Dylan kept throwing surreptitious looks at Jenna during the journey and was relieved to note the tension in her body had begun to ease as they headed out of Cheyenne. As they wound along the route that led to the reservoir he kept an eye out for a place with a vantage point overlooking the lake. He gave a grunt of satisfaction when he found just the spot, and brought the car to a stop beneath some trees.

Through a gap between the trunks, the lake gleamed like highly polished mirrored glass, reflecting the surrounding rock formations and flora in a perfect echo of their surroundings.

Dylan got out of the car and opened the trunk, unloading a large rubber-backed blanket and a picnic hamper. He passed the blanket to Jenna.

"Here, find us a spot. I'll bring the food and drinks."

She took it without a word and headed a little closer to the water. When he joined her she'd spread it out in a sunny spot in a small clearing.

"I…I'm sorry. For before," she said in a stilted tone. "I'm sure my reaction probably appeared over the top to you."

"A little, but that's okay. No apology needed."

"No," she said vehemently. "You were trying to be nice and I threw it back at you. I just…"

She averted her gaze out over the water, as if searching for something to draw strength from to help her get her words out. Dylan waited quietly, watching the internal battle reflected on her face.

"I just don't like it when people think they can buy someone else with things, or when other people accept them."

Dylan scratched his jaw as he played her words over in his mind. Sounded as if there was a story behind that statement. Would he ever hear it from her? He hoped so.

"Fair comment," he answered, putting the hamper and the small drinks cooler down at the edge of the blanket. "And duly noted for future reference."

"You're mad at me, aren't you?"

"Not mad. Disappointed, maybe, that you don't feel you can accept the car from me, but hey, I'm a big boy now. I'll get over it."

And, he added silently, *I'll find a way through that wall of yours, one day.*

He opened the cooler and handed Jenna a bottle of mineral water before snagging one for himself.

"Italian?" she asked, looking at the label. "Is there anything you do normally?"

"Define *normally.*"

She chewed on her lower lip a moment before speaking. "Well, inexpensively, then."

"Why should I?"

"Because one day you might wish you had, for one. What if the bottom drops out of steak houses and the Lassiter Grill Corporation goes down with it?"

Dylan shook his head, a smile playing around his mouth. "It'll never happen. People like food, especially good food. Plus, they're more conscious these days of how their food is raised. The cattle on the Big Blue are free range and grass fed. Only nature's goodness. The beef served in the Grills is the best in the country, probably the world, and I ensure our staff and our dishes live up to that promise."

"You're very confident."

He paused a moment, thinking about it. "Yeah, I guess so. I haven't always been this way. Being raised by J.D. made a big difference, though. It took a while, but we got there."

"You lost your parents quite young, didn't you?"

"Sage was six and I was four. I don't remember too much about them, but Sage—" Dylan sighed "—he took it real hard. Kind of put himself in opposition to anything J.D. said or suggested from day one."

"I always wished I had a brother or sister," Jenna said wistfully, taking a sip of her water.

He found his gaze caught by her actions, riveted by the movement of her slender throat as she swallowed.

"Only child?"

"Only and lonely," she said lightly, but even so, he heard the truth behind her words.

"Where did you grow up?"

"All over. I was born in New Zealand and grew up there before my mom and dad broke up."

"New Zealand, huh? I thought you had a bit of an accent."

"Hardly," she snorted. "When we heard my mom had died, Dad packed us up and brought us back here to the States. Any accent soon got teased out of me at school."

"Back to the States?"

"My father's American. We traveled a bit and eventually I got to settle here in Cheyenne. The rest, as they say, is history."

Painful history by the sound of things. What she didn't say spoke louder than what she did. Dylan turned to the hamper in a bid to break the somber mood that had settled over them. He reached past the cooling pads he'd packed around the food and lifted out a couple covered containers. He popped the lids off, revealing in one, sandwiches made with freshly baked whole grain bread, and in the other, a selection of sliced fruit.

"I can promise you I prepared these myself and that I carefully studied what you can and can't eat in pregnancy," he said, putting the dishes down between them on the blanket.

Jenna picked up a sandwich and studied the filling. "You mean you washed and dried the lettuce in here yourself?"

"With my own fair hands," he assured her with a grin. "But don't tell any of my kitchen staff that or they'll expect me to do everything myself."

They ate in companionable silence and Dylan quietly cleared up when they were done.

"Tell me why you've never been on a picnic before," he suggested, interrupting her contemplation of the lake's beauty.

She remained silent for a while, and so still he began to wonder if she'd even heard him.

"I guess I just never had the opportunity before," she eventually said, but he could tell she was leaving plenty out of that trite little answer. "It's nice, though. Thank you."

He'd have to be satisfied with that, he told himself, and filled in the gap in conversation that followed with his own tales of the times he and Sage had raided their aunt's kitchen to take a picnic outdoors. He loved it when he made Jenna laugh. It lifted the shadows from her eyes and showed a different side to her than the one that constantly met him head-on and tried to thwart his every attempt to spoil her.

It wasn't much later that Jenna lay down in the sunshine and closed her eyes. She was asleep in seconds. The day's temperature was still pretty mild, but the wind had a bite in it, so Dylan got his sweater from the trunk of the car and gently put it over her as she slept.

He stretched out beside her, wishing they had the kind of relationship where he could pull her into his arms, curl around her body and keep her warm with his heat alone.

All in good time, he assured himself. All in good time.

Jenna woke with a shiver as a shadow passed over the sun. She opened her eyes to see a cloud sailing overhead. She realized that she had something covering her and lifted it to see what it was. Dylan's sweater? When had he done that? A warm sensation filled her at his consideration.

For a minute or two she just lay there, absorbing the

sounds of the insects and birds, and relishing the peaceful surroundings, before she became aware of a deep steady breathing that came from close by. She turned her head and saw Dylan lying on his back beside her. Well, that answered one question, she thought. He didn't snore. His arms were bent up under his head and even in sleep the latent strength of his biceps were obvious. She observed the steady rise and fall of his chest. His T-shirt had risen above the waistband of his jeans, exposing just a hint of his lower belly.

At the sight of his bare flesh a tingle washed through her, and her fingertips itched to reach out—to touch and trace that line of flesh with the faint smattering of dark hair. She didn't dare give in to the temptation, though. Things were already incendiary between them. They didn't need any further complications and right now, to her, a relationship with Dylan was a complication she'd rather avoid.

She looked past him to the Caddy, sitting in all its shiny glory under the trees.

What kind of man did that? she asked herself. Who on earth bought a classic car on a whim for someone he barely knew from Adam, just because she said it was a dream of hers? The thought triggered a memory of the day her dad had come to pick her up from junior high. They were living in Seattle at the time and he'd rolled up in a brand-new 5-series BMW, looking like a cat that got the cream.

Soon after, she'd met the reason behind the car. His latest conquest had bought it for him when he'd admired it one day as they'd passed a dealership. It was payment, he'd said flippantly, for services rendered. Jenna hadn't fully understood, at the time, just what he'd meant by that. Just as she'd never understood, until she got older, why all the women he dated had at least ten, sometimes more, years on him. Or why he was always turning up with expensive things. Even back then it had made her uncomfortable. It hadn't seemed right, especially when her dad never appeared to hold down a real job. But her father had just laughed off her concerns when she got brave enough to broach them.

He'd never stayed with anyone for long. All of a sudden she'd wake one morning and they'd be on the move again. Sometimes clear across the country in pursuit of his next happily-ever-after. She'd had no idea that even while he was dating one woman, he was casually grooming up to five others via the internet. Nor did she know that when they'd moved to Laramie when she was fifteen, and she'd shaved her head as part of a school-run fund-raiser for one of their cancer-stricken teachers, that her father would use that picture to create a whole new set of lies to fleece his victims with.

Lies that eventually saw him hauled off to jail for fraud and caused her to be placed here in Cheyenne with Margaret Connell. Jenna squeezed her eyes shut. She didn't want to think about that time—about the gross invasion of her life by the media, the reporters who'd accused her of being complicit in her father's schemes. She'd been just a kid, with nowhere and no one else to turn to. When child services had taken her, she'd wondered if she was going to end up in prison, too. After all, she had no one else. Her mother was dead. They'd learned she'd died less than a year after she'd left them, choking on her meal aboard ship. And there'd been no other family to come in and pick up Jenna's fractured life.

Mrs. Connell had been a much-needed anchor and a comfort. For the first time in her life Jenna had been able to stay in one place for more than what felt like five minutes. It hadn't broken her reticence about making friends, though. Even now she found it a struggle to get close to anyone. She'd learned growing up that it was better that way, better than having to say heart-wrenching goodbyes every time her life turned topsy-turvy again.

She studied Dylan's strong features. Even in sleep he looked capable, secure in his world. What would it be like to take a chance on him? To just go with the flow and let him take control of her and the baby's worlds?

Even as she considered it, the idea soured in her mind. And what about when he lost interest and moved on? she asked herself. As her father had moved on so many times? As Dylan himself had moved on from various publicly touted relationships in his life? She wouldn't do that to her child, or to herself. They were both worth so much more than that.

Self-worth. It was a hard lesson to learn, but it was one Margaret Connell had reinforced every day Jenna had lived under her roof. It was why Jenna could never accept anything that was a facsimile of a real life, or a real love. She'd been there already and she still bore those scars. Probably always would.

Dylan's eyes flicked open and he turned his head to look at her. "Nice sleep?" he asked with a teasing smile.

"Mmm, it was lovely. Thank you for this. It was a great idea."

"Even though we had to do it in that?" He nodded over toward the Cadillac.

"Yes." She heaved a mock long-suffering sigh. "Even though we had to do it in that."

He rolled onto his side, facing her. "You certain you don't want it? You're allowed to change your mind, y'know."

"No, thank you. I don't want it. Besides, there's no anchor point for an approved child restraint," she said soberly, reminded anew of how much her life, her dreams, would change in a few short months' time.

"Good point. Maybe I'll keep it for date nights."

Jenna felt her entire body revolt at the statement. Here she was contemplating approved child restraints for *their* baby, and he was busily planning his next night out with some woman.

"*Our* date nights," he specified with a wicked grin that told her he knew exactly what she'd been thinking.

"We won't be having any of those," she said in an attempt to suppress his humor, especially since it was humor at her expense.

"I think it would be good for our kid to see our common interests don't just revolve around him or her. I've seen too many couples lose sight of what they feel for one another when they're crazy busy with their kids and with work. They lose themselves, and worse, they lose each other."

His words, spoken so simply, ignited a yearning inside her that made her heart ache. He made it sound so simple. But she knew to the soles of her feet that life just wasn't like that.

"You're forgetting one thing," she murmured. "We aren't a couple."

He leaned a little closer. "We could be."

And with that, he inched a tiny bit nearer and closed his lips on hers.

Seven

The second their lips touched, Dylan knew it was a mistake. If only because they were in a public place and there was no way he could take this all the way. Not here, not right now—even though his body demanded he do so. He should have waited until they were behind closed doors. Someplace where they could relish their privacy and take the time to explore one another fully. Enjoy one another without fear of discovery.

It didn't mean he couldn't make the most of the moment, though, and he slid his hand under Jenna's head, cradling her gently as he sipped at the nectar of her mouth. Her lips were soft and warm, pliant beneath his. A rush of need burst through what was left of his brain, urging him to coax, to plunder, to take this so much further than a kiss. But he held back.

He wanted her, there was no denying it. But he was prepared to take this slowly—as painful as that would be—if that was what he had to do to convince her he was serious.

Jenna's hands lifted up to bracket his face, and he took that as permission to use his mouth to tease her some more—to open her up and taste her, their tongues meshing, their teeth bumping. How he wished he could see all of her, and touch and taste every inch.

She was pregnant with his child and he'd never seen her naked. Just the idea of it made his nerves burn with raging heat, and urged him to go further. But still he held back, eventually forcing himself to ease away, to create at least a hand span of distance between them. It wasn't enough. There could be an entire continent between them and it wouldn't deaden how he felt about her. How much he wanted her.

"Think about it," he said, rolling away and standing up.

"Think about what?" she asked, looking up at him with a dazed expression in her eyes.

He fought back a smile. Maybe that's all he'd have to do to convince her they should get married. Kiss her senseless until she simply said yes.

He offered her a hand and helped her to her feet, then picked up and folded the blanket, slinging it over one arm. "Us. Together. You know—a couple."

She started to shake her head, but he reached up and gently took her chin between his fingers.

"Think about it, Jenna. At least give me a chance to prove to you how good we could be together. Not just as lovers, although I know that will take us off the Richter scale—again. But as a couple." His hand dropped to the slight mound of her belly. "As a family."

Before she could respond, he grabbed the cooler and turned and walked to the car. He didn't want to see rejection in her eyes. Not when he'd realized, even as he spoke, just how much he wanted this. He'd lost his parents when he was only four, Aunt Ellie—his adoptive mother—only three years after that. He was luckier than most. He'd had four parents in his lifetime, five when he counted Marlene as well, and each one had left an imprint of devotion. An imprint so indelible it had made him promise himself that, when he eventually had a family, he would be a part of his children's lives. They would know the security of parents who loved them unreservedly. He'd had that, and he would walk over flaming gas ranges if necessary, to make sure his kid had it, too.

Jenna appeared beside him, handing him the now empty hamper as he stowed the cooler and blanket in the trunk.

"Will you at least consider it?" he asked, closing the trunk with a solid thud.

She looked up at him, vulnerability reflecting starkly at him from those dark brown eyes of hers. "Okay."

One small word and yet it had the power to change everything about the life he lived, about the choices he'd made. It should be daunting and yet it made him feel excited on a level he hadn't anticipated. Made him almost feel a sense of relief that he could, maybe, stop searching for that one ephemeral thing that he'd always felt was missing from a life rich in so much already. The thing he'd sought in travel and women and had yet to find. He shoved his hands in his jeans pockets to hold himself back, to stop himself from giving in to the impulse to grab her and twirl her around with a whoop of satisfaction.

"Thank you."

The drive back to her home was completed in silence but it was a comfortable one. With one hand on the wheel, he'd reached across and tangled his fingers in hers for most of the journey. It wasn't something he'd ever stopped to consider before with anyone else but, right now, he felt as if the connection between Jenna and him had solidified just that bit more. And it felt strangely right. By the time he dropped her off and saw her into her house he was already formulating plans for tomorrow. Plans that most definitely featured Jenna Montgomery.

Monday morning, the smell of fresh paint and new carpet filled Dylan's nose the moment he strode in through the front door to check on progress at the restaurant and was pleased to see the delivery of the new furniture was well under way. He stopped a second to inhale the newness, the potential that awaited. The excitement that had thrummed quietly inside of him built to new levels. It was happening. He'd felt excited about each of the previous three Lassiter Grills to date but this one was even more special to him than the others.

Hard on the heels of his excitement came a thrust of regret that J.D. couldn't be here to see their dreams become a reality. It was still hard to accept that his larger-than-life, hard-as-nails father figure was really gone. At moments like this, it was that much worse.

God, but he missed that man. And as much as he grieved for J.D. with a still-raw ache, he owed it to the old man to make sure that everything about this new restaurant would match, if not eclipse, their existing venues. That meant keeping up his hands-on approach to business and proving that J.D.'s faith in making him CEO of the Lassiter Grill Corporation was well founded.

With a nod of approval, he walked past the massive polished wood bar to the double doors that led into the kitchen. As much as he loved the front of the restaurant, this was the hub of what made the Lassiter Grills great. This was where he belonged, amongst the stainless steel countertops and the sizzle and steam and noisy organized chaos of cooking. The last of the equipment had been installed a week ago and his team had spent the past week trialing the signature dishes that would be specific to the Cheyenne steak house, along with the much loved

menu that made the Lassiter Grills so popular in L.A.,
Las Vegas and Chicago.

It was ironic, Dylan thought as he surveyed the hand-
picked team, that he'd spent the better part of his adult
years running away from responsibility and family commitment and yet in the past five years he'd embraced
every aspect of both of those things. Clearly, he was
ready to settle down.

The very idea would have sent a chill through him not
so long ago but over the past few months, well, it had tickled at the back of his mind over and over again. Maybe
it was losing J.D. so suddenly that had made him begin
to question his own mortality and his own expectations
of life. Or maybe he was finally, at the age of thirty-five,
mature enough to accept there was more to life than the
hedonistic whirlwind that had been his world to date. It
was a sobering thought.

Satisfied that his staff had it all under control, he
drove over to Jenna's store. He pushed the door open
and stepped in, his nostrils flaring at the totally different
scents in the air, compared to those back at the Grill. As
before, there was no one in the front of the store, but he
could hear off-key humming coming from out back. The
humming came closer and he saw Jenna walking through,
carrying an armload of bright fresh daisies. She'd pulled
her hair into a ponytail today, lifting it high off her face
and exposing her cheekbones and the perfectly shaped
shells of her ears. He imagined taking one of those sweet
lobes between his teeth and his body stirred in instant
response.

"Oh, I didn't hear you come in," she said, placing the
flowers on the main counter.

"No problem. I haven't been waiting long."

He studied her carefully. She looked tired, a little pale.

As if she'd had about as much trouble getting to sleep last night as he had. He couldn't help himself; he lifted a hand and skimmed the back of his fingers across her cheek.

"You okay? You're not overdoing things, are you?"

She pulled away from his touch. "I'm fine, Dylan. Trust me, I won't do anything to harm this baby. I may not have planned for it, but now that it's a reality, there's nothing I want more in my life."

There was a fierce undertone to her voice that convinced him she was telling the truth. It didn't stop him worrying, especially when she bent to shift a large container filled with water to another spot on the floor.

"Here," he said, brushing her aside. "Let me do that for you. I thought you had staff to help you."

Jenna stood back, a quizzical expression on her face. "I do, but they're part-time. I open and close the store each day."

"Then let me do the heavy stuff today."

"No problem, but I'll be back to doing it again tomorrow. Unless you plan on being here for me every morning to help me rearrange everything in the store?

"If that's what it takes," he said as he straightened. "Or I could arrange that you had someone here first and last thing to do this if you'd rather."

She shook her head, a rueful smile pulling at those kissable lips of hers. "I'd prefer to do it myself."

"Hey, can you blame me for wanting to take care of you? You're carrying precious cargo there."

A wistful expression settled on her face. "Yeah, I am, aren't I? But I still have a job to do. Now, I guess you're here to see what I've worked out for the flowers for the opening? I've sketched a few ideas and also thought I'd put something together quickly with what I had out back."

She grabbed a square of burlap and some twine, and

wrapped them around a plastic-lined cardboard base. She then moved around the store, selecting stems of greenery and laying them on the counter next to the daisies. Before his eyes, she used the assortment of items to create a vision of beauty.

"Hmm, needs some berries, too, I think," she muttered, more to herself than anything. A second or two later she turned the arrangement around to face him. "There, what do you think?"

He eyed the compilation of color and texture and decided he liked it very much. She had a genuine talent for this. There was nothing generic about what she'd created. She'd taken his minimal instructions and put together what he'd wanted without his fully understanding it himself.

"That's great. So these would be for the tables?"

She nodded. "And then I'd do something bigger, maybe in a crate propped on some hay bales, in the foyer. What do you think?"

"I think you're an artist."

She gave a little shrug. "I have a knack, I guess."

"Don't sell yourself short, Jenna." Dylan cast his eye over the arrangement again. "I'm thinking, though, that the colors need to be bolder. These might disappear in the decor. Why don't you come back with me to the restaurant for lunch? You can get a better feel of what I mean."

"You're going to feed me again? Three times in three days? This is getting to be a habit."

"We need live subjects to try the menu, and some of our waitstaff need the experience, too," he explained, even though it was more a case of now that he'd seen her again, he didn't want to let her out of his sight. "You'd be doing me a favor."

He didn't fool her for a second, that much was obvious

from the smile that spread across her face. "A favor, huh? Well, since one of my workers is due in shortly, I think I'd be able to slip away for an hour for lunch."

"Just an hour?"

"I do have a business to run. Besides, won't it be better for your team to get used to working with customers who are in a hurry?"

"Good point," he acceded, even though he wished he could just whisk her away for the afternoon and keep her to himself.

"I'll come at one, okay? I have some orders I need to put together for our delivery guy and—" she glanced at her wristwatch "—I need to get to work on them now if they're to be ready on time."

"That's great. I'll be waiting."

Jenna watched him leave, surprised at herself for agreeing to lunch today. Despite all her tossing and turning last night, and her resolve to try and keep things purely business between them, it appeared she wanted to see him again more than she'd realized. True, this visit was under the guise of checking the decor of the restaurant, but the prospect of spending more time with him, even if only an hour, made her bubble inside, as if the blood in her veins was carbonated.

Valerie, her assistant, came in through the front door.

"Wow, tell me the guy just leaving wasn't an apparition."

"Oh, no." Jenna smiled. "He's quite real."

"Just my luck to be running late today, or I could've served him."

Jenna looked at her long-married friend, a mother of four, and raised a brow. "Seriously?"

"Well, a girl's entitled to her dreams, isn't she? He

looks vaguely familiar. What did he want? Please tell me he wasn't ordering flowers for his girlfriend."

"That was Dylan Lassiter," Jenna said with a laugh, "and he's ordering flowers, through us, for the latest Lassiter Grill opening."

"He is? Wow, that's got to be good for business. You think they'll keep us as a regular florist? It'd be a fabulous lift for our profile."

"I haven't discussed future work with him, but we have a good start. Which reminds me, if I don't get my work out of the way this morning, I won't be able to make it to the restaurant for our next meeting at one."

"I could always go for you," Valerie suggested with a wink.

"I'm sure you could," Jenna said, still laughing, and imagining Dylan's face if she took Valerie up on her offer. But an unexpected surge of possessiveness filled her. She didn't want anyone handling Dylan's requests but herself. Dragging her thoughts together, she briskly continued, "C'mon, help me with these orders before Bill gets here for pickup."

The balance of the morning flew by. While she worked, Jenna considered the ramifications of having a regular corporate account with the Lassiter Grill. The exposure for her business would be great, there was no denying it. She made a mental note to raise the subject with Dylan, and went to get ready for their lunch date.

She was running late by the time she arrived at the restaurant but luckily found a parking space just around the corner.

Dylan was waiting by the front door as she jogged up the sidewalk.

"I was beginning to think you'd stood me up," he said, opening the door for her and guiding her inside.

"Just a busy morning, that's all."

"We have company for lunch. My brother, Sage, is joining us, together with his fiancée, Colleen."

Jenna immediately felt at a disadvantage. "Oh, I wish you'd said so. I'm not dressed for company."

Dylan turned his gaze to her and she felt him assess her from top to toe. "You look mighty fine from where I'm standing."

Heat bloomed in her chest and flooded all the way up to her cheeks. Great, now she'd look like a little red fire engine when introduced to his family.

"I mean it, Dylan," she said awkwardly.

"So do I. Seriously, you have nothing to worry about. They're my family and they'll love you any way you're dressed."

He grabbed her hand and led her inside. Her eyes darted around the dining room, taking in the design features that were such an integral part of the pictures she'd seen of each Lassiter Grill. While the building had a stone exterior, the interior walls were log lined. Her eyes roamed over the high ceilings, hung with massive iron fans, and down to the wooden plank floors. A huge floor-to-ceiling stone fireplace held a place of dominance in the center of the restaurant. What they'd sacrificed in space they'd more than made up in character. She loved the ranch-style atmosphere. It was realistic without being over the top. An idea popped into her head.

"I've been thinking about the opening and about how you'll dress the tables for the night," she began.

"Uh-huh?"

"What do you think of burlap table runners on white linen?"

He paused a moment, considering. "That sounds like a good idea. D'you have pictures of what you're thinking?"

She nodded.

"Good, we can talk about them after lunch. C'mon over and meet my brother."

Her nerves assailed her and she tugged at Dylan's hand, making him stop and turn to face her.

"Do they know?"

"Know?"

"About us, about the baby."

"Not yet. Do you want to tell them?"

She shook her head vehemently. It was enough that Dylan knew, but she wasn't ready to share the news with others.

"Okay, but they're going to find out sooner or later," he warned.

"Just not yet, okay?"

They crossed to the table where the couple were seated. Sage rose to his feet as they approached. Slightly taller than his brother, with medium brown hair sprinkled with a touch of gray at the temples, he looked like a man used to being in control. He also didn't seem like the type you could hide anything from for long, and the way his gaze dropped to her hand clasped in Dylan's larger one, and then back to his brother's face, told her he saw a great deal more than what lay on the surface. She pulled free of Dylan's grip as a frisson of unease wended its way down her spine. She so wasn't ready for this.

"Jenna, this is my brother, Sage, and his fiancée, Colleen. Sage, Colleen, this is Jenna Montgomery."

"Pleased to meet you," Jenna said, taking the bull by the horns and stepping forward with her hand outstretched. "Dylan's asked my firm to do the flowers for the opening. I hope you don't mind my crashing your lunch, but he wanted me to see the restaurant before we confirmed a color palette."

She knew, as soon as the words left her mouth, that she'd overcompensated. As if sensing her discomfort, Colleen rose from her chair with a welcoming smile and shook Jenna's hand.

"I'm pleased to meet you. Didn't you do the flowers for—"

"Angelica's rehearsal dinner, yes," Dylan interrupted, his swift interjection earning him a curious glance from his brother.

"I was going to say for a friend of mine's dinner party a couple of weeks ago," Colleen corrected smoothly, still holding Jenna's hand. "She was thrilled with what you did. I know you'll do a great job for Dylan."

Jenna began to feel herself relax as Colleen took over the conversation. It didn't mean that Sage stopped his perusal of her, but she allowed his fiancée to distract her as they turned the discussion to the pair's upcoming wedding and what the best flowers and style of bouquet might be. Across the square table, Dylan and his brother bent their heads together in deep discussion. Despite the differences in their coloring, their eyes were very much the same and the shape of their jaw and their mannerisms spoke of their strong familial connection.

Dylan looked up and flashed Jenna a smile before shifting his attention back to his brother, and she felt herself relax a little more. Colleen was very easy to talk to, and by the time they'd ordered off the menus and awaited their meals, Jenna found herself beginning to enjoy the other couple's company. Sage, while appearing a little standoffish at first, was clearly very much in love with his fiancée, and Jenna had to quell a pang of envy.

What would it have been like to meet Dylan and let a relationship with him progress the way most normal couples started? She shoved the thought aside for the piece of mental candy floss it was. She couldn't afford to indulge in thoughts of what might have been. She had been dealt large doses of reality in her lifetime, and coping with those, while keeping her wits about her, was paramount.

When their orders came Jenna applied herself vigorously to her serving of smoked baby back ribs with fries and grilled corn on the cob, which certainly beat a hasty sandwich grabbed in between customers at her shop. It felt strange being the only diners in a restaurant, waited on so industriously by the staff there, although the other three seemed to take it in stride. Jenna took her cue from Dylan and tried to act as if she was used to this kind of thing.

About thirty minutes later, when Sage made his apologies and rose to leave the table, Jenna decided she should do the same.

"No, wait for me here while I see Sage and Colleen out," Dylan insisted. "We still have those colors to discuss, as well as the table dressing you mentioned."

She nodded and turned her attention to the glass of mineral water Dylan had ordered for her. The water reminded her she needed to find the restroom. She got up and moved to the front of the restaurant, but before she could reach the facilities she overheard Sage talking to his brother.

"She's pregnant, Dylan. I hope you know what you're doing."

"I know she's pregnant. It's my baby."

"It's what?" Sage couldn't hide the shock in his voice.

"It's my baby and I'm going to marry her."

"Don't be a fool, man. It's not like you were even dating. You don't *know* her or anything about her. You don't even know for sure if the baby's yours—it could be anyone's. Shouldn't you at least wait until it's born, so you can do a paternity test?"

The sour taste of fear filled Jenna's mouth. This was exactly what she'd hoped to avoid. She didn't need Sage's censure or his implications. Yes, she had behaved like a tramp that Friday evening back in March. But so had Dylan. It was unfair that there was always one set of rules for guys and then another for women. The fact remained that they were dealing with the outcome of their dalliance, but the last thing she wanted was for it to become common knowledge. Not when she'd worked so hard, for so long, to wash away the taint of her father's behavior from her life.

She was where she was and who she was despite her upbringing. And, dammit, she would make a great mother even if juggling her business and motherhood would be a challenge. Jenna knew, to her cost, that life wasn't about easy solutions. It was about making the right choices and working hard to hold on to them.

"I don't like your insinuation, brother. Be very careful what you say about Jenna. I plan to marry her and I will raise my kid with her."

Dylan's tone brooked no argument and Jenna's spirits lifted to hear him defend her.

"Look, I didn't mean to offend you, but let's be realistic about this. At least have her investigated. If you won't, I will."

Ice cold sensation spilled through her veins. Investigation? It wouldn't take much to unearth her past, a past she'd fought hard to put behind her. Dylan's voice was raised when he answered his brother.

"I am being realistic about this, Sage. You know what family means to me. You know what *you* mean to me. I am not walking away from my son or daughter, and I'm not walking away from Jenna."

She held her breath through the tense silence that developed between the brothers, but she couldn't help but shift slightly. She really needed to pee. Her movement must have made some sound, because Dylan turned his head, his eyes spearing her where she stood.

"Um, I was just looking for the restrooms?" she said, horribly uncomfortable that she'd been caught standing there, eavesdropping.

"Through there," he said, pointing.

She scurried in the direction he'd indicated. After she relieved herself, she washed her hands under cold water, and then assessed her reflection in the mirror. She'd faced condemnation before and survived. It wasn't pretty, but she'd do it again if she had to. She dried her hands and returned to the restaurant. Dylan stood waiting for her.

"I'm sorry you had to hear that."

"It's okay. It's only what everyone will think, anyway." She brushed it off, but a note of how she was feeling must have crept into her voice.

"Jenna, I—"

"Look, let's just leave it, okay? Thank you for lunch. Now that I've been here I think I'll have a better idea about what you'll need for the floral designs, and I agree, bold and strong colors will be best." She flicked a look at her wristwatch. "I need to get back to the store."

"What about the other matters we were going to discuss?" he asked, searching her eyes. But she found herself unwilling to meet his.

"I'll email you."

"That sounds suspiciously like a brush-off." He cupped her shoulders with his big strong hands, the warmth of them swiftly penetrating the thin knit jacket and silk blouse she wore. "I'm not giving up on us, Jenna."

"Dylan, there is no *us*."

"I refuse to accept that," he said succinctly. "And one thing you need to know about me is that when something or someone is important to me, I never give up. You are important to me, Jenna Montgomery. Don't doubt it for a second."

When had anyone ever said anything like that to her before and meant it? She'd tried these past few days to keep Dylan at a distance, emotionally at least, but those few words wedged a tiny crack in the shell that had formed around her heart and began to split it apart. And when he lowered his face to hers, and caught her lips with his own, she felt herself reaching up to meet him halfway, as needy as a flower seeking rain on a drought-parched prairie. Wanting his promises, wanting his attention as she'd never wanted anything from anyone before.

Eight

Two days later Dylan paced the confines of his L.A. office. He was restless. Something had shifted inside him last Monday at the new restaurant. From the second he'd seen Sage take in Jenna's presence at his side and come to the correct conclusion about her pregnancy, he'd known he would defend her to anyone for any reason. For all time.

During his training in France he'd heard people refer to a *coup de foudre*—love at first sight—and he'd eschewed it for the fantastical notion it was. But thinking about that split second when he'd first noticed Jenna back in March, it was the only way to describe how he'd felt and behaved that night. It certainly described how he felt now. His family would just have to struggle to understand. Hell, even he struggled to get a grip on just how much one woman could turn his world upside down.

Since he'd walked back into her world five days ago, his every thought had been consumed by her, his every action taken with her in mind. Now, instead of focusing on the business and meetings to discuss the commencement of their planned East Coast expansion that had called him back to L.A., he was resenting the fact that it had taken him away from Cheyenne—away from Jenna.

He'd called her last night, but he'd sensed a reserve in her again, as if overhearing Sage's words had somehow erected an invisible wall thwarting the tentative connection they'd been building on. If only Dylan hadn't been forced to let her leave on Monday. If only he'd been able to pursue that kiss they'd shared at the restaurant just a little further. Instead, she'd all but fled from him and he'd had to let her go, his cell phone ringing in his pocket even as he watched her flee.

It was as if she was too scared to trust him, too scared to allow him into her life. But there was more to it than that. So many more layers to Jenna Montgomery that his hands itched to peel away. He'd have to bide his time, though, at least until Saturday, when he was due back in Cheyenne.

Dylan came to a halt at his office window and looked down over the sprawling metropolis that was Los Angeles. This had been his home, his city, for the past five years, and he'd fit in here. After training and cooking in restaurants in continental Europe and the United Kingdom, he'd been ready to come back to the States, ready to take on his next role in his career. But with J.D.'s death he'd been forced to take stock, to reevaluate his belief system and what was important in his life.

Right now, he missed Cheyenne. More to the point, he missed a certain woman who lived there. The perfect solution would be to take her and simply transplant her here into his life, his world. But even he knew that wouldn't be fair to her. She had a life in Cheyenne, a business and a home. Until he'd shown up in her store, she'd had everything worked out quite perfectly, Dylan had no doubt.

He forced his mind back to work, back to the task at hand. He'd get through these days because he had to, and because, ultimately, doing so would let him return to where he most wanted to be right now.

His phone chirping in his breast pocket was a welcome interruption to the frustration of his thoughts.

"Lassiter," he answered, without checking the caller I.D.

"Hey, Dylan, it's Chance. How are you?"

"I'm good, thanks, and you? How're things at the Big Blue?" Dylan smiled as he spoke. A call from his cousin was always a welcome break from everything else.

"I'm thinking of putting a barbecue together for Saturday. Think you could handle someone else's cooking for a change?"

Dylan laughed out loud. "Sure. For you, anything."

"Great. I was also thinking you might have a certain someone you'd like to bring along with you?"

"You been talking to Sage?"

"I might have."

Dylan could hear the smirk that was undoubtedly on his cousin's face.

"Chance—" he said, a grim note of warning in his voice.

"Hey, I promise I'll be on my best behavior, truly. I just want to meet her."

"And if she doesn't want to come?"

"I guess I can probably feed you, anyway," Chance drawled teasingly as if doing so would be a great hardship.

"That's big of you."

"But I'm sure, with your charm and skills, you'll manage to get her to come along."

"I'll let you know. What time do you want us?"

"Let's make it early. Hannah is visiting with her little girl, Cassie. She's the cutest tyke."

Since the discovery that Chance had a half sister—his father's secret daughter—the family had been getting to know one another, with great results. Now Hannah was engaged to Logan Whittaker, the lawyer who had been responsible for finding her when the contents of J.D.'s will had become known, and their family continued to expand. It was a good thing, Dylan thought privately.

"You getting ready to settle down, cuz?" It was Dylan's turn to tease now.

"Not likely," Chance replied, "but it's hard not to love her. She's a good kid. Anyway, come around six."

Dylan did a little mental calculation. By the time Jenna closed shop on Saturday and he picked her up, they could just about make it.

"We might be a little late," he said, "but we'll be there."

"Great, I'll let Mom know. She loves having family over. The more the merrier, right?"

Right, Dylan thought grimly as he disconnected the call. Now all he had to do was convince Jenna she wanted to meet more of his family, when all they probably wanted to do was subject her to the third degree. Damn Sage and his flapping mouth. Still, when push came to shove, his family was the backbone of who he was today, and Dylan wanted Jenna to see that, to be a part of it and to want their baby to be a part of it also. This gave her a perfect opportunity to see just what his family's lives were like.

Dylan had never been happier to leave L.A. and take the flight that brought him back to Cheyenne. As he pulled up in his SUV outside Jenna's house, he saw her at the front door before he could even get out of the car. He'd toyed with bringing the Caddy—he hadn't quite been able to bring himself to part with it just yet—but he knew it would probably make her uncomfortable. Besides, with the temperatures tonight set to drop to around fifty degrees, they'd probably welcome the climate control in the SUV instead.

He got out from behind the wheel and walked around to open her door for her, his eyes drinking in her appearance. He hadn't seen her for four days, but it felt like four weeks. Was it his imagination or was her tummy just that tiny bit rounder, her breasts that much fuller? Everything inside him tightened up a notch.

"Hi," she said, ducking her head as if she was a little shy.

"Hi back," he replied, bending his head to kiss her on the cheek. She blushed a pale pink when he did. He loved that he could do that to her, unnerve her like that. "I missed you."

She flicked her gaze up toward him and he saw her bite her lip, an action that sent heat rushing to his groin.

"I missed you, too."

She sounded puzzled by the fact and it made him quirk his lips in a smile. Dylan handed her into her seat and closed the door, suppressing the urge to punch the air and give a primal whoop of satisfaction. Progress. At last he was making progress.

He filled the time during their thirty-mile drive out to the Big Blue with what he'd been doing in L.A.

"So your sister lives in the house in L.A., too?"

"Yeah. Dad bought the property about twenty years ago and Angelica has really made it her own. She has a knack for decorating, for making a place feel like a home." He sighed inwardly. "It's always good to see her, but she's been pretty angry since Dad died. Things are strained between all of us."

"Angry?"

"Yeah." Dylan suddenly wished he hadn't brought the

subject up, but it probably deserved airing. "Dad was pretty old-fashioned, but I always thought he was fair. What he did to her when he left a controlling share in Lassiter Media to her fiancé, rather than to her, was a slap in the face. It's really upset her, especially since she'd basically been the one running Lassiter Media up until J.D.'s heart attack."

"Wow, I can see why she'd be upset. Is that why the wedding got called off?"

Dylan nodded. It still made him sick to his stomach. "Lassiter Media was Angelica's life, and now she's left wondering if the whole reason Evan asked her to marry him was so he could gain control of the company. Not exactly the basis for a good start to marriage."

Jenna was quiet for the rest of the journey, until Dylan reached across the center console and laced his fingers through hers.

"You okay?" he asked, flicking her a glance.

"Just a bit nervous."

"Don't be. Chance is a great guy."

"Who else will be there?"

"His mom, Marlene—she'll love you, don't worry. And his half sister, Hannah, is visiting with her daughter, Cassie. And look, we're nearly there."

He pulled in through the gates to what had, in his mind, always been home. After his parents died, J.D. and Ellie had brought him and Sage here to the ranch. Originally, the main house had been far more modest, but as the Big Blue had become more successful, it was replaced by the two-story wood-and-metal structure they were now approaching. Wraparound porches with hand-hewn wooden railings graced both levels.

"Wow, this is quite a place," Jenna commented, sitting up a little straighter in her seat. "You and Sage grew up here?"

"Lucky, huh? Just think, all this land and these big wide-open spaces for two little boys to burn their energy off in. I had a great childhood."

It occurred to Dylan that she hadn't talked much about her own upbringing. Aside from knowing she was born in New Zealand and had, for the most part, grown up in the U.S., he still had a lot to find out about her.

They got out of the car and walked up to the entrance. Dylan pushed open the front door and guided Jenna inside, yelling out a "hello" as he did so. Footsteps sounded in the hall and an older woman came forward.

"Dylan! Great to see you!" She enveloped him in a huge hug.

"Aunt Marlene, I'd like you to meet Miss Jenna Montgomery. Jenna, this is my aunt, Marlene Lassiter."

"Mrs. Lassiter, I'm pleased to meet you."

"Oh, go on now, we don't stand on ceremony here. Call me Marlene and I'm going to call you Jenna. Head on through. I've still got a few things to see to in the kitchen. Hannah and Cassie are outside on the patio and Chance is fiddling with the grill, as if he thinks he knows what he's doing."

"No Logan today?" Dylan asked.

Marlene shook her head. "No, he called me to apologize and say he'd been called out of town for legal work for some high-profile corporate client but just between you and me I think he's ducked away to avoid the wedding planning." She finished with a wink and a sparkle in her eyes that took the sting out of her words. "So, go on outside. They're waiting for you."

Jenna appeared to hold a little tighter to Dylan's hand. He guessed it was a bit overwhelming when you came here the first time. He looked around the house he'd grown up in. Maybe the second time, too. Out on the patio she seemed to relax a bit more. The expansive gardens stretched out before them.

"Is that a pond?" Jenna asked.

"It's a saltwater pool designed to look like a pond. When Sage and I were younger we used to swing from a rope tied to a branch on that tree there—" he gestured to the limb in question "—and drop into the deep end."

"Wow, you really had it all, didn't you?" she said, almost to herself.

A little girl bounced toward them, her bright red hair hanging in disordered ringlets around her pretty face and her green eyes sparkling with mischief.

"You're my uncle Dylan, aren't you? But Mama says you're more like a cousin something-removed. What's that?"

"Cassie! Let Dylan and his guest say hello to the rest of us first, before you start bothering them," a woman's voice called from the patio.

Dylan watched as Chance's half sister, Hannah, rose from her seat and came over to greet them.

"Hi again," she said to him before turning to Jenna. "I'm Hannah Armstrong."

"Jenna Montgomery," she said. "Is that your daughter? She's adorable."

Hannah beamed with pride. "Yes, that's my little treasure. She's quite the character. Here, you leave Jenna with me and go and see what Chance is doing over by the grill."

Dylan gave Jenna a glance to see if she was comfortable with that. She inclined her head slightly.

"Sure, I'll be fine," she said, but he could see by the pallor of her cheeks that she was still a little nervous, as if, given the right provocation, she'd turn and run like hell back to Cheyenne.

"I'll say hi and then I'll be right back."

"It's okay," Hannah assured him in her gentle voice. "I won't bite."

Jenna let Hannah draw her over to where she'd been sitting a moment ago, and they relaxed in the late afternoon sun.

"I'm gonna help Grandma with the horse derves," Cassie announced importantly, before skipping back inside the house.

"Wow, she's full of energy, isn't she?" Jenna commented, her lips still pulled into a smile over the little girl's mispronunciation of *hors d'oeuvres*.

"Sure is. Has been like that from the day she was born. Never a dull moment with her around, and I wouldn't have it any other way."

There was a steely vein of pride running through Hannah's voice. One that made Jenna press her hand on her lower belly. Yes, that's how she felt, too. As scary and unknown as what lay before her was, she wouldn't have it any other way, either.

"It's so beautiful here," she remarked, looking around again, trying to take it all in.

"I know. When I first saw the place it totally blew me away."

"You didn't grow up here?"

"No, I'm from Boulder, Colorado. But I'm getting married next month and Cheyenne will be our permanent home after that. In the meantime, Cassie and I are staying here. She's loving having an uncle she can twist around her little finger, not to mention a Grandma who just adores her."

Jenna tried to put all that information together, but something was still out of sync in her mind. "Marlene's not your mom?"

"It's complicated. Chance and I share a dad," Hannah explained with a wistful smile. "But they've all been so welcoming since we found out about one another. Especially Marlene, which was so much more than I could have hoped for."

"They seem very tight-knit," Jenna observed, watching Dylan and Chance laughing together over something one of them had said.

"But inclusive at the same time. Don't worry." Hannah patted Jenna's hand. "I wondered what I'd be letting myself in for, but they made me welcome from the start. You'll fit right in."

Would she? Her heart yearned for stability; she'd created as much as she could herself by working hard and buying her own home. She was almost fanatical about establishing roots, about grounding herself in familiarity and routine after her younger years filled with instability. From what she saw here, the Lassiters were clearly just as invested in permanence.

"Here you are, ladies. Some icy cold lemonade for you, honey," Marlene said to Jenna as she returned, putting a tray with a couple of frosted pitchers and some fresh glasses on the table in front of her. "And margaritas for us."

Jenna felt uncomfortable. So they knew already that she was pregnant. She murmured her thanks and watched Cassie carry a tray with inch-high edges to Chase and Dylan.

"Used to be a time she'd serve me first," Hannah commented with a rueful smile. "But now it's all about her uncle."

"She might have him wrapped around her pinky," Marlene observed, "but it's mutual. It's good to have a child around here again. It's been too long since those boys were growing up."

The older woman turned to face Jenna, a warm glow lighting her hazel eyes. "How are you keeping with the baby, Jenna? Well, I hope?"

Jenna's upset that news of her pregnancy had preceded her must have been evident on her face.

"Oh, I'm sorry, hon. Is it supposed to be a secret? Chance told me and I just thought the whole family knew."

Jenna hastened to reassure her hostess. "No, really, it's okay. I'm just not used to people knowing just yet." She smiled to soften her words. "As to how I've been? I've been pretty lucky. A little nausea in the early stages but my main problem has been tiredness."

"You're in your second trimester now, aren't you?" Marlene asked. When she nodded, the other woman said, "You should notice you're feeling better again soon. This is where you get to experience all the fun of a pregnancy, without the sickness or the aches and pains. Is your family looking forward to the baby's arrival?"

Jenna squirmed a little. She was totally unused to someone being so inquisitive, though friendly. "I don't have any family locally," she settled on saying— unwilling to admit to anyone here that her father was doing time at the state penitentiary in Rawlins.

"Oh, you poor girl," Marlene clucked sympathetically. "Never mind. If you'll let us, we'd be glad to help you out. If you have any questions, anything at all, you just ask away."

"Thank you." Jenna blinked back the burn of tears at the kindness of Marlene's unexpected offer. Her eyes hazed over again and she lifted a hand to wipe at the moisture that began to spill.

"Don't you worry, honey," Marlene said softly as she handed Jenna a crisply laundered, lace-edged handkerchief. "We'll take good care of you."

Jenna wiped her eyes and fought to get her ridiculous emotions under control. She was a virtual stranger to these people. Yet because of one impulsive accident, they were prepared to open their hearts to her. She'd been so closed up, so reluctant to let anyone in, that she felt slightly off-kilter at the prospect of even thinking of accepting help and support. She didn't deserve this. Didn't deserve their trust or their generosity.

Even so, the idea of it dangled before her like a tantalizing, yet forbidden, fruit.

Nine

Dylan looked over to where the women were talking. Something tightened in his chest when he saw Jenna's expression and recognized the distress on her face. He went to step toward her, but was arrested by Chance's hand on his shoulder.

"Don't," his cousin said.

"She's upset. She needs me."

"Mom will look after her. Trust me. She'll have everything under control."

Dylan watched as Jenna recovered her usual poise. And as the women seemed to grow closer and enjoy one another's company, their laughter floated toward him on the light evening breeze.

"Do you want some more horse derves, Uncle Dylan?" Cassie asked from beside him, shifting her weight from one leg to the other.

"No, thank you," he replied, squatting down to her level. "But thank you for taking such great care of us. How about you offer some of those to the ladies?"

"Okay!" the little girl said brightly.

He watched as she strutted importantly to the table where the women sat. A sense of wonder stirred deep inside him. Would his kid be a boy or a girl? Would it one day be right here, playing on this patio like he had?

"So when did you knock her up?" Chance's voice interrupted his reverie.

Dylan's hackles rose. He didn't care for his cousin's turn of phrase. "I don't think that's any of your business."

"Of course it is. Sage thinks it isn't yours—that she's maybe pulling a fast one on you."

"Sage should keep his thoughts to himself," Dylan growled. "It's mine. And so is she."

His cousin nodded, clearly satisfied with that response. "You going to be a hands-on dad?"

"Every chance I get," Dylan replied emphatically.

Chance looked pensive. "I often wonder what life would have been like to have grown up with my own dad around longer, y'know?" His father had died when Chance was eight years old. He, too, knew what it was like to grow up without his natural father.

"Yeah. It's why I'm going to be there for my kid, through thick and thin."

"And Jenna? How does she feel about that?"

Dylan took a swig of his beer and rolled the brew over his tongue for a moment before swallowing. "She's coming around to the idea," he said with a grin.

Chance gave him a punch on the arm. "Thatta boy. Besides, with all you can offer, why would she refuse?"

"That's the thing. She doesn't seem to want what I can offer. She's fierce about her independence, and from what I can tell, she's worked hard for it. I just need to convince her that it's okay to share the load."

"Well, good luck with that. I'd rather rope a steer in a bad mood than try and convince a woman of anything."

"Good point," Dylan concurred, before gesturing to the platter of raw steak waiting to be cooked. "Hey, you going to do anything with those or are you waiting for them to cook themselves?"

The seriousness of their discussion broken, they turned to the matter of cooking the meat. But a niggling thought remained at the back of Dylan's mind. What if Jenna wouldn't let him in? What if she wouldn't share the load? What then? He knew he could use his power and his money to get what he wanted, but the very idea soured his stomach. No, he wanted her to come to him willingly and wholeheartedly. Not because she had to, not because she was being coerced. But because she wanted to as much as he wanted her.

It was late when he drove Jenna home. Dylan had fully expected her to want to leave soon after they'd enjoyed their meal, but it seemed that the longer she spent with his family, the more she wanted to stay. It made him begin to hope that she could see herself being a part of his own close circle. Part of his life.

"Thank you for taking me tonight. I really enjoyed it," she said softly.

"It was my pleasure. I'm glad you came."

"They're all so lovely. And Cassie's so sweet. I loved how she crawled into your lap after dinner and just fell asleep there."

He'd loved it, too. Had welcomed the little girl's trust in him. It had been a precious gift, and he'd missed the weight of her little body when Hannah had eventually lifted her and carted her off to bed. It made him yearn even more to be a father, to cradle a child of his own in his arms.

"Kids are special. No doubt about it."

Dylan drove onto Jenna's driveway and got out to walk her to her front door. He waited on the porch as she fitted her key in the lock, the breeze bringing a teasing hint of her fragrance toward him. Roses. She always carried that sweet scent on her. It suited her. The flower was so beautiful yet could be prickly at the same time.

She pushed the door open and hesitated a second or two. He saw her shoulders lift and then drop, as if she'd drawn in a deep breath.

"Jenna? You okay?"

She turned to face him. "Do you…?"

She bit her bottom lip, the action having the exact same effect on him as it had the other day. Fire licked along his veins as he waited for her to finish her sentence.

"Do you want to come in for a nightcap?"

Hell, yeah, a little voice all but screamed at the back of his mind. He didn't want tonight to end. She'd softened, somehow. Her defenses seemed lower than before. He pushed the screaming voice aside. He needed to tread softly. He certainly didn't want to scare her or damage the tentative closeness that had grown between them tonight.

"One more drink and I'll be over the limit to drive," he said quietly—asking her the important question without putting it into so many words. He'd go if that's what she wanted. He wouldn't be happy about it. But he'd go.

Jenna took a step closer to him and placed her hand on his chest. "Then perhaps you should stay."

His breath caught in his lungs. Could she feel his heart all but leap from his chest at her words? "Perhaps I should," he managed to reply, and hooked an arm around her waist.

They headed in together. He let her go as she walked around her sitting room, flicking on the occasional light.

"I'm not even sure what I have in the way of spirits, but I'm bound to have some wine. Would that be—?"

Her voice broke off as he caught her hand and drew her to him.

"I don't really want a drink, Jenna," he said, his voice a low rumble.

"You don't?"

"No, I just want you."

"Oh."

It was all she got time to say before he kissed her. The taste of her lips almost blew his head off and ignited the slow-burning embers within him to flaming, ravenous heat. His kiss was hungry, demanding, and to his delight she met his need with corresponding passion. Her hands slid upward, from his chest to his neck, then cupped the back of his head, not letting him break the kiss.

"Bedroom," he demanded against her mouth, not wanting to remove his lips from hers for even a second.

She pointed down the hallway. "At the end, on the right."

He scooped one arm behind her knees and the other behind her back and lifted her, holding her body against his. She snaked an arm around his shoulders and caressed his cheek with her free hand, as if she was as reluctant to break their connection, their kiss, as he. He covered the short distance down the hall and pushed the door open with his foot. Her bedroom was small, with minimal decoration. Simple in its design. A plainly covered bed took up most of the space, a solid plank of blond wood serving as a headboard.

Dylan let Jenna slide to her feet.

"I want to see you this time," he growled, moving away from her for the brief second it took to switch on the bedside lamp.

He turned back to her and reached to lift her loose-fitting tunic from her body. His mouth dried at the sight he revealed, his untaken breath burning in his chest. Her skin was smooth, with the lightest touch of summer in its tone. He let his gaze track down her throat, across her shoulders and to her breasts, which spilled from the lacy cups of her bra.

"I told you you were beautiful. I was wrong," he said, his voice thick with emotion. "You're so much more than that."

His hand reached out to trace a faint blue vein on her breast, and he heard her sharply indrawn breath. He followed the line to where it disappeared beneath the pale blue scalloped edge of her bra.

"I'm going to kiss you there," he promised, lifting his eyes to hers—his stomach clenching at the heat he saw burning back at him. "But first, I'm going to see all of you."

He took his time removing her sandals and slim-fitted capris until she had only her bra and panties left. Fine tremors quivered through her body as he let his hands drift up her arms to her shoulders. Her skin was so soft, and sweetly fragrant, and he trailed fine kisses along her shoulder and then up the side of her neck.

"Let me get the bed ready," she said as he nibbled on her earlobe, just as he'd imagined doing a few short days ago.

"It looks pretty damn ready to me," he said when she pulled away with a small laugh.

Still, he was happy to use the time she took turning down the comforter and tugging back the sheets to shuck off his clothing—something he managed with record speed. His erection strained at the cotton of his boxer briefs and he rubbed his hand down his aching flesh. Soon, he promised himself, soon. But first there were more important things to attend to. Such as examining the woman in front of him from head to foot. Getting to know what made her breathless with desire. Making her scream with pleasure such as she'd never experienced before.

Jenna lay down on the bed and held out a hand to him. He took it, stretching out next to her and marveling at how perfectly formed she was. He traced the curve of her collarbone again—such a delicate line—and followed his touch with the tip of his tongue. She rewarded him with a sigh of pleasure so he did it again, his tongue lingering in the hollow just at the base of her throat. Her pulse leaped against him, as avid and hungry as his own.

Dylan continued his voyage of discovery, his fingertips tingling as they met the swell of her breasts. He swept over their shape before letting his hand travel to her shoulders, slipping first one, then the other bra strap down, and reaching beneath her to unsnap the clasp.

"Should I be worried that you did that so easily?" Jenna teased, but then her voice ended on a gasp as he traced the pale blue line of her vein to where it collided with the dark pink distended nipple.

"Never," he said, before using the tip of his tongue to meet that pink tip.

She shuddered beneath him. "Do that again, please?"

"Your wish is my command," he promised, and did as she asked.

Her moan of delight drove a fierce spear of lust straight to his groin, but he forced himself to ignore it. To dwell instead on her pleasure, on her. He took his time with the rest of her body, lingering over her breasts, her ribs, her belly button, and then moving down to the small firm swell of her belly.

His hand hovered there and he willed the connection between them to go beyond skin, beyond sensation. His baby. His woman. His life. He pressed a kiss against her skin, his hands now skimming her panties, tracing the outside edge of the fabric where they met the top of her thighs. Her legs trembled at his touch, her pelvis thrusting upward toward him. He cupped her, marveling at the heat and dampness that collected at her core.

"Dylan, please!"

He pressed his palm against her, felt her shudder against him.

"You're teasing me. It's not fair," she cried, her voice a strangled sound.

"All's fair," he said easing her panties down her legs and punctuating his next words with firm kisses on her thighs, then the junction where they met. "In." Kiss. "Love." Kiss. "And." Kiss. "War."

His mouth found her center and he saw her hands knot into fists on the sheets as his tongue flicked against her glistening sex. The scent of her was driving him crazy. A delicious blend of rose and musk.

He couldn't stand it a second longer. He had to have her, be inside her, be one with her. He shoved his briefs down and settled between her legs, feeling her jolt as he nudged the blunt tip of his erection at her entrance. She lifted her hips in welcome and he slowly let himself be absorbed by the tight warm heat of her body. Slowly, so slowly, until he was buried in her. Until he was exactly where he needed to be.

His hips flexed and she met his movement with her own, her inner muscles holding and releasing him in time with their actions. Her irises darkened to near black, clouded with the fog of her desire. He tried to make it last, to make it even more special, but when her body began to pulse around his, when her eyes slid closed and she released a keening cry as her body shuddered toward its peak, he lost control—his hips pumping until he, too, reached his climax.

Lost in the power of wonder and emotion that swept over him, Dylan let his body take him on the ride as he crested wave after wave of pleasure. His entire frame shook with the force of what he'd just undergone—with the perfection of how it had felt. He rolled to one side and gathered Jenna against him, waiting for his heartbeat to return to anything approximating normal.

It was a long time before he could speak.

"I think we just proved our first time wasn't an aberration," he said with a huff of breath. He felt her chuckle ripple through her.

"Yes, I think we did."

He could hear the humor in her voice, humor mixed with a languid satisfaction that made him feel even better, knowing he'd contributed to her well-being. Everything was right in this moment. Perfect. He knew he'd never tire of this. Of the feeling of her in his arms, of the curve of her sweet bottom beneath his hand. Of this sense of connection he'd never shared with another woman.

He wanted this—forever, with her. It took all his self-restraint not to press her again to agree to marriage. To agree to committing to one another forever.

Deep down he knew she still had reservations. Understandable, given the short length of time they'd actually known one another. But they had the rest of their lives to discover all those finer points that kept a relationship interesting. What they shared was a gift beyond compare. He should know—he'd sought perfection wherever he went in whatever he did.

Jenna Montgomery was that perfection for him. He just needed to convince her of that fact.

Ten

Jenna could hear Dylan's heart racing beneath her ear, and her lips curved into a smile. He might be the CEO of the Lassiter Grill Corporation, he might be a world-renowned chef and playboy, but underneath it all he was still just a man. A pretty damn fine one, that was for sure. And, right now, he was hers.

Her man forever? She was beginning to believe it could be true. She'd loved spending time with him and his family this evening. Could she find the courage to reach out from behind her safe fortress and grasp what he offered? Only time would tell.

Dylan's fingers traced a lazy trail from her hip to her shoulders and back again, his touch setting off tiny shivers beneath her skin. She stretched beneath his touch, like a cat, almost purring.

"Tell me what you like," he asked softly. "This?" He firmed his touch. "Or this?"

"Hmm, let me take about the next twenty minutes or so to get back to you on that," she replied.

He laughed and the sound filled her heart with happiness.

"Twenty minutes? That's quite a commitment."

"It might be," she said, realizing that if she really wanted this—really wanted *him*—she needed to take the bull by the horns and open up to him.

But whenever he started talking about commitment it still struck a knell of fear inside her. He knew virtually nothing about her but the face she presented to him right here, right now. The person she was today was a far cry from the person she'd been eleven years ago.

Pretty much everything about Dylan and his life was an open book. Yes, he'd had sorrow in his life with the death of his parents and then his adoptive mother, and more recently, J.D. But with each loss, he'd had the advantage of family, of someone else willing to step up to the plate and fill that yearning hole in his life.

With the loss of his parents it had been J.D. and his wife, Ellie. With the death of Ellie, Jenna had learned tonight, Marlene had stepped into the breach to provide mothering to Dylan and his brother. What had Jenna ever had growing up, except a will for survival? That will had gotten her through her parents' arguments, their one-up-manship and then her mother's desertion.

It had gotten her through the news that her father was taking her to America, away from everything and everyone she'd ever known or allowed herself to anchor to.

Did she dare anchor herself to Dylan?

"You're thinking so hard I can just about hear the cogs turning in your brain," Dylan said teasingly. "Wanna share?"

She began to say no, but then realized that this was a perfect opportunity to give him some of her truths. What he did with it would define what happened between them in the future.

"I was just thinking about how different our lives were, growing up."

"How so?"

"You had such stability, such strength behind your

family. It's like everyone has a place and they fit there, y'know?"

"Uh-huh. It's not always a bed of roses but we get along pretty well."

"Pretty well?" she said, tweaking one of his nipples with a pinch that made him yelp.

"Okay, very well. But we work at it."

"That's part of what I mean," she said, smoothing her hand over his chest to soothe his injured flesh. "You do work at it, together. I guess I've never had that sense of community within a family. From what I know, my parents were both only children, and their parents died before I was born. It should have made them closer to one another, but instead it always felt like they were tearing each other apart."

"Doesn't sound comfortable, for them or for you."

"No, it wasn't. It was confusing, unstable. I never knew from one day to the next if they'd be happy and loving or morose and picking a fight. When my mother left us, I almost felt a sense of relief, y'know? But by the same token I was distraught because she didn't take me, too. Dad said she felt like we were holding her back."

Dylan sighed. "That was unfair of him for saying it and, if it was true, of her for feeling it. You can't do that to a kid. Your job as a parent is to nurture, to support and love your children. Yes, that means putting your own needs last a lot of the time, but I reckon there's a time and a place for everything and everyone, and when your kids are young it's *their* time, *their* place."

Jenna closed her eyes as a swell of something rich and true buoyed up inside her. His words were so simple, yet they rang with such a deep certainty about what was right and wrong. Tenets she held dear to her own heart.

"Well, obviously they didn't feel that way."

"Do you stay in touch with your dad now?" Dylan asked.

Jenna shook her head. She didn't want to tell Dylan that her father would be locked up behind bars for at least another two years. He'd probably have been out on parole by now if the prison staff hadn't discovered he'd begun grooming wealthy widows for future cons during his computer time inside.

"No. We lead totally separate lives. To be honest, I don't want anything to do with him," she said emphatically.

"Will you tell him about the baby?"

"No. I don't want him anywhere near us."

"Family is family, Jen," Dylan said, still stroking her skin, his actions soothing the anger that had risen in her as they discussed her dad. "I wouldn't be where I am now without mine."

She laughed, but it was a bitter sound. "Nor would I. But I've learned the hard way that just because someone is family doesn't mean they have your best interests at heart. My foster mum gave me more care and stability than my parents ever did. Thanks to her, I've learned to do very well on my own and I like it that way. I work hard, and what I have is my own. Okay, so I can't provide luxuries like saltwater ponds with swinging ropes, or private jets and silver spoons. But I can provide what counts—stability and constancy in a loving home. I've set down roots here. I finally belong somewhere and I'll protect that, and my baby's right to that, with every last breath in my body if I have to."

Dylan was silent for a while, but then he spoke. "And do you see any room for me in that life of yours?"

She rolled on top of him, her legs tangling with his

and her hands on either side of his face as she rose up to kiss him.

"That depends," she said, pulling away so they were inches apart.

"On what?"

"On whether you plan to keep telling me what to do, or whether you want to be an equal partner in what happens in our baby's life."

Tiny twin frown lines appeared between his brows as he looked into her eyes. "I can do partnership," he said carefully. "But I'd rather do marriage."

This time, when he said it, it didn't send quite the same shaft of anxiety through her. Instead, she felt a sense of curiosity—a need to take his suggestion and examine it more closely instead of rejecting it out of hand.

"I'll think about it," she said, hardly believing it herself as the words fell from her lips.

"Thank you," he answered simply.

His strong, warm arms closed around her and she caught his lips again, letting herself and her fears go in his touch until once more they were lost in each other.

The air had grown cool around them and Dylan shifted to drag the covers up over their naked forms. Jenna had fallen asleep almost immediately after the second time they'd made love, but he'd continue to lie there turning over her words.

Her family had hurt her, had made her doubt and fear closeness. Chipping away at her barriers would take time and care. And love? Yes, and love. Love and dependability. Those had been the backbone of his upbringing. He wanted those attributes to be the backbone of his kid's upbringing, too, and to do that he needed to woo Jenna with those promises. He'd known all along that courting her would be a challenge. They'd done everything from back to front, for a start. But he'd get there, he decided as he finally drifted off to sleep. What he and Jenna had between them was far too important. Failure was not an option.

In the morning Dylan eased himself from the bed-sheets without disturbing her. Dragging on his jeans, he padded through to her kitchen to see what he could rustle up for breakfast. He eyed her appliances with interest. Everything was new and in near pristine condition. Either she was a fanatical housekeeper or she didn't do a great deal of cooking in here. From what she'd said about TV dinners, he suspected it was the latter.

He opened her fridge and confirmed that she didn't do a great deal of cooking. His brow furrowed as he considered his options. A quick check of the vegetable drawer revealed a red pepper that was just about past its best by date, and some fresh mushrooms. He made a sound of satisfaction. Further rummaging in the kitchen uncovered potatoes and onions in matching earthenware containers.

So, with these items combined with the eggs in the fridge, he could do a Spanish omelet with red pepper and a side of fried mushrooms. His mouth was already watering at the thought. But when it came to slicing the potatoes, he eyed Jenna's knives in despair and wished he was in his own kitchen with his quality steel blades honed to perfection. Still, he'd made do with worse, he thought, testing the blunt edge.

He fried the potato and onions together in a pan while he went to work slicing mushrooms and beating the eggs. By the time he was ready to turn the halved omelet onto two warmed plates he heard a sound in the hall.

"Good morning," he said as Jenna stumbled into the kitchen, wrapped in a fluffy long bathrobe.

She looked as though she'd forced herself awake. Her hair was mussed and her eyes had a sleepy look about them that almost made him abandon their breakfast and take her straight back to bed to wake her up properly.

"Good morning," she said as she went over to the fridge and grabbed a bottle of water and screwed off the cap. "Something smells good. Are you feeding me again?"

"Spanish omelet. You hungry?"

She groaned. "Hungry? I'm always hungry lately."

"Then," he said, scooping up the sliced mushrooms he'd fried in a little butter, and sharing them between their plates, "you'd better wrap yourself around this."

She gave him a puzzled look. "You did this?"

He waggled his fingers in front of her. "With my own fair hands."

"Did I actually have the ingredients or have you been out?"

He laughed. "You had everything here. I haven't left you for a moment."

Nor did he plan to for the rest of this weekend, or any of the time he had free until the official opening of the Grill next week.

"Hmm," she said, quickly setting the small table she had in the dining area and transferring their plates onto the table. "Maybe you should give me some lessons."

His mouth quirked in a smile. Lessons? Oh, yeah, he'd love to do that. His mind filled with the possibilities, starting with Jenna wearing an apron…and nothing else.

"Sure. Shall we start today?"

"I was kidding, but if you're serious…"

"I never kid about food."

"Okay, today would be fine."

"Good, I'll take you back to my place. We'll have more to work with there."

She returned his smile and he felt as though the sun had just risen again. "Thank you, I'd like that."

Dylan heard his phone beep. "Excuse me a second," he said, sliding it from his pocket and checking the display.

It was a message from Felicity Sinclair, Lassiter Media's queen of PR, confirming her arrival in Cheyenne tomorrow morning. He tapped in a quick acknowledgment and turned his attention back to Jenna.

"Sorry, work," he said by way of explanation.

"Do you always work on weekends?"

He shrugged. "When it's necessary. With the Grill opening next week everything has become more time sensitive. That was just a text from our PR executive. She's flying in tomorrow. I'll bring her by your store and introduce you."

"That'd be nice. Hopefully, she can make sure that Connell's Floral Design's logo is featured prominently in your advertising," she said with a cheeky smile.

Jenna leaned forward as she scooped up a mouthful of omelet, her action making her robe gape open enough to give him a glimpse of one pink-tipped breast. Any thoughts of work and the people associated with it flew from his mind as he allowed his gaze to drift over her. She continued eating, oblivious to his perusal, until her plate was empty and she lifted her attention to him—and realized just what had caught his attention.

Her eyes darkened, as they had last night, and her cheeks became tinged with pink.

"Not hungry?" she asked, her voice a little husky.

"Starving," he replied, putting his fork down and pushing his plate away.

He eased from his chair, dropping to his knees and

sliding one hand inside her robe to cup her breast. Her nipple instantly tightened against his palm.

"Ah, now I see why you're feeding me so well," Jenna said, drawing in a deep breath. "You want to keep my energy levels up."

"Among other things," he drawled, letting his thumb graze back and forth over the taut nub that just begged him to take it in his mouth.

Never a man to ignore his instincts, Dylan did just that. Jenna's fingers tunneled through his hair, holding him to her as he nibbled and sucked her flesh.

"Well, it's a good thing I've eaten then," Jenna managed to say before he pushed aside her robe and lavished her other breast with equal attention. "Because I have a feeling I'm going to need the extra calories."

"Them and more," he murmured against her skin.

They didn't get out to his place until well after lunchtime and by then they were both famished again, for each other and for more sustenance. How they even made it into his high-tech kitchen bemused him, when all he wanted to do was take Jenna to the dizzying heights they'd shared, over and over again.

Instead, he supervised her as she put together a simple lunch for them both. Jenna surveyed the assembled ingredients on the island in the center of the kitchen.

"You always buy this extensively from the grocery store?" she commented as she tore up some romaine lettuce and threw it into a bowl.

"When I'm in the mood for Greek salad, yeah. What's wrong? Didn't your family ever cook?"

As soon as the words were out of his mouth he wished them back again. He already knew talking about her family created an invisible barrier between them, one he'd unwittingly put back in place.

"I can remember baking cookies with my mom once or twice when I was little, but aside from that, nothing really. Dad was big on takeout, or eating out. He often wasn't home for meals anyway, so I just learned to make do."

It was what she didn't say that struck him. How old had she been when she'd been left to fend for herself come mealtimes? Dylan moved around the granite-topped island and slid his arms around her waist, pulling her gently back against him.

"I'm sorry," he said, pressing a kiss against the back of her neck. "I didn't mean to bring that up."

"It is what it is," she said, studiously concentrating on slicing the red onion and then the red and green bell peppers she'd laid out in a row on the countertop in front of her.

"Here, do you want me to do that?" he offered, wanting to do anything to change the subject and shift her focus to something else.

"Actually, no. I'm enjoying this. I never thought I would, but it's true."

She flung him a smile over her shoulder and kept chopping and slicing until the bowl was filled with the earlier ingredients, together with tomatoes, olives and cucumber. Her hand hesitated over the feta cheese.

"It's okay," Dylan said. "I checked. It's made from pasteurized milk."

"Are you sure?"

"Hey, leave it out if you want to. It's not a food crime." To save her the hassle, he swept the packet up and put it back in the fridge, substituting it for a sliced cooked chicken breast. "Use this instead. There's no reason why we can't play around with tradition."

"Thanks," she said. "I'm sorry, I just don't want to do anything that will potentially harm the baby. He or she is all I have."

She placed one hand on her belly and Dylan could see the love in her face. He put his hand over hers. "You have me now, too. I want you to remember that, because I'm not going anywhere, Jenna. Not unless you're coming with me."

Eleven

She wanted to believe him. With all her heart she wanted it to be true. But she'd heard such platitudes from her father's mouth all the years she'd spent with him. He'd used them with her and also with his many lady friends. He'd always made it sound so sincere, as if the words truly came from his heart, but they'd come from a place far more closely associated with his wallet.

"Seeing is believing," Jenna said, trying to keep her words light. But she knew they'd struck to Dylan's core.

"You don't believe me?"

He reached to take the knife from her and turned her to face him. His hands framed her face and forced her to maintain eye contact with him.

"I didn't say that, exactly," she hedged, knowing to the depth of her soul that she wanted to be certain of him, to be able to trust what he said without looking for an ulterior motive.

Still, aside from the baby, and obviously the incredible sexual chemistry they shared, what else was there? A marriage took so much more than those two things. Her parents had been the perfect example of that. A marriage needed commitment, togetherness and mutual minds. What motive could he have to want to be with her? It wasn't as if she had something he needed. He had it all and then some.

"Jenna, I meant what I said. Yes, I know we haven't known each other all that long and, yes, we've gone at this all the wrong way. If I could, I'd turn back the clock and take the time to woo you, to prove that you can rely on me. Something brought us together, I firmly believe that. And we're meant to be, Jenna."

"I wish it could be that easy." She sighed.

"It can be. If you just let it."

"I'm trying, Dylan, honestly I am. I...I want to trust you."

"Then that's progress. I'll take it. We're halfway there, right? C'mon, let's get this salad finished and I'll show you around the house."

The next morning Jenna was happily reflecting on her day with Dylan when Valerie knocked on her office door and popped her head in.

"You have visitors. Mr. Drop-Dead-Gorgeous and a woman who looks as if she walked straight off Rodeo Drive. They make a nice couple," Valerie said, closing the office door behind her as she returned to the showroom.

A couple? Jenna didn't think so, not after the very thorough loving Dylan had given her yesterday. But even so, she felt a twinge of jealousy and insecurity. This PR chick, whoever she was, was certainly more suited to Dylan's world than Jenna ever could be. And she'd lay odds that she didn't have any dark or shameful secrets lurking in her past, either. Insecurity made Jenna uncomfortable as she rose from her desk and checked her appearance in the mirror that hung on the back of her office door.

Well, there wasn't a hair out of place and her makeup hadn't disappeared since she'd lightly applied it this morning. There was nothing else to do but go out and face them.

Her heart skipped a double beat when she thought about seeing Dylan. He'd been so attentive yesterday and had made her feel so incredibly special. She wished she was the kind of person who could simply embrace that and not constantly read between the lines of everything he said and did for an ulterior motive.

There was another knock at her office door.

"Jenna?"

It was Dylan. She pasted a smile on her face and reached for the handle. She felt her heart thump as she saw him. He was all sartorial corporate elegance today, dressed in a charcoal-gray suit, white shirt and striped tie. Her eyes skimmed past him to the tall, slim, golden-haired woman who was examining some pink hollyhocks. No wonder Valerie thought they made a cute couple. With the woman's tailored suit and high heels—Louboutin by the looks of them—she and Dylan looked as if they'd stepped out of the pages of *Forbes Magazine*. Jenna tugged at the loose-fitting tunic she'd teamed with a pair of stretch pants this morning, and wished her wardrobe had extended to something a little sharper for this meeting.

"Good morning," she said as brightly as she could.

Dylan didn't waste a second. He surprised her by swooping down and planting his lips on hers. Jenna put her hand on his chest to steady herself as her blood instantly turned molten. Two seconds in his presence and she was already starry-eyed. Man, she was so gone.

"Now it's a good morning," he said with a smile that crinkled his eyes at the corners. He linked her arm through his and drew her to his side. "Come over and meet Fee."

As he mentioned the other woman's name, she lifted her head and smiled in Jenna's direction. She took a few steps toward them, her hand outstretched in greeting.

"Hi, I'm Felicity Sinclair, but call me Fee," she said warmly. "Are these your designs? They're fantastic," she said, gesturing to some of the more artistic pieces the store had on display.

"Yes, mine and Valerie's," Jenna said, feeling a little more charitable toward the newcomer.

"You'd be very popular back home. I wish we had someone like you doing the flowers for our offices and functions. Dylan tells me you've got everything under control for Saturday's opening?"

"Yes, would you like to see a mock-up of the table settings?"

The next twenty minutes passed swiftly as Jenna went over her plans for the floral displays at the restaurant. By the time they left she felt a whole lot more confident in herself and her ability to hold her own with women like Fee Sinclair.

Dylan whispered in her ear as they were leaving, "Ready for another cooking lesson tonight? I was thinking of something along the lines of dessert, maybe with chocolate sauce?"

Fire lit inside Jenna, flooding her limbs and making them instantly feel heavy and lethargic. Her cheeks flamed in turn, earning her a considering glance from Valerie.

"Sure, your place or mine?" she asked, keeping her voice low.

"How about your place. It's closer to here for you in case we oversleep in the morning."

She nodded, not trusting herself to speak. He kissed her again, taking her in a hard and swift embrace that promised everything, but left her hanging in a daze of sensual awareness that clouded her already foggy mind.

"See you after work," he said, ushering Fee from the store.

After the front door had closed, Valerie zoomed straight to her side.

"And just when were you going to let me in on the secret?" she demanded, waggling a playful finger in Jenna's direction.

"Secret?"

"You and Mr. Drop-Dead-Gorgeous. You never told me you were an item."

Jenna smiled. "An item?"

"Sweetie, I saw the way he looked at you." She fanned herself theatrically. "And the way he kissed you? Well, suffice to say it had my hormones racing, and it wasn't even me he was kissing!"

"We're friends, Valerie. Good friends," she amended.

"He's your baby's daddy, isn't he?"

Jenna felt her cheeks drain of color. Aside from Dylan, and obviously his family, no one else was supposed to know yet that she was pregnant.

"I've had four kids of my own, remember. I know the signs. Look, I can understand you wanting to keep it quiet, especially with him being a Lassiter and all," Valerie continued. "I just wanted to say, good on you, girl. You work so hard, it's about time you had a bit of play. If there's one thing life has taught me, it's to grab what's offered and make the most of every darn second. You never know what's around the corner."

Valerie's words continued to ring in Jenna's ears as she forced herself to focus on her work for the day. Was she being a fool for trying to play it safe with Dylan? For not jumping, boots and all, into a future together? She didn't doubt he'd take care of her, but did she want to be taken care of? She'd fought to be independent, to be able to stand on her own two feet. Did he accept her as an equal? She weighed the thoughts in her mind, along with the realization that she was learning to trust him, to accept who he was. Could she take that final step and agree to marry him?

"So, what did you think?" Dylan asked as he drove Fee back toward the restaurant.

"Of the designs or of Ms. Montgomery?" she asked with a twinkle in her eye.

"Both. Either. Hell, I don't care." Dylan laughed. "By the way, I'd like you to see that her store gets linked to the Grill in the advertising push over the next few days."

Fee raised her eyebrows but took out her planner and made some notes. "Sure, no problem. The floral work is going to be fantastic—a perfect complement to the opening and the restaurant in general. About Jenna—she seemed familiar to me for some reason. I can't figure out where from. I'm not sure if it's her face or her name."

"She did the flowers for Angelica's rehearsal dinner. Maybe that's where you remember her from," Dylan said offhandedly.

"No, I don't think it's that. Not to worry, it'll come to me soon enough."

At the restaurant Dylan found it difficult to remain focused. All he wanted to do was race back to Jenna's store and sneak her home. Fee kept him occupied for the better part of the day, though, walking him through a couple of interviews she'd scheduled for tomorrow, among other things, and by the time he left the restaurant he was itching to get to Jenna's.

He'd barely thrown the car into Park when the front

door opened and she stood on the porch, waiting for him. He couldn't hold back the smile of satisfaction that wreathed his face. So, she'd missed him today as much as he'd missed her. That was definitely a step in the right direction. He snagged the bag of groceries he'd picked up on the way over, and raced up the path, sweeping her into his arms and delivering a kiss that he hoped showed how much he'd looked forward to seeing her again.

When he set her back down she looked a little starry-eyed, but a stab of concern pierced him when he saw how pale she was.

"C'mon, let's get you inside and off your feet. You look as if you've been overdoing things today."

He shepherded her through to her living room and sat her down on the long sofa, making her laugh when he picked up her feet and swiveled her around so she was fully reclined.

"Dylan, don't. It's not necessary. I just had a full day, that's all."

"And now you can relax. I'm here."

He said the words with a quiet authority he didn't really feel. In fact, with Jenna, he was never too sure just how close he was to overstepping the mark. He wanted to take care of her, to lift her problems from her slender shoulders and onto his broader ones. Especially when he saw her looking like this.

Despite her protests, he noted that she didn't make an effort to move off the couch, so he took the groceries through to the kitchen and poured her a glass of water, bringing it back immediately.

"Did you get off your feet at all today?" he asked, sitting at the end of the sofa and picking up one of her feet in his strong hands.

He began to massage her arches, and smiled when she groaned in delight.

"Oh, that feels good," she said, effectively dodging his question. "I'm thinking of keeping you on if you can promise you'll do this for me every day after work."

"You only have to say the word and I'm yours," he answered.

"The word?"

"Yes. And in case you've forgotten, that would be a yes to the will-you-marry-me question."

He deliberately kept his tone light.

"Okay, duly noted, and I consider myself fully informed," she teased with a tired smile.

Dylan picked up her other foot and began to massage it, as well, watching as she let her eyelids drift closed. When he stopped she didn't even move, so he gently placed her foot back down on the sofa and rose to go and prepare their evening meal. It worried him that she was so tired. Was that normal? He needed to do some research or talk to a doctor or someone. Maybe Marlene could help, or Hannah. He made a mental note to call the ranch in the morning, and then eyed the ingredients he'd bought for dessert before deciding to put them away for another time.

He worked quickly and efficiently in Jenna's kitchen, combining ingredients to form the spinach and pesto stuffing for the plump, free-range chicken breasts he'd purchased. He placed them in a shallow glass casserole dish, on top of quartered red potatoes that he'd tossed in olive oil. Then he smothered the breasts with the leftover stuffing before placing the lid on the dish and sliding it into the oven.

Just as he turned back from the oven, Jenna's home phone began to ring. He cursed the noise it made and dived for the handset on the kitchen countertop, hoping he'd get it before the sound woke Jenna.

"Hello?"

"Um, hello. Have I dialed the right number? Is this Jenna Montgomery's house?"

Dylan recognized Valerie's voice from the store.

"Yes, it's Dylan Lassiter here. Jenna's resting."

"Oh, good. I was just calling to see if she's okay. She took a dizzy turn in the shop today, and while I tried to encourage her to head home early, she flat out refused. Tell her that I've arranged for someone to keep an eye on the kids for me, so I'll open up for her tomorrow, would you? She can come in a bit later."

Dylan promised to pass the message on and placed the phone back on its station. A dizzy spell? No wonder she'd been looking pale. Clearly, she was overdoing things. His gut twisted in frustration. He was in no position to tell her what to do, but every cell in his body urged him to take charge and to make it clear that her health, and that of her unborn baby, should take greater precedence over her work.

But he was beginning to understand what her work meant to her. Without the support of family, she'd grown up missing the markers of encouragement and success that most other kids enjoyed. He thought about what he'd had growing up, and how he'd had the luxury of traveling and finding his niche in the world. How he'd taken all that for granted.

There were still huge gaps in what he knew about Jenna's past, not least of which being how she'd gone from living with her father to living here in Cheyenne with Margaret Connell. Dylan could only hope that eventually she'd trust him enough to tell him everything, to help him know her that much better so he could prove to her that spending the rest of her life with him was the best thing she could do for them all.

"Was that the phone?"

Damn, the call had disturbed her. By his reckoning she'd had only about twenty minutes or so of sleep, and judging by the darkness that underscored her eyes, she needed a whole lot more than that.

"Yeah, it was Valerie. She phoned to check up on you and to say she'd open for you tomorrow."

"She doesn't need to do that. I'm perfectly capable of opening the store myself. She has four kids to juggle in the morning," Jenna protested. "It's why she starts later."

"Clearly, she's juggled them so she can help you out. Why didn't you tell me you weren't feeling well today?" he asked, coming back into the sitting room and parking himself on the sofa again.

He lifted her legs and positioned her feet in his lap. Jenna got a defensive look on her face.

"I felt fine. I'd been bending down and when I stood up I just got a little bit dizzy. That's all."

"Have you felt dizzy before?"

"No, never. Seriously, I'm fine. Please don't fuss."

"Maybe I want to fuss over you," he countered. "Maybe I think you need a little fussing in your life."

She gave him a reluctant smile. "Oh, you do, do you?"

"Tell me, when was the last time anyone paid attention to you, real attention of the spoiling variety?"

Her grin grew wider. "I think that would have been last night, in bed, when you—"

"That's not what I mean, and you know it. Jenna, sometimes it's okay to let someone into your life, to let them share the load. I want that someone to be me."

Her face grew serious again and for a while she was si-

lent. When she spoke, her voice trembled ever so slightly.
"I want that to be you, too. I just—"

He leaned over her and placed a finger on her lips.
"No, don't justify anything. I'll take what you said and I'll
hold on to that for now, okay? Remember, I'm not going
anywhere. I'm right here for you, whether you think you
need me or not."

Twelve

Jenna stretched against the sheets in Dylan's bed, relishing the decadent luxury of the high thread count cotton against her bare skin. Last night they'd been out to the Big Blue for a family dinner, where the Lassiters had celebrated Hannah's engagement to Logan Whittaker. Again she'd been struck by the genuine love and warmth shared within the family. Love and warmth that had included her.

The siren call of being a part of all of that, the whole family thing, was growing louder in her mind, especially when combined with Dylan's attentiveness to her since Monday. He'd remained true to his word and shared her load; to be more accurate, it felt as if he'd shouldered the whole thing. Jenna still found it hard to accept gracefully, but she was learning. God, how she was learning. He'd delivered breakfast in bed each morning before driving her to work, his argument being that he didn't want her to suffer a dizzy spell while driving. And he'd collected her at the end of each day, to return to his or her home for dinner and to sleep.

And sleep they had. He hadn't made love to her since last weekend, insisting instead that she rest, and somehow, cradled securely in his arms each night, she'd slept better than she ever had before. She'd been unable to argue in the face of his logic, and had promised to follow up with her doctor if she felt the slightest bit dizzy again.

It was a novelty being so thoroughly spoiled. She couldn't remember a time in her life when she'd ever felt so pampered.

Or so loved.

He might not actually say it in so many words, but with every meal, every gesture, Dylan was using his attentiveness and care to prove that he'd meant what he said about wanting to be there for her in everything. Maybe they really could make this work, she thought, stroking the small mound of her belly through the sheets. Maybe they really could be a family.

She looked up as Dylan appeared in the doorway to the bedroom. He looked so sexy in just a pair of drawstring pajama bottoms slung low on his hips. His jaw was unshaved and his hair disheveled, and she had never wanted a man more in her life than she wanted him right now.

"How are you feeling this morning?" he asked, putting the tray with her breakfast on a bedside table and sitting down on the bed next to her to kiss her good morning.

"Fantastic," she answered with a smile. She raised a hand to trace the muscles of his chest, letting her fingers drift low over his ridged abdomen until they teased at the waistband of his pants. "In fact, any better and I think I'd be dangerous."

"Dangerous, huh?" He smiled in return.

She nodded. "I think I should show you how dangerous. Actions always speak louder than words, don't you think?"

Jenna rose up onto her knees, letting the sheet fall away from her body and exposing her nakedness to his hungry gaze. The look on his face empowered her. He made her feel so beautiful, so sexy, so very much in love. The realization should have hit her like a blow, she thought, but it felt right to admit it. To play around with the idea in her mind and to accept that with Dylan she could let go of the rigid control she'd developed to direct her life.

She pushed him back down on the bed, tugging at the drawstring of his pants and pushing the fabric aside to expose him to her gaze, to her fingers, to her lips. Then she showed him, slowly and lovingly, just how much he'd come to mean to her—imbuing every caress, every stroke of her tongue, with all that she felt and all that she wanted for the future. Their future.

Afterward, as they lay side by side, spent, their heart rates slowly returning to normal, Jenna looked across at the man who'd inveigled his way behind her defenses and come to mean so very much to her.

"Yes," she said simply.

Dylan's eyes narrowed and he looked at her intently, rolling onto his side. "Yes? Is that what I think it means?"

She nodded, suddenly shy and a little bit scared. This was letting go of her last vestige of control. But it would be okay, wouldn't it? With Dylan?

He reached for her hand and linked his fingers through hers before drawing them to his lips and kissing her knuckles.

"Thank you," he said with a reverence that brought tears to her eyes.

"Do you think your family will be okay with it? I mean, we haven't known each other all that long."

"They'll be more than fine, don't you worry. I'd like to announce it soon, though. No more secrets. What about at the opening the day after tomorrow? Everyone who matters to us will be there. Okay?"

No more secrets. Yet she still held one very close to her

chest. One that might change the way he thought about her forever. What the hell should she do? Tell him, and hope like mad that it wouldn't make any difference? Or keep it hidden away where it would hopefully never see the light of day ever again? It was impossible to know, but at least she didn't have to make a decision right now. After all, hadn't she just made the biggest decision in her life by accepting Dylan's proposal?

There was a time and a place for everything, and right now was not the time for the past. Right now was all about the future.

She slowly nodded. "Okay."

"Then I'd like you to wear this."

He slid open a bedside drawer and removed a pale blue ring box. Jenna's heart raced in her chest. Was that what she thought it was? Dylan slowly lifted the lid and showed the contents to her. A giant solitaire diamond, set high on a band embedded with smaller diamonds, winked at her in the morning light.

"Dylan, are you sure?"

He lifted the ring from its cushion and reached for her left hand, sliding the ring firmly onto her finger.

"I've never been more sure of anything in my life."

Dylan glanced around the restaurant. It looked, in a word, *perfect.* Jenna and her weekend girl, Millie, had delivered the table centerpieces, and they'd just left after putting together the massive tiered floral design in the foyer. Jenna had come up with an idea to use three up-ended logs of different lengths, and cunningly secured them so they wouldn't fall over. Her colorful floral displays cascaded over the logs in a tumble of nature's beauty.

It had given him a new appreciation for her talent as a

floral designer, and made him realize there was so much more to her than simply her ability to tweak a few wildflowers in a vase and make them look appealing. An ember of excitement burned deep inside him. He couldn't wait to announce to all the world tonight that she was his, that they were to be a family.

Today really was turning into the culmination of so many years of hard work, so many of his dreams. God, he missed J.D. and wished the old man could have been here to witness it all. He'd been at Dylan's side for the opening of each of their previous Grills. Dylan had to hope J.D. was here with him in spirit today. He would have been so proud.

"Dylan?"

Sage's voice interrupted him, dragging his attention back to the here and now. Dylan turned with a welcoming smile, surprised to see Sage here. But the serious expression on his brother's face wiped his smile clean away.

"Problem?" he asked.

"Mind if I talk to you for a minute?"

"Sure, fire away."

"In private?"

Dylan looked around at the hive of activity that buzzed about them. Waitstaff scurried back and forth, checking that the tables were all set to perfection and that every glass glistened. Through the serving window a similar hum of commotion came from the kitchen. If they wanted privacy, they'd need to go into his office.

Once they were inside, Sage made a point of closing the door behind him.

"What is it?" Dylan asked, getting the distinct feeling that he wasn't going to like what he had to say.

"Look, I don't quite know how to begin this."

"How about at the beginning," he prompted.

Sage's expression was stony. He drew in a deep breath before speaking. "I got that report back."

"Report?"

"The investigation into Jenna."

Dylan's blood hit boiling point in an instant. "You had no right—!"

"I had every right, as it turns out," Sage interrupted. He shook the contents of a large envelope onto Dylan's desk.

"What's all this?" he demanded, even as his eyes skimmed the words on one of the sheets that had fanned out.

Thief of Hearts! a headline proclaimed. The story went on to detail the trail of heartbroken victims a scam artist had left in his wake across the length and breadth of the country. Dylan continued to skim the article until his eyes jolted to a halt on a name: James Montgomery.

"Just because this guy shares her surname doesn't mean there's any connection," Dylan said, even though he had the distinct impression he was now grasping at straws.

Jenna had said she didn't see her father anymore. No wonder, if he'd been caught, tried and incarcerated for perpetuating such calculated crimes against innocent and vulnerable women.

"Keep reading. You ought to know," Sage said.

A knock sounded at the door and Fee popped her head inside.

"Am I interrupting?"

"No," Sage said before Dylan could answer. "Come in. You need to know this in case there's any fallout tonight."

"Know what?" she asked, coming into the room and closing the door.

"It seems my little brother's girlfriend is not who she appears to be."

"You don't know that," Dylan argued.

"Don't be so quick to judge me, Dylan. There's one thing I do know. That baby she's carrying *is* most likely yours. My investigator couldn't turn up any dirt on her in all the time she's lived in Cheyenne. Which begs the question, why did she suddenly latch on to you? Did she plan to get pregnant all along?"

"You bast—!"

Dylan lurched closer to his brother, only to have Fee step in between them. She looked from one man to the other.

"Guys, this isn't going to get physical, is it? I'd rather not be forced to explain black eyes at the opening tonight."

Her words compelled Dylan to relax the fists he hadn't even realized he'd made.

"You overstepped the mark, Sage," he growled.

"Can you blame me for wanting to look out for you? Read the articles then make up your own mind."

Through the fury that clouded his thinking, his brother's concern for him filtered through.

"Fine," he agreed, his jaw clenched tight.

"I'll leave you to it. Fee, you might need to read those, too." As Dylan began to protest, Sage overrode him again. "If my guy could discover this information, bear in mind others could, too. People who might want to cause trouble."

After Sage turned and left, Fee let out an audible breath.

"Wow, that was intense. What's it all about?"

Dylan swallowed back the bitter taste that had risen in his throat. "Some information he has on Jenna."

"Jenna? Really? Should we…?" Her voice trailed off as if she wasn't sure if going any further would be stepping on his toes.

Dylan sighed. "Yeah, we should. Here," he thrust half the papers in her direction. "Read."

Dylan finished reading the article he'd already started, feeling a sense of anger rising against Jenna's father for his callous behavior toward the women involved. Many of them were widows, women who'd lost their husbands and had sought male companionship, even love, only to find their bank accounts emptied and a pile of debt left in his wake when Jenna's dad left them. Imagine if something like that had happened to his aunt Marlene? Anger welled inside Dylan like a boiling cauldron.

He resolutely picked up the next article. Daughter In On It? questioned the headline. A photo of Jenna, much younger than she was now and with her head shaven beneath a tight headscarf, dominated the page. Even though she couldn't have been older than fourteen or fifteen, her beauty was easily apparent—perhaps even more so as she'd had no hair, so that the picture highlighted her large brown eyes and sweet smile.

Dylan's anger burned into a glowing mass of molten rock as the facts were grimly detailed. Jenna's father, the so-called Thief of Hearts, had used this photo of her and created an online fund-raising profile, saying she was dying of cancer and that they'd needed funds for her treatment. Dylan could barely believe what was there in stark black-and-white. While it was never proved that Jenna was a willing accomplice, questions still remained as to the depth of her involvement in that specific scam, as well as what had happened to all the money her father had conned out of his targets.

The article further revealed that as a minor, under the

care of the state when her father was sent down, Jenna would be put into foster care. That certainly explained how she had arrived in Cheyenne and ended up under Margaret Connell's roof—even though Mrs. Connell had never been known to foster anyone before then. Dylan reached for the printed single page report that summarized the investigator's findings. It went into interesting details about her financials. She'd attended the University of Wyoming without incurring any student loans and she'd also used a large cash deposit when buying her own home. A business loan had helped her buy the florist business. On their own, he could understand and accept each point, but the report raised far more questions than it answered. Like, where had Jenna gotten the money to attend university and buy her house?

Dylan reread the paragraph of the second article that talked about the sum of money that had been donated toward Jenna's "treatment." It was a hefty sum, reflective of the good will that had been shown by their community, and then abused and stomped on by her father. Apparently, the fund had been augmented by a six-figure donation from the woman Jenna's father had been known to be seeing at the time. Somehow, though, before the full investigation into her father's behavior, all that money had been withdrawn from the account set up in Jenna's name, and no amount of investigation had been able to reveal what had happened to it.

By the time he and Fee had finished reading the papers, a worried frown creased the PR manager's brow.

"Do you want to can the Q&A this evening?" she asked. "It might be best."

"It would be a complete break in our usual format. Wouldn't it raise even more questions if we do that?"

Fee pursed her lips. "You're probably right. I guess

we'll just have to hope that we can steer off any awkward questions, though I have to admit, I'm worried. As Sage said, if he could get this information, so can anyone."

Again that sense of being duped hammered at the back of Dylan's mind. It was information he'd have discovered himself if he'd been more diligent. If he hadn't been so swift to see only what he'd wanted to see.

"Let's just deal with it if it arises. Jenna's involvement in her father's scams was conjecture only."

Even as he said it, he felt his own doubts rise in his throat to choke him. Fee worried at her bottom lip with her teeth as she scanned the papers one more time.

"Are you sure that's how you want to handle it? In fact, are you sure you even still want Jenna there tonight?"

No, he wasn't. What he wanted was answers from Jenna. Answers he should have had from her before now. The fact she'd hidden all this from him hurt at a level he didn't want to discuss right now.

"Again, that would probably raise more questions than if she wasn't there. So, yes, I'm sure," he said firmly.

"Okay, then. I'll see you tonight."

Fee rose and left the office. He'd go to Jenna right now, he decided. He had to talk to her, to ask her for the truth behind this whole story. Determined to have this out with her face-to-face, he started to rise from his chair.

A loud crash sounded out in the kitchen, and within seconds a rapid knocking started at his door.

"Chef! Chef! We have a problem!"

Dylan groaned out loud, knowing that whatever was happening outside was far more urgent than talking to Jenna right now. He had more than a problem, he thought, as he shot from his office and into the kitchen to deal with the latest crisis. He had potentially opened up his whole family to someone who could be an accomplished scammer. One to whom he'd be inextricably connected for the rest of his life through their child. One who'd inveigled her way into his heart so securely that even entertaining the suspicion that she'd been a willing accomplice in her father's scheme caused a physical pain in his chest.

Sage had cautioned him about racing into this full-on, and Dylan hadn't listened. Had he been thoroughly duped? Had her playing hard to get all been part of her act? He didn't want to believe it could be true, but a devil of rationality perched on his shoulder told him he needed to consider all his options before taking this any further. As far as he knew Jenna had lived an exemplary life here in Cheyenne. Finishing high school, attending college, working hard and buying a home and a business. On the surface, it all looked so perfect. Too perfect maybe?

"Chef! We need you."

The shout spurred him into action. Right now, the kitchen was his priority; unfortunately, just when it looked as if his life was jumping out of the frying pan and into the fire. Deep down, though, Dylan couldn't help feeling a sense of betrayal. The other night, when she'd finally accepted his proposal, they'd agreed—no more secrets. And if this wasn't a breach of that agreement, he didn't know what was.

Thirteen

Jenna stepped from the car Dylan had sent for her, her gown falling around her in a delicate swirl of fiery-orange. The halter neck and empire waistline drew attention away from her bump, although she doubted she'd be able to continue to hide it for much longer. She thumbed the diamond ring on her finger with a small smile. Once their engagement was public knowledge it would be okay to let the news of their baby leak out.

She ducked her head shyly as some of the assembled media took her photo as she walked toward the front door.

"Name please, miss?" the stylishly suited young man at the door asked, before referring to his clipboard and ushering her through when she'd told him.

Dylan was part of a receiving line in the entrance. She drank in the sight of him in a dark pinstripe suit that looked as if it had been tailored specifically for him.

He was hers. The idea filled her with a sense of completion she could hardly dare believe. She really was the luckiest woman on earth. After all she'd been through, he'd become her light in the darkness. Her true north.

He looked up and she beamed at him, covering the carpeted distance between them as quickly and gracefully as her high heels would allow.

"Dylan, this looks amazing!" she breathed as she reached his side and lifted her face for his kiss.

She was surprised when his lips just grazed her cheek, but put it down to the swell of people pressing behind her as they came through the main entrance.

"I won't take up your time," she said quickly. "I'll leave you to your duties."

"No, wait just a second." Dylan caught her by the hand and turned to the man beside him.

"Evan, could you look after Jenna for me? Just until I can get free, okay?"

"Sure, absolutely no problem whatsoever."

"Jenna," Dylan continued, "this is Evan McCain, CEO of Lassiter Media. He's come in from L.A. for this evening. You'll be in good hands."

Jenna had recognized the ex-fiancé of Dylan's sister, Angelica, the minute she'd walked in the door, and said as much.

"It's good to see you again, Evan. I'm glad you could make it," she added.

"I wouldn't have missed it for the world." He smiled, his hazel eyes crinkling at the corners. "So, shall we go and see what the waitstaff are serving on those ridiculously large trays they're carrying around? I don't know about you, but I'm starving."

He offered her his arm and Jenna took it with a smile. She glanced back at Dylan, who was watching her with that little frown between his brows.

"I'll be fine. Just looking forward to when you're free," she said with a small wave.

He gave her a nod and turned his attention to the next newcomers in the line, welcoming the mayor and his wife with his accomplished smile and polite patter. As Evan led her away toward the dining room, Jenna couldn't help but feel that something was amiss. Aside from getting the message, through Fee Sinclair, that he'd be sending a car for her instead of picking her up himself today, she'd not had a single call from him. That in itself had been unusual.

Still, she silently reasoned, he was under a lot of pressure for tonight. In her call, Fee had mentioned the accident one of his staff had suffered in the kitchen earlier today, and Jenna knew he'd stepped into the breach. Did that explain the undercurrent of tension she'd felt? She hoped that was all it was, and that once he knew everything was running smoothly for tonight he could relax.

There was a loud murmur of activity at the entrance and Jenna turned her head in time to see Angelica Lassiter arrive, accompanied by a striking man. Tall, with dark brown hair and eyes that appeared to miss nothing, he looked incredibly handsome and yet had an air of ruthlessness about him that set her on edge. On his arm, Angelica looked absolutely stunning. Her shoulder-length hair was swept up into an elegant chignon that exposed the delicate line of her neck.

Jenna could feel Evan's tension as he watched his ex-fiancée's entrance. "Him? Of all the people she could have come with, she chose him?" he muttered.

"Who is he? I don't think I've seen him around here before," Jenna said, allowing Evan to turn her away from the newcomers and toward a waitress carrying a tray of canapés.

"No, you wouldn't have. No disrespect to you, but you don't move in Jack Reed's exalted circles."

Jenna couldn't help but recognize the bitterness in his voice. Evan continued, "He's from L.A., and has a hard-earned reputation as a corporate raider—all of which makes me wonder why he's even here. Unless Angelica did this to deliberately annoy me."

Jenna's first instinct was to refute what Evan had said.

She'd met Angelica again at Hannah and Logan's engagement dinner, and Dylan's sister had been gracious and charming. She certainly hadn't struck Jenna as malicious, even though there was clearly some undercurrent between Evan and Angelica's date. But then a tiny voice reminded her of something Dylan had said several days ago, about how upset Angelica had been when her father had cut her out of Lassiter Media in his will, leaving the controlling share to Evan.

"Well," Jenna said quietly, "I guess whatever the reason, the best thing for now is to make do with my company and show her that you don't mind who she's shown up with."

"Make do? Having your company is far better than making do," he said with a charming smile that lit up his face. "I apologize if I made it sound any other way."

Jenna laughed, the sound drawing the attention of the newcomers—in particular Angelica, whose set expression and sharp-eyed glare at Evan showed she was about as happy seeing him here as he was in seeing Jack Reed at her side. A swell of people moved between them, breaking the moment, and Jenna felt a wave of relief sweep through her.

Evan led her through the room, circulating among the gathering guests. The crowd consisted of Lassiters and members of the local chamber of commerce, interspersed with a few celebrities and a smattering of media. Jenna received many compliments on her floral displays and, from the number of business cards she was given and was asked for, would be rushed off her feet with work in the coming weeks. Things were really looking up, she thought, as everyone was invited to take their seats.

Evan showed Jenna to a seat at a table near the large stone fireplace in the center of the restaurant. The placeholder next to hers showed Dylan would be seated on her right, and Evan slid into the chair at her left. It took some time for the room to settle into quiet and for everyone to be seated. The lighting dimmed until only a podium near the front was well lit. She smiled through the gloom as Marlene and her date, Walter Drake, whom Jenna had also met at Hannah and Logan's engagement dinner, sat down opposite her.

Dylan took the floor, introducing his new Lassiter Grill team with pride. Jenna squirmed with excitement. Any minute now he'd be closing up the official business and inviting her to join him to share their news—their happiness—with everyone assembled. It felt odd, after so many years of keeping her head down and struggling to remain unnoticed, to be looking forward to being the center of attention. But as she watched the man she loved with all her heart standing there in front of everyone, she knew she could do anything in this world as long as he was by her side.

She thumbed the engagement ring he'd given her two days ago, and felt a swell of love build inside. She'd never been happier than she was right at this moment.

Dylan wound up the formal section of the evening, thanking everyone for being there, and asked if there were any questions from the floor. He smoothly fielded a number of questions relating to the restaurant before the tone began to swing toward a more personal note.

"Dylan, you've been spending a lot of time in Cheyenne lately. Aside from the restaurant, is there something or some*one* else responsible for that?" one of the female reporters asked with a sugary sweet tone.

Dylan nodded his head. "I've been seeing someone, yes, that's true."

The same reporter asked, "Are you going to tell us who that someone is?"

Fee, standing slightly to one side of Dylan, whispered something in his ear. He nodded and addressed the reporter.

"Jenna Montgomery. Many of you will know her already. She's responsible for the stunning floral designs here tonight."

A prickle of unease crept across Jenna's skin. That was it? Nothing about their engagement? She thought tonight was when he'd wanted to make the announcement. To shout it, loud and proud, that they were getting married and having a family together.

A different voice, a man's this time, rang out.

"Is it true that Jenna Montgomery is pregnant with your child?"

How on earth had some journalist heard about the baby?

Dylan kept his composure. "That is true," he answered smoothly as if the news was of no consequence.

The same man persisted. "Are you and your family aware that the woman carrying your baby is the same Jenna Montgomery who faked terminal cancer to help her father swindle nearly a quarter million dollars from a fund set up in her name eleven years ago?" the reporter persisted.

The room exploded in an uproar. Jenna felt the world tilt and a sensation like icy cold water ran through her veins. Through the haze of terror in her mind she heard Dylan's voice asking for calm. As the room once more fell quiet, Jenna found herself—like pretty much everyone else there—hanging on a thread waiting to find out what he would say.

"Yes, I am aware of Jenna's past and of the unproved

charges against her." He paused and whispered something to Fee, who went immediately across the room to two men standing to the side in dark suits. Together with them, she walked toward the reporter who had asked the questions. Dylan turned his attention back to the assembly as the reporter was quietly ushered from the restaurant. "Now, if there are no more questions, let's enjoy dinner."

An eerie silence filled the room like a vacuum as all eyes turned to Jenna. Across the table, Marlene looked at her in concern, a question in her eyes that Jenna had no wish to answer right here and now—or ever, if it could have come to that. She wanted nothing more than to run, and glanced around the room for the nearest exit, feeling like a cornered creature with nowhere to hide. Beside Marlene, Sage Lassiter's eyes bored into her as if he could see right through her to the woman he'd thought she was all along.

Her gaze flittered past them all, frantic to find a compassionate face, but everyone simply looked at her in a blend of shock or accusation. Here she was, a viper in their midst. Someone they'd accepted, welcomed—someone they really shouldn't trust.

Eventually, she looked at Dylan, silently begging him to believe in her. To *know* that she had been an innocent party in all that had happened. She should have told him long before. Her silence now made her appear complicit. Finally, his eyes met hers and she felt every last glimmer of hope for a future together fade into nothing. In his gaze she saw no trace of the teasing lover who'd shared her nights, nor the conscientious and caring soul who'd paid such devoted attention to her this past week. No longer was he the man who'd determinedly suggested marriage and then cajoled her into love—into believing in a time ahead where they could be happy together, be *parents* together.

A shudder rippled through her body, numbness taking her over until it was a struggle to draw in a deep enough breath. This was her worst nightmare. Her darkest, most shameful secret had been exposed to everyone here. People she admired and had come to trust. People who had come to trust her. Now that trust was crushed to smithereens, her hard-won reputation scattered to the corners of the county. She'd truly thought she'd managed to put all that behind her, but now, well, nothing could ever be the same again.

Dylan's eyes flicked from hers to someone else nearby, and seconds later she heard Felicity Sinclair's voice in her ear.

"Come, let me take you home. This can't be good for you or for the baby," she said in her capable, no-nonsense manner.

"Th-thank you," Jenna said gratefully, rising to her feet as Dylan continued to field a melee of questions from the media who'd been asked to cover the opening.

Fee guided her past the beautifully dressed tables—tables Jenna had helped decorate herself, in excited preparation for tonight—and the accusatory stares of the people gathered here punctured her as though each one was a spear of loathing. She couldn't believe how her world had turned on a dime, from one filled with joy and expectations to one where the future once again appeared bleak and lonely.

It seemed like forever, but eventually they were at the front of the restaurant and out the main doors. Fee ushered her immediately into a waiting car. Jenna didn't even stop to wonder how the woman had arranged for the driver to be there so quickly. Instead, she sagged against the seat, locked in a cocoon of loss, as Fee slid into the seat beside her and instructed the man to take them to Jenna's home.

Fee's hand slipped into hers. "Take a deep breath, Jenna. And another. Okay? Leave it to Dylan. He'll take care of everything."

How could he take care of everything? Why would he even want to? Jenna squeezed her eyes shut, but his image still burned there, especially the look on his face just before Fee had led her from the restaurant. The numbness that encased her slowly began to recede—replaced instead by a tearing pain deep inside her chest.

"It's going to be okay," Fee soothed. "You're out of there now."

Sure, they were out of there, but nothing was ever going to be okay again. Jenna had seen the questions in Dylan's eyes, the hurt and mistrust that had replaced the warmth and the love she'd already grown accustomed to seeing in him. Inside she began to mourn what they would never be able to share again.

She should have known better than to hope, known better than to reach out and take what he'd offered her so tantalizingly. She thought about all she'd undoubtedly lost. His trust, their future, his family. She would miss it all. Would she ever be able to look at him again and not see the accusation in his eyes? The knowledge that, of all the things she'd shared with him, that piece of her past was the one she should have shared first?

A discreet buzz came from Fee's delicate evening bag and she slid out her phone.

"Yes, we're on our way to her house."

Jenna could make out a muffled male voice at the other end.

"She's okay, for now. I'll stay with her until you can

come, just to be sure." Fee popped her phone back into her bag. "Dylan will be over as soon as he can get away."

Jenna nodded, but knew it wouldn't make any difference. What they'd had would be gone now. A man like him—a family like theirs—didn't need the notoriety that being with someone like her would bring. She'd known that all along, and yet she'd foolishly dared to dream it could be different.

Now, she knew, it would never be.

Fourteen

Dylan parked at the curb outside Jenna's house, leaving the driveway clear for the limousine that remained parked in the drive. He nodded to the driver as he walked past and up to the front door.

Fee opened it before he could knock.

"How is she?" he asked, his voice tight.

"She went to lie down as soon as we got here. Do you want me to head back to the Grill now?"

"If you don't mind. I guess you've probably already worked out a strategy to cope with any fallout over tonight?"

Fee smiled. "Of course. Leave it to me. This will blow over, you know. It won't affect the Lassiter Grill Corporation. If anything, the notoriety might even be good for you."

It might not affect the company, but it certainly affected everything else that was important to him, he thought as he escorted Fee out to the limousine. He watched as it drove away, and then turned and went back inside Jenna's compact home.

She was standing in the living room when he got inside. He was shocked to see how her dark eyes stood out in her eerily pale face. She hadn't changed from the gown she'd been wearing tonight, and it looked crumpled. His eyes drifted over her graceful shoulders, over the fullness of her breasts and lower, to where his baby nestled inside her. His gut twisted.

"Are you all right?" he asked, concern for her and the baby uppermost in his mind.

"A bit upset," she said, her hand fluttering to her belly. She gave a humorless laugh. "Actually, a lot upset."

He wasn't surprised. It had been a shock for him, too. First of all to discover that secret in her past, and then to have it laid out in front of everyone at the opening tonight.

Why had she kept it hidden from him? She could have told him at any time over the past few days, especially once she'd agreed to plan a future together. Did she honestly think that if she was an innocent party, he'd have felt any differently about her? Hell, she'd been so young she *had* to be innocent. Even if she'd participated in the scam, surely she would have been compelled to do so by the one person who was supposed to have been taking care of her.

Unless the real answer was all too damning. In general, people didn't hide the truth—which left an alternative that Dylan found distinctly unpalatable.

"It is true?" he asked. Everything depended on her answer.

"What part, exactly?"

He bit back the frustration that threatened to overwhelm him. How could she be flip about this? How could she continue to avoid telling him what he needed to know?

"All of it? Any of it?" He bit out the questions.

"There is some truth to it," she said softly, ducking her head.

"So you were involved."

Something passed across her face, something he couldn't quite define.

"Yes," she said, lifting her chin and meeting his scrutiny. "I was involved, but not voluntarily. I didn't know what my father was doing."

Could he believe her? He wanted to, but all the evidence, especially her silence on this very matter, suggested he shouldn't.

And it still didn't answer the question why she hadn't told him.

"What about me?" he asked.

"What do you mean?"

"What am I to you?"

"Dylan!" She sped across the carpet to stand directly in front of him, placing a hand on his chest. "You know what you are to me. You're my lover, the man I want to marry. You're the father of my baby. The man I love."

It sounded so sincere, and yet there were still shadows in her eyes. Truths that couldn't be told because maybe they weren't truths, after all. The questions that had been tumbling around in his mind all day were as irrational now as they'd seemed when they'd first evolved in his brain. Yet they still spewed forth from his mouth before he could have time to weigh them properly.

"Did I come across to you as an easy mark? Is that what it was? Did you see me at the rehearsal dinner setup and target me then? Or maybe the idea came to you later, when you discovered you were pregnant. Was that it?"

He saw her flinch beneath his onslaught. Felt her pull her hand away from his chest, and in its place felt coldness invade that part of him where his heart had beat steadily for her.

"I can't believe you'd think that of me," she said, her eyes wide with horror.

"Seriously, Jenna? We agreed, only two nights ago, no more secrets. What am I supposed to think?"

She stiffened her shoulders. "I can't tell you what to think. Look, perhaps it would be in the best interests of everyone concerned, especially your family and the Lassiter brand, if we didn't see one another again. I won't stand in your way when it comes to access to the baby, I promise you that. It's what I expected to do from the first, anyway."

She took one step back, then another, her fingers frantically working off the engagement ring he'd chosen with all the love he carried for her in his heart. She dropped the ring onto the occasional table beside her.

"Take it," she said bluntly, determination overlaying the anguish that still reflected in her eyes. "Just take it. I don't want it anymore."

He looked at the ring sitting on the table—its beauty an empty symbol of all his hopes. He scooped it up and put it in his suit pocket and turned and walked away.

"Fine. Since you still can't be honest with me, I'll go," he said bitterly. But nothing was fine at all. At the door he hesitated and turned back to face her. "You know what the worst thing about all of this is?"

She stared back at him, mute.

"The worst thing is that you wouldn't trust me enough to tell me the truth. I love you, Jenna. I really thought you'd learned to love me in return. Last chance. Tell me the truth."

She shook her head, her arms wrapping around her body, her cheeks glistening with the tears that ran freely down her face. Every instinct in his body urged him to go to her, to take her in his arms and to tell her that they could still work this out. That everything would be okay.

"Please," she said, her voice thick and choked. "Let yourself out."

She wheeled on her feet and fled down the hallway toward her bedroom. A second later he heard the door slam in finality. Raw pain, the likes of which he'd never known before, clawed viciously through him. Somehow he managed to walk out the door and get to his SUV. He sat there in the dark, staring at her house for a full five minutes, before starting the car and driving away.

Anger bubbled up from beneath his agony. Why couldn't she just tell him? Why couldn't she share that part of her that had now effectively driven them apart? Dammit, she'd chosen doing what was right for his family—even the Lassiter brand—over sharing the truth with him. What about his feelings? Didn't she care about them? Didn't she care that she'd let them both down?

Somehow he drove back to the restaurant, where the opening night party was still in full swing. He slid in through the rear entrance, but Sage caught him when he was in his office, about to put Jenna's ring in the safe.

"You all right?" his brother asked.

"No, I'm not all right," he growled, one hand swinging open the safe's door while the other closed in a fist around the ring in his pocket. It cut into his palm and he welcomed the pain. It matched how he felt inside. He flung a glance at his brother. "So, are you going to gloat? Tell me you were right all along?"

Sage shook his head. "You didn't see her face when that reporter threw that question at you. She looked as if her entire world had blown up."

"Her fabricated world, you mean," Dylan said bitterly.

"No," Sage said firmly. "Her real world. Maybe I was too hasty in showing you that report. Maybe we should have delved a bit deeper first. I agree," he said in response to his brother's snort of disgust, "it was my idea. But, Dylan, you didn't see how tonight affected her. Give it a few days. Go back to her. Talk it out."

He shook his head. "Not going to happen. She doesn't want to see me anymore."

He pulled his fist from his pocket and uncurled his fingers from around the ring, exposing the glittering piece before hurling it into the back of the safe and slamming the door shut.

"I didn't mean to hurt you, Dylan. You deserved to know the truth. But think on this. If she really was what those articles say she is, she'd still be wearing that ring."

Dylan weighed his brother's words. "You're probably right," he said with a sigh. "But until she's prepared to be open with me, I can't see us working this thing out. Besides, she'll probably never forgive me for what I said."

"What exactly did you say?"

"I asked her if I was her latest mark. I couldn't help it. It just came out. I was so mad that she'd kept something so important from me. Nothing about her life adds up, Sage. Nothing. Not unless she really was a part of her father's scheme and has been happily living off those proceeds all this time."

He didn't want to believe his own words, but without proof, without Jenna's own testimony, how could he think anything different?

Jenna walked on aching legs to her office to tally up the day's receipts. So much for today's cashless society, she thought, as she extracted the float to go back into the cash register, and then counted the notes to go to the bank the next morning.

She'd been beyond worried that after the disaster of Lassiter Grill's opening night, her business would slowly dwindle and die off. Instead, the opposite had been true. She'd barely been able to keep up with demand, and had been forced to increase her orders from the wholesalers. She and Valerie had been swamped working on special orders, and the foot traffic coming in through the front door had doubled over the previous week.

"Why don't you let me finish that up," Valerie offered as she entered the office. "You look dead on your feet."

"No, I'm halfway there already," Jenna insisted, even as a wave of weariness swept through her.

It wasn't the first time this week she'd felt weak and slightly disoriented. Considering she'd barely been able to force herself from bed each morning, or to eat or drink properly, it really was no wonder. Logically, she knew she had to look after herself, to look after the baby. But just now everything to do with herself fell into the "too hard" basket. She was glad they were crazy busy. At least at work she could get lost in the oblivion of one order to fill after another.

Valerie sat in the chair opposite Jenna's desk and studied her. "Have you heard from him yet?"

"What? No, I haven't. And I don't expect to, either."

"Never?" Valerie sounded regretful.

"Never, at least not directly," Jenna responded. She could hear the flatness in her voice and tried to inject some life back into it. "It's better that way."

"I don't see how. You're still pregnant with his baby. That takes two."

"Valerie, please. This week's hard enough as it is," Jenna implored her friend. "Can you just let it go?"

Valerie studied her from across the table. "Not when you look the way you do. I'm sorry, but I care about you. In fact, no. I'm not sorry. I *care* about you, Jenna. I've watched you go all the way from sweeping floors to taking this business over from Margaret and getting us to where we are today. You're bright, you're clever—but most of all you're honest. I know people have been saying things about you, and yes, I remember the stories about your dad from back when. It's shameful what he did to you and it's shameful that it's coming back to haunt you. You're not the person they said you are. The past belongs right there, in the past. I believe in you, Jenna. I just wanted you to know that."

Jenna gave the other woman a weak smile. "Thank you. I appreciate it."

"But it's not enough, is it? You still love him."

Jenna felt the all too familiar burn of tears in her eyes. She resolutely blinked them back, again. "That doesn't matter. What matters is this little person in here." She patted her tummy and was rewarded with a ripple of movement.

"Honey, trust me, it matters. You're killing yourself over this."

Of course it mattered. It mattered enough that barely a minute went by without her thinking of Dylan. Without seeing again and again the pain she'd inflicted on him and the disappointment that had been etched on his face before he'd left her on Saturday night. She drew in a deep breath. It would get better, eventually. She had to hold on to that thought.

Valerie persisted. "I think you should see him. Talk this out some more."

"He's gone back to L.A. At least that's what I heard."

"So pick up a telephone."

"No, really. It's over, Valerie. If I can accept that, I think you should, too. In fact, I'd appreciate it if you didn't mention it again."

Never would be too soon, Jenna thought as Valerie reluctantly agreed to her request.

"At least come to my house tonight for dinner. You can put up your feet. I'll make sure the kids wait on you and I'll cook you up one of my famous chicken casseroles."

"It sounds lovely, but to be honest, I'm beat. I just want to go home and go to bed."

"And have something to eat," Valerie added.

"Yes, yes, and have something to eat." Jenna gathered up the cash and checks and handed Valerie the float to put back in the cash register. "I'll do the banking on my way in tomorrow. Will you be okay to open up?"

"Sure. With my eldest and her best friend happy to mind the younger kids for a few extra dollars while they're on summer vacation, life's a whole lot less chaotic for me in the mornings. Don't rush in."

"I'll be here just after nine, I hope. We have another big day ahead."

"Which is exactly why I don't think you should be rushing around," Valerie teased with a laugh.

"Okay, okay. Don't you have enough mothering to do with your kids?"

"Hey, once a mother, always a mother."

Valerie went to put the spare cash in the register and then walked out the back with Jenna. "You take care tonight," her friend said, then got in her car and drove away with a cheerful wave.

Jenna watched her go with a wistful smile on her face. She'd never stopped to think all that much about Valerie's life beyond what she saw on the surface—married for sixteen years, with four great kids. Jenna was hit with a near overwhelming sense of envy for the simplicity of Valerie's world. For the security within it. She tightened her grip on the steering wheel and breathed in deep. She could do this. She'd been on her own for a long time now and she didn't need anyone else.

But even as she thought it, Dylan's face swam into her thoughts and with it a feeling of loss so devastating it made her head swim. She leaned back on the headrest and dragged in one breath after another until the woozy sensation left her. Then she turned on the ignition and put her car into gear, easing it out of the parking lot and onto the street, heading home.

She'd get through this. She just had to.

Fifteen

She was dragging her feet from the moment she got up the next morning. It was as if no matter how much time she spent in bed, or resting, it was never quite enough. Jenna surveyed the miserable offerings of food she had left in her fridge. Nothing worth eating for breakfast, she realized. She'd pick something up at a drive-through on the way to the store. She filled her traveling cup with drinking water, picked up her bag and went through to her garage.

Just as she pressed the garage door opener a wave of vertigo hit, and she put out a hand to the doorjamb to steady herself. It took about a full minute to pass.

"Pull yourself together," Jenna chastised herself out loud, adjusting her bag on her shoulder and stepping toward her car. "You ate a decentish meal last night. You can survive until after the bank."

She took a sip of her water, then another. There, she was feeling better already, she told herself, and walked the short distance to her car.

Driving to the bank, she felt fine. She found a parking spot close by and then went inside to wait for a free teller. Despite the early hour, it was busy for a Thursday. She hadn't been waiting terribly long before she felt the earth tilt beneath her feet once more.

"Not again," she muttered under her breath.

"What's that, miss?" said the older man in the line ahead of her.

"Oh, nothing, sorry."

"Are you sure? You look a bit—"

That was all Jenna heard before the blackness came out of nowhere to swallow her whole. She never even felt it when she hit the floor, nor did she hear the concerned cries from the people around her.

"You look like crap, man," Dylan's second in charge, Noel, said as he came into his office on Friday morning.

"Why, thank you," he replied in a voice loaded with sarcasm.

Truth was, he knew he looked like crap. Felt it, too. Since leaving Cheyenne he'd felt as if something—or more precisely, someone—was calling him back. He'd tried to tell himself he'd done all he could, that he'd overseen the opening to the best of his ability and that he'd left things in his executive chef's and restaurant manager's capable hands. Hell, he wouldn't have hired them if they weren't up to the job in the first place. It was time to pour himself back into what his job called for here in L.A.

Even so, his mind kept turning over that last conversation with Jenna, and with it, all the questions that remained unanswered between them. He'd done some more research and discovered that her father, James, had quite the reputation with the ladies. Exactly when he'd started fleecing them for every penny had been unclear, but when a couple of widows had begun comparing notes about their new beau over a game of bridge at their country club one afternoon, they'd seen and heard enough from one another to realize they were dating the same man.

After pressure from their families, they'd been the ones to bring the original complaints to the police, instigating the investigation into James Montgomery's habits. An inquiry that had unearthed a string of similarly swindled lovers in his past. Women who'd been too embarrassed to bring their situation to the attention of their families, let alone the authorities.

It made Dylan furious to think of so many innocents being duped by the charmer. A man whose first priority should have been the care and raising of his daughter. Dylan didn't understand how anyone could be so remiss in his duty to his own flesh and blood.

Speaking of *his* flesh and blood, he wondered how Jenna was doing. She'd be sixteen weeks along by now. When had she been due next for a scan? He huffed out a sigh and forced himself to relax his hand around the Montblanc pen he was strangling to death over the papers he was supposed to sign, and which Noel was waiting so patiently for.

"Your EA asked me to bring these in to you," Noel said, putting some pink message slips on Dylan's desk.

His eye scanned the papers, but it wasn't until he picked up the Cheyenne area code on one that he sat up and took notice. It wasn't like Chance to call him here at the office; his cousin usually called him direct on his cell phone, Dylan thought as he flourished his pen across the necessary pages and then passed the stack of documents over the desk to Noel.

"Was there anything else you needed from me today?" he asked the younger guy.

"No, I'm pretty sure we're up to date with these," he said, flicking through the pages. "I'll call you if anything arises from them."

"Thanks." Dylan nodded absently. He checked his cell

phone as he picked up the office handset to dial home. Two missed calls from Chance—yesterday. Whatever it was, it had to be urgent. His cousin picked up on the second ring, his voice gruff.

"Chance Lassiter."

"Hey, just the man I wanted to speak to. How come you're not working?"

"I wish I wasn't working. I'm going through the ranch accounts before handing them over to the accountant. But that's beside the point. Where have you been, man? I've been trying to get hold of you since yesterday."

"I had my phone on Do Not Disturb and forgot to change it back. What's up?"

"Have you heard about Jenna?"

Dylan stiffened in his chair. "Heard about her? Why? What's happened?"

"She collapsed in the bank yesterday morning. They had to rush her to the hospital."

"She collapsed? Do you know why?"

Dammit, he shouldn't have left Cheyenne. He shouldn't have walked away from his responsibilities to his unborn baby or to its mother.

"Mom called the hospital as soon as she heard, but they wouldn't give her any information other than to say Jenna was stable."

Stable was good, wasn't it, he consoled himself. At least she wasn't in serious or critical condition. "Has anyone tried to contact Jenna directly?"

"Sure. But her cell must be turned off. A woman called Valerie answered at the store, but she was about as forthcoming as a clam when Mom asked after Jenna."

Dylan mentally calculated what he had to complete today to be able to get back home to Cheyenne. Home. When had L.A. stopped being home for him? he wondered briefly, and then realized it never really had been. Sure, it was where he lived, but it wasn't where he belonged. Right now he belonged back in Cheyenne.

"I'll be there as soon as I can. Thanks for the heads-up, Chance."

"I knew you'd want to know. Hey, man. You're going to sort this out, aren't you? The rest of us don't care what happened to her in the past, or what she was involved in. We do care about who she is now, and she's going to be the mother of one of a new generation of Lassiters. She's one of us, whether she wants to be or not."

"Yeah, I'm going to sort this out," Dylan said, ending the call. *Somehow.*

But it was as if the world conspired to prevent him from getting to Cheyenne, from getting to Jenna and finding out what was wrong with her. He was as gnarly as a wildcat with a thorn in its paw by the time he dumped his remaining work onto Noel and instructed him that if anything else urgent came up, he'd have to handle it himself. To the younger guy's credit, he didn't so much as blink.

Dylan's executive assistant filled him in on the booking details for the flight she'd just managed to squeeze him onto at short notice. It would mean a stop in Denver, but at least he'd arrive in Cheyenne before midnight tonight. He cursed the fact that the company jet was down for routine maintenance. While he waited at the airport, he called the hospital and asked to be put through to Jenna, but was surprised to be told she'd already been discharged. That meant she had to be home, right?

In the departure lounge he tried her home phone number, but there was no reply. He tried her cell—again, no reply. He looked at his watch; her store would just about be closing. He dialed the number, only to hear the final

boarding call for his flight. A security guard gave him a
strange look as Dylan muttered a string of curses before
grabbing his briefcase and heading to the gate. He'd have
to stow his impatience and his concerns until he got to
Wyoming and could see her for himself.

A delay in Denver saw his flight into Cheyenne land
well after midnight. Dylan was chafing at the bit to drive
straight to Jenna's house, but logic and reason told him
that would be stupid. If she was home, she'd be sound
asleep by now. The morning would have to suffice.

Once he arrived at his house Dylan shrugged out of
his suit jacket and tore off his tie. He poured himself a
generous measure of aged Scotch and threw himself into
one of the large chairs in the living room. Sleep was the
furthest thing from his mind right now. From the moment he'd received the news about Jenna, his primary
focus had been on getting here. He hadn't really stopped
to think about what he'd do when he arrived. Sure, he
wanted to see for himself that she and the baby were okay,
and he most definitely wanted to know what had caused
the collapse that had sent her to the hospital in the first
place. But what then? What came after that?

He still had questions to which she was the only one
who held the answers. It had hurt him deeply when he
learned she'd been holding back and made him say things
he never would have under normal circumstances. But
then again, their circumstances had never been normal,
exactly, had they? That said, he'd been upfront about his
desire to want to take care of her from the beginning. To
build a future for her and their baby. Seeing her again,
after their first encounter, had proved to him that their
attraction was definitely not the kind of thing that crossed
a person's path more than once in a lifetime. In fact, for
many people, it never entered their life at all. He'd be-

lieved, down deep in his soul, that she was the one for him. Had that changed?

Aside from his natural concern for her, how did he feel now? Had knowing what lay in her past changed his emotions when it came to Jenna Montgomery? He took a sip of his whiskey and rolled the liquid around on his tongue before swallowing it. The answer to his question took a long time coming. No, he didn't love her any less. Sure, he was stung that she hadn't told him, but it didn't change how he felt about her at his core. He'd accused her of not trusting him with the full story about her past, but wasn't he just as bad not trusting her when she had told him she hadn't been knowingly involved in the cancer scam? Had he been so hurt by her withholding the truth that he hadn't even wanted to listen—had somehow wanted to punish her for that secret and therefore hadn't been prepared to believe her?

This past week had been hell without her. Without hearing the sound of her voice, the husky timbre of her laughter, the delicious hitch in her breathing when he kissed her intimately.

Could he imagine life without her? Hell, no, he couldn't. Every night since the opening he'd tried to see how his future would evolve without Jenna being an intrinsic part of it, and it had been a dark and harrowing place. He wanted her. More than that, he loved her with a passion so great he knew he could never settle for anyone else but her. Ever.

Which left him in a difficult position. He'd known from the start that their relationship was fragile, that it needed careful tending to bring it to its fullest and most exciting best. Had he crushed that tender seedling when he'd asked her if she'd thought him to be an easy mark? Could they revive the bond between them? She'd looked so battered, so bruised. He'd been so locked in his own anger and disbelief at what he'd perceived as disloyalty, not to mention dishonesty. He still wanted to know the truth, the full truth this time. They couldn't move forward until everything had been laid bare between them.

What was it she'd said, exactly? That she couldn't believe he'd think that of her. Somewhere along the line he'd earned her confidence, which was a far cry from where they'd been that day he'd swanned into Connell's Floral Design and back into her life. And, with a single comment, he'd destroyed it. But trust was a two way street. If she couldn't be 100 percent honest with him, too, then they didn't stand a chance.

He had his work cut out for him if he wanted to get her to open up to him fully, that was for sure. But he was driven to succeed in this, to surpass his success in everything else he'd wanted in his life to date. She'd said she wouldn't stand in his way with the baby, but he wasn't satisfied with that. He wanted them both.

What Chance had said resonated with Dylan. Whatever she'd done or been involved with in the past wasn't who she was now. Why should it matter? She was the mother of his baby. She was the woman who held his heart. That was all that counted. The rest, well, he'd deal with it one way or another, provided she'd let him. The morning couldn't come soon enough.

It was only ten o'clock and already Jenna was exhausted. Millie hadn't shown this morning, too hungover, if the garbled text message she'd sent had been anything to go by. Had Jenna ever been like that? she wondered. No, of course not. She'd been too busy trying to be invisible, yet invaluable at the same time.

A call to Valerie, to see if she could come in, even if

only for a couple of hours, had revealed that during the night she'd fallen victim to an apparently short-lived, but virulent, stomach virus that was ripping through their household. There was no way she'd come in and risk infecting Jenna, even if she could tear herself away from the bathroom right now.

Jenna had assured her tearful friend that she'd cope—after all, they'd completed most of the work for today's wedding client yesterday and by working back about three hours last night—but her head swam a little and she leaned against the counter, taking a swig of her water bottle and reaching for the salty snack the doctor had told her to introduce into her diet. She certainly didn't want a repeat of what had happened the day before last, and especially not at a time when she was on her own at the store. She'd had three bouquets to finish for the wedding today—now thankfully completed. With no Millie and with Valerie laid low with that stomach virus, it was all up to Jenna to handle those last-minute things, the things she'd counted on Millie helping her with so she wouldn't overdo it, she thought with a grimace. Not to mention walk-ins.

She heard the buzzer out front in the store. Ah, good, hopefully that'd be her wedding people in to pick up their table arrangements and the bouquets and boutonnieres. She forced a smile onto her face as she left the workroom.

Her smile faded the instant she saw who'd arrived.

"What are you doing here?" Dylan demanded. His face was a taut mask of control but she could see fire glinting in his eyes.

Jenna took a step back. "Where did you expect me to be? And what business is it of yours, anyway?"

"It's my business because that's my baby you're carrying. I went around to your place this morning, expecting to find you there, but you weren't."

"Well, obviously," she said drily, even as her heart rate picked up several beats at seeing him again.

"Why aren't you at home, resting?"

Oh, so he'd heard. She sighed.

"I just fainted, that's all." Jenna reached toward some roses she had on special in a tubular vase next to the cash register, and tore away a few damaged petals.

"Why? Have you been looking after yourself?"

"You're not my mother," she snapped. "I'm perfectly capable—"

"Don't give me that, Jenna," he growled. "I've seen inside your refrigerator. I know you don't cook for squat. Why were you hospitalized?"

"My blood pressure's a little low, that's all. I have to be careful not to let myself get dehydrated, and they recommended I up my salt intake. So you see, there's nothing to worry about."

"And the fall? You didn't hurt yourself?"

"No, and the baby's fine, too. Seriously, Dylan. I'm okay." Someone else came in through the front door. Ah, the father of the bride to pick up the flowers. "I'm also very busy, so if you'll excuse me?"

He didn't leave. Not through her discussion with her customer, nor when it came to helping the guy load the flowers into his van. Dylan even had the temerity to insist she stay in the store and sit down while he helped instead. She was seething by the time he came back inside.

"I don't need babying and I don't appreciate you coming in here telling me how to do my job."

"You're working far too hard. Aren't you supposed to have help here today? Where's Millie?"

"She couldn't make it, and…oh, there's a customer."

He waited while Jenna dealt with the woman. Then helped the client out to her car with the flowers she'd ordered.

"What do you mean, Millie couldn't make it?" he asked the second he and Jenna were alone again. "Don't you have backup?"

"Well, yes, sometimes Valerie will come for an extra day, but she's sick and she's already been doing most of the heavy stuff for me since my little incident."

"Little incident?"

Jenna could see he wasn't impressed by the terminology.

"Look, I fainted at the bank. The staff called an ambulance because that's their procedure. I was checked into the emergency department, and kept overnight for observation. I was rehydrated and then released in the morning with a set of instructions that I promise I've been following." *Mostly.*

It was as if he could hear her thoughts.

"Not completely, if I know you. What are your plans for lunch today?"

"I was just going to grab a sandwich—"

"How, when you can't leave the store unattended? How are you supposed to have a decent break if you don't have an assistant?"

"Well, I didn't know that she wouldn't be here until I got in this morning, did I?"

"Are you expecting any more customers today?"

"There are always a few walk-ins on a Saturday, but I have no more orders to fill."

"Good, then you won't mind me doing this."

He strode out back and she heard him locking the back door.

"What are you doing?" she asked.

"Get your bag."

"I won't do any such thing!"

"Fine. I'll do it myself." He shot through to her office and came out with her handbag slung over his shoulder. She'd have laughed at the sight he presented if she hadn't seen the look of absolute determination on his face.

"Dylan…" she started, but her words trailed away when he swept her up in his arms and carried her out the front door, hesitating only a second to turn the sign around to Closed. The door banged shut behind them.

"Key," he demanded, and she reached into her bag for her set, and while he still held her in his arms, turned the lock.

A group of people began to gather on the sidewalk.

"Hey, look at that! Isn't that Dylan Lassiter?"

"Yeah. Go, Dylan!"

To her chagrin, he flung them a beaming smile and began to walk toward his SUV, parked a few spaces down the street. As he went, the crowd grew larger, and began to applaud and cheer. Someone raced up to open the passenger door for him and another cheer rose into the air as he gently slid Jenna onto the passenger seat, before reaching around her to secure her seat belt.

Jenna was certain her cheeks were flaming. Dylan closed her door and marched resolutely around to the driver's side.

As he got into the car she flung him a murderous glance.

"This is kidnapping, you know."

"I know," he responded succinctly, right before he reached out to cup the back of her head and draw her to him.

Sixteen

His lips closed on hers with familiarity and yet with a sense of newness and wonder that tantalized and terrified her in equal proportions. On the sidewalk, the crowd went wild. Dylan broke away and reached for the ignition. For a second Jenna thought to protest once more, but the set of his jaw convinced her any argument would fall on deaf ears. She'd have to wait until he got her to wherever they were going.

It didn't take long to figure out. She recognized the route out to his home immediately.

"Dylan—" she started.

"Don't mess with me, Jenna. We'll talk when we're home."

He said it with such strength and distinctness it echoed in her mind. His home was in L.A. now, but from his tone it sounded as though he'd chosen the word quite deliberately. As if he meant to stay here. Her heart leaped in her chest even as her stomach dropped. The prospect of seeing him more often would be both torture and an illicit pleasure at the same time. She'd told him all along that she'd give him free access to their baby, so did this mean he meant to make his visits more frequent? Another more frightening thought occurred to her. Did he mean to get permanent custody? He had the funds at his disposal, and the family support.

She shoved the idea from her mind as quickly as it had bloomed there. He'd never once spoken along those lines. Why would he start now? Her thoughts flew back to last Saturday night at the opening—to the exact moment she'd felt her world come inexorably apart, like a dandelion destroyed in a powerful gust of wind. She simply couldn't go through all that again.

When they arrived at the house, he surprised her by parking in the garage rather than out front. She was even more surprised to see the red Cadillac gleaming under the overhead lights in the four-bay garage.

"You kept it?"

"I couldn't let it go," he answered simply as he lifted her from her seat and into his arms again. "A bit like you, really," he added cryptically.

He carried her inside to the casual family room off the massive kitchen, and put her down on a long L-shaped couch in the corner.

"Stay," he commanded, then wheeled around to the kitchen and went straight to the fridge, where he started pulling things out. In no time, he'd made a couple sandwiches on what smelled like freshly baked bread. He came back over to her and put a plate on her lap. "Eat."

She looked at him in annoyance, tempted to tell him where to stick his sandwich. But her mouth watered at the sight of it and she knew she needed to eat. Heck, she wanted to eat this layered concoction filled with freshness and flavor.

Once she'd finished, he took her plate, poured a glass of mineral water and handed it to her.

"Yeah, yeah, I know. Drink," she said, her voice dripping with sarcasm. This dictatorial side of Dylan was already starting to get old. "I am capable of taking care of myself, you know."

He just looked at her, his derision clear in those blue eyes that seemed to be able to stare straight through her. She couldn't hold his gaze. She might be capable of taking care of herself, but being capable and actually doing it had been two very different things.

"Things are going to change, Jenna," Dylan said, once she'd drained her glass and he'd taken it from her. "You are too important to me to leave either your health or the baby's to chance. You could have really hurt yourself in that fall, and what if it happens again?"

"It won't. I'm more aware of how I'm feeling now, and despite what you might think, I plan to take better care of myself." *It's just that everything else in the past two days has gotten in the way,* she added silently.

"Planning isn't good enough. You need more help if you're going to look after yourself properly."

"I know," she admitted. It was something she'd thought about a great deal this morning. One other person could make all the difference.

"So you'll hire more staff at the store."

Jenna's mind raced over the logistics of employing another full-time staff member—with wages, insurance and paperwork—and how that would upset her careful budget.

"At my expense—I insist on it," Dylan continued.

"Oh, no," she resisted firmly. What if he then decided to try to call all the shots when it came to her business? "Besides, it's not that easy to find a good florist. They don't just grow on trees, you know." The ridiculousness of that statement struck her at about the same time it struck him, and they both laughed. The sound lightened the mood, clearing the air as if by magic. Jenna let her barriers down. It *would* be great to hire another florist, someone who was innovative with design, yet didn't mind throwing together the traditional bouquets and arrangements that remained the backbone of her business.

"I'll look into it," she acceded.

"Thank you. I appreciate that you won't just get some walk-in off the street, and that in a business the size of yours, finding the right person might take some time. Can you get a temp until you find the right one? Do they even have temps for this kind of work?"

"I'll find out on Monday."

"I could do that for you," he offered.

"I said I'll do it and I will." She didn't want to relinquish an ounce of control to him if she could help it. This was her business and while, yes, he had a very valid point about her needing help, she would be the one looking for that help. Not him. Besides, didn't he have enough on his plate already? Jenna swung her feet to the floor and started to get up from the chair.

"Right, now that we have that sorted out, perhaps you could take me back to work."

"No."

Dylan stared back at her, his feet planted firmly on the floor and his arms crossed in front of him as if he was some kind of human barrier.

"Dylan, please. You've fed me, again. I've rested. Now I really need to get back."

"We need to talk."

"We've talked," she pointed out. "And I've agreed to get more help at the store. I thought—hoped—that would settle your concerns."

"On that score, yes. But there's a whole lot we didn't discuss last weekend that needs to come out in the open."

Jenna felt a fist close around her heart. So, they were back to her father. Would she never be free of his crimes?

Dylan reached out and took her hands in his. "I reacted

badly last Saturday. It hurt more than I wanted to admit when I learned you'd withheld stuff from me and in turn I hurt you back. I'm sorry for that. But I need to know everything. If you can be honest with me, Jenna, I believe we can work things out. Don't you want to at least try?"

She studied his beautiful face for a long time. He looked tired, with lines of strain around his eyes and those parallel creases between his brows that told her he was still worried, deep down. Could she do it? Could she share her shame with him and come out on the other side intact? There was only one way to find out.

"Okay," she said softly, dipping her head.

He let go of one hand to tip her chin back up again.

"Don't hide from me, Jenna. Don't ever hide."

Tears filled her eyes, but she blinked them back and drew strength instead from the reassurance in his voice.

"At first it was okay when Dad packed us up and brought us here to the States. We settled in Austin, Texas, where he was originally from. He met a lady, fell in love, but when it ended he just packed us up again, and off we went, somewhere else."

"It must have been hard, shifting around like that," Dylan sympathized.

"It was. I'd just get settled somewhere and the same thing would happen all over again." Jenna sighed. "I retreated into myself more and more, made friends less and less. His girlfriends started getting older and wealthier, and he started receiving more extravagant and expensive gifts from them. I would, too, because he always introduced them to me—maybe having me there in the background gave him some degree of respectability. They were usually nice to me, some more than others.

"One of them in particular, Lisa Fieldman, was especially lovely and she lasted the longest of all his girlfriends. There was a stage when I began to wonder—to even hope—they'd get married. That I'd have a mom again. She used to say she'd always wished for a daughter and that we'd do together very nicely.

"Lisa always had time for me and showed an interest in whatever I was doing. She even got my dad to come along to a school recital I was in when he'd never been to one before. I can still remember the big wink she gave me when I saw them in the audience. Lisa gave me a stock portfolio for my thirteenth birthday. She told me it would be something to fall back on—my 'rainy day fund.' I had no idea what that was and promptly forgot about it. I vaguely remember Dad trying to cajole her for control of it straightaway but she was adamant its management remain in the hands of her investment advisers. That was probably when Dad realized that she could see right through him. Despite that, I'm pretty sure she loved him, faults and all, but she wasn't a complete fool and kept a pretty tight rein on her finances. Of course, by the time the penny dropped for Dad and he realized he couldn't get any more out of Lisa, we moved on. It just about broke my heart. I'm pretty sure it broke hers."

Jenna paused a moment to swipe at her eyes.

"Your dad sounds like a real piece of work."

Jenna gave him a wry smile. "You have no idea. Anyway, I'd forgotten about the portfolio until I turned eighteen and some lawyer tracked me down to say it was mine to do with what I wanted. I couldn't believe it. Suddenly, I had funds that if I managed them carefully, could see me set up for life. I cashed in enough so I could get my degree without a student loan, and I kept working weekends at the store to meet my other expenses. I eventually sold off the balance a couple of years ago and used it toward buying my house."

She felt Dylan shift at her side and she gave him a piercing look. "You thought I'd somehow used the money my father swindled to buy my house, didn't you?"

He had the grace to appear shamefaced. "It was starting to look that way. The sums just didn't add up."

She nodded. "Yeah, I guess you're right. Anyway, I was able to use the house as collateral to borrow the money I needed to buy out Margaret when she was ready to retire. The repayments make things tight, but as long as I can keep afloat I'll get there in the end. The business will be all mine."

"That security is important to you," Dylan commented. "Owning your own home, your own business. Being answerable only to yourself."

Jenna nodded. "It became everything to me. It's the antithesis of what my life had been like up until my father was put in jail and I was sent here to Cheyenne to live."

"You were in Laramie when your father was investigated, weren't you? How did you end up here?"

Jenna rubbed at the mound of her belly absently. "Dad's arrest was national news and Lisa heard about it. Despite Dad ditching her the way he did and all that he'd put her through, she was still fond of me. Turned out she had a recently widowed college friend who lived here. That was Margaret. Lisa contacted her about taking me on. It was only supposed to be until I was eighteen, when I was theoretically supposed to be cut loose, but we got on well. I worked hard and she appreciated that. Plus, I also loved working with her and with flowers. We ended up being a natural fit. I have so much to be grateful to Lisa for, but I'm particularly grateful to her for using her influence to convince the authorities to send me to Margaret.

"Being here was a gift that I certainly wasn't going to

throw away. It gave me a chance to start over in a town where people barely knew of me. I hated every second of the publicity that surrounded my father's arrest. It was even worse when the media began to point a finger at me, saying I'd been complicit in his behavior. If I was guilty of anything, it was of ignorance. Maybe by the time I was fifteen I should have been asking questions about how he made so much money when he never appeared to work, but my head was filled with school and teenage stuff, so it never occurred to me to question any of it.

"One of my teachers got sick with cancer and the student council came up with the idea of a sponsored head shave to raise money to help her family out while she had treatment. When my dad saw me he was horrified at first. But then he took some pictures of me while I was visiting my teacher in the hospital. Without my knowledge or consent, he used those pictures to create a fake profile online, and used his imagination for the rest. It didn't take long for investigators to clear me of any involvement, but mud sticks and for me it stuck hard."

She thought back to that time when she'd been too afraid to leave the house and face the media assembled outside. Her father, then out on bail and awaiting the case to be brought before court, had simply taken it all in his stride, even laughing and joking with the reporters when he'd gone out. But for Jenna, who was still growing her hair back, every moment at school had become a trial by her peers, each day more unpleasant than the last.

"When Margaret placed me in school here I just did what I'd always done. Kept my head down and focused on my grades. By the time I attended the University of Wyoming people had begun to forget. Sure, I crossed paths with a couple of the kids I'd gone to school with in

Laramie, but time has a really good way of blurring the edges of people's memory."

Jenna studied Dylan's face again, and was grateful he'd listened without passing judgment. When given the chance, she'd grabbed the opportunity to forge a new life for herself, with both hands holding on tight. Sure, in hindsight she could see that her father had always believed he'd tried to do his best by her. That he'd obtained all those things under false pretenses was his cross to bear, not hers. Jenna knew that now. It didn't mean that she forgave him for it, but it was who he was.

"As to the money he raised, I have no idea where it is. He managed to hide it somewhere. No doubt he'll use it to seed his lifestyle when he gets out and the instant he does I hope the police will be back onto him. I'm sorry I didn't tell you all this before," she said softly. "I should never have accepted your proposal without doing so, but I guess a part of me was scared that you'd believe the worst of me when you knew."

"And then I did, didn't I?" he said ruefully. "Or at least it probably looked that way to you, huh?"

"In part. You have such a wonderful family, Dylan. I sullied them and your opening night at the Grill by bringing my life's ugliness into it."

"No, don't say that. What you went through made you who you are now. And we love you for it. All of us."

She searched his eyes to see if he was telling her what she thought, and hoped, he was saying. Sharing her past with him had made her feel lighter inside, as if it was no longer her burden to carry alone.

"Yes, Jenna. I do love you. I shouldn't have walked away from you last weekend. I was so angry and so hurt when I learned you'd kept such an important piece of yourself from me. I shouldn't have reacted the way I did.

You needed strength and support from me, and I didn't give it to you. But if you'll let me try again, that's what I'm offering you now.

"Everything, Jenna. My heart, my soul, my life. Knowing what you went through in your past just makes me want to create a better future with you, one for all three of us," he affirmed, placing his hand on her belly. "So I'm going to ask you again. Jenna Montgomery, will you marry me?"

Seventeen

Dylan's heart beat double time as he waited for her answer. He wanted this, her, the baby, more than anything he'd ever wanted his whole life. His happiness and his future hung now on Jenna's reply.

When it came, her simple *yes* was the most magical word he'd ever heard.

"I promise to make sure you never regret it," he vowed as he leaned forward and took her lips in a kiss that transcended every previous contact they'd ever had before. Nothing stood between them now. Their lives and their love were laid bare to one another.

"I know I never will, Dylan. You offer me so much, it makes me wonder what I offer you in return," she said uneasily as they broke apart.

"Everything," he said, and it was heartfelt. "I thought it was just a fluke, the way you made me feel the first day I met you, but you never left my thoughts. Through J.D. dying, through Angelica's wedding being called off... even when I was working hard on the Cheyenne Grill's opening, you were always there."

Dylan shifted on the couch so he could pull her into his lap, one arm wrapped around her while his other hand rested on the mound that resulted from their first meeting.

"I couldn't stop thinking about you, either," Jenna

admitted with a rueful smile. "It was…quite uncomfortable at times. I knew you were back in Cheyenne on and off, while the restaurant was being built. I guess I was a bit like a crazy teenager with a crush, hoping I'd get a glimpse of you. Your world, your background, is so different to mine. I convinced myself that you were unattainable for me, that our lives were too far apart and that I was happy not to hear from you or get in touch with you myself. But then I discovered I was pregnant, and it made me reassess everything. Made me wonder if you'd even be interested. After all, it's not like we got to know each other before we—"

"Shh," he said, pressing a short kiss to her lips. "So we didn't do things the conventional way. That doesn't mean we can't be as old-fashioned as we like, if we want to be, for the rest of our lives. Let's not wait to get married. I want us to be together, as husband and wife, as soon as we can."

"But what about where we're going to live? I—"

"I've been thinking about that. I have a strong team at my back. I can afford to work from here in Cheyenne, at least until the baby's born. After that, we can decide what we're going to do next, although I'd like to think I can make the move home permanent. I'd like to see our baby raised here, closer to my family's roots. So, what do you say? How does next Saturday sound?"

"Are you sure? That's a lot of organizing in a short period of time."

"We can do it, if we want to. I have contacts in the catering business," he said with a cheeky grin, "and I know someone who has a real way with flowers. If you're okay with it, I'd like to keep it small and invite family and close friends only. What do you think?"

She nodded. "That sounds perfect. Do you think we

could get married out at the Big Blue? It's an important part of your past and your family. I think it would be so special to be married there, where you grew up."

"I think that would be perfect," he said, kissing her again. "And I'm sure Chance and Marlene would be thrilled. So, shall we do it? I'll get the license on Monday and we can be married by the end of the week."

"I can't believe it's true, that it's really happening."

"Believe it, Jenna. Believe me. You are all I've ever wanted, you and our baby. I had some wonderful examples of love growing up. First my parents, and then J.D. and Ellie. Losing Aunt Ellie crushed J.D. He never stopped loving her until he drew his last breath.

"Even as a kid, I knew I wanted to know that kind of love with another person. I'm thirty-five years old, Jenna, I was beginning to think that kind of love wasn't out there for me, and God only knows I looked. I never expected to find it, to find you, right here under my nose in Cheyenne. And now that I have you, I'm never going to let you go."

"I'm going to hold you to that, Dylan Lassiter. Every day for the rest of your life," she promised, her eyes burning fiercely with her love.

"I can't wait."

It was a dazzling afternoon out at the Big Blue. As Dylan had expected, Marlene had taken the initiative and organized the wedding with the flair and efficiency he'd always known her to have. Strange how he'd thought he'd be wildly excited about today; instead, he was filled with a deep sense of rightness and calm. Everything he'd ever done to this point in time had led to this moment, this day, where he would declare his love for Jenna in front of their nearest and dearest.

He looked out the window of the second floor of the house and down toward the garden, where a hastily erected bower of flowers on the patio marked the spot where he and Jenna would become husband and wife very soon. A handful of waitstaff from the Grill circulated among the small gathering with trays of drinks and hors d'oeuvres, and he knew his executive chef had taken over Marlene's expansive kitchen to create a wedding supper that would rival anything he'd ever done before.

A knock sounded at the guest room door and his sister stepped inside. A smile wreathed Angelica's beautiful face, but he could see the concern in her eyes.

"Hey," she said, moving across the room to give him a quick hug.

"Hey, yourself," he answered. "I'm glad you could make it."

"Well, it was rather short notice, Dylan. Seriously," she teased, "a girl needs time to plan for these things."

"I figured if the bride could be ready in a week, our family and friends could, too."

"Good point," she said, stepping back and assessing him thoroughly. She flicked a tiny piece of lint off the lapel of his suit. "Speaking of which, this wedding is all rather sudden, don't you think? To be honest with you, I can't believe you're actually going through with it. Are you absolutely sure you're doing the right thing? It's no small step you're taking."

"I've never been more certain of anything in my life."

"Dylan, you don't have to marry her to be a father. You know that, don't you?" she pressed. "We hardly know anything about her."

"I know all that I need to know for now. I look forward to spending the rest of my life discovering the rest. As to not having to marry her—Angelica, I want to. I want her to be my wife more than I've wanted anything else in the world. It's a destination that I know, deep in here—" he thumped his chest "—we would have come to anyway. Having the baby, well, that just speeds it along."

"What if things go wrong?" she persisted. "Even when you think you know a person…"

Angelica's voice trailed off, leaving her bitterness and anger toward her ex-fiancé to hang in the air between them. Another knock at the door interrupted what Dylan was going to say, and Sage came into the room.

"You scrub up pretty well," he teased his younger brother.

"You don't look so bad yourself," Dylan replied, taking comfort in the usual banter.

"I never expected you'd beat me down the aisle," Sage commented lightly. But then his face grew more serious. "It's not too late to change your mind."

"Not you, too," Dylan groaned. "Look, guys, I appreciate the concern, but I know I'm doing the right thing. She's going to be one of us now. I'd like you to respect that. Can I have your promise you won't say anything about it again, please?"

Angelica and Sage each agreed, and the conversation turned to other matters.

Sage spoke first, directing his attention to their sister. "Since the three of us are together, I wanted to discuss the rumors that you're moving forward with contesting J.D.'s will."

"You're not still going ahead with that, are you?" Dylan asked.

"Of course I am," Angelica said with a stubborn look that the brothers knew all too well. She might have all her mother's beauty and grace, but deep down inside she was

J.D.'s daughter through and through. "As I recall, Sage, you were originally the one to suggest it."

His eyes reflected his frustration with her. "Yeah, but I also realized early on, and advised you, that continuing with the idea would prevent J.D.'s other wishes for inheritance from happening. Did you really want to see Marlene unable to live here? Or for any of the other bequests to be frozen while you battled this out? I thought you understood that it was more important to observe J.D.'s wishes in the end than to persist in something that's only going to cause bigger and bigger problems."

"Oh, sure." Angelica laughed, but the sound was insincere. "Nothing like the good ol' boys backslapping and agreeing to hush the little woman on her ideas, right? We all know Lassiter Media should have been mine. I did all the hard work. I picked up and carried on when Dad started to pull back from the day-to-day operations. Me! It's my baby and I want it back."

Dylan interrupted before things could get any more heated. Sage was right, but he could see where Angelica was coming from, even if he believed she was wrong. "I would have thought you'd want what's right for Lassiter Media. We all know that while we didn't agree with everything J.D. did, he was a brilliant businessman. He made his decision. Think of the wider picture, Angelica, if you even can anymore. You've become so dogged about this that your behavior is damaging the company. Is that what you want?"

She sighed and her shoulders sagged beneath the couture gown she wore. "No, it isn't what I want at all, but I have to fight for what's right. For what's *mine*."

Dylan put an arm around her. "We're going to have to

keep agreeing to disagree on this, Ange. This obsession isn't good for you, isn't good for any of us."

"That's easy for you to say," she retorted. "You got what you wanted."

"And I'd walk away from it all today if I knew that was what was best for the corporation."

The air was thick with the conflict until Angelica shook her head. "Let's not talk about this today, okay? We're here to celebrate you getting married."

The men grunted their assent, but Dylan knew the subject would not be forgotten. It was far too important to simply try and sweep under the rug. But for now, they could pretend there was nothing contentious simmering between them. He looked out the window once more, noting that the white folding chairs on the patio were filling with guests.

"Let's go do this," he said with a smile at his siblings.

Downstairs there was a hum of excitement in the air, yet it did little to ruffle the calm that wrapped around Dylan like a cloak. He'd spent every day in the past week looking forward to this moment, and finally it was here. Everything was coming right in his world, and he only hoped his sister could one day be as happy as he was.

Dylan took his place under the floral bower and smiled at the celebrant they'd booked to conduct the ceremony. Then he turned and looked down the aisle at the eager faces of the people he loved most in the world. All except for one, and she'd be coming from the house any moment now.

Jenna had elected to walk alone toward him, stating that she'd stood on her own two feet for so many years, she didn't need anyone to give her away. She was coming to this marriage freely and wholeheartedly. In response,

Dylan had elected not to have a best man, although they'd asked Sage and Valerie to be their official witnesses.

After a flurry of activity at the doors leading onto the patio, Marlene appeared with Cassie, who was dressed in mint-green organza and carried a basket of petals. Marlene flung Dylan a smile and gave him a thumbs-up. Until then, he hadn't realized he'd begun to feel nervous. No, it wasn't nerves, exactly, it was more anticipation. He couldn't help it; a big smile spread across his face.

Marlene took her seat and the music began. Cassie skipped her way down the aisle, throwing handfuls of petals on the ground, in the air and toward anyone who looked her way. Everyone was quietly laughing by the time she took her seat beside her mother.

And then silence fell upon them all as Jenna stood framed in the doorway. Dylan's breath caught in his chest as his eyes drank in the sight of her. Dressed in a simple white gown, with a broad satin sash under her breasts that lovingly contoured her slightly swollen belly, she looked radiantly beautiful. Her dark hair was swept up on her head, with tendrils drifting loose to caress the sides of her face and throat, and the diamond drop earrings he'd given her last night sparkled in the late afternoon sunlight. If he could have frozen this one moment in time forever, he would have. She was perfection, and she was about to be his.

Their gazes met and held as she began to walk slowly toward him, a smile on her face and her love for him beaming from her eyes. Then, finally, she was at his side, where she belonged for the rest of their lives.

The celebrant began to speak, and Dylan and Jenna made their responses, pledging their vows to one another. And Dylan knew, without a doubt in his heart, that he now had the family of his own he'd always wanted.

And as they turned to the assembly of guests as husband and wife, he looked at everyone's loving faces and knew this was the family he, Jenna and their baby deserved.

* * * * *

MILLS & BOON®

Why shop at millsandboon.co.uk?

Each year, thousands of romance readers find their perfect read at millsandboon.co.uk. That's because we're passionate about bringing you the very best romantic fiction. Here are some of the advantages of shopping at www.millsandboon.co.uk:

* **Get new books first**—you'll be able to buy your favourite books one month before they hit the shops

* **Get exclusive discounts**—you'll also be able to buy our specially created monthly collections, with up to 50% off the RRP

* **Find your favourite authors**—latest news, interviews and new releases for all your favourite authors and series on our website, plus ideas for what to try next

* **Join in**—once you've bought your favourite books, don't forget to register with us to rate, review and join in the discussions

Visit **www.millsandboon.co.uk**
for all this and more today!